CW01670017

An Alien Invasion at the Pub

2021 Anthology
from
Michael Terence Publishing

Michael Terence
Publishing

First published in paperback by
Michael Terence Publishing in 2021
www.mtp.agency

Copyright © 2021 Michael Terence Publishing

Each author has asserted the right to be identified
as the author of their work in accordance with the
Copyright, Designs and Patents Act 1988

ISBN 9781800941878

All rights reserved. No part of this publication may be reproduced,
stored in a retrieval system, or transmitted,
in any form or by any means, electronic, mechanical,
photocopying, recording or otherwise,
without the prior permission of the publisher

Cover images
Copyright © Linda Bucklin, Michael Rosskothen
www.123rf.com

Cover design
Copyright © 2021 Michael Terence Publishing

To writers and readers everywhere…

With love to my friend
[illegible], [illegible] x x x

Introduction

This collection of short stories is taken from the Michael Terence Publishing 2021 Short Story Competition.

Entries were received from across the world – which perhaps helps to explain the wide and stimulating range of subjects covered.

We extend our sincere thanks to the judges for their hard work and diligence. The panel was, as always, truly impressed by the overall high standard of the submissions – so it's a big thank you to all of the wonderful authors.

Here we publish the prize-winning story plus works that were highly commended by the judges.

Each has been published as it was received, without further editing.

We hope you will enjoy reading them all.

About Michael Terence Publishing

In the past, the founders of MTP experienced the frustration of having a great manuscript but meeting a brick wall when trying to find a traditional agent/publisher.

Quite simply, MTP was founded to give worthy authors a platform to publish their works, earn 100% royalties and to achieve the best sales for print books and eBooks.

Today, submissions of new works in all genres are being gratefully received via our website.

Find out more about publishing *your* book at:

www.mtp.agency

Contents

PRIZE-WINNER: Sandra Srivastava - An Alien Invasion at the Pub

An alien spaceship landed in a pub car park. The door opened slowly, there was a hiss of steam and six aliens climbed down the steps. As the first alien (wearing the fanciest clothes and therefore the leader) reached the ground, he nearly jumped out of his skin as he spotted six yobs revving their motorbikes. The other aliens had to stop suddenly, and collided with each other.

"Take me to your leader," said the chief alien.

"I'm the leader around here," said the biggest yob, puffing himself up to look even bigger. A couple of heads whizzed round to glare at him, as if they weren't so sure about that. Neither were the aliens. The yob stuck his nose in the air and continued, snootily, "I'm the biggest, my motorbike is the biggest, my boots are the biggest, and I have the longest hair. Therefore, I'm the leader. That's obvious. And *I* say you can't park there because our mates will be here in a minute and they'll want somewhere to park."

"Somewhere to park *or* some entertainment," said a particularly greasy yob. "It's not very big, is it?"

"Er … It's bigger on the inside than on the outside. Yes, that's it," said the chief alien, nodding triumphantly. But, unlike the aliens, the yobs had not seen *Doctor Who*, and didn't know what he was talking about. They all mounted their motorbikes and sped around and around the spaceship, whooping and jeering as they went.

"Run!" yelled the chief alien. So the aliens ran across the car park and climbed over the wall into a field. The chief alien stepped in something and lifted his foot to see (and smell) what was on it. He screwed up his face and asked, "Yuck, what is *that*?" One of his companions pointed towards some cows, who were still doing it. The chief alien said, "Right!" He marched up to them and, hands on hips, commanded, "Take me to your leader."

"Mooo," said one of the cows. All the cows moved slowly towards the aliens. All the aliens moved slowly away from the cows.

"Run!" yelled the chief alien. So they ran across the field and climbed over the wall into the next field.

A flock of sheep stood close together, gazing at the aliens. "Take me to your leader," said the chief alien. As the aliens moved slowly towards the sheep, the sheep moved slowly away from the aliens, still in a tight group. This annoyed the sheepdog, after all his hard work to get the sheep where he wanted them, and he began barking indignantly at the aliens. "Are you the leader?" asked the chief alien.

The farmer strode up to them and, red with rage, boomed, "Who do you think you are, scaring *my* cows and *my* sheep and *my* dog?"

"Aha, so you're the leader!" cried the chief alien. "I've got a bone to pick with you."

The farmer raised his shotgun.

"Run!" yelled the chief alien.

So the aliens ran across the field and climbed over the wall into the next field. Coming towards them on the footpath was a hardy-looking hiker, carrying a long stick and a big rucksack. "I've been watching you. You people think you can come here from other planets and wander around the English countryside as if you own the place. What are you doing here, anyway?" asked the hiker casually, picking his fingernails as if he didn't really care.

"Wouldn't *you* like to know!" crowed the chief alien.

"Well, I don't like it. How would you like it if I went to your planet, parked in your driveway, played football in your garden, went into your kitchen in my muddy boots, helped myself to beer and pizza from your fridge, kissed your wife, patted your children on the head, stroked your pets and settled down to watch *Deep Space Nine* without so much as a by-your-leave?" asked the hiker, catching his breath after all that.

"You'd find it difficult to do any of that on our planet," said the chief alien.

"Oh, you think so, do you?" jeered the hiker, waving his stick.

"Run!" yelled the chief alien.

So the aliens ran across the field until they came across a pretty village with a few little cottages with whitewashed walls, thatched roofs and roses around the doors. A black cat sat washing itself in front of one of the houses. By this time the chief alien was a bit nervous, so he went up to it carefully and asked, politely, "Er – excuse me – are you the leader 'around here'?" The cat looked at him for a moment and said nothing, then ran along the path and jumped over a high fence into a garden.

"Do you think we're supposed to follow?" asked one of the aliens.

"I don't really know," said the chief alien, "but we don't want to annoy it so, to be on the safe side, we'd better follow."

The aliens scrambled up the fence, which swayed quite a lot with six of them on it, and they had to cling to it tightly until they plucked up the courage to jump down into the garden. The cat was sitting on the roof of a rabbit hutch, arching its neck and looking upside down at the occupants. "Oh, I see," said the chief alien. "It wants us to rescue those trapped lifeforms. And there are more in another container over there."

After quite a bit of fumbling, the aliens managed to open the hutches. Six rabbits went hopping around the garden, some of them taking quite a lot of interest in each other.

Suddenly a little boy appeared. "No, no! They'll have babies!" he cried.

"What do you mean?" asked the chief alien.

"Um … I don't really know," said the little boy.

Then his big sister came up, sighing and shaking her head. "When a male and a female love each other very much …" she began, wearily.

The little boy clamped his hands over his ears and shouted, "Lalalalalala! I don't want to hear it! Lalalalalala!"

Their mother rushed out of the house. "Olivia!" she whispered, urgently. "I've told you not to tell him that story again. He's not old enough!"

"But I'm not telling it to *him*. I'm telling it to the *aliens*! They asked! How else are they going to learn?" asked Olivia, innocently.

Two little dogs came running into the garden to see what was happening. To defend their humans, they began biting the ankles of the aliens, who had to hop around, trying to shake them off. The cockerel was confused and began crowing in the middle of the day. The cat fled up a tree and hissed menacingly at everyone else, from a safe distance.

A large man appeared from around the corner, brandishing a spade and demanding to know what on earth was going on.

"Run!" yelled the chief alien. So the aliens rushed at the fence, which fell over, and ran for their lives. The family scuttled around the garden separating the rabbits, but it was too late.

The aliens ran back along the footpath, breathed a sigh of relief that the hiker, the farmer and the dog had gone, climbed over the wall, tip-toed slowly past the sheep, climbed over the next wall, crept gingerly around the cows, and climbed back into the pub car park. The yobs' mates had arrived, leant their motorbikes against the spaceship, and gone into the pub.

The aliens didn't like the look of any of the local species. They weren't going to get anywhere with these lifeforms. They boarded their spaceship and whooshed off, leaving the motorbikes in a heap on the ground.

Alan Bryant - Praying for Feathers

She was short, plump, "frumpy", some said, with an outgoing disposition and instinctive dependence on early revenge. It was not her first relationship, nor her first violent breakup. Now she had to get out, be a different person, set a new perspective on her being. But first she needed to discover what her being really was.

It was never her intention to look like a real vicar. Her clothing appeared too casual for piety. The collar was a piece of card cut from a shoebox. On close inspection, the words, "nude heel", could be seen in one corner. A black cotton bed sheet made an almost convincing cassock. She had taken it from her ex-partner, an ardent experimenter of new bedroom experiences. He thought black was exotic.

On becoming a lady of the cloth, albeit one with improper thoughts, she would have preferred purple silk. However, she believed it courteous to start at a more humble level. And for a vicars and tarts evening, the outfit suited well enough. When dressed, she posed in front of her full length mirror, running her hands over the material, smoothing out memories of past exertions and worthless prayers.

The new sheets worked so well for her ex-boyfriend's libido his enthusiasm for dark erotica surged. Walls were pasted with life-size silhouettes of ancient Greeks gratifying themselves in positions no self-respecting contortionist would consider. He lined the ceiling with mirrors, then the headboard and the wardrobe doors. Sound activated cameras were situated in strategic and inventive places to record events for future reference. And there were a lot of sounds.

She was flattered he spent so much on her behalf. Did this mean true love existed? She tried to blush but coyness had never been a natural emotion for her and one she found difficult to portray. So she rubbed her cheeks hard to make them red and forced a weak smile. But when she fluttered her false eyelashes they cooled her face and her paleness showed again.

His erotic merchandise stimulated him, compounding his love for her, he said. He sent for toys that buzzed and bent in odd shapes, oils and body creams in Asian flavours. Every day another parcel arrived. Furry handcuffs, blindfolds, silk ropes littered the bed. He told her he was a new man, Superman, soldier, even a fire-fighter holding his hose. The outfits kept coming. With sculptured chest and foam filled biceps he threw himself into action. A polyester rash caused a hiatus in in the courtship. A self-confessed altruist, he stopped spending on himself. His main concession to economy was staying nude. He told her his body was allergic to most materials, except her skin which had qualities to both soothe and excite him in turn. She tried blushing again, rouge helped this time.

"My Very Own Beginner's Set of Whips" arrived with a small but comprehensive booklet. She stopped him at that. Pain was only enjoyed by those who never had to walk home with bunions, she said. She did not want it as a hobby and suggested he looked for a less inflaming project. He sulked for an hour before agreeing to return them, but on condition he could remain on the company's mailing list.

His alternative choice was a water bed. He said it was worth spending money on what made them both happy. She agreed but wondered just how happy he wanted to be. Insisting the bed was a present for her, he said they must fill it together. It would be their shared ocean of amore. The two lovers would sail on waves of passion, float across oceans of rippling ecstasy. But as it was too heavy for her to take home when full, it must stay in his apartment. It came with expensive underwear consisting mostly of strings and tassels, in black obviously.

His extensive collection of adult toys worked especially well for him. He reached such incredible highs his excitement caused his willpower to last no more than twenty-three seconds. She knew this. She timed him with the watch he bought her.

On discovering that all the gifts and equipment for these steaming, though speedily completed, romps were paid for with her credit card she ran at him screaming. The cameras clicked on and saw the bread knife raised high in her hand. It was her personal choice of weapon. He locked himself in the bathroom, crying for mercy. She cried too as she slashed the water bed into small, wet strips in a rage that would have loosened Lucifer's bowels. Wrapping her belongings up in his black bedding she slung the baggage over her shoulder to carry it through the streets, sobbing like a lost, manic cartoon character. The fire-fighter's costume dangled from the pack, a flat gigolo refusing to let go of his dragging hose.

At home, she hung the sheets against windows to keep the world in its dark place while she hid away and cried, and dried her eyes with a matching set of strings and tassels till she slept.

Waking up, she felt reborn. From that day forth it would be a new life for her. Tired of being used for someone else's benefit, of choking on honeyed promises and soured emotions, and of course running at people with bread knives, she sought meaning in her existence. Possibly she needed to find faith in something intangible but intrinsic. Her first thought was gold and diamond jewellery, but she reasoned this might be considered too consumerist. Something more abstract in its aesthetic appeal would be required. She made a list, meditation, yoga, tai chi, mindless graffiti. None would give her the serenity she craved. She waited for the answer to appear.

That evening, when she switched on a table lamp the light haloed around her. Peace hovered above her microwave as it hummed with its meal for one. Ten seconds later when the oven pinged, the light-bulb blew. It was a sign. Religion must fit the void. And if ever her reverence faltered, (as she believed it would) the threat of Heaven-sent retribution did not overly concern her. In her experience, suburban thunderbolts were rare and not noted for pinpoint accuracy.

She was a changed woman.

***

He was tall, bony, "gawky", they said. But he had the figure to flaunt a red leather mini skirt. And in the kaleidoscopic lighting of a thrusting nightclub, fishnet stockings adequately camouflaged his jutting knee-caps and hairy calves. Getting the seams straight had challenged him. He once read of a female bird in the Andes that could see backwards. Maybe, he thought, this was a talent solely attributed to ladies. After failing to twist his neck around a hundred and eighty degrees he stood between two mirrors to ascertain his rear reflection.

His outfit had been left by an ex-partner who bought the clothes on a whim of potential seduction. It was her intention to steam up their nightly activities. She remained a disappointed bedfellow. Their bustling exertions were tapering off at an exponential rate. His interests in the pleasures of her flesh had waned in favour of watching ornithological documentaries in bed. Male birds puffed themselves into rainbow arcs to strut through shimmering rain forests showing off their beauty. These winged Don Juans attracted drab toned females who flocked to their sides with blatant physical intentions.

Their ability to attract a mate impressed him so much with he made himself a bird costume from vivid ostrich feathers and a paper beak. On finding a snapped branch in the park he took it home to practise walking along it barefoot whilst whistling come-and-get-me calls.

Until then his girlfriend had been vegetarian. Becoming second best to various tropical fowl she became a fervent devourer of poultry, lying beside him eating chicken nuggets and pickled eggs. Very soon this new diet caused her to outgrow the seduction clothes. In her opinion, those strutting birds had a lot to answer for. She dieted with a vengeance.

One morning he woke and stretched out his arm to touch her. His hand landed on the flat leather skirt of his failed temptress. For a second, he thought she had deflated. He got up and looked for her in the bathroom but all he found was his snapped branch wedged down the toilet. Only by watching back-to-back episodes of chaparral mating rituals for sixteen hours did he ease the loneliness of this unforeseen abandonment. He punctuated his day with peanuts, paracetamol and sips of rain water.

When he switched the film off, his brain radiated with visions of multi-coloured preening. He collapsed on his *Wings Over Windmills* duvet. This was too much. He must start acting like a normal person having normal fun, whatever normal fun might be. It must be time to leave his crumpled, crumb filled bedroom to seek a different world with real people who did not strut along branches chewing worms, collecting twigs or eating chicken nuggets and eggs in bed.

Adapting to a new lifestyle would not be easy with his conversation limited to tail feathers of the world. Though a comprehensive, some might say, fascinating compilation, the subject was finite in provocative scope for the uninformed and no matter how animated his revelations, none of this dialogue could qualify as pillow talk.

He saw the poster, "Vicars and Tarts, all welcome".

The wearing of women's clothes had occurred to him previously when studying online catalogues of female underwear. But he had avoided the temptation in the belief that cross-dressing was best left until elderly. By then, a paunch and sagging breasts would add some natural gravitas to the overall effect. However, his situation now spurred him on to try it before the encroachment of senility. He reasoned that it would be better to wear ladies' clothes when in his prime than wait until he was sitting on a vinyl armchair in a room full of soup stained cardigans buttoned up the wrong way.

He would have preferred to go out in his bird costume but when he went through his wardrobe it was missing. A trail of feathers led from the bedroom and out to the street. Maybe it had flown. Possibly for the best, he thought. He needed to prove he could do more than flash bright plumage for the benefit of genetic heritage. So he wore the seduction clothes discarded by his ex. Putting on her underwear surprised him when it caused immediate but uncomfortable arousal. This discomfort increased when he tried bending and his thong stretched, seemingly transformed into a cheese-wire.

Once fully dressed, he was curious as to what his girlfriend wore when she left. Either she was naked or had stolen his clothes. Over the radio came reports of a five feet high psychedelic bird flitting through the town centre throwing pickled eggs at pretentious statues and squirting spray-cream over car windscreens. The news disappointed him. Some birds were without decorum.

Stilettos were not his preferred footwear but he persevered and with the use of a breadknife shortened the heels by two inches, still managing to maintain the wiggle when he walked. But as he did not cut the heels in equal measure this also gave him an awkward limp. And being so tall and thin, the sway of his body exaggerated perpendicular movement to fearful degrees.

He could not be described as pretty in the way a woman would be termed pretty, but in a red leather skirt, scarlet blouse, purple wig and sparingly applied make-up, he wondered if his air of eccentricity might create a colourful attraction for ladies of a certain flighty type. He checked himself in the mirror. His ensemble gave him the appearance of a chirpy gadabout, ready to enter into the merry melange of the night. And if he, at least, made the effort to project the charismatic effect of a fun loving personality (though this would be difficult, he was not a man to mingle freely) then who knew where the evening might lead?

***

She approached him at the bar. "Unusual shoes," she said.

How could a tart like him resist a cleric ready wrapped between the sheets?

She took his hand.

He smiled.

She smiled so much …

He called a taxi.

Sex resulted in more of a rushed flight through clouds than a heavenly ascendance. They stayed in bed till noon to the sound of jungle bird calls.

"I'm hungry," she said.

"Do you eat worms?" he said.

"If you could be someone else," she asked, "who would you be?"

"Icarus," he said, "or Audrey Hepburn. Such aerodynamic handbags. Who would you be?"

She slid out of bed, put on his skirt, blouse and wig then checked herself in the mirror. "Look at me," she said, adjusting the purple fringe over her eyebrows.

"Those clothes don't suit you," he said.

"Why not?"

"Because you aren't a real tart."

She blew him a kiss and wiggled her leather-clad bum. "It's two hundred for the night."

He tried to blink the disbelief from his eyes. "You mean …?"

"It's cash only," she said.

He sat up. "But you're too good a person for that."

"You really don't know me."

"I can't pay you."

She smiled and wagged a naughty boy finger at him. "You must. I need the money."

His arms flapped up and down at speed. "Can we talk about this over breakfast?"

"I'm open to a narrow window of negotiation," she said.

His flapping slowed to a relieved glide. When he was grounded, he took a deep breath, looked her in the eyes and made the sign of the cross.

"I will pray for you."

Her cheeks flushed with a rose glow. "That's so sweet," she said. "I'll make some toast. Where's the bread knife?"

Alanna Cramer - Ethics Amongst Parasites

"Kelly, just make the incision." The unconscious woman's relaxed tongue is heavy and hard to talk around.

"Ok. You're sure it's right here?" she asks. The knife blade is cold on the woman's skin.

"Yeth," I slur, "YES. Make the damn incision. I'll be out in a minute."

"Don't you want to keep an eye on her levels?"

"No, she's fine," I lie. *She got to us too late and I don't want to die in here.* "I'm coming out now."

I slip back into my own body and release the Connector just as Kelly makes the incision. It's a messy extraction and we have to remove the appendix too to get the whole thing out. The parasite writhes, a small black mass of vessel-like tentacles in my gloved hands, splattering blood up my covered forearms. I secure it in a disposal container. Kelly is still dealing with the wound. I consider telling her not to bother. Perhaps if we can keep the woman's heart going I could try to stabilise her. Then again the organ damage was... Well, Kelly needs more practice anyway.

"You remember how to finish up?"

"Sure."

The parasite's screeches fade as I slam the furnace door closed. I dispose of my gloves, covered in darkening blood and sticky tentacle residue, and change into fresh scrubs.

When I return to the room the large black body bag is by the door, ready for the morgue. Inevitable, but such a waste. She was only in her twenties.

Kelly is still in her surgery scrubs. She's soaking the sheets from the operating table in the old bathtub. The water is ruby pink.

"You forgot to tie off the feeder artery again, didn't you?"

"Yeah, well," she huffs, wringing the sheet out. "Her chances weren't great anyway. She should have come here sooner."

"Hmm." Half of those that survive the parasites long enough to get to us die on our operating table or in our makeshift ward. Still, it would be nice if we could improve our survival rates.

"I was planning on going into oncology," Kelly sighs, "Not surgery."

She is the third student the government has sent me. So far, she's shaping up to be as useless as the previous two. Afi quit after two tough days. Chrissy didn't get a parasite into a disposal case quickly enough. It attached itself to her carotid artery. She had a stroke. There was nothing I could have done.

We ran out of properly qualified surgeons during the second wave. None of us anticipated the masses that descended on the hospitals. Combine that with the mere minutes you have between a patient dying and the parasite emerging to violently infect a new host… Things spiralled pretty quickly after that. Most of us were sent out to what are generously called 'field hospitals' like this one. Years mastering the ability to internally diagnose everything from rabies to osteosarcoma felt wasted. Here we are, the un-graduates, all that knowledge rotting away as we train the would-be freshman to dig demons out of living corpses. What skills will any of us have to care for the survivors when all this ends? If all this ends.

A sob outside pulls me back into the room and causes Kelly to jump.

"That sounds close?" I ask.

Kelly nudges the curtain aside. "An elderly male and a young girl. Best suit up."

I pull a pair of blue gloves out of the dispenser. It chimes to signal it needs refilling, the red light blinking on below the logo.

"Shit, mine ran out this morning too." Kelly fidgets, examining her blood-splattered scrubs. "I'll stop by the store room on my way back, I'll need to change first."

She leaves, and I prepare for the patients. Clipboard and consent forms out, my notepad out, two working pens. Apron secure, mask secure. Connector in place around my right wrist. Ready.

I step around the doorway to beckon the patients in, examining them externally as I hand over a clipboard and pen. The girl is likely in her mid-teens, tanned skin taut over bone but otherwise the first healthy face I've seen for months. The man is elderly, but something in the way his muscle is wasting away denotes that he was previously in very good health for his age. Most of the people in this county were farmers; he was likely still working up until a few days ago. However, the external signs of infection are evident: darkening around the eyes, sunken cheeks, the vasculitis with the telltale macular rash spreading up the neck and across the mandibular margin, the oedema beginning in the extremities. I waste no more of his time.

"How long ago were you exposed?"

"Three days," he croaks. "Came off one of our sheep, jumped onto my shoulder and down my shirt 'fore I could catch it." He lifts his shirt to show me the puckered, erythematous entry mark on his lower abdomen.

I nod, making notes. I've seen enough from out here. "Happy with the consent form?"

"As I'll ever be." He hands it over, a scribbled signature across the bottom.

"Read through the risks?"

"Well aware I'll have two extra beings rooting around my insides."

"I'd hope one is more welcome than the other," I laugh. He says nothing. The girl shudders, crossing her arms. I put down the notepad, picking up the Connector remote and sitting opposite him before extending my gloved hand. "May I?"

He shrugs and reaches back. I click the remote just before our hands join, feeling the cool metal cage expand out from my wrist, around our joined fists before shrinking to fix them in place. I take a deep breath in as I slip away, shakily exhaling through his nose. He groans as I adjust to the searing pain he has grown all too used to in the last few days.

It's been this bad the whole time?

"Yes," he responds, fighting me as I grit his teeth.

"Grandad, are you ok?"

"Fine, sweetheart, the doctor is just seeing what the damage is."

And the breathing trouble, when did that start?

"Last night."

Bear with me, I just need to locate it then I'll be out of your hair.

"Literally," he chuckles, a weak but unmistakably jovial sound. Hardly any of our patients still laugh.

"How long will this take?" asks the girl.

"Not long, sweetheart." I feel the vacuum pull of another body as he takes her fidgeting hands in his. I cling on where I am until he lets go. "Why don't you get some air, Abbie?"

I feel the tension around his heart as he watches her go, the strain of adrenaline and the flood of hormones that make up 'love'.

Granddaughter?

"Yeah. She's a good kid really. Only has me left now. Not sure what to do if…" He clears his throat. "You found it yet?"

Yes.

I feel the adrenaline hit his system as he asks, "You'll have to operate, right, doc?"

The network of blood vessels around the parasite is immense. It's latched onto the aorta. Shit. One of the worst I've seen in a while. An alarming portion of the blood supply has been diverted from most of the organs in the area. It's going to be almost impossible to get out. I'm genuinely surprised he's still alive. Best not think that too loudly.

I slip back into my own body, taking a few deep breaths before I speak. "Yes, we will. It seems to have settled very near to your kidney so there's a chance…"

"You'll have to take the kidney out with it?"

I nod. Does he need to know about the other organs? Does he need to know that, given his age and the advanced infection, he's unlikely to survive the anaesthetic? 'Do no harm' can't just mean physical harm. How much psychological harm do I cause this dying man?

He smirks, unaware of all of this. "Well, God gave us two for a reason."

I force myself to chuckle politely. I must remember to order more body bags tomorrow.

The door slams open behind us and I only realise it can't be Kelly when I hear the first gunshot.

"Murderers!!" screams our assailant as I collapse to the floor. Warmth is pooling somewhere beneath me. She's blurry but I vaguely recognise her. I think she came in with the woman who died this morning.

I'm going to die this morning too.

Where the hell's Kelly when I need her?

"Doc?"

My tongue feels heavy.

"Doc? Are you ok?"

I shake my head to clear my thoughts. I check my own vitals quickly and see that I've lost a lot of blood. The bullet went through an artery. This body is done.

I'm not done. I'm blacking out. *Please, I'm not done.*

"Where did Abbie go?"

My body twists around to look at the door. Why am I twisting to look at the door? With some effort I turn my head to look at the body of the old man next to me, still joined by the hand.

Not the old man.

Me. My body.

I'm not in there anymore.

I'm a dead man inside another dying man's body.

Shit.

"Doc?" The old man's voice is tremulous. "You're in here?" He taps his temple. I'm not calm enough to ascertain my exact location yet, but I confirm. *Yes.*

"How?"

It wasn't intentional. I'm not sure.

"No. But…" He takes a few struggling breaths, "What happens to us both when…?"

We both… I don't know. This is why we use the Connectors. To prevent anyone getting stuck in a… dying body.

Tears are running down his cheekbones to the ground. "Town's het up over all this. People aren't acting as they should." He scoffs, "Shame she hit me too, else I s'pose you could've carried on doctoring in my body for a while. Save a few more folk, eh, doc?"

That would be unethical.

"Hmm. Be unethical to leave a dying town with no doctor."

Arguably. *Kelly will manage,* I think, but even I don't believe it. *And there are other doctors they can send, right?* Useless trainees with a higher death rate than me.

He takes a rasping breath and clutches one of the wounds in his abdomen. After a moment, he speaks. "I was going to die today anyway, wasn't I," he states rather than asks. I feel no need to answer.

"GRANDAD!?"

I'm in no mood for theatrics right now, so I go about checking the damage while the girl wails at us. He's been hit in the stomach twice. One miraculously missed almost everything, but the other has taken out a big blood vessel that was feeding the parasite.

The parasite is not happy about this. It will be out in minutes. I should really warn the girl.

Sorry to interrupt but…

"…the parasite is going to exit this body in a couple of minutes," I speak through his mouth, "You've got to go."

"NO! I am NOT leaving you to die alone."

"He won't - I won't - Listen, you'll die if you stay here. Please go."

"No, I'm staying with you!"

I give up. I let him take back over his mouth. He's softer with her than I am. "Abbie, you remember what happened to Dylan? He stayed by your mother too long…"

I let them talk and keep a watch on the parasite as it begins to disconnect itself, ready to exit and infect the next host. I have to give it credit, it's certainly perfectly designed to fulfil its role in the world. Not like me. What have I ever done to fulfil my role? I was a difficult child, a brash, headstrong student, a selfish, neglectful spouse if my divorce record is any measure of judgment. I was a brilliant diagnoser, but all of that went out the window when the pandemic started and suddenly diagnosing anything else didn't matter. If there is anywhere other than the void waiting for me now, how will my heart measure on the scale?

The girl grabs ahold of his hand and I anchor myself in place against the whirlwind pull of her body before I realise what it is.

A way out.

That would be unethical.

Those were my thoughts seconds ago. And it would be unethical. Not to mention completely stupid and probably pointless. How long could I last in someone else's space? My med school roommate's best friend ended up spending seven hours in a patient for a surgery, and he was markedly not himself after that experience. The medical board recommends no longer than four hours inside an external body following several studies. No one has ever properly tested anything longer. It's considered unethical to subject people to human testing.

Unethical. 'Do no harm', right?

Is it…

But is it arguably unethical to leave her in this room, where in approximately one minute a parasite will be bursting out of her then dead grandad and springing onto her? Am I causing harm to her by *not* taking over her body to get her away from the danger of that mad woman with the gun returning? I don't know where she is. The girl is too focused on her grandad to consider the danger of either situation. Would I be causing her less overall harm by getting her away from here?

After all, I might just fade away after a few hours. Dissolve, or assimilate into her system. All sentience faded, no thought, no feeling, just a wisp of what was 'Jordan' waving like a flag in the plasma flow of her bloodstream. Perhaps I would have no effect on her, but I would have saved her life.

Just as I begin to give in to the pull, I grip on again. How would I even go about getting consent for this? Excuse me, but I'm stuck in your dying grandad and if you don't run you'll die too, by parasite or bullet wound, so please do you mind if I take over your body for a few minutes to get you the hell out of this death trap, and then I'll just chill out in your liver until I maybe probably fade away?

I'm not sure it would go down well.

But then neither would sneaking in. The ramifications for my career if anyone ever found out…

What career would I have anymore? Even if somehow any lasting vestige of myself remained in there, I'd still certainly have to retrain. But what harm would there be in that? I need the extra surgery training anyway. I could be back out in the field in a few years, more skilled than before, saving more lives. One girl's life sacrificed to save thousands. Hundreds of thousands maybe.

And who would actually find out anyway? Who is this girl? A farmer's daughter. What connections does she have? Most of this rural community are dead, by a parasite's mouth or my unskilled hand. Her grandad said they're the only ones left, so once he dies she'll have no one. Her only carer will die on my watch. A girl her age wandering the streets is a target for the trafficking gangs. Do I have a duty of care to look after her, to prevent harm in whatever way I can?

The parasite is cauterising the last few blood vessels attaching it to this body. There isn't much time left.

I move closer to where their hands are joined, feeling the energy whip past me, tugging at me but I pause, digging in. Do the ends justify the means? Will I be no better than this parasite here if I invade her system? Just another creature seeking a body to support it, draining and suppressing the life of its host.

An odd nausea sweeps over me, despite my lacking a stomach of my own. I can't do this. I can't take another life on purpose, even potentially.

But I did already. I was so apathetically certain the patient this morning was going to die that I never gave her a chance to be saved. I evacuated before the incision was made and left an inexperienced physician to finish off, as 'practice'.

Maybe I am a murderer. Maybe I deserved to die.

The tile floor is cold against the skin of the old man's arms, the hair pricking up with goosebumps. There is sweat forming along his forehead. His heart is hammering, violently trying to compensate for the blood he's losing, his lungs working hard to maintain failing oxygen levels. Adrenaline gives every feeling a sharp edge. It will all fail soon. I will never feel any of these sensations again. I will never see these blurred colours and shapes, never hear any voice, like a distant radio broadcast now as he begins to fade.

As we begin to fade.

Where will we go? How will we go? Will there be a stronger pull into the other place when we die? Or will it be a slow fade to black and nothingness? Distant stars flash overhead and all go out at once. The end of the universe, for us at least.

The parasite is disconnected now and has started eating its way out. She'll be infected in less than a minute unless she runs right now.

One arm lifts off the cold tiles as he reaches to grasp her hand with both of his, leaning in to impart his final wisdom to his beloved granddaughter.

I should let go. Fade away into oblivion and let them have this final moment. Let other doctors save the world. I played my part. I did as much as I could.

Didn't I?

He rasps in a breath to speak. He's fading fast.

"Abbie…"

"Yes, Grandad?"

I start to slip away.

"…I always thought you would make a wonderful doctor."

Amanda Parrott - But for the Grace

He stepped into the booth. The room fell silent as two officers followed him closely and positioned themselves on either side of him at the back of the dock. The glass that formed its walls from waist-height upwards was unnaturally clean, except for an oval-shaped smear in front of his mouth. He wore black; black suit, black tie, with a white shirt. Helen had no idea whether the outfit was a ten-a-penny Primark effort or a carefully-sourced investment – how could they tell, she'd always wondered, when someone described a suit as 'beautifully-cut'?

"Court rise."

Thirty seconds later the bench at the front of the courtroom was occupied. Helen's attempts to prepare herself for this moment now felt absurd, since nowhere in the imagined scenarios that haunted her had a plump, middle-aged woman appeared. The judge's eyes swept her audience.

"Ladies and gentlemen of the jury, this is a criminal case." Her voice was gentle, with a trace of a Manchester accent.

"You will be asked to decide if the defendant is guilty or not guilty of the offence with which he is charged. You have been instructed how to proceed should you require clarification or if for any reason you should find yourself in difficulty. Please raise your hand if you have not received or understood these instructions."

The jury's collective attempt to mirror the behaviour of the professionals was laudable, if a little ridiculous, as they straightened their backs and nodded raised chins, whilst maintaining their solemn expressions.

She softened her voice further. "You will hear accounts that contain some distressing details."

Helen's breath left her lungs as her heart raced.

"You must listen carefully to all the information presented to you, in order to reach a fair conclusion. A young man has lost his life. You must decide whether that life was taken from him unlawfully, and whether the defendant was responsible."

Did this woman have a child?

Helen had a child.

Helen stood in a small, cluttered kitchen, the lives of neighbours above and below an ever-present sound track. She liked knowing that the two of them were sandwiched between secure families with the right balance of people. The weak February sun was already low in the sky, striking the perfect angle to highlight the sticky handprints that marked ownership of everything below waist level. Plastic farm animals consorted with dinosaurs on the lino floor behind Helen, as she spooned sweetcorn and cauliflower from a saucepan onto a scratched melamine plate. Mickey and Minnie disappeared as the vegetables, then a spoon of pasta covered them.

"Feeding time," she said, placing the plate on a table, then scooping up the nineteen-month-old farmer, who squealed and clutched a triceratops closer to him.

"It's OK, he can have some too." She expertly squashed the resistance by standing the three-inch dinosaur next to the plate. The child replied with the cherished babble that demanded her full attention at every meal time. She breathed it in, along with his light blue eyes that concentrated on hers as he struggled to explain why his triceratops couldn't eat sweetcorn. Everything about him was pale, her white-blond, ivory-skinned little doll of a baby. Precious, people called him, and he did have the air of a fragile ornament, a delicate work of art that would shatter if it were knocked. Appearances were deceptive though, and Helen was proud of her son's self-assurance. He would happily babble to anyone, adult or child, and Helen liked to think that his confidence was somehow her doing.

"At least no one else can take credit for how he turns out," she'd reminded herself wryly on the days when she would have readily accepted a helping hand, whatever form it came in. No offers were forthcoming though, unless a mercifully brief liaison with a financial advisor sixteen years her senior counted.

"All down to me."

"I invite the Counsel for the Prosecution to present their opening statement."

One of the black-gowned barristers in the centre of the courtroom rose and bowed briefly to the coat of arms behind the judge. She was an imposing figure, tall and broad-shouldered, her sharp features made all the more striking by unapologetic make up. In contrast to the judge, she made no attempt to soften her manner for the comfort of the jury.

"Ladies and gentlemen, the defendant is charged with murder. Should you find him guilty, you will have concluded that he, whilst of sound mind, unlawfully killed his victim.

A twitchy elderly man in the front row of the jury was nodding vigorously.

"His victim. A twenty-one-year-old man. An ordinary, law-abiding Business student in the second year of his degree. A boyfriend, a friend. A son. A promising footballer and a popular, valued member of the university. I don't wish to paint the victim as exceptional – quite the opposite. I suggest that he was unremarkable; your neighbour, your daughter's boyfriend, the son you chastised for trampling mud on your floor. His murder has left a tragic hole in the lives of those who loved him, which will never be filled." The banality of her words did not diminish their truth.

Helen's other senses had faded in order for her hearing to intensify; the words were all she was conscious of, a torch-lit text in a pitch-dark room. She absorbed every one, as the judge had instructed, and her eyes closed in an unconscious attempt at a deeper concentration on the description of this beloved, perfect, imperfect boy.

"He's been!" The tiny whirlwind flung open Helen's bedroom door. "Look, look what he brought me!" He pushed a small blue box, bits of its gaudy wrapping paper still attached, under her nose. Helen pushed herself up to sit against the pillows and reached for the bedside lamp. 4.47am, shouted the red digits on her alarm. Three hours sleep was really absolutely fine, though. Better than fine.

"Merry Christmas, baby!"

She pulled him up onto her bed as he tore open the box.

"Can we make it now?" he begged, already pulling at the clear plastic to get at the Lego.

"Hang on, we need to see if he's brought anything else first. And have you been for a wee yet?"

She carried him to the bathroom, brushing off his protests that six was too big to be picked up, then together they burst into the living room. The little room didn't have much of a fireplace - just a dated tiled effort from the 80s - but it did at least have a mantlepiece, boasting one bulging, red stocking.

"Thank God for that," Helen thought. Her struggles to fix the brimming stocking to the mantlepiece at 1.15 that morning hadn't been wasted. She handed it down to him and took her chance to make a quick coffee, watching through the open door. Breakfast could wait – his "Wow! That is so cool!" with the same surprise every time, was priceless. Helen sat close to him on the thin grey carpet as her coffee went cold.

The stocking empty, she gathered the pile of red paper and almost scooped up the paper plate underneath too. A silver foil mince pie case sat next to a few crumbs of carrot. He picked up the plate in silence and stared at it with reverence. Without looking at Helen, he leaned as close as he could get to the back of the gas fire and called upwards, "Thank you, I love everything. Thank you!"

Helen dropped her pile, hugged him and covered his squirming face with kisses. She felt something - guilt? - at how lucky she was. Her one wish was for that feeling to return every year, forever, a ritual that never came to an end.

She opened her eyes and looked at the young man in the dock, just for a second, keeping her head bowed. Christmas. She dropped her gaze and studied her fingers. She'd noted the open shoulders and strong posture so practised to him that he couldn't drop it, even in that exposed glass cage. Or maybe especially in that exposed glass cage. He was listening intently to the Prosecution's outline of the case. Was he working hard to maintain an image he'd been advised to portray? He was doing a good job. Taken out of the current setting, he'd have been described as calm, measured. Pleasant, perhaps. He nodded slightly at some of the lawyer's words, confident his approval was relevant. The composure showed no sign of wavering as the prosecutor arrived at the details of the murder.

"At 1.35am on Saturday 17th of May this year, the victim suffered a violent attack outside the Firefly nightclub in Templeton Street. He played no part in initiating the attack, nor did he provoke his attacker. The victim sustained two broken ribs, a fractured skull and injuries to his face in the initial attack. I would ask you to turn to page six of the file you have in front of you."

The jury members reached for their white lever-arch folders, glancing sideways to check the page matched their neighbour's. A colour photograph of a man's face. They winced. The same photograph appeared on the screen behind the judge but Helen's eyes remained on her hands. She'd seen it before and had no need to refresh the image already in her head.

"The injuries you see left the victim unconscious. At this point his attacker used a kitchen knife with a three-inch blade to stab him repeatedly in his abdomen, causing his abdominal aorta to burst and resulting in massive internal and external bleeding. Paramedics who attended the incident confirmed that he was dead on their arrival.

Medical professionals, whose testimonies you will hear this afternoon, describe the force required to cause such injuries as 'brutal'."

She paused and turned away from the jury a fraction, towards the judge.

"It is the Crown's case that his attacker was the defendant."

Helen watched the judge. She wasn't surprised to see the serene expression maintained throughout, and had registered the barely perceptible nods as she made the odd note on her pad.

"They could at least have given her a decent pen," sprang to Helen's mind as she fixed on the lidless black biro. She resisted her brain's attempt to lead her towards the safety of a mundane frame of reference and forced her attention back to the judge's eyes.

Did she have a son?

Helen had a son.

The night before, she had ironed her clothes again. The choice had been made long before, after endless sessions of trying on everything she owned, as though it mattered. She would struggle to sleep, like every night since. At 3.12am, the radio still playing, she had finally slipped away to a past that should have brought comfort.

The same dream. Celebrations of a new millennium. In the bedroom of her flat with his father, reliving the only night they had ever spent together. The party next door was still in full swing and Helen was flying high on tequila-fuelled, new-millennial hope. Could this be it? Could he be her future, this man who had noticed her, flattered her and now kissed her? The dream amplified her euphoria, but also her terror of shattering the embryonic promise of happiness. The radio was ploughing through the decade's number ones and she pulled the embodiment of her hopes to his feet to dance with her. They both giggled when the opening bars of Robbie Williams's 'She's the One' gave them almost no choice but to move the story on. Nearly every night, she felt that thrilling anticipation build again, only for it to be crushed in an even ruder conclusion than twenty-two years earlier. He would abruptly cancel the start of their future before it began, walking away before he had slept with her.

"It's for the best," he would smile, closing the door behind him and leaving her empty. However else the dream's narrative varied, conception never took place.

Helen would wake soon after, and every time readjust to the reality that he had left her pregnant. Her son did exist.

Her son had always been fascinated by dreams. He would confidently attribute meanings to his quests - often naked, always heroic - to outrun wolves or snakes or whichever wild animal had pursued him this time and would always land on an explanation that granted him another superhero character trait. Helen never disagreed, more than willing to bolster his infallibility He never asked about her dreams.

As he grew, and one by one, discarded each mark of childhood in his wake, Helen gathered them all in her arms, hurrying to keep up behind him. She held every hug, every smile and every tear. Far from forgetting the arguments and harsh words, she cherished those too, holding on tightly to all the pieces that fitted together to complete her son.

The defendant's expression had changed. His jaw was clenched and Helen could see his chest rising and falling as his breathing quickened. The prosecutor was talking about the girl.

"Her two-year relationship with the defendant had ended six weeks before the attack."

The man in the dock swallowed.

"We should be clear that at the time of the attack she was not in a relationship with the defendant. Having recently begun a relationship with the victim, she was a witness to the attack, having spent the evening with him at the Firefly nightclub."

Helen watched the jury while they shaded in the black and white image of the girl in their heads. She wondered if their conclusions matched her own. She knew what the girl looked like, of course, but what else? The jury's guess at her essence, her role in the catastrophic convergence of the two relationships was as good as Helen's.

Dates, locations, times. The product description of a kitchen knife. When the court adjourned for lunch the details still filled Helen's head as she shuffled along the bench with the other occupants of the public gallery.

"Sorry"' she muttered, as she reached the end of her row at the same time as a couple leaving the bench in front.

"After you."

The woman, leaning slightly on her husband's arm looked a little older than Helen. She held Helen's gaze and the rest of the scene fell away as the moment froze. Her eyes sent Helen their undisguised message. I pity you.

Helen walked out into the car park. She wasn't prepared for the crisp sunshine, and blinked; the December darkness had only just begun to lift as she'd stepped out of the cab that morning. Her eyes on the pavement, she crossed the square and walked. Feeling no compulsion to do anything except walk, that's what she did, subconsciously counting the footsteps. An hour and a half later, as she walked between the last of the red-brick gables of Watergate Street, she knew she wouldn't be returning to the court. The river was in front of her, on the other side of Brunswick Street. She raised her eyes at last and waited for the wall of traffic to break, then crossed all four lanes, her eyes on the river.

Turning right, she followed the water, icy blue in the low winter sunlight, until she reached the ferry terminal. She hadn't been conscious of her destination until then.

Helen leaned heavily over the rail that enclosed the deck, flecks of once-white paint peeling away against the sleeves of her jacket. She stared down beyond the surface of the water, imagining herself falling contentedly to the river bed. The ferry had always been her place, the scene of her earliest treasured memories. It would spirit her away with her grandad to the same locally-foreign shores each time and she adored it. The round-trip ticket let them stay on board all day if they chose. All the way along the bumpy road of childish fall-outs, teenage angst and the pain of her grandfather's death when she was seventeen, the ferry never broke its promise of escape, of whipping away her worries on the one-way wind. She hadn't been back for years.

Eventually, the earthy rumble of the engines came close to drowning out the court transcript. She still didn't move, breathing in the sharp air methodically, willing the familiar mix of metallic and marshy odours to supplant this with a pain that was ordinary, bearable. When they docked for the last time, the sunshine was long gone and the noise of rush hour traffic had replaced the engines. The only passenger, she crossed the narrow gangplank, exhausted, and barely registered the protest from her legs at the solid surface beneath them.

The exit route herded her first into the coffee shop with its cold metal chairs, uninviting at the best of times but positively forbidding in the early evening gloom. There were no customers as Helen stepped in, just a waitress, who had stopped wiping the

counter to concentrate on the TV on the wall, her attention caught by its red 'breaking news' banner. On the screen facing Helen, a reporter was nodding empathetically towards a couple, as they stood together on the concrete steps outside a court. The woman was maybe a little older than Helen.

"We're satisfied with the verdict," the woman whispered into the reporter's microphone, then turned away, leaning on her husband's arm.

The picture changed. Helen reached for the back of a chair. The face she hadn't seen for seven months was in the centre of the screen. Handcuffed to an officer, he looked straight at Helen. The blond hair and ivory skin were indistinct against the white wall behind him. The waitress, the café, the river – the world beyond his face – was lost to Helen as blackness closed in on everything except his ice-blue eyes.

Pity.

Andrew Sutherland - The Infinite Book of Alder Shy

I listened distractedly as the man with the shiny face lectured his young companion. He kept stressing the importance of her following his "big-picture blueprint". She should put aside any misgivings, he told her, and trust to her innate ability. From time to time he reminded her – and me, obliquely – how much money he'd invested in the project, and in us. The money was the only reason I'd agreed to this meeting.

'Only three very particular people can do this, and we're sitting right here. Let's get it done.' He stared hard at the two of us then stood as if to leave the pub, but did not remove his leather hat from the table. 'I'm going for a pee.'

'He doesn't wash!' Rose, the Japanese American girl with blue-black hair rolled dark, scandalised eyes in my direction. 'He smells and his hands are not clean.'

This is true. Alder Shy carries with him the mildewed scent of old forest floors. A musty odour soiled the air even after he'd gone. I shrugged. Though my heart wasn't in it, there were more important things to talk about just then.

'How did you find him?' I asked her.

'I did not. He found me! He came into the university saying he wished to meet me. I had already heard of him, of course…'

We have all heard of Alder Shy, the strange man with stranger ideas. Certain quarters of the internet are alive with rumours of his absurd mathematics. None are able to throw any light on who he is, though. And in the closed world of theoretical physics, provenance is everything.

'Did he come and find you, too, Mr. Clive?' Rose blushed and looked down at her neatly folded hands. 'If you don't mind me asking.'

'Yes, Rose, he did.'

*

Nobody strolls into XeneX Systems and sees the boss without serious references. It can't be done. Yet my PA, a shrewd judge of character, had fielded a telephone call a couple of weeks ago and promptly granted a diary slot: *Alder Shy plus one, funded proposal, fifteen to twenty minutes.* At the appointed hour Alder had sailed into my office towing a waft of sour air and the venture capitalist, Barlow Bain in his wake.

I'd wrinkled my sensitive nose. 'Barlow? If you're involved this must be big!'

'It is.' The great financier had clasped my hand. 'I'm so sorry to hear about Lilly, Clive. If there's anything I can do…'

'Thank you.' There's nothing anyone else can do. The worst of it is, there's nothing I can do. 'You're very kind.' I'd listened carefully, then, as Barlow told me he had no hesitation in underwriting my visitor's project. After a few more pleasantries he'd consulted his watch, shaken my hand once more and rushed off to another meeting. At Barlow's level a man's word is very much his bond.

I'd raised an eyebrow at Alder Shy.

'Well, we both heard him. What do you propose to do with Mr Bain's money?'

'I'd like to commission a range of top-end, bespoke items, Clive.' Alder had pulled a folder from a brown leather briefcase. 'And I'll give you half a million just to hear me out.'

'Yeah, right. All credit to you for winning such impressive backing, Mr Shy, but what could you possibly want from XeneX? We develop specialist processors for – '

'Alder, please. And I know what your company does.' He'd pushed the folder into my hands. 'Read this.'

I hadn't believed that the unhygienic man before me would actually hand over half a million, but moved by his chutzpah I'd waved him into a chair and skimmed the folder.

'This is some shopping list, Alder. Very specific. You've clearly done your homework.'

'When it's ready I'd like to have it delivered to an address in the East End.' Alder had poised his greasy fingers over an expensive-looking laptop. 'Let's settle up in advance. How much should I transfer to your account?'

*

'He came to see me, Rose, and gave me an astronomical sum of money to custom rig a van-load of components.'

Rose nodded. 'I think he must be very rich, Mr Clive. When my professor at the university said there was no question of him "borrowing" me for his project, Mr Shy paid off our research application for the whole year! He says I'm the only student he's ever interested in.'

'Ever interested? So, he's borrowed you to…?'

'I am a super-conduction engineer studying quantum applications. He wants me to help him build something.' The girl glanced up at me. 'Mr Shy says you have made the parts and he will tell me how to put them together.'

'Did he mention – '

'Right, drink up and let's get going.' Alder appeared beside us, wiping his hands on the front of his trousers. 'Unless there's somewhere else you'd rather be.'

Somewhere else? At Lilly's graveside, perhaps, with my head pressed against her stone to help block out the pain. The grief doesn't fade. A cancer stole my daughter from me and to shore up my soul, to stop myself falling into ruin, I'd gone back to work. To cut the deals just like the old days. But not exactly like, though. A colleague, her eyes brim-full of disapproval, had wondered why I was at my desk again so soon after the funeral.

I'd told her, business is chess. I'm white, they're black. I move, they move, I counter. To win you have to concentrate and that concentration wipes everything else away. Not long ago Lucy's swift leukaemia took a steak knife and rammed it through my face - in one cheek and out the other - leaving the blade to click between my teeth. Concentrate on *that*, Clive. I'm back in the game in search of distraction, thanks for asking, and being as brave as I can be.

We drove to the East End in my classic Jag. Rose perched beside me, somehow managing to look uncomfortable amid the Connolly and walnut whilst Alder stank up the back seats alone. The directions he gave me took us through a light industrial estate to a damp basement lock-up beneath an abandoned sports hall.

'A bit dramatic, Alder.' I said.

'Nice and secluded, Clive.' Said he.

Stacked inside, we found the specialist items I'd supplied him, a crowbar lying invitingly atop the nearest crate. Next to them were the materials he'd sourced for himself: a diesel generator, drums of copper wiring, a lot of other stuff I didn't recognise and, in the centre of the floor, an enormous glass fish tank.

Alder caught the direction of my gaze. 'It's not what you think,' he said. 'Glass resists ageing, and that will be important later.'

'Mr Shy?' We both turned in surprise as our quiet, retiring Rose finally addressed the elephant in the basement. I'd actually been about to do it myself. 'Why are we here?' She wriggled in embarrassment.

Alder Shy gave her a thoughtful look before taking a seat among the boxes. 'Some background might be helpful, I think.' He tossed his hat into a corner. 'Essentially, would you think me mad if I said matter and energy should be regarded purely as information? And that this universe, the one in which we find ourselves, is just one of countless billions?'

'You're preaching to the converted, Alder. Rose is researching quantum physics and my own background's in AI software. These are familiar concepts.'

'What if I suggest that the infinite universes are like the pages in a book, pressed together one next to the other in intimate contact. Everything in this and every other universe is information, yes? Happy with that? But the information on one page does not transfer itself to the next, nor does a change in the information on one page cause an adjacent page to rewrite itself.'

'Again, nothing new.' Rose folded her slender arms. 'A version of multiverse theory. The various realities are discreet and cannot interact with each other.'

'Am I mad, then, if I suggest they enjoy a common denominator?'

'Deluded, anyway.' I headed for the stairs. 'Our business is concluded, Alder. Thank you for your patronage and are you ok about getting a taxi back?'

'You never stay to help, Clive. Don't worry, Rose and I are quite capable.'

'What?'

He grinned at me. 'My little joke.'

*

I assumed that would be the end of it.

I made several assumptions: That Alder Shy and Rose would fiddle about in a fruitless search for God knows what till the money ran out. That Barlow Bain would chunter about failed tech investments for a while, but we'd still do business afterwards. That I'd carry on taking my wife to the graveyard in Silverthorn Lane to grieve for our Lilly.

That we'd carry on failing to deal with the aching hole in our lives.

I assumed I'd never see Alder again, but I was wrong. He asked for another appointment a few days later and my PA, not so shrewdly judging that it would do me good, admitted him. He came alone.

'Would you like to see what we've done, Clive?'

'No.'

I told him I was busy and really couldn't spare the time but we ended up in the Jag anyway, bowling through the rain on our way to the Docklands because I hadn't the strength to keep it up. Halfway there I pointedly hung an air freshener on the rear-view mirror.

He pointedly wound his window down. 'You people get sick all the time because you constantly strip away your skin's bacterial defences. It's not natural. I can't imagine how you stand the chemicals.'

At the heavy steel door beneath the sports hall, Alder paused. 'I like you, Clive,' he said, 'I always do. And I'm truly sorry for your loss. I've never met Lilly but… you know. Look, once you've seen this remember that I want to help. From my point of view it works out the same every time; Barlow Bain's a wealthy vampire looking for a good investment, Rose is a young genius looking for the great leap forward and you,' he turned the key, 'you're a nice man who makes useful stuff.'

Inside, the basement reeked of mould. At first glance it was all but empty, the piles of equipment and great spools of wire that had previously filled it were no longer there. The only light now seeped from the large glass fish tank that still stood in the centre of the room. As I moved forward I could see it was full of a pearlescent, white-ish fluid.

'Mind your feet,' murmured Alder, pointing downwards at the thick ridges of verdigris and corroded metal that covered the floor.

'What's in the tank?'

'The common denominator.'

'Which is…?'

'The one thing common to an infinity of incompatible realities. The one thing that cannot be physically influenced, described or measured.' He smiled. 'Time.'

'My watch measures time, Alder,'

'It certainly does not. Your watch records a series of arbitrarily chosen intervals.'

Irritated, I poked a toe into a nearby slurry of rust. Beneath the surface, exposed by my casual digging, the ivory corner of something familiar came into view. I bent closer.

'Each of the infinite universes is similar to, but not exactly the same as its immediate neighbours. They in turn are similar to their immediate neighbours and so on, getting more and more peculiar the further out you go.' Alder's voice carried to me from where he stood on the far side of the tank. 'Although different to each other, Clive, the one thing they share in common is time. It flows through them and between them. An eternal, homogenous, unifying plasma.'

The ivory, I saw, was a piece of plastic that had once been white. Another twitch of my foot and the thing fell to powder. It must have been old. Very old. But therein lay a conundrum.

'By swimming in that flow I've found it's possible to cross from one universe to the next. It's the funniest joke. Time travel doesn't move you forwards or backwards. It takes you sideways.'

'Well, if you say so.' I worked my shoe deeper into the mess, dislodging bits of ceramic insulator, a laptop hard drive and the crumbling remains of a high tech motherboard. All of it as aged and rotten as if it had been dropped there a century ago. Other, equally derelict shapes lay beyond. I turned to face Alder. 'You're not from around here, are you?'

'I'm English, if that's what you mean.' He hoisted himself awkwardly over the edge of the glass tank and lowered his legs into the fluid. I watched as tendrils of whiteness began crawling up his clothing. 'Just not *your* England. I'm a traveller, Clive. From one page to the next page and the next. On each page I find a Barlow to lend me the money, a Clive to sell me the parts and a Rose to build me an onward route.' Gently, Alder raised his knees and the pale threads that had covered them dissolved into the air. 'This stuff won't be useable for long. I'd best be off.'

'Going to London?'

He grinned. 'One of them. Sorry about the mess. The device Rose assembled for me soaks up time and condenses it. Hence the white goo in here and the decay out there.'

'On the subject of whom…'

'She's around somewhere.' Alder laughed. 'There's always a Rose around when you need one.'

I nodded. I'd seen the long bones back in the shadows. 'You were absent when she switched the device on?'

'Of course. Each universe is similar to the next, Clive. Some of the details are different but the nature of the people never changes.'

Alder left soon after that. He closed his eyes and let himself slip beneath the glowing surface, and when the fluid was still again I could see that barely half of it remained.

*

It stopped raining as I eased the Jag onto the wide road heading west. The grey Docklands fell away behind me to the soft hiss of Firestones on wet tarmac. Driving slowly, I stared through the windscreen and tried to think of nothing at all. Just drive. Look only at the road ahead and not at the two hands gripping the wheel. Not at the curved wooden dash with its back-lit gauges. Not at the little tree-shaped freshener lying next to the ashtray, still in its cellophane wrapper.

An hour later, under the elms at the end of our driveway, I park and climb out. Sometimes in life you have to make a decision without first having the time to properly consider it. I'm feeling very old, very tired. Time, like life itself, is over and gone so soon. If you choose to turn aside and walk a different path, to suffer a different pain, is that such a bad thing?

The door to our house is oak inset with round, bottle glass panes. Candle light shines through the glass, yellow and warm and welcoming. And behind that light a woman moves to open the door, a girl-child in her arms.

Anthony Slone - The Laws of Metaphysics

They say that every action has an equal and opposite reaction, and I know what they mean: good luck is paid for with bad; wicked behaviour is rewarded with a suitable punishment. You steal a bike, you're taken hostage. That sort of thing. Logic.

They? The scientists of course. They who would have us not repeat a failed experiment. Yet that is what I'm doing. I am one day free from a year of captivity, and as I reflect on the moment I was taken, all I know for sure is that the signs I'm given now are as compelling as they were then.

I can see myself still, standing outside the baker's shop, thinking about Dolly and Beacham and shopping, and a currant slice for a treat to take home; not exactly looking for signs but receptive to them perhaps. If anything, I was a bit reticent, I see that now, a newbie too conscious of how not to do it wrong, and consequently not doing it right. That thing about good timing being to do things just before you're ready for them.

There I am, on Fleet Street, next to two women with whom for a moment I made a line of three, contemplating purchases. Purchases added for them, stop at contemplating for me. Like me, they sported an air of unused education. Like me! A pang of longing strikes. I was once like them.

One of them pointed at a display in the window and said, 'They'll do, thirteen of them,' and giggled, which would not have been remarkable, had I not been thinking about that time me and Dolly bought a dozen of the same cakes, and Gibson had thrown in an extra one but charged us for it anyway. I get that feeling again, which tells me something about providence. I think a word, and someone says it; I read a word and there, at that very instant, it's said on the radio. Like someone near but far away is trying to tell me something. That I should keep going.

'What are they,' asked the other, and one said *macaroons* as the other said *75p aren't they*? And the two of them exchanged that guttural giggle again which seemed to say that the whole world was mad and only they had noticed.

As the proposer of the purchase disappeared into the shop, I said to the one left outside, 'Nine pounds seventy-five by the way,' and to this day I cannot understand why I said it in a Scottish accent. The thought of it anew strikes me like a punch in the stomach.

We watched her friend lean into the window to point to the tray she wanted, and as she did, she pulled a face at Outsider unseen by the shop assistant. I saw it though, so I said to my new confidante, 'Some peep holes think I'm bonkers, I just think I'm free.' I think it went like that; it was from a pop song I'd heard somewhere or other.

I see her reaction clearly now. I see now how the world saw me then. I swallow hard. 'Nine pounds seventy-five,' I wheeze out, airless, shamed at the memory, in a wee squeaky Scottish accent, as if I'm appalled at the prospect of paying nine-seventy-five for something so palpably worthless. I lean back my head and face it up to the sky and shout, 'Oh God. I'm sorry,' but it doesn't help, and just dissolves into a muffled sob. A van pulls away slowly from a few yards behind me. I'm in a lay-by on the A12. The passenger leans his head out of the window and shouts 'Get a grip you iron.'

I wasn't filthy, only grubby. I remember, I hadn't looked closely until I engaged with the women. One of them was wearing an expensive blue gilet – the sort of thing I'd wear if I ever. Mmmh. I see myself concentrating on the baker's window looking at our reflections – carried away with my thoughts about Dolly and a currant slice for a treat out of those big rectangular metal trays, like the ones school dinners came in. I can't remember whether I said 'nine pounds seventy-five' to the reflection or to the person now that I think about it. Though I do recall that I had that tune in my head, *Sing me a song, Laugh me a laugh,* which you might know better as the theme tune to the Cannon and Ball show. *Give me a slice, of currant slice, I think it's very nice*, but I couldn't get it to end. I sensed that there was significance in the missing ending. That's why I persisted with it, I suppose.

She comes out of the shop and decides that she doesn't want the little extra that she's bought for herself because she's on a diet. She sees me and hands me her purchase with a smile. She's one of those ambitious types with a big jaw. I don't realise that it's an act of charity towards a tramp until they've gone.

Outsider flashes a look at her, but Jawbone doesn't notice it as she organises the big purchase into her bag.

'What's six eights?' Jawbone says.

Outsider goes, 'Fixty-six,' then a few moments later she says, 'oh I think so. Is it?'

Jawbone goes, 'I thought it was fifty-four actually,' like it could be negotiated.

I've known what six eights are since I was six, or eight.

'Six and eight, sixty-eight.'

They both looked up at me at the same time. Then scarpered.

I held onto the new bounty and continued to examine my image, pretending that I was deciding what to buy. By the way, if ever Baden-Powell's seminal work is to be brought up to date for the Twenty First Century, then Item 1, page 1, of *Tramping for Men*, must be, *Always carry a bottle of washing up liquid. A cheap serve-all that works for the skin as well as the clothes.* I cannot stress that too strongly. Anyone who tells you that tramping is easy simply doesn't understand the game.

Look at my anorak for example. I called him the *man for all seasons.* He had been inexpensive, but had a robust and easy to clean exterior which was acceptable come winter, come summer. Plus, it looked a bit nautical and supported the student look I was trying to cultivate. Summer come loudly. He's always making a big deal out it, not like winter who just turns up and says 'Deal with it, I'm here'; there's summer, promising to come, then not, and then he expects a round of applause when he finally turns up. I'd bought it in a French supermarket for ten units. Francs and cents – whatever. I demur as to the date; it was another time, a Golden Age.

I'd have to start wearing him loose so that he didn't draw attention. He was on the wane. The hard plastic weave of outer material made the flaps on the pockets curl up slightly. I tried tucking them in but that only revealed the tear that had started in the corner of one of them. The same curly effect was starting on the stand-up collar. It chafed less that way, but the curly plastic edges were wearing away to its base material and they were permanently black now. Proper ones softened into charming artefacts as they weather-in, but my cheap imitation would eventually decay into a misshapen hard black plastic lump to reveal the coarseness that underlies all commercial enterprises. It also had a design fault in that it had this sort of breathable lining that was supposed to allow you to wear it fully buttoned up against the rain without sweating. In breach of this covenant, it did the opposite. When it rained, it ran through the coat and mixed with the sweat to create a noxious compound. Rain smells nice. Rain on roads. We were standing outside the front door after a rainstorm and my mum sang, 'I can sing a rainbow to you,' then the rag and bone man came so I had to run in and hide. But rain on clothes, giving off that rainy, pissy, old man smell. Stinking of urine. Did we all, or was it just me? Once it's dried in, it's part of your smell and no amount of washing up liquid will keep it at bay. And the *man for all seasons*, perspicacious as his acquisition had been, frankly I expected better of him.

My mark had one. His was red too and it wasn't dissimilar to mine from a distance, though when you got up close to him you could see that his was made out of a sort of sailcloth that weathers-in nicely instead of going black. He worked in this place that sounded like a pet's name with 'bank' tagged on the end, in a sort of merchant's house thing – as I imagined a Mayfair hedge fund – but this was Fleet Street. And there was something casual about his time keeping too that suggested he did something easy and useless. We saw each other face to face once, about a yard apart. He'd done his usual. He went down the side of the house, leant the bike against the wall, entered the building, went to the bathroom or something like that, came out un-helmeted a few moments later, got the bike and took it in the building. Always the same. I was down there once. There were bins and things there, so I could easily have been a proper person doing something in the real economy. Did I have my hand on the bike? Recall says I did – I think I made it look like part of the movement of squeezing past him. It feels like we analysed each other for a minute or so, but we probably just met eyes for a fraction of a second. He'd turned out like I was supposed to. Hair, teeth, skin; indoor-ablution type. Pink and fleshy like a ham.

I opened the paper bag. Mute, immobile, petrified, I stared entranced at a currant slice and saw providence glaring right back at me. Suddenly I knew that I needed to start responding to the signs if I was to learn their meaning, so I set off after them. Were they not my transhumant conduits to the lush pastures at the top of the mountain? Angels, perhaps? Not Arcs, obviously, there'd have been more light, but something from the ranks maybe?

I could see them in the distance, no longer in flight, but back among the pedestrians, behaving just like them. And whether or not they knew it, they were heading inexorably towards my patch – quartier clochard.

I sort of lived between the LSE and the Inns of Court at the time. Don't let anyone tell you that a tertiary education is not worth the money. I had access to some of the best, short notice, bathroom facilities in London. Security was tighter at the LSE, but it was labyrinthine and once in, you could disappear for days on end; the Inns were more comfortable, but I always felt more conspicuous there. As soon as I thought I was attracting too much attention in either place, I switched venues. You know, middle-aged man hangs around in the showers. Jimmy Savile has ruined that game for us. There were mature students in both places of course, but not enough of them and they (we) stood out like novelties. The real ones had this purpose about them too, which made me all the more conspicuous. That's why I had to get away.

You see I had to steal a bike. This bike, his bike. Boffin I call him, d'ya like him? Once executed though, it would mean riding around on him close to his original owner wearing a jacket that from a distance looked like his. So, it was not just a bike theft I was planning but an entire change of scene. And then I entered a classic planning conundrum, the bane of the project manager's lot - in a nutshell, that once the bike was mine, I was committed to getting out of town, but I needed to know that it was a plausible scheme before I made the move, and I could not know that without … you know, round like a circle in a spiral, like a wheel within a wheel, like the memories you find, in the windmills of your mind. I think I've missed the last four summers now that I think about it. It can't be windmills, can it? The windmills of your mind? I have it on very good authority that were it not for the extra syllable, recesses would have got the job.

I had decided on the University of the East of England by the way. A campus university that was reachable with a couple of hard days in the saddle. It first came to mind when I recalled that thing I did there as an undergraduate on a sports outing. That was when I remembered that it was basically in a field somewhere, away from the competition, in a part of the country where I could perhaps pass the long vacation on a traditional British holiday camp, with toilet blocks. Et cetera. Further, and the clincher for the deal as far as I was concerned, it was the sort of place to which nobody else would want to go.

So, compare and contrast, if you will, the London School of Economics and UEE, site, situation, form, and function: the essence of analytical analysis – copyright geography, prince of the humanities. To have a game of something at the LSE involved a bus, the tube, a train, and a long walk through what is considered to be the haven of London's suburban commuter belt. UEE on the other hand was a self-contained slab of concrete, where sports administrators went round in golf buggies like they do in science fiction films, forcing you stay outside and play on the green. It's not unlike one of those places in which the hopeless are re-homed. You see the appeal now?

They'd slowed outside a jeweller's shop but maintained a crucial momentum; I was within a hundred yards of them when Jawbone saw me again, she nudged Outsider, and they were off again. It didn't matter, they were on my turf and I knew all the outruns off by heart.

'Come by Glen,' I shout, and start whistling for them. There's a wicket gate to the Inn just a bit further along, if they go through that I'll have them penned up without even trying. It's busy, and some pedestrians coming my way notice me shouting and waving and try and get them to stop. But they eschew their solicitations, as they fear mine, shake them off and roll on again. Strange behaviour for Angels I know, but I suppose they could have been trainees. I'm only going to ask them who they are and where they're from, they needn't look so worried about it. I get closer but still have ground to make up when the mark flashes past in front of me and goes down the passageway.

Providence. *Success on a plate for you.* This is why they've brought me here. You cannot plan good timing. You take the opportunity when only you can see it. I knew the routine. I'd be parking my new bike outside the library building before he'd managed two shakes. I divert. I grab. I purloin. I push the bike along the passageway with my left foot on the pedal, ready to swing my right leg over and away. I worry about scattering the pedestrians as I emerge back onto Fleet Street, so I push still. Gaze set forward. Don't look back you might trip up.

Bang! I'm down. 'Oh God.' I try to get up, but people are helping me and it prevents me from doing it properly. I want to drag the bike out of the view of the passageway, but I'm restrained from doing so. I'm saying, 'The bike, the bike,' not, 'My bike' just in case I'm revealed. I'm not injured but I can't get up and run. I'm trying to get up, but I can't. There's too much going on. I think they're trying to help. It's busy and there's a scene but there's something efficient about it that I can't grasp. Pedestrians are walking round me and continuing on their way. I don't see the mark. My view's obscured – I don't know whether he's there or not. Suddenly I sense that I'm being dragged. I am. And there's more than one of them. They're trying to help me up but they're going too fast and I can't get back on my feet. I'm going backwards fast. Then suddenly I'm up in the air and into a van. They're treating me like I'm injured but I'm not. I think I heard words. 'Evidence,' or something like that. Maybe it's someone's name.

One of them is in the van with me. I'm face down and his knee is in my back. I'm under a sack facing the front of the van. I get the faint aroma of garlic, and a weird sweet soapy smell. There's another shout then the bike is thrown in too. The door is closed and the van drives away.

It feels like this is the next day. In many ways it is, in others it's another lifetime. But the same external forces still compel me onwards, telling me that it will be alright in the end. I guess that we just aren't close enough to the end to know yet.

All I do know is that if I stop, I may never start again.

Arlene Smith - The Body

Murder is a subject that not many people care to consider. The idea of losing a loved one by the hands of a murderer is a chilling and unwelcome possibility. The idea of being a murder victim is one of the most terrifying prospects imaginable. The idea of being a murderer is very rarely contemplated by sane minded people.

Maybe that's why I am in complete disbelief. My eyes have begun to water and sting, yet I cannot draw them away from the empty shell of what was once a human being that lays on the cold ground before me. The Body has lost all essence of life already. Within the minutes that have passed the skin has become waxen with an almost bluish tinge. The face is expressionless, the eyes closed, and the mouth relaxed into a natural grimace. No matter how long I study the subtly changing features, I cannot convince myself that It is just sleeping.

My stomach convulses and I heave. It comes to me that I have become the last glimpse of the living world to a human being. I recall how that last glimpse was filled with terror and, what had to have been, an excruciating amount of pain. I suddenly need to be away from the alleyway, and I clutch my excitable stomach as I run out into the dark street. I am relieved to find the night is deserted and I can throw up amongst a pile of discarded rubbish, undisturbed. It takes me a few seconds to regain some composure before I realise that Steven has not come after me. I could run, faster and further, beyond my usual capabilities. I could run far away from this situation, from this city, this entire country if I wanted to. If anything, I could lose some weight in the process and be less recognizable to the authorities.

I feel a migraine begin to brew in my head and I shake away the completely inappropriate thoughts that crowd my brain. Of course, I will return to that alleyway. How could I do anything else? I do not consider Steven a friend in the conventional terms of the word, but he is the only thing I have that comes close. I now realise why he has not called after me or come to drag me back. He expects me to return.

Steven, it appears, has discarded the contents of his stomach, too. His face is flushed, his hands shake, uncontrollably. As I stagger back into the nightmarish scene, he looks away from The Body and searches my face with concern.

"Ok?"

His voice shakes with suppressed emotion. I do not trust my own vocal cords at that moment and simply nod.

"Ok… ok, we can sort this. We can fix it…" Steven is walking around the alley now. He examines The Body from various angles and swears a few times. I carry out my own, swift, inspection and my eyes move upwards. I realise that there are two windows from the opposite building that overlook the alleyway. There are no lights behind them at the moment, but should someone decide to peer out into the night…

"We need to call the police," I say in little more than a whisper.

With a spontaneous burst of energy, Steven leaps across The Body and shoves me, hard. I am caught, completely, unaware and fly backwards. My back slams into the hard plastic of that large, industrial bin and I am momentarily winded. It is my turn to swear.

"What'd you do that for!" I snap.

Steven marches towards me and I take a protective stance. He slams his hands on the bin at either side of my head and I wince.

"Will you shut up! Do you want to wake up the entire street?" he hisses.

"Well, then, don't go throwing me all around the place!"

"Well, then, don't go saying stupid things!" Steven snarls. "Call the police? Do you want to go to prison? Do you? Are you really that desperate to ruin both our lives? You stupid-, you naïve-, you dim little- "

"Ok!" I snap.

"You'd drag us both down just to salve your own guilt you pathetic- "

"I said ok!" I whack his arms away from me and rub my throbbing back. I catch sight of The Body once more and I am shocked to find I had completely forgotten its presence on the scene.

"What're we going to do, then?" I ask.

Steven runs his fingers through his, already, tousled hair.

"We're going to have to move it…"

I wish I had run away when I had the chance.

"How?" I say, weakly. "Should we just… grab a leg and an arm each or…?"

"Don't be stupid. How d'you think we'd look walking down the street like that?"

I want to tell him we'd look like any other group of mates after a night of drinking in the city. But I decide now is not a good time.

I stand, silent and awkward, as Steven concocts a plan in his head. He paces the short space available, muttering to himself, pausing, occasionally, to consider The Body. Finally, he rubs his hands together and announces that we, "need the Iron Beast" before he rushes off into the night.

In the fifteen minutes I am left alone with The Body I am sure that I struggle through several panic attacks. I have no means of determining the time, but I feel like it has been night for too long. I am expecting the sun to rise any minute and a swarm of morning pedestrians to crowd the streets. When I hear the Iron Beast approach, I feel no relief. Steven seems to have gathered his wits together more effectively and when he comes to stand across from me, The Body in-between us, and says "Ok, now you can grab an arm and a leg", I comply with no arguments.

Somehow, I hadn't expected The Body to be just as heavy in death as it was in life. Our first two attempts are unsuccessful. On the third, I misjudge the gap and the head whacks against the bumper with a sickening thud. I take a step back and refuse to engage in a fourth attempt.

"This is ridiculous," I gasp. "Look at what we're doing right now… I'm sorry but after everything that's happened tonight… I don't think I can bring myself to drive around town with a body in the boot of the car, ok? It just… it feels like too much of an insult."

Steven is, clearly, arriving at the end of his patience with me. He considers my face, set into a defiant scowl, and strides around the car to open the passenger door.

Another fifteen minutes later and we are driving along the steadily, brightening street with The Body strapped into the back seat. Steven relays the rest of his plan as we drive. I'm heartily grateful for his decision to drop me off at the shops to 'pick up a few things'. I am less pleased by his request for me to meet him at the riverside.

"We're going to dump it in the river?" I ask, revolted.

"Why not? It'll just join the millions of other bodies and road signs that are already there. Unless you've got any better suggestions?"

My mind races. We could take it outside the city, burn the Iron Beast with The Body inside. Dig a ditch and bury it. Dump it down an embankment and let the squirrels and foxes have their way with it. Then I realise that the sun is rising, and we have no time to do any of these things.

"Fine…" I mutter, like a grumpy child.

The supermarket has just opened its doors and the aisles are vacant save from the very few early morning shoppers and grumpy staff members. Everything seems far too clean and bright. I realise I am sweating, and my hair is a frizzy mess. I move to flatten it before I realise my hands are filthy and I stuff them in my jacket pockets. My eyes flit towards the security cameras. I cannot tell if they are actually turning to follow my movement or if I am imagining it. The cashier gives me a contemptuous look as I toss the two packs of black bin bags onto the conveyor belt. I see, quite plainly, her eyes moving over my torn leggings and filthy t-shirt and I fold my arms, self-consciously.

Beep. The first pack moves across the scanner in a swift motion. I can't help but tut, impatiently, as the cashier struggles with the shopping bag. I watch her ridiculously, perfect, manicured nails fumble with the opening and my patience snaps.

"I don't want a bag."

She continues to rub the plastic between her fingertips.

"I said I don't want a bag. Ok? Just leave it. Why would I need a bag to carry some bags? I thought all you big corporations where into saving the planet and being green and all that. Just leave the bag, ok?"

I realise I am rambling and bite my lip to stop. The cashier stares at me, completely unconcerned with my distress. Her eyes don't leave my face as she passes the second pack across the scanner and holds out a hand for payment. Only when the money, soaked in the sweat from my palms, touches her skin does she look away, making no effort to disguise her disgust.

By the time I reach the riverside the streets have become more active. I, suddenly, regret my refusal to accept a shopping bag. Every stranger I pass is a potential witness and the items I hold in my hands are incriminating evidence. I try not to seem too conspicuous as I clamber over the fence and make my way down the embankment to the water's edge.

Steven is on the edge of sanity when I arrive. I am pleasantly surprised and most relieved to find he has chosen a decent location, with plenty of cover from the trees and the bridge above us. The Body lays in a straight position in the dirt. The skin has lost any hint of colour and is now a waxy grey. The ground around it is littered with cigarette stubs. I guess that more than half of them have come from Steven's own hands.

"What took you so long?", he hisses at me as I approach. I noticed he has stopped shaking but his eyes are still manic with anxiety. He snatches the bin bags from my hands and inspects them with unnecessary fixation before turning his face up to look at me.

"You are the biggest idiot I have ever had the misfortune to know." He sounds completely calm all of a sudden, and it is this that unnerves me.

"What are you talking about?"

"Of all the times to make a stupid mistake!"

I open my mouth, already equipped with an angry retort, when Steven rips apart the packaging and tugs one of the bags free. He shakes it in front of me and, as the air fills inside it, I realise what I have done.

"Yeah, these would be helpful. If we were disposing of a bloody midget!" Steven snaps, tossing the bags at my feet.

I had been far too preoccupied to check in the supermarket, although it had never really occurred to me that bin bags came in different sizes. In my mind I can see the shin-high metal bin in my mother's kitchen and suspect the bags would line the inside of it quite snugly.

"Oh…"

I am sure Steven would have hit me then, if he hadn't lost his footing on the uneven ground and fell on his backside.

"Fuck this day!" he whines. "Ok, we need to get an axe…"

"An axe?" I squeak.

"Or a really big knife."

I understand what he is proposing but the thought of even witnessing such an act makes my empty stomach heave again.

"We can't…" I manage to whisper.

Steven bites his lip and I can see his is not particularly partial to the idea either.

"No… no, I don't think we can," he concedes. His hands move over the pebbles on the shore and I can almost hear the gears working in his brain.

"Steven?"

"I know what to do. Grab a couple of those bags. We need to start acting quicker…"

It seems to take no time at all before we have several bags filled with pebbles. Our fingers steady themselves long enough to allow us to attach our makeshift weights to The Body and roll it, none to gracefully, into the murky waters. We watch with shuddering breaths as the head bobs just above the surface for a few seconds then, slowly, sinks into the icy-cold depths of the river.

Ash Miller - The Groundsman

Albert was busy sweeping up the fallen leaves of autumn, blown around by the wind that afternoon, they had become scattered across the graveyard. Several large piles had amassed in his wake, heaped at the edge of the pathway, awaiting collection. A gentle breeze drifted listlessly in the evening air, rippling the leaves with its lazy touch. Albert was hoping that it wouldn't become any stronger, scattering the leaves before he could collect them. Once he had half a dozen neat piles, he set off for his wheelie-bin. It was a good routine, and Albert always stuck to his routines.

Completely lost in the stream of thoughts that were spinning around in his head, he worked away, his mind locked on other things. It wasn't unusual for him to drift off like that, it was something that happened all the time. Looking up for a moment, he spotted Penny Morgan ambling along the pathway. "Hi Penny." He called out, without thinking. He waved briefly in her direction, but she didn't react. Should have shouted louder, he thought, and turned back to focus onto the task before him. There was work to do, and he was quite happy to be doing it.

Scooping the leaves into the bin that he'd dragged up, Albert set off to the next section of the graveyard. He had a routine that he kept to at that time of the year. One quarter of the site every evening, that way he could cover the whole place once a week. At that moment, he stopped in his work and glanced back down the pathway. Something was bothering him, but he wasn't sure what it was.

It was later, once he returned home, that Albert remembered having caught sight of Penny. That memory came as a surprise, he was pretty sure that Penny had been dead for at least three months. He'd become used to noticing odd things around the graveyard, but he had never seen Penny there before. The more he thought about it, the more he was convinced that she had returned his wave, if vaguely. He recalled spotting the two opposing arrows tattooed on her forearm. Could it have been someone who happened to look like Penny, he asked himself. It was the only explanation that he could come up with and did she have that tattoo before, he couldn't remember for sure.

The job at the graveyard had arrived in Albert's lap by pure luck. One evening he had been sitting in his local bar, as his routine dictated, pondering what to do with himself. At that moment the vicar of St

Nicholas Church turned up looking for someone to take over from Dom Cresswell, who had recently left the job. Andy Blair, the vicar, was a little bit of an eccentric character, but didn't care what people said about him. He wound some of his parishioners up with his ideas, but he still managed to draw new people to the church, all the time. The one thing that he asked was that the upkeep of the graveyard wasn't carried out during the day. Old Dom had always worked nights and whoever was to take his place would have to do the same.

The vicar had come to the bar planning to recruit a new caretaker, as he would only work with people in the local community. Any time he wanted a pair of hands, his first stop would be one of the nearby bars. He would be looking for people who needed the work and, in his words, "had the right type of soul". When Albert heard about the job, he grabbed the vicar by the elbow and offered to buy him a whiskey. The vicar was unlikely to resist the offer like that, the staff knew him well and his drink appeared on the bar as if by magic. Clicking glasses, Albert tendered his services and found himself being hired on the spot.

As they sat at a table in The Goose, the vicar explained what the job entailed and the hours that would be expected of him. People drifted through the bar, occasionally speaking briefly to the vicar as they passed. Generally, they ignored Albert, few of the bar's customers spoke to him, but he was happy with that. It all fitted, it was exactly what he had been looking for. The schedule of the job would take getting used to, but that was fine. The important thing for Albert was the regular wage; in fact the job paid far better than he could have hoped for. For once, it appeared as if he had fallen on his feet.

Several days after seeing Penny Morgan, Albert found himself being stopped in his work by an elderly man swathed in a long dark trench coat. "Where do I go?" The man asked in a vague way. Albert looked up at him, the street lights casting a deep shadow over his face. The wide brim of his hat added to the shadows and obscured all but his unshaven chin. "Sorry?" Albert replied, stretching his back after having been crouching down for so long.

"The vicar. . . where do I go?" The man asked again. As he spoke, he extended an arm causing the sleeve of his jacket to ride up, as if it was a little too short for his arm.

"Andy, oh, he's in the church, is he expecting you?" Albert enquired, glancing at the man's sleeve. The sharp point of an ornate arrow head stuck out against the pale skin of his arm. The vicar had explained that people could turn up for meetings and that they might not know their way around.

"Huh! Yeah, I, I think so, I . . ." The man stumbled on his words and left the sentence hanging. Noticing that Albert had spotted the tattoo, he tugged his sleeve back down to cover his wrist. It left the impression that he was ashamed of the artwork.

"Follow the path round to the right. The side door should still be open. He'll still be there." Albert said, pointing to the far corner of the church.

"Thank you, I . . . I . . ." The man shook his head. He strolled off in the direction indicated without finishing whatever he had been about to say.

Albert was a conscientious worker, he turned up five evenings a week, regardless of the weather. It was a routine and he lived by his routines, they kept him focused. The vicar had told him not to turn up if the weather was too bad, but he wasn't going to let something like that stop him. He was enjoying his new job and it kept him out of The Goose for much of the evening, which was a bonus. Not only was he being paid well, he was happy to have a mission, something to his mind.

Every few days someone would appear in the graveyard. Some of them would walk straight past him as if he wasn't there, others would stop and ask him for directions. Albert had never been comfortable with churches, but he was happy to work for the vicar though. His job meant that he didn't have to actually enter the building, which was fine by him, if Andy needed his assistance, he would come looking for him. The shed in the far corner of the graveyard, housed all of the tools that Albert could possibly need.

***

Several months passed and the same old routine rolled on. Albert had to admit that he was enjoying himself, it was the best job that he had in years. One evening, while he was working, Albert came across a young woman sitting in the graveyard. Glancing over, he guessed she was around eighteen or nineteen, certainly no older. She was sitting on one of the benches, her head in her hands, balling her eyes out. The moment that he saw her, Albert put down his rake and walked over the bench; he knew that he had to do something, he couldn't ignore someone in a state like that.

"Are you alright?" He realised it was a stupid question the moment he'd asked it, it was obvious that she wasn't, but he didn't know how else to draw her attention.

Glancing up, the girl tried to control her sobs and brushed tears away from her eyes with her sleeve. "No . . . not r, really." She stuttered. "I just feel empty, tired . . . Oh, I don't know . . ."

Sitting on the bench beside her, Albert hesitated briefly but then put his arm across her shoulders and gave her a hug. "Is there anything I can do?" He asked.

"No, no, there's nothing anyone can do." She replied, taking a deep breath, she added. "Unless you can bring Peter back."

"Peter?" Albert repeated.

"Yeah . . . my boyfriend. He, he died, la, last week."

"I'm sorry, that can be hard to deal with. You know, this probably isn't the best place to be hanging around in. Do you live nearby, I'll walk you home if you like." Albert offered.

"Oh, I'm not far away. I should go, thank you for caring. What's your name? Mine's Eva."

"Albert, my name's Albert. Take care of yourself Eva. It will get easier; I know it's hard right now, but it will . . ." He left the sentence unfinished, aware that he had no way of backing that statement up. Sometimes it didn't get better, he knew that for himself, sometimes it held on and on.

As Eva got up and walked away, Albert collected his brooms and other tools together. He'd had enough for one evening, tonight he needed to stop at The Goose for a pint. One of the things he liked about the job was that he could pick his own hours. The only rule he'd been given was that he should start no earlier than seven o'clock in the evening. From there he had a twelve-hour window, as long as the graveyard was tidy, he could do what he wanted.

It was a few days since he'd been in The Goose, but he always felt comfortable there. Sitting in the corner of the bar with a pint, Albert watched the regular customers coming and going. People tended to ignore him there, leaving him along, which was fine by him, sometimes it felt as if he wasn't really there. That evening, he overheard a conversation on a nearby table and listened to someone talking about the tragedy of Peter and Eva. Although he didn't want to eavesdrop, he couldn't help focusing on the exchange.

The couple had only become engaged a month ago but then Peter had been involved in a major car crash. Despite the hospital's emergency team working on him for over an hour, he had died from his injuries. The woman relating the story continued by say that Eva had taken the whole thing especially badly. Several of her friends, including the woman telling the story, couldn't help worrying about her state of mind.

Albert turned back to his pint, going over his encounter with Eva in the back of his mind. She'd been in a real state at the time, but was there anything that he could do to help, he asked himself. In the end he decided that all he could do was keep an eye out for her. If she returned to the graveyard, he would try chatting to her again. Talking about problems could help, it didn't always work, but sometimes it did. The vicar had told him that when he'd first met him, told him that there was always someone to help.

It was several days before Albert spotted Eva again. Although she wasn't crying that time, he could see that her eyes were red and sore. She attempted a smile when she saw him approaching but it was a forced smile, one that didn't quite reach her eyes.

"Hello." Albert said, trying to appear bright and cheerful.

Eva waved a hand at him but didn't say anything, so Albert sat next to her on the bench. "How are you feeling, Eva?" He enquired.

"Oh, okay . . . I, I suppose." Eva replied in little more than a whisper.

"That's good, I . . ." Albert was going to say that he'd heard about Peter but suddenly thought better of it. "I was worried about you." He stated, instead.

"Oh, don't waste your time worrying about me, Albert." Eva said, looking up at him. "I'll be fine, once the funeral's over, I, I'm sure I'll be fine."

"They're never an easy thing, Eva. Have you got family to support you?"

"No. No, they're all up north, Manchester, never met Pete. They wouldn't come down anyway; it would be too much trouble."

"Oh, I'm sure they'd want to help you."

"Ha! You don't know them. Anyway, I haven't told them. So, so they won't be coming. It'll be me and Peter's family, seems to be loads of them." Eva said, shaking her head a little.

"Well, if you wanted someone to be there, I could go with you." Albert found himself offering, without thinking about what he was saying.

"Thank you, Albert. That's very sweet of you, but I couldn't put you through that." Eva said.

***

Over the next ten days, Eva turned up in the graveyard regularly, always making her way to the same bench. When he saw her, Albert made the time to sit and talk to her, trying to take her mind of her problems. During that time Eva talked and talked, telling him all about her life with Peter. She spoke about everything they'd done together, and the things that they had been planning to do. As the days passed, she slowly began to change.

The redness in her eyes disappeared, and they became bright and powerful, glowing with life once again.

On the tenth day, the day after Peter's funeral, Eva actually laughed at one of her stories, it was the first time Albert had heard that magical sound. She had been telling him about how Peter had been determined to learn to play the guitar. Initially it was just a smile that crossed her face, as she explained how awful Peter had been at playing the instrument. When she told him about Peter's struggle to play a song for her, *The Lady in Red*, her face came alive. Within a few moments she was laughing and once she started, she couldn't stop. After a while, Eva managed to calm herself but the smile didn't leave her face.

"Thank you, Albert. I can't remember the last time I laughed like that." She explained, wiping tears from her eyes, but this time they were not tears of sadness.

"It's good to see a smile on your face, Eva." Albert said.

"I like your tattoo, Albert." Eva remarked, pointing to a spot on his arm.

"My tattoo?" Albert replied, wondering which one had caught her eye. Looking down he saw that she was indicating the two opposing arrows on his forearm. The arrows were large and elaborate in design, they virtually came alive on his arm. It was strange but Albert couldn't remember having them done, in fact, he couldn't recall having seen them before. In an odd way, they resembled Penny Morgan's tattoo, rather than one of his.

Climbing to his feet, Albert said. "I . . . I've got to see Alan about something. Keep smiling, Eva. You've got a lovely smile, people should see it more often."

Eva watched him stroll along the pathway, heading towards the side door of the church. At that moment a gust of wind blew through the graveyard causing her to blink. Looking up again, she saw that Albert had gone.

A few minutes after having noticed that he'd disappeared, the church door opened and the vicar stepped out. Taking one look up the path, he spotted Eva and made his way in her direction.

"Albert was just going to find you, you must have missed him." Eva said, when the vicar grew near. She knew that there hadn't been time for him to go inside and speak to the vicar.

"Oh, Albert's gone now, Eva." The vicar said, looking down at her.

"Sorry. What do you mean, he's gone?"

"These people I get to work here, they all have their jobs to do. Albert's job was to take care of you, to help you get through your problem. He's done his job to perfection; I can see that in your eyes."

"But, where's he gone. I don't understand."

"Albert was never really here. I don't know what these people are, in truth. Spirits of some kind, I guess. They come to me looking for something and I try to help them along the way."

As the vicar turned back towards the church, he added. "Oh, and he told me to tell you that Peter loved you just as much as you loved him."

Benjamin Asman - Mirror Image

Dan stared at his mirror and it displayed him, as it always did. Brown hair and tough skin for his age of 30. He touched his face, running his short stubby fingers over his one closed eye, down his cheek before finally they fell from his chin. At first he sighed, then smiled. Assuming the face looking back was his, he brushed his teeth and went to bed.

The next day, at 8 am, his alarm buzzed and squealed and Like a low iron teenager, he got up dizzy, and fumbled to get ready. He washed his face then satiated his hunger with a slice of toast before gulping from a refrigerated bottle of cold brew coffee. He rushed out his door and headed to the train line. At the station, he waited on the platform. The tracks were 4 feet below him over the yellow line. He always noted the Samaritan posters that were at train station platforms.

What an odd way to end it. 4-foot drop, roll your ankle and get hit by a train slowing to a stop. He smiled.

I couldn't do that. Apparently, suicide is for the cowardly. But that method requires bravery, I don't have.

"Are you alright, dear?"

Dan turned, jumping back like an excited rabbit. A woman had startled him from thought. He composed himself for a split second, hiding behind a long blink, searching for an answer, and then spoke.

"Yes, I am, yes. Thank you." The woman smiled, her eyes though sat still, worry making them glassy.

She thought I was going to jump. The woman walked away, her handbag beside her; she pretended to rummage, an excuse to turn her head and look Dan's way again.

"Off to Linark also? Are you sure you're okay? I don't mean to pry." The woman rubbed her hands for warmth and moved away after a moment of silence. *She still thinks I'm going to jump.*

Dan's thought moved on as a loud horn signalled a trains' coming. however, it wasn't Dan's because the train was on the other track; it went east, not west. As it approached, Dan saw his reflections in each window again. The train's windows were polished like mirrors and Each reflection felt uncanny. Dan stared at his reflection, and the reflection stared back. One image disappeared as a woman on the train pressed herself against the window as a fat man sat beside her. The train blew its horn again and steamed away. Dan never smiled at his reflection this time. It had stared too long.

Dan avoided reception and waited outside. After eight minutes, he was called. He followed the receptionist and looked at the three seats. The receptionist left.

"You can sit there," the psychologist said. His name was Dr Pond. Dan didn't know his first name. Dan sat. "So, how has your week been?" Dan inhaled. To someone adept in studying human behaviour, Dan's sigh may have indicated that he was about to answer, maybe even with a lot of information. Dan didn't answer. He was silent.

"Dan?"

Dan stared at a box of tissues that sat upon the table between him and the psychologist. Dr Pond noticed.

"Do you need a tissue?"

"How would you offer me one?" Dr Pond tilted his head to the side. Silence in the room. Dan knew to further explain. "A tissue, how would you offer me one? An individual tissue or the entire box?" Dr Pond inhaled this time. Shifting his seated position to recompose.

"I'd gesture at their position and wait for you to take one. Why do you ask?"

"I read people like you, spend days studying whether to hand the box or the individual tissue. The individual is more intimate but may cross a boundary, the box can appear cold, but, also less awkward as the patient may need more than one tissue." Dan watched his psychologist process what he had said.

"I never learnt such a thing, Dan. So, will you tell me how your week has been?" Dan sat back. He steepled his hands and looked about the mirrorless room.

"I'm spending too much time with my reflection."

"Describe me."

What?

"Describe me." Dr Pond repeated, as though he read Dan's mind. Dan leaned forward, his elbows on his knees, hands still steepled.

"You're old, your hair is white, and you comb it a lot. Your hands have liver spots on them, and you love to wear suits that match a younger man. Despite all that, you fit the role of a psychologist, you look approachable."

"In you, I see a young man who believes he's older. He doesn't change his clothes nor shave enough. Your hair is brown, but stresses have sprouted some grey by the ear. Your fingers are long, perfect for many instruments. You're wearing a plaid jacket and blue jeans," Dr Pond finished. He took a mirror from his briefcase and held it in front of himself. Then he turned the mirror to Dan. "So, what do you see?" he asked. Dan took a moment, analysing his reflection. It copied him, looked like him too.

"It's me, it's my reflection," Dan said. Dr Pond flashed his eyebrows, a snippet of a 'well yes, obviously' attitude.

"When you're home, or out and about, describe your looks to yourself before seeing your reflection." Dr Pond had returned the mirror back to his briefcase. "You need to try hard to understand what you're seeing. You logically know your mind can struggle. Fight your mind with logic, it's your best weapon."

The session was over. It had lasted only 17 minutes. Dan left the gloom of the building, with his next appointment written on a note of paper; he used to write the appointment times on his hand, but he always forgot them as they would rub off in the rain. He returned to the train station. Greyness filled the surroundings Dan looked upon. The rain brought the high skies' smog down to eye level, and the gravel floor soaked it in, the only break from this bleak reality was the yellow line at the train station platform. Dan walked up to it. Down below, on the tracks and amongst the stones that lay between them, he saw a shadow. It copied his movements, if not a little behind in speed and accuracy. *Another layer to the conundrum*, Dan thought. He looked up, catching drops of rain in his eye, but no sunlight.

"Are you okay, dear?" It was the same woman. She had purchased a pair of white woollen gloves. Dan moved back from the yellow line. He looked at the woman. Behind her, out of focus, was a Samaritan poster.

"Yes, I'm fine, thank you." She smiled and walked over to the shelter. The train arrived. Dan couldn't find his reflection as the train slowed past him. Each window looked matte and showed only the detail and texture of rain, except one. One window offered a reflection looking back. It was clearly his, apart from the obvious grin Dan felt sure he wasn't flashing.

Dan stopped at his front door. His apartment, on the bottom floor, had waited for his return. Letters like uneaten food hung from the door's mouth. Dan opened the door and closed it behind him. He shook the water from himself and hung up his jacket.

"Brown hair, a little grey, blue jeans." His hands feathered his face like a blind man would. He studied the intricacies and memorised them before heading to the bathroom. He washed the acidic rain from his face that had collected dirt as it fell and looked into his mirror. There he was. Dan smiled.

He walked to the living room. The TV painted the room a hazy white, Dan hadn't left it on. His eyes narrowed. On the couch, a man was sitting, he relaxed, watching the Tv. He had brown hair; he was wearing a wet plaid jacket, blue jeans also. Dan crept back, into the kitchen. He grabbed a knife and returned. With the knife out of view behind his back, he approached.

"Who are you?" Dan said. He spoke with thunderous authority, but lightning strikes of doubt cracked his voice. The man turned. His face now in view.

"It's me. Dan." The man's voice was blurry. It felt like oil pouring into Dan's ears. This man's name especially felt muffled and demonic, almost. *He's me*, Dan thought. His eyes were wide now. Dan raised his hand and without hesitation ran at the man on the couch. Vaulting the low backrest, Dan's sudden burst of angered pursuit jellied the man's legs; he fell off the couch and Dan dived on top of him.

"You are not me, there is only one Dan!" He plunged the knife into man's face several times as he cried. "I knew you were playing with me, you bastard. On the train, no light. No sunlight to bounce reflections at me, you couldn't hide. I saw you on the train." The man was not responding. His face was now unrecognisable. It resembled a mushroom pulsated by a hand blender. The blood was thick, and brain matter painted the wooden floor. Dan's face was hot and coated red with blood. He stood up, dropped the knife beside the man, and ran to the bathroom mirror. He saw himself. Perfectly following each movement, his reflection was the perfect mirror image. "Only one of me now," Dan said. His mind now felt awake. Voices or thoughts screamed at the doppelganger's demise. Screams of jubilant praise for the body they controlled. Dan hid the body that night. Medical science would not find this otherworldly presence near him, someone would not experiment upon him.

The next week Dan sat again across from his psychologist, Dr Pond.

"So how was your week?" he asked.

"Good" Dan replied. A brow raised on Dr Pond. He took from his briefcase a mirror, like he had many times before.

"Describe me." Dan sighed, but obliged.

"You're about 32, curly ginger hair, it's messy, you don't comb it or look after it. You don't wear clothes befitting a psychologist, chinos and a polo top, like you're ready for golf," Dan said. Dr Pond sighed.

"Have you succeeded this week, Dan? Have you accomplished something? You seem relieved," Dr Pond asked. Dan leaned in. He wanted to talk. His hands were steepled.

"Can you explain doctor/patient confidentiality to me again?" Dan asked.

"This is all private unless you tell me you have a plan to kill yourself or someone else," Dr Pond replied. Dan leaned back. Closing his eyes, he walked through the palace of his mind. He battled the weight he dragged behind him, wrapped in black bags. He looked at the body. The face flashed between normality and decomposing mush.

"Maybe at another session," Dan said. The rest of the session passed slowly. It was like wading through water silted black with thick gunk.

"Dan," Dr Pond said as Dan stood and went to the door. His hand on the handle, ready to leave. "I want you to come back. I believe I have an explanation for your reflection problems." Dan turned to the psychologist. The ginger-haired man gulped.

"I've already found the solution," Dan replied. Dr Pond began again, rummaging inside his briefcase. From it, he retrieved some printer paper.

"Tell me what you see, Dan," Dr Pond said. He turned the paper around. Upon it, a full-colour image of a macerated face boldly sat. It was the man Dan had slain. The Doppelganger. Dan's breathing increased. He saw the evil behind the bloodied mess; it flashed back and forth, as it had in his mind.

"This was Todd, Dan. Your flatmate. They found him last night." Dan couldn't keep his eyes off the picture Dr Pond still held. "He was sixty miles from his… your flat." Dan shook. His hand holding the door handle made it rattle he trembled so much. Dan's brain pumped chemicals throughout his body to calm him down, while also juicing him up with fear and adrenaline. His mouth was dry, and his eyes watered. *It wasn't Todd. It couldn't have been Todd.*

"It wasn't Todd," Dan said. Tears warmed his cold cheeks. All the blood in his body had rushed to his heart and organs like a fierce swarm of bees protecting the hive.

"Did you do this?" Dr Pond asked. Dan looked away and locked eyes with Dr Pond.

HE KNOWS, HE KNOWS. NO NO. CALM DOWN. FUCK JUST TELL HIM. TELL HIM NOW, IT WASN'T TODD.

"I didn't kill Todd, no. But that." Dan pointed at the picture. "I did that, yes. B-but it was the solution," Dan stammered.

"Solution to what?" The Doctor remained calm, but Dan could hear his heart beating.

"My reflection, my mirror image. The troubles are gone. It wasn't Todd. It was a Doppelganger," Dan and Dr Pond were silent. The room was full of tense air stoked by fluttering, humming hearts.

"A doppelganger, Dan, for goodness' sake. These fantasies are not real. You're psychotic." Dr Pond lost professionalism. For a moment he acted as a father, not a psychologist. He had stood to Dan's height. A flicker of thought crossed in Dan's mind. Could the others in the building hear this discussion?

"WHAT THE FUCK DO YOU MEAN?" Dan hurled back his words. His tormented mind breaking. Dr Pond stood silent controlling his breathing, his chest rose and fell, deep breaths to calm himself. He nodded. Adjusting his tie, he sat back down. Dan stood at the door still. Dr Pond took several tissues from the tissue box.

"Here," he said. Dan turned and took them. Dan's mind flooded with the meanings behind the actions of his psychologist as he wiped away his tears and blew his nose clear. The two sat in silence for another 25 minutes. The silence was needed. Sometimes words don't suffice, occasionally there are barriers only silent meditation can break through.

Dan rocked a little, cradling his wearied mind and lost in visions of captivity. The 25 minute silence had not calmed his breathing. His chest rose and fell as he stooped further into panicked thought. Dr Pond sighed.

"I told the police you were with me, that you are not capable of killing anyone, Dan." Dr Pond's voice sounded melodic, calming and nurturing. Dan looked up at the psychologist and saw his father looking back. "The session is over, Dan. I want to see you next week, same time." Dan wrote the appointment on his hand. At the door, Dr Pond squeezed Dan's shoulder. "I will see you next week." He concluded the session. Dan's mind painted the walk back to the station black with deep thought. He passed the Samaritan poster. Its poster box had been smashed and rain had beaten it muddy.

"Are you alight, dear?"

The yellow line crossed his sight. Hence forth, he moved with courage.

Beth Marston - Black Holes

Otto Parks spent most days confused. You see, although Otto was well-behaved and extremely well-mannered, his parents never seemed to pay him much attention. His older brother Nash, on the other hand, despite being described by his teachers as 'a firecracker, ready to explode', was very clearly Mythica and Cedar Park's pride and joy.

What Otto called his bedroom; the rest of the world would recognise as a cupboard. However, Otto loved space and had decorated the exceptionally small room perfectly to his liking, with aliens made of toilet tubes and a bed that almost resembled a rocket ship.

His best friend, Simbi, had once given him a tub of glow-in-the-dark paint to draw stars on his ceiling, but when Otto got home from school, he slipped and spilled every drop in to the dog bowl. To this day, Nash's dog, Spider, still has a glowing tongue.

Otto had earned the nickname 'dim-wit', given to him by Nash. In recent months, his parents had even started joining in, and there had been times when Mythica and Cedar momentarily forgot what Otto's real name was!

Everything in Otto's room, or 'The Cosmos Totalis' as he called it, had been broken and fixed at least twice. Plasters, string, glue, cardboard, even chewing gum, were amongst the hundreds of items he had learnt to utilise whenever he had his calamitous moments, and, though he knew there were certain things he could never fix, like his Mother's scowl, or Nash's bad breath, he knew he could always mend the smaller things. The truth was, Otto's parents had no idea just how much their young son had repaired around the house, and put it down to their 'good luck' when the fridge suddenly became cold again.

One evening, after cooking himself two boiled eggs, Otto sat down to read his SpaceLife magazine. He had scanned each page a hundred times, but never got bored of reading about the volcano on Mars that was three times the size of Mount Everest, or that one day on Venus is longer than one whole year on Earth.

"Rumble in the jungle!" Nash screeched, as he flung open the door, preparing to play his favourite game of performing wrestling moves on Otto, and after a particularly rough rumble that involved an elbow to the nose, and Mum screeching because 'dim-wit got blood on the carpet', Otto checked his injuries in the mirror.

As he squeezed the broken skin together and applied his homemade 'Hold-and-Heal' ointment, he noticed something strange. There, on his left cheek, was a hole the size of a pin prick, but before he could take a closer look, it began to change.

It burned and fizzed, bringing tears to his eyes as he watched it grow to the size of a strawberry seed. Without warning, a heavy weight crushed in to his chest, and he crumpled to the floor, suddenly unable to breathe. The room span as he closed his eyes and attempted to control the thumping in his head. Otto had no idea what was happening to him, but he knew he had to try to fix it.

The following morning, Otto's head was still pounding, and though he knew he had to get up, an overwhelming feeling of sadness seemed to be laying heavily on top of him, stopping him from moving.

Otto could only remember feeling sadness twice in his life; once when his pet woodlouse, Martin, had died, and again when Nash had jumped off the garage roof, landing on his neck. However, on both occasions, the sadness had swiftly disappeared when he realised that there were in fact hundreds of woodlice in the park, and that Nash wasn't quite so rough with a back brace on.

It was the sound of Nash's blaring music that forced Otto to peel himself off the floor. He got up slowly, and as his eyes focused on his reflection, he felt dizzy again. There, in his cheek, was a hole the size of a five pence piece.

Otto quickly began searching for all the things he could gather together in his room to try and fix the fleshy void, but he had never come across something quite like this before.

He had several jars of his 'Hold-and-Heal' ointment for broken noses, large tubes of 'Gouge Glue' for feuds with Nash's fingernails, and splints, ready to straighten broken digits. What he didn't have, was medicine to fix a hole.

Otto laid on his bed in defeat and looked at the black hole he had painted on his ceiling. Planets, stars, even spaceships swirled around it, preparing to be sucked in and lost forever. A constant stream of purple space dust, rushing in to a void that was impossible to fill.

"That's it!" Otto thought. "I don't need to *fix* this hole; I need to *fill* it!"

He leant down, taking a box of knick-knacks from under the bed. Over the years, Otto had filled this box with anything he knew his family wouldn't miss. Offcuts from the hessian curtains that no-one had bothered to measure, soap that Nash refused to use, beard trimmings from when Mum made Dad shave off his beloved goatee. Otto was sure he could find something, and sure enough, after a few experiments, that's exactly what he had done.

"I'll cut the cloth and soften it, with Spider's dog shampoo, scrunch it up, really small, and cover it in glue! Squish it in and mould it, so it stays in place, then hopefully I'll have filled, this big hole in my face!"

Otto's hands were shaking. As he lifted the mass of sticky fabric to his face, he realised he had never fixed something quite so scary as his own head. He gently pushed the slimy ball in to the hole, pinching and flattening it in to place. Once it was sitting flush against the rest of his cheek, he began to dry it. It wasn't long before the glue had formed a tacky outer layer, and although it was no longer painful, it had become a constant ache.

The 'BOOP BOOP' of the school bus jolted Otto in to action. Grabbing his rucksack, he made it out of the front door just in time.

Otto loved the school bus. It was his favourite part of the day. It was never full, meaning he always got a window seat, and at about two thirds of the way in to the journey, the bus entered a tunnel and plunged everything in to darkness.

As the tunnel lights flew past in a blur, Otto imagined he was travelling through space. Instead of going to school, he fantasised that he was completing an important mission to find life on Mars.

"What's that?" asked Simbi, plonking herself next to Otto and staring at his cheek.

"Nothing." shrugged Otto.

Simbi and Otto had been best friends ever since Otto had given her his 'Slow Down Spray' when she was panicking on the first day of school.

She saw him turn away with tears in his eyes, but took a plaster from her bag and gave it to him, shrugging, to let him know that she was just as unbothered by it as he was.

When Otto got home from school that day, he noticed something was different. Nash's music wasn't on and Spider wasn't barking. It was completely silent.

"Mum?" Otto called out. "Dad?"

"In the kitchen" said Nash, making Otto jump. With a sick feeling in his stomach, he followed Nash in to the next room.

"Dimwit!" Dad said, causing Mum to snicker. "We have something to tell you."

"We're going to SPACE WORLD!" Nash blurted out, the saliva around his mouth bubbling with excitement.

Otto had read about Space World in his magazine, but not in a million years did he think he would actually be going.

He wondered whether he would be tall enough to get on The Saturn Spinner, or brave enough to ride The Asteroid, a rollercoaster famous for being the highest, and therefore closest to space, in the world.

"When?" Otto squeaked.

For what felt like minutes, there was silence, which was suddenly broken by Nash screeching with laughter. Mum joined him. Dad couldn't help but smile, as did Otto, who wasn't quite sure what for.

"We are leaving in 10 minutes. You are staying here." said Mum, through hiccups of laughter.

"I don't understand." said Otto.

"Well, I was in your room today, and imagine how disappointed I was to find that you've been stealing from us."

Otto closed his eyes. He had been in such a rush to get on the school bus that morning, he had left his box of knick-knacks on the bed.

"Oh." Otto whispered, not knowing what else to say.

"Nash was so upset when we told him that his own brother was a thief, weren't you Nashy?" sniped Mum.

Otto looked at Nash, who was nodding, but making no attempt to cover up his smile. Suddenly, Otto felt the same sensation he had experienced the night before. It was sharp and painful, and right in the centre of his stomach. Then in his hand. Then in his shoulder. He could barely breathe.

"Now look, there's no use getting upset. What's done is done. We'll be back in a couple of days. Do you think you can handle that?" said Dad.

Otto managed to nod as he made his way to his bedroom. He could hear his family continue to laugh as they packed up the car. The pain in his body became so intense that he found himself on the floor once again. He could feel that more holes were forming as he heard the front door slam shut. For the first time in his life, Otto let out an almighty scream.

It seemed whenever he thought about Nash at SpaceWorld, or Mum laughing at him, or Dad staying silent, another hole would begin to form. The pain was always incredibly intense at first, but eventually died down to an ache. Of course, now that these aches were all over his body, it was crippling Otto, sapping him of energy and leaving him feeling as though he was going in slow motion.

The next morning, as Otto walked around the empty house, nothing seemed to matter. There was nothing of interest. Things were neither good nor bad.

Otto got himself a glass of water and sat at the kitchen table. The SpaceWorld brochures had been left as a reminder of what he was missing. He could feel his face turning red and his ears burning as he filled with anger.

An envelope poked out from underneath a brochure, catching Otto's eye, and he was surprised to find a ten-pound note inside. Still bubbling with rage, he marched to his room, emptied his school bag and filled it with supplies, before making his way to the front door. As he took one last look back at the many 'family' pictures of Mum, Dad and Nash on the walls, he realised that all he was leaving behind were bad memories.

A few hours later, Otto was sat in the pouring rain under a tent he'd constructed from branches and one of Mum's old tablecloths. It was cold and loud, and he missed his room. He regretted not bringing more things with him to make the tent his own.

He took his SpaceLife magazine from his bag and began flicking through the pages. His stomach dropped. Nash had scrawled the word 'LOSER' in thick black marker over every picture.

Right on cue, the burning started, fizzing away a tiny portion of his hand. This time, Otto just stared at the hole as it formed. He had become almost used to the pain, and as he closed his eyes, he thought about how easy it would be for a black hole to swallow him up.

"Otto!" said Simbi, poking her head in. "As soon as I saw a funny little tent in the middle of the park, I knew it would be you!".

Otto opened his eyes.

"What are you doing here? Are you camping?"

"Yeah" croaked Otto.

"You're so lucky you're allowed to go camping on your own! Dad only ever lets me camp in the garden."

As Simbi took a breath, she realised she wasn't getting any response.

"Do your parents know you're here?" She asked, gently.

"No." he mumbled, "They took Nash to SpaceWorld. He ruined my magazine."

Otto brought his knees up to his chest, and began to sob. Simbi sat down next to her friend and put her arm around his shoulders.

They didn't talk; they just stayed huddled together for what felt like hours, only moving when they heard Simbi's Dad call her name.

"I have to go now" She said, sadly.

Otto nodded. "Okay. Are you coming back tomorrow?"

"Well Mum's not very well at the moment, and Dad wants us to spend time together."

"What's wrong with her?" asked Otto, before being interrupted by Simbi's Dad sounding very concerned that he couldn't see his daughter.

"I should go. I'll see you soon, okay?"

Otto watched Simbi run over to her Dad. He scooped her up, not angry that she'd been out of sight, but relieved that he had his daughter in his arms.

Otto spent the next few hours thinking about all the times he had tried to help his parents, but had been branded a 'busy body'. He slumped over and stared at his reflection in a puddle that had found its way inside the tent. "Maybe it's me" he told himself.

Mum's tablecloth had done a dreadful job of being waterproof, and now everything was slightly damp, including Otto.

Suddenly, he heard a cry that froze him solid, and a light that had not been there seconds ago. A shadow flew past and the sound echoed again. It was high pitched, and as it latched on to the wind, it seemed to stretch further than was humanly possible. Perhaps it was an animal, or a monster, or his Mother coming to find him.

The light suddenly went out, plunging Otto in to darkness once more. He was aware of something lurking outside the tent, and quietened his breaths as he heard the ground crunch, closer and closer.

He watched as the lining of the tent opened and fingers wrapped around the material.

"Otto? Are you in there?" a voice said.

The light came back on. He closed his eyes and held his rucksack to his chest, not sure what he was preparing for. When Otto eventually opened his eyes, there, in front of him, was a woman. A woman who was covered in holes.

"Otto? I'm Hallie. I'm Simbi's Mum."

Otto couldn't stop staring at all the holes covering her hands, neck, and face.

"You can see them, huh?" said Hallie, with the gentlest voice Otto had ever heard.

"Maybe I could borrow some of that?" she said, pointing at Otto's cheek. Otto lifted his hand to the first hole that had ever formed.

"Can I come in?" Hallie asked.

There wasn't nearly enough space, but Hallie smiled as she scrunched herself up in a corner, narrowly missing the puddle.

"What happened to you?" Otto asked, not able to stop himself tearing up. "What happened to me?"

Hallie smiled and offered a hand to Otto. He took it, thankful for the warmth. They both became aware of the sound of water, as it dripped on to the tent floor.

"You know, if that water keeps dripping, it will eventually make a hole in the tent."

Otto watched as more drips fell, landing in the same place each time. He was confused.

"It's true. Even mountains wear away and, *change* shape when the same wave crashes on them every day."

Otto nodded. He knew that was true; he'd learnt about it in school.

"So, if I asked you to think of something that keeps happening to you, like wave that keeps crashing on you, what would it be?"

Otto thought hard, and said something he had never said out loud before.

"My family. My family keep making me feel sad. I think it's because they don't love me." he sobbed.

Hallie squeezed Otto's hand.

"Am I wasting away?" he asked.

"No, you're not. I promise."

Otto turned his face away from Hallie.

"What would you do if there *was* a hole in the tent?" she asked.

Otto shrugged. "Try to fix it."

"And it would still be a tent, right? Even with a hole?"

Otto nodded.

"And when a wave changes the shape of a mountain, does it stop being a mountain?"

"No."

"No. So, maybe we could figure out a way to start fixing these holes. Maybe we can stop our shapes from changing too much. Do you think we could do that together?"

Otto looked at Hallie. He was relieved to see she wasn't smirking, or asking him a question just to trick him.

The short burst of a car horn made them both jump. Hallie laughed, which made Otto feel completely safe for the first time ever.

"It's a lovely tent you've made here, but maybe a bed would be warmer? Less puddles?"

Otto didn't think twice as he followed Hallie out of the tent and in to her car, where Simbi was waiting.

"This is for you" she said, as soon as he'd fastened his seat belt, placing the latest SpaceLife magazine on his lap. Otto looked up and met Simbi's Dad's eyes in the rear-view mirror.

"You ok lad?" he asked.

Otto nodded, as a wave of relief, uncertainty, hopefulness and sheer exhaustion forced his eyes closed, and he was asleep before the car had even started moving.

Caspie Harriet - Navy Blue

Dragon
and you hold him
Dragon
and you ride him
like a horse
left to lye
in a coffin
full of hose spit
bare arms
Dragon
you place a hand on my left knee
please look at me
Dragon

Dragon
he watched you perform
firing your breasts
as you arch over him
look down at him
but never lower to his disperse
Dragon
until he comes
like a bullet in your loaded gun

Teaching men the use of water, because we are ghosts and clay no longer. Transpire and crack in an orthodox manner when you perceive my ribs. Where the eyes are black and no one knows me, no omen, take the fleshy dreamy softness and the hard skins that you can water in me. Trace the spine that is bent, faint with your finger tips and be weary when the back is turned. Dark becomes the colour in my vision so I cover the air with a purity powder to soften.

He drains out all my self-doubt but I ask him not to hang me dry. Stripped bare and the bachelor is uneven; when we could be tiny old plastic people in love, or something that they want to talk about. The political incorrectness in a household of fear, a neighbourhood of sirens and streets of sadness, where the men stood before me - no sexual desires. In this secret life of a mythical madness that places me as the centerpiece, in a game I don't quite know how to play I still think you always look so wonderful, like no matter what happens. In your own little way, you're out there fighting as hard as you can even if other people can't tell just by looking at you. You've been fighting all your life. You're not fighting for me of course, well at least I don't think you are. You're falling all over yourself and fooling around, trying to wrestle with this big whatever-it-is, and I can't comprehend why you're doing it.

There is no point in me getting all hot for you anymore. When you do these kinds of things I get all anxious and nervous, and lose my train of thought, and every word I want to say to you leaves me feeling totally tired and exhausted. If I had to bet on it, I think I would win on this statement, but I wouldn't want to go poor. I don't want to watch you going under either, losing sleep and tiring yourself out for reasons you do not know and I don't want to sweat for you anymore than I already have.

I've got a dozen pencils, all sharpened and laid out in neat little rows. There's an eraser and a sharpener too in case I make any mistakes. They're all brand new; I've only just bought them today - especially for writing to you. I am going away to a world that is a little less crazy, and a little more ordinary. But if I hadn't met you, things would have never turned out this way. But despite my move, I have every bit of faith in you, and you will be bigger and better than ever - in every single way possible. When I feel the naked rain upon me, I will tell the Wolf that I'm home, in a place where sanity is rare. Would I dare to press my lips on your shoulders? Would I care to place my hands on your chest? My fingers dance a melody to the sound of your voice, as it reverberates through my naked body. As you look down at me those blue eyes roar. Whilst you imprint my sheets with your body, I'll lay in your arms for a while.

Dear London,
You love him. Dear London, he adores you. The great escape of a dream tendency forever coming true. Smart and beautifully presented, holding a stare and smiling. Hipster facial shapes and waist-coated warmth is the time, the theme, and the style as the wireless radio fulfils the warm air of the dynamic bird garden. His scent is beautiful and his eyes so blue. Eastern secrets and herbal glass jars; tea and sweet leaves and an essence of incense that dress the room with a promise to never break. I remember

why I like it here; a place I once called home.

Turning my head, taking a glance at the fountains behind me, I feel the temperature is falling and the people around me fade into the distance. There's a slight chill in the air, which makes my body tense and the hairs rise on my bare arms - escalating to a shiver. I cross my arms tightly and lower my chest to the table. I don't know how or when it happened but for me my home is nothing more than 'your world', and when I'm in my safe space with you, it's nothing more or nothing less than 'the me contained within you', except I'm not in your world at all, I just place myself there from time to time. It's not your fault of course. That's why I had to come and find my own world if I can't be in yours completely. I can't have half of you anymore, so I thought long and hard about it and finally decided where I had to go. The past few years have quickly overtaken my world and you're in it too, consuming every little bit of me. Don't get me wrong, I'll still think about you, I'll still look at your face imprinted on my Instax and I will still ask myself the same questions like the prodding of a hot iron rod.

The juniper berries are growing, and sprouting at an instant yet I'm running behind the vastly slow moving vehicles. We were always so close. The city is calling my name, and the smoke is filling my lungs. The battery is draining on my phone and shortly no one will reach me – I'll feel the fresh air on the other side soon. I light a cigarette in memory and hope that one day you will call me by my name.

I hear a faint snare and Soul Eyes tunes in with the unexpected yet apparent legato piano arpeggios. Coltrane's contagious efforts to ease the one with the pain – every doll tolling like a tale of receptors inside. The melody takes over and I cannot hear anything anymore. The beloved beat is back yet drowning in three four time. It's black and white, and I hear my mother's voice on repeat;

"Feed yourself and clean your mess, those sheets must stay white".

Light me up and watch me burn, slowly as I enter your mouth. Like a pooled haze of tastes and a feeling that won't last more than 11 minutes. As you breathe me in I breathe you out, but remember, I am the only one who can make you fall to your knees and beg me for more. When I release you, release me too and stub me out gently like the post orgasmic settings of the seconds before. I stand alone in the room where all that is heard is the aftermath; the overwhelming silences and fluttering worlds and words of your inner self that only escape sometimes, like a recurring nightmare –

one self's unconsciousness in the public domain. This is me and mine. Yours and your own fueled by the self. Undertaken and forever underestimated. The cloud quickly catches the sun and it hibernates like a terror-stricken snail to a shell. It's all a little darker, duller, desperate as the evening draws in. I lower my head slowly to the table, resting it on top, timidly.

I see darkness as the floor trembles. The butt of the cigarette glows its golden glow again as Dexter draws near. There's a party in my something percent capacity. I guess its higher than 20. Twisted and turning she stands alone and needing more. Alone she stares into the smoke, like a bird of the night, caught by the wings inside the smog of the city in her cosmopolitan colours amongst uncanny colleagues. He asked me if I love him. The emptiness burdening upon like a ton of steel falling from great height. He already knows that I do. She's cold but dives in. Invisible, but bold, she leaves a distinctive trace of herself. Floating on the surface she's calling for help although utters no more than ten terms or so. Small words exit her mouth;

"Thank you for being there when I needed you the most, now everyone can applaud."

I suddenly wake up to a jolt. Coughing and shaken. I was drowning, deeply and quickly to the very pits of the awakened seabed. Swallowing all that enters and overflowing with mixed up worlds and words as the hollow voices play on repeat, but I can't quite understand what they're trying to say to me anymore, although I must call mum, she'll be worried.

The underground is deafening. The morning commuters struggle and he's taken by stride as I stand slightly off central – more so maybe something to do with last night. My head is a little heavy; eyes dry, fuzzy and delicate, and the sickness is swirling around the pit of my empty stomach. Bloated but I remember I haven't eaten, again, and my eyes are stinging like the slicing of a dozen red onions. He has an untucked shirt and untied cuffs that suggest he's not in for the morning ride either. Shaking his paper upright, he buries his head to read the blurred lines. I close my eyes and hide my sleepless dark circles behind my little blackout dark shades. My head is too heavy to keep upright, the pain is pounding like a foot to a high-hat, so I rest it on the cushioned bag behind me and press play on my music. My hair droops down over my sunken cheeks as I stare at my reflection through the window. I can't even find the drive to bend down and tie my shoelaces. I do it anyway with great difficulty, and somehow put my finger through the side of my boot. I wondered why my socks were wet. On my way up, I look in the opposite direction. The other male authority sits back, upwards, straight and crossed legged, with his head tilted slightly to the right. My left, focusing on the text above my head, the small print.

"You could be anywhere in the world but you're here".

A silver oval pattern silk tie and coal black shades. Smoked blue lenses, stunning. His shoes shine slightly, brown calf leather Oxford punched-toe-caps, remarkable, but too bright for my delicate eyes to look at for too long. His bag sits upright between his legs, loosely, *Bottega Veneta*, the leather portfolio of perfection. *Tudor* on the wrist and the timing is so right. Seamaster Diver. Black Bay fifty-eight, navy blue, 300M co-axial. Born-to-Dare, this gentleman oozes elegance, style, grace. Double breasted knee length coat – detailed with notched lapels and a single vent from *Versace* with *Tom Ford* French cuffs. I'm not comparing and sculpting my own male figure but I'm too fixated on the second as opposed to the first. He reminds me too much of you, elegant and beautiful. Fatigued and weak, my hands begin to tremble. I question if it's the effect that you are still having on me, or the second wave of motion sickness kicking in, in sync with the music to my ears;

"If you hate the taste of wine, why do you drink it 'til you're blind? And if you swear that there's no truth and who cares how come you say it like you're right? … We are nowhere and it's now".

Bright Eyes - your gift to me when discussing the functions of bodily fluids, or the lack of when it's cold. But making some kind of beautiful mess, that no one understands except the two of us, like poetry, where every sentence becomes music to our ears but each time it's spoken it's always a different hymn. We always did it, and we would tell the same story more than once with a bit of hope that we might eventually just be on that same page, because it makes every single sense of the world to place untold words into the shape of something like a book, or a caressing hand placed comfortably on your forearm as I read you. But I've filled myself up with expectations of you and how perfect you are, you're a good man, you really are, and I sincerely adore you. I can still smell you. I can still taste all of you in this stillness, but my eyes don't see you like they used to. My words don't move in you, and my hands don't touch you like I want to. It's cold but the sounding of the rain keeps my thoughts warm inside a safe space with you. I'm leaning on the beat of your chest where desires override conceptions of reality. The electric ocean of sound is drowning, and through the glass we cannot touch. My heart is pressed to the memory when I used to read to you as you slept, the same passage without a second thought, unaware if you could hear me.

> "Your cravings fill me and your scent becomes me, and I hear you screaming in the silence and your voice rises in the mute as waves crash before you. So, silent and still. Where you embedded my head with your hands. My mouth is filled with earth like a blow against the wind, stopping myself from measuring myself with your breath. And I name you softly, and I know that you hear me, and I think of you in my always. You've moved me and my touch, and I know that you reached me …"

***

7 months have passed since I read to you for the last time. In 12 days, this junction will become two-way traffic, and there will be live train times in the palm of my hand. This all seems beneficial for the one with the electrical device. The trains arrive every two minutes anyway, don't they? And my question is why are you still running? You find that you have missed the train you aimed to catch - the Northern Line to High Barnet - but do not ponder any longer, there's another in two minutes. Two whole minutes for you to catch your breath. The ability to cross amongst the oncoming traffic with one approachable run is a success.

10 days to go. I'm waiting for you. You appear like no other, but it's different than before. You're a mystery as Beth Gibbons sings; *I'm adoring life and I'm adoring you*. She can ask for more but I cannot. If I were a colour it would be grey, and scaled as a picture or a measurement of weight, time, and distance, of what this heaviness but apparent light of fullness is that drifts within me, it floats. An ease, a grace, and a warmth of belonging, in a certain place that you exist. You, you're a mystery and needing more, and my knowledge of you characteristically differ within the silences that approach me often.

Scoring on a better day, the moments that I enjoy are filling my senses with a burden of a smokiness haze, resulting in a walk that becomes alone, and full of light from the streets where warmth is no more, but please be there anytime. I wear the headphones hoping to hear some neutrality. It's an illusion. You sit there alone and I see you. You and no one more. I guess it's 8 days now…

Nail biting wanderer. You're nowhere to be seen and they didn't visit either. Now I'm here again, and as promised, I returned for you. Returning weekly, with a heavy dread of sickness. Where ones' idea of good conversation are the explicit and often unfortunate events of the night before. Personal endurance, a physical test, an addiction for further craving. Burning and heavy breathing and a level of self-control before entering. Enjoying the hunger, remaining in a starved state that becomes another level, and a high degree of self-control. Solitude and silence where no other dares to enter. I don't let anyone inside anymore, you taught me well. I flew the entire 136 steps towards you and counted every single one out loud, but upwards I always walk alone. If I say it again will it have further meaning? The repetition repeats like a fucking broken record; it spins and it sins, in circles, as deep as the ocean that we always dive into.

I dream about it often, and I've noticed you hadn't been yourself of late – I just hope that wherever you've gone you feel free. You lose yourself in the process of someone else, but when I fall in and out of love with you, I still push down your zipper under moonlight night skies and collect washed out droplets on the window pane. I still smell you on this 20:46-night train. As you compress to me I caress every inch of your chest and I hope to confess you by name. I drop lower to loosen your thighs, your eyes no longer visible as you close them slowly. Inside darkened desires I close my eyes too, and secretly smile inside your mouth. I want you to feel everything and depend on my touch, and tell me what kind of night this is and I'll shout out loud my affection.

The beautiful monuments of a memory.

David Goodfellow - On the Ledge with Elvis

Johnny stood on the ledge peering down, his stomach shooting bile up his throat. Eighteen storeys below the people looked like ants on sugar. His toes curled over the edge and panic shuddered through him as the wind pushed him forward. Arms outstretched, palms pressed into the rough brickwork, his fingertips made a meal of the thin mortar lines.

"Excuse me mate." Johnny did not register the upbeat mockney voice. It came again, "I said, excuse me mate."

Johnny looked towards the voice but saw only a tabby cat; white fur under its chin with large aqua eyes peering up at him. The wind pulled his focus back to the balancing act keeping him alive.

"Listen, mate," Johnny snapped back to the cat. It was definitely the source of the voice, "you're obviously busy, but here's the thing, you're in my way. Three windows along," the cat raised a paw to gesture, "there's a lady. My Spanish milkmaid, I call her, we have a thing, a routine. I climb through her window, rub against her legs, pretty please and all that. And she gives me milk, it's all good and thank you very much, that's the deal. Not just any milk, mind you, gold top, like Derick used to give me. So if you don't mind I've got places to be."

Johnny's heart jackhammered as the cool morning air rushed into his heaving lungs. In his mind, he was dropping like a wingless angel, past the seventeenth floor, sixteen, fifteen.

God made Adam and Eve but floor fourteen belonged to Adam and Steve. It was their view of the vanilla sky Johnny would interrupt as he briefly flickered past their window. It was, wow, thirty years ago he'd first met Steve and moved in.

"Knock knock, I hope you don't mind? The door was open."

"Come on in, you must be Johnny. I would shake your hand, but…" Adam waved his hands, covered in oil paint. "You've caught me red-handed."

"This place is amazing, I can't believe you guys squatted the whole building. The ceilings are so high and the windows let in—" Steve emerged from the bedroom, looking like Noel Coward in a dressing gown.

"The natural light." he finished his sentence and the three men smiled, "You know what Johnny? Flat eighteen is empty. We could be neighbours, comrades, amigos, brothers in paint…"

But of course Adam and Steve were long gone. Johnny had no idea who lived on fourteen anymore.

Johnny imagined rotating his arms, clawing the air, cycling his legs as if sprinting to the ground.

"Listen, mate," Johnny snapped back to reality, still on the ledge, tensing every muscle. Like defectors ignoring the battle plan, his fingers clamped onto some old guttering. "This here ledge," the cat continued, "is a thoroughfare, rather than a place to stop and soak up the view. As in, I use this ledge to get from A to B, one flat to another. Comprende?"

Thirteen, twelve, eleven. Ten was Outsider Mark's floor.

"Hi Mark, I got some odds and sods. A loaf, some Yorkshire Gold, a couple of chicken bits from the reduced shelf at Sainsbury's," Johnny said, making his way across the floor, tiptoeing between piles of old motherboards, hard drives, wires and screen.

"How much do I owe?" Mark asked, the joint wedged in the side of his mouth bouncing with every word.

"Don't be silly. What's all this?" Johnny plonked himself down in the battered leather chair made from an old Range Rover seat. He looked about, taking it all in.

"See these?" Mark grabbed a circuit board examining it under the lamp. "Stunning, see how the light catches these bits here, that's real gold, I'm not joking."

"Yah man, I guess I never really took a close look at what makes a computer tick.

What are you doing with them anyway?"

"It's obvious, isn't it? I'm going to tile the bathroom. And see here, look at this lot," he sent a stained tote bag sailing through the air into Johnny's lap. "Spoons, forks, knives man, look at them." Johnny fished out a clutch of bent cutlery.

"These are pretty mangled dude, they get run over with a car?"

"Something like that, I got them out a skip in Tottenham Court Road, someone actually threw them out, can you believe it?"

"But you can't eat with these."

"Of course not." Mark's voice shouted back from the kitchen as he clanged about making tea, "they're too gorgeous for anything as humdrum as that. I'm thinking chandelier—but only if I can magic-up a bowling ball or an anvil to hang along with them; to balance out the composition, you see?" Was Mark an outsider artist or a hoarder with a glue gun? Johnny felt ashamed that Mark had died before he worked out the answer.

"Comprende? Comprende?" the cat repeated.

"Cat, cat, bloody cat." the words rose out of him like an incantation. "Flip." the cat said matter of factly.

"Shoo, shoo." Johnny carefully raised his left foot and waved it, "shoo." The cat observed the foot, moving his head left and right, tracking it through the air.

"Flip." The cat repeated, unperturbed. "I reckon if you tried," he took a lazy swipe at the foot before losing interest and looking back down, "If you really put your back into it, you could do a full flip before you land." Johnny loosened a few fragments of brick as he planted his foot back down on the ledge. He watched as a small cluster of debris showered to the ground before tipping his head back against the wall.

"Forget about the flip. Probably not the best idea for someone like yourself. I've never been that impressed with, how should I put it, the acrobatic ability of humans." Johnny clamped his eyes shut with the conviction of a child wishing away monsters. Johnny was falling in his mind again. Nine, eight, seven, floor six. Amy. That's where she lived when they were a thing.

"What's that smell?" Johnny said, breathing deeply.

"Tofu and green lentil curry. There's lemongrass and fresh chillies in there." Amy bounded towards him, barefoot, her body bouncing inside her overalls. "But forget about that. You've got to read this, Johnny," Amy thrust a leather book under his nose. Johnny turned it over in his hand.

"William Blake?" Amy took the book back.

"Here, let me read you this…

> To see a World in a Grain of Sand
> And a Heaven in a Wild Flower
> Hold Infinity in the palm of your hand
> And Eternity in an—

"Listen, I'm sure it's great. But I can't stay. I'm working on a canvas. I think I'm getting somewhere. I'm making something—I'm only here to pick up my brushes."

"Johnny," Amy deflated like a balloon. "The curry, my parents are coming round. I wanted them to meet you. And I wanted you, you know, to stay afterwards."

"I should have stayed with Amy, not for the curry but for the rest of my life." "What curry?" the cat asked as if being summoned back from a meditative state. "Balls— I was talking to myself."

"That mate, is a matter of opinion. Who's Amy?" "Just — somebody I used to know."

"If you say so." the cat turned in circles before lying down with one paw casually flopped over the ledge.

Johnny retreated back into his mind. He fantasised; how might the local paper cover his demise? An article near the sports section perhaps? The headline: Local Artist Leaves Behind Great Impression. The journalist would bullet point a small clutch of victories to summarize his life. The well-received portrait of the ArchBishop, his landscapes of the Heath. Perhaps they'd mention the coffee table book that bore his name, `The Impressionist Paradox'. Most who read his obit would not understand the reality of his life. The bedrock truth: dying on the edge is not enough. If you don't live on the edge as an artist you're guilty of taking up too much room.

"Pass one will you?" Mark pointed to a pile of dismembered doll parts. "A leg, an arm or a head?"

"A head." Mark glued it to the iceberg emerging from the carpet.

"Doesn't it bother you, that hardly anyone sees your work?" Johnny asked while pouring the millionth cup of over-brewed tea from Mark's filthy, stainless steel teapot.

"Do you mean, am I disappointed my work isn't cluttering up some gallery instead of my living room?"

"Well, I wouldn't put it quite like that, but yes."

"What do you think goes on in museums? Why go to all the trouble of collecting— packing-in and framing as many masterpieces as possible?"

"Efficiency, I guess, it makes things easier for the public. And safety; frames protect the artworks."

"Right, it's all very utilitarian is it? Despite the fact that one masterpiece is more than enough for a room, or building, or even an entire postcode. Frames, museums, galleries; they're all desperate attempts to confine greatness. We gather masterpieces, like dragons hoarding gold because deep down we're scared. We fear that even a single spark of escaping divinity might burn our lives to the ground. You see Johnny, the burning bush speaks to us all but most of us reach for the first extinguisher when we hear it. We can't afford to see the wonder of a diesel slick across the road, smell heaven as the butter burns or fully hear the roaring silence with intent. We have places to go, people to see, work to do. Society can't afford for us to stumble upon beauty willy nilly."

On the final part of Johnny's journey, he'd smash through the once brilliant red, now faded awning, proudly announcing Mario's Cafe to the world in big white letters, before he reached the ground. Five feet from Mario's door, in plain sight of the rickety tables packed with people eating smashed avocados on toast. For an instant, the adrenaline would cause the world to slow and flood in through his senses. He'd hang inches above the patchwork pavement, carefully examining the contours of each crack. A handful of discarded sweets, balls of prime colours, half crushed on a painter's palette. He'd see once intensely loved but now discarded cigarette butts and discarded lottery tickets sailing down the gutter. He'd smell the rich and primal power of Mario's freshly roasted coffee beans. He'd hear a child's laughter drowned out by the high-pitched squeal of a speeding scooter. He'd finally see the bigger picture, like a witness to Jehovah he'd see the unframed masterpiece held within the moment of his death.

Finally, it would be done. He'd pound into the pavement in front of the building; once full of friends now full of God knows who. A thud he'd never hear, a crumpled mess of limbs he'd never see. An homage to Pollock or Francis Bacon? It would be street art after all, so perhaps in the end he'd be a budget Bansky?

The cat pulled him back, rubbing against his leg. Johnny released the vice tight grip on his eyelids. His eyeballs flickered up and down, taking it all in.

"You remind me of Derick. You smell like him; ripe, if you get my drift?" "Who's Derick?" Johnny was fish hooked by the conversation despite himself.

"He was my human for a while. We lived together. We had a flat over the road. He was a home-body, didn't get out much. But he was a nice fella, I slept with him most nights. I'd let him feed me when he asked nicely. That sort of thing."

"What happened to Derick?"

"Damned if I know. I went back one day and he wasn't there. I never saw him again.

I'm guessing he finally left. Poor geezer, I hope he's happy, wherever he ended up. Haven't thought about him in years, you smelling like him, reminded me."

"I'm sorry about— It's hard alone."

"It can be hard together. That's just life innit."

Johnny examined the four-legged interloper. His delicate white whiskers arched out either side of his coal-black nose. He had neat white paws like a child's Sunday best. His thick fur was rippled black with a dozen shades of grey. The way the light reflected off his coat, he was a Dürer canvas come to life. Johnny forgot about dying and his mounting credit card debt. The compounding numbers that bullied him from sleep at night. The dark coldness they brought in their wake. First the electric and now the gas bill left unpaid. He forgot about the letter on his coffee table that had forced him out on the ledge.

> Dear Johnny Anderson,
> We regret to inform you that your failure to pay six months of rent arrears for the address listed above violates your tenancy agreement. Failure to make full restitution by the end of the month will result in your eviction. A court order will be enforced by bailiffs…

Johnny forgot it all. Johnny wanted to— run his finger through that fur, feel it purring close to him. As they stared, revealing worlds to one another, the cat slowly raised his leg like a ballerina, before plunging his head deep into his nether regions. Johnny smiled. He couldn't help it.

"I'm Johnny," he said like an awkward teenager on a first date. His demons rattled their chains inside his head.

"I'm Elvis. Nice to know you." The cat responded cheerily. "Elvis, like the singer?"

"The singer? Can't say I've ever heard of a singer called Elvis." "Elvis Presley, you know, you ain't nothing but a hound dog—"

"Never heard of him. Presley? Hound dog? What you talking about mate. I'm a cat." "Clearly. Yes, I can see that," Jonny pedalled backwards, "'Hound Dog' it's an Elvis song." Elvis the Cat looked up at him. Johnny knew that look, even from a cat. It meant, 'what kind of nutter are we dealing with here?'

"Well," Elvis spoke as if explaining the world to a child, "I don't know about Elvis Presley or any hound dogs. I'm Elvis the Cat. Any other Elvises out there are like me, not the other way around. As in, I am a local legend, the sun if you will, around which all other Elvises orbit. Don't take my word for it, you can ask anyone in this building or even that one across the road." Johnny laughed.

"How about we, um, go inside? I could get you some tuna fish. I think I have a can." Elvis stretched his neck and peered along the ledge.

"I suppose my milkmaid can wait. Tuna you say? That would hit the spot right about now." Very carefully Jonny inched his way along to the sash window. Gripping the frame with both hands he pushed his body inside crumpling onto the hallway floor.

"Estas bien? Sorry, English. Are you ok?" a woman's voice asked. Johnny felt a hand on his shoulder. He looked up to see an olive-skinned woman with a brown fringe and hot chocolate eyes.

"I, um—" Elvis elegantly slipped through the open window. His white paws made no noise as he sauntered up and pushed his head between them. "I was on the ledge with Elvis." He said as casually as he could muster.

"Ingleses locos," The woman shrugged and turned her attention back to Elvis.

"Ven aqui Elvis. I worry about you." she started speaking as if to a baby, "te quiero gatito Elvis. Who's the best cat in the world?" she tapped a finger on Elvis's nose. As she fussed and stroked him, Elvis looked over as if to say, 'I told you so'. Johnny found his feet, "You must be Elvis's Spanish milkmaid."

"Pardon?" she looked at Johnny, confusion etched across her face.

"That is to say. I meant to say, you—you must be the kind lady who feeds Elvis gold top."

She faced Johnny with Elvis in her arms, "How do you know that?" she asked. Her accent curled up and nestled in Johnny's ear.

"Well, Elvis is something of a superstar around here. He's a special cat. We all—um— want the best for Elvis". Johnny ruffled the fur between Elvis's ears, "he's got no home at the moment. Poor little guy. In fact I was, maybe— I was going to feed him some tuna." As if on command Elvis jumped to the floor.

"Well ok then, maybe I see you later Mr Elvis."

"Yes, I'm sure you—and perhaps we might grab coffee sometime? You know downstairs at Mario's?" Johnny tried to keep up with his words as they fell out of his mouth, "Fresh arabica beans. It's great coffee," he paused before adding, "and they have smashed avocado on toast."

"I'd like that," she smiled and picked up her bag, "I'm Catrina by the way."

"Nice to meet you," he shuffled on the spot, "And I'm Johnny, and you've met Elvis," he slapped his forehead as Catrina disappeared around the corner. He turned and opened the door to his flat. Elvis sprinted in between his legs.

"What a dump." Elvis sniffed as Johnny turned to look down the hallway before following him inside.

Eileen O'Donoghue - Over the Shop

Technically, she wasn't eavesdropping. She just happened to be in the hall, searching various coat pockets for her keys when she heard Adrian talking to his mother in the front room. She just wanted to find the keys and get out for a run with the dogs. Then she heard her name.

'It's always Jane's fault with you.'

It wasn't a deliberate deceit, to stand there listening, was it? She caught the two dogs by the collars and shoved them in through the door that led from the hall into the shop. Aisling, the part timer, was in there and she was always sneaking ham from the deli for them, so they raced in drooling, tails in the air. Jane shut the door quietly to keep them in there.

She went back to her search, rooting around in the pockets of jackets lined up on several hooks inside the front door where she could hear her mother-in-laws wheedling, Hannah's thin voice somehow surrounding her in the hall, curling around her neck. Jane could picture her perched on her window seat in that sitting room, watching the goings on of the village, an occupation that prevented Adrian from extending the shop fully across the front of the building. Ye can do what ye like when I'm dead and buried. Ye won't have long to wait was the long-playing mantra.

Her hand found the keys, tangled up in the Charlies lead, in the pocket of her fleece. She stood perfectly still, keeping her hand in the pocket, the steel edge of the keys imprinting on her palm. If Adrian came out suddenly, she could still be looking. She pressed her cheek against his rally jacket, which hung shoulder to shoulder with her fleece, inhaling him while she listened.

'Adrian, love, you're too soft. She runs rings around you.'

'Ah, Mam. Will you leave it?'

'I won't leave it. I heard ye last night, the jist of it anyway.'

'And stop blaming Jane. It's hard for her living here and working in the shop too. And then there's the girls and their kids with a free run of the place whenever they want.'

'And why shouldn't they? Are your sisters to stay out of the house they were reared in now too?'

'Well, that's just it, Mam. I never meant for it to go on this long. We need our own place. Do you know what I am trying to say? It's all a bit claustrophobic.'

'Claustrophobic how are you. You wouldn't hear the likes of it on Doctor Phil. That's one of her fancy words.'

In the hall, Jane's cheeks reddened with swallowed rage and she buried her face in Adrian's jacket to supress any sound.

Adrian tried again. 'Look, Mam, I'm trying to hang on to my marriage. The boys are small. They need Jane. I need her. I'm doing my best for the business, but I have to think about my family.'

Lowering his voice, he said, 'We're going to see a therapist.' He was interrupted by some outburst from Hannah that she didn't quite catch but continued, 'I'm telling you, so you won't feel the need to snoop around trying to find out what's going on. And I'm only telling you, so I better not hear it back.'

'Who would I be telling?'

'The girls, who else. You know they will find a way to needle Jane about it. Can you just stay out of it?'

'I will. But I'll give you one piece of advice whether you want to hear it or not.'

'Go on.' She heard her husband's weary reply.

Grabbing her fleece off the hook, her hand still wrapped around the keys, she left the hall soundlessly and went into the shop. She couldn't stand to hear another word.

Aisling was busy stocking the crisp shelves near the counter. She had her earphones in and was oblivious to Jane slipping out through the shop onto the street, leaving the dogs behind.

*

Adrian took in the room around him, unchanged since he was a child, still dominated by the patterned, wool carpet, as indestructible as it was ugly. It was like a different country outside. The June sunlight poked through the heavy lace curtain in bright pin pricks at odds with the brown interior of the room. It hadn't rained for three weeks and the village had gone from sodden to parched. Outside, the street had a faded look, like a pale skinned Irish girl trying to wear the summer dresses of an olive-skinned beauty. An olive-skinned beauty, like Jane.

He turned his focus back on the cluttered room, regarding the small steely woman sitting in her straight-backed chair by the window. She was twisting a cloth hanky, dark liver spots and raised blue veins moving with her hands. The old, flat, wedding band she still wore was loose but kept in its place by a swollen, red knuckle. Because she had always been old in his eyes, she had never gotten older. He raised his eyes from her hands to her face and took in the pale wrinkled skin, the lash-less eyes, the immovable set of her sparse grey hair. The room was airless and choked by a confusion of photos and ornaments that were propped for admiration at every turn. There were several framed photos of his mother with the four of them surrounding her. His father only appeared in two, their wedding photo, on one side of the Sacred Heart, and his mortuary card on the other side.

Hannah shifted slightly in her chair and brought him back to the moment. 'If you go to a therapist, it will go on a medical record somewhere and it might come against you sometime with the bank.' She raised her hand refusing any interruption, 'Now let me say it! My advice to you is to get Jane to go to the therapist on her own. She's a bit depressed, hardly surprising with her history. How could anyone be right never knowing their mother and raised by so called grandparents that aren't even related to you. Say that it will be good for her, that kind of approach. That way if anyone's mental abilities are called into question, it won't be yours.'

'I already said we'd go, last night. I promised.'

'Well, promise her you'll go after she does a few sessions on her own. Now, don't be cross! That counselling is all a racket and those that dole it out are all a bit cracked themselves. It doesn't work and it leaves a stink.'

He moved to the window, pulling the lace aside a fraction, looking out, not answering.

Hannah stood up, indicating that their talk was over. 'What are doing this morning, so?' she asked.

'I'll give a run to the Cash n Carry for some stock.'

'Who's in the shop?' she detained him a moment longer.

'Aisling is in there.'

'That one,' said Hannah, rolling her eyes.

'Ah, she's alright. She won't burn the place down.'

'I caught her on the mobile phone behind the counter the other day. Sharing a post she was, something viral, whatever that means. Nodding dogs, all those young ones. I'll go in myself for a while.'

Leaving his mother to her rant on the useless Aisling, he went into the shop to hear the same girl singing, 'So you had a bad day,' at the top of her voice. He almost felt sorry for her. She stopped mid-screech when she saw him and smiled, taking our one ear bud, 'Did you say something?'

'Aisling, remember I asked you not to let the dogs into the shop?' Charlie, followed by his slave Bertie, bounded up to him, wagging their tails, and pushing each other out of the way.

'Oh, sorry.'

'Did Jane go out?' he asked casually.

'I didn't see her,' she said, leaning over the counter to look outside, 'but her car is gone, see?'

'Right. I'll be back after lunch. Will you be ok? My mother said she'll give you a hand.'

'Great,' said Aisling, her smile fixed.

'And will you put the dogs outside, please?' He stepped in behind the counter and took a pack of cigarettes and a cheap lighter, put them into the breast pocket of his shirt before stepping out into the sunshine.

It was strange that Jane hadn't taken the dogs to the beach. She hated running without them. He got into the jeep and headed away from the shop. The summer holidays were fast approaching and that meant crazy kids and cranky women. All under the one roof.

Instead of turning for the Cash n Carry, he drove to the beach and parked the jeep in the top carpark, knowing Jane always ran from the other end. He got out, inhaling the soft, salt breeze and locked the car with the remote as he turned. His work shoes were slippery on the sand as he climbed the back of the dunes. On the downside, he sat a while and gazed at the shimmering sea. The light was hitting the water in blinding spots, the waves dancing to the choreography of the sun. He took out a cigarette and lit up, squinting in the light.

*

Jane ran but her legs were heavy. Without the dogs, it was half-hearted anyway. Fine grains of sand carried on the soft breeze grazed her face, brushing her cheeks and eyelids. She gave up, stopping with her hands on her waist, bending a little to catch her breath and made her way to the edge of the dunes to sit. Her mind was pulling her backwards and she surrendered to it.

She hadn't really known Adrian or his sisters growing up. They were all older, already in college when she went away to boarding school. She had always been a little afraid of Hannah, had always felt the woman inspecting her whenever she was in the shop with her grandparents. Her childish fantasy was that her mother would come back for her and everything would be perfect when they were together in London. All she knew, was that Jim and Ann had adopted her mother Ellen as a baby, that she herself had been born in London and Ellen had brought her home to Rossmore, when she was six months old. The only time she had ever heard Jim talk about her mother was just before she was sent away to boarding school. Her grandparents, who never raised their voices to each other, were arguing in their bedroom and shed heard her Gran say, 'Ah, Jim. Would you have the house so empty again?'

'Better to have her away in school with other girls, than here with every boy in the place hanging around. They're already looking, Ann.'

'She's not Ellen, Jim. She's her own person.' she answered him softly, and in that moment, Jane understood that her mother was never coming back.

***

Watching the seagulls soar and dip, Adrian didn't care what time it was. His mother and Aisling could fight it out in the shop in their mutual reign of terror, for all he cared. At forty-five his body felt old and tired. Was the age gap becoming more of an issue between them? He had gotten over it a long time ago after the initial ribbing about being a cradle-snatcher. He had not intended anything that night in the pub when she came back for Jim's funeral. She had stayed away after Ann died, must have been five or six years before that. She came into the pub that night with a bunch of local girls, like a dark swan trying to hide in a group of hens. She was sleek and stunning in a short denim skirt and white top, no sleeves, her skin tanned with a golden sheen to it. Her hair was cropped and dark and those eyes she kept slightly lowered, were pure Audrey Hepburn when she levelled them at you. He had only wanted to give her a bit of space from the circling lads and their stupid chat up lines. The other girls were busy flicking their long highlights laughing and talking together while she was just still and somehow shining.

That first time, a few nights after Jim was buried, she had shocked him with the urgency of her physical need for him. They were barely inside the door when they were pulling at each other's clothes. They only made it halfway up the stairs. Whenever he thought about it, he felt guilty, as if the old man had somehow witnessed their blatant lust on the turn of his stairs, and him barely cold in the ground.

*

She wanted the space and light to devour her so she could become invisible. What would it be like, not to be seen at all? Never to be looked at. Adrian had sensed her panic that first night in the bar. With a gesture, he had offered her a seat and a way out of it. The others backed off and before either of them realised it, they had been paired off as an item.

The first time with him, she'd never wanted anyone like that. The sex on the stairs had been bare and honest, without an agenda. Afterwards, when she took him by the hand up to her spartan childhood bedroom, he gently pushed her into the doorframe, kissing her, his hands slowly opening the buttons on her top. They moved together, stumbling to her small bed and skin to skin she knew she wanted to be joined to this man, to inhabit him, to never be separate again.

Looking up now, she saw that that the tide had turned, and the water would soon make its way back up the beach, reclaiming it. She became aware of a figure, coming from the top side of the beach and knew him by the set of his shoulders. A silence had stretched between them over the shop, and she did not know how to begin again with him. As she watched him draw nearer, she owned that she, herself had allowed this. She had allowed it by always agreeing to everything, always trying to fit in or fade into the crowd. She could have refused to sell Jim's house. She could have said no to moving in with Hannah. She could have said no to something.

He sat, landing heavily next to her, and picking up fists of the pale, golden sand, he said, 'How did you forget the dogs?'

She shrugged and looked out to the water, waiting for whatever was to come. It would at least be honest, like those first moments between them.

He took her hand in his, turning it palm up and kissed the inside of her wrist. She let him.

'Jane, you know I love you and I'll do anything to make it work between us. I never meant for it to go on this long, living with Hannah. She's a tough old bird. She'll manage.' He smiled a tight, thin sort of smile, 'But the counselling – do you really want that? I think you were just trying to shock a reaction out of me last night.'

She moved her hand away from his, ripped and relaced her runners while he continued talking.

'If I'm really honest, I think there are things you might want to deal with yourself, first. You know what I mean, growing up with Jim and Ann, not knowing your mother, all that. Look, our house was far from perfect, but at least I don't have unanswered questions.'

She didn't speak. He pressed on.

'If you still think we need to go together at some point, we can talk about it again then. Okay? And I promise we'll get out of the shop and get our own place, go on a few holidays, whatever you need.' He stopped then, taking a ragged breath.

'What changed your mind, about the counselling?' she asked.

'I had some time to think this morning, that's all. I'm tired, Jane, that's all I know right now.'

He closed his eyes and stretched back on the sand, drained. He exhaled and covered his eyes with the back of his arm. A rainbow of colours flashed and faded on the back of his eyelids and a low breeze whispered through the rushes behind him, the sound of it shushing his busy head. He was glad of the moment, the sunshine on his face, Jane still and quiet beside him.

Then, sensing she was no longer there, he sat up, scanning the beach both ways until he found her, a small figure between him and the sea, running on the vast stetch of sand.

Eric Olsen - Gemma

It's a funny feeling, travelling on a train with thirty million in your pocket. You know it's there, no one else does, but you're sure everyone's looking at you. Anyway, I arrived in Hatton Garden with only a hopeful gesture from 'The Big Issue' vendor.

Gemma and me, we've been together for thirty years, not married. One day, we promised the girls.

She's easy-going - when she gets her way. That's one reason we're back in England. It fits her business plan; imports from Southern Africa. Containers of animals welded from scrap metal or carved from hardwood. Quite elegant, some of them, but if I see another windmill, I'll divorce her. Ah, I'm ahead of myself.

Containers, that's where the trouble started. We'd unpacked it, the Romanian guys and me. The driver did fuck-all got a bad back; he said. That's why he smoked the funny stuff. Gemma busied herself, deciding where everything should go. I suppose that's fair, seeing as she bought the place.

Friday. I thought we'd finished. Two days later, my phone beeped.

"Smith," I answered.

"Mr Smif?"

"It's Smith."

"Sorry, sir. I'm from the removal company.

"There's been an accident. After the truck left you, it went off the road into a ravine."

I grunted some suitable commiseration.

"No, they're discharged from hospital, sir.

"We wouldn't bother you, but the assessor went out there. He brought back package seventy-two. It must have tipped out when the truck rolled over.

"We found the delivery documents; everything's ticked, but perhaps you overlooked that box. Did you receive number seventy-two, sir?"

It's Monday today. Two days ago, seventy-one counted, thirty-nine still left, how would I know?

"I can't be sure," I said. "I'll ask the boss, but she's in the shower if you'll hold a minute."

"Look, we've got a rep coming your way to do another quote. He'll drop off the package. It must be yours. If not, you'll let me know, won't you?"
"Who was that, Hon?" Gemma padded from the bathroom, tucking a towel the way women do.
I gave it a playful tug. Thirty years on, there's more of Gemma than there used to be. Takes me longer to check it all. I forgot about number seventy-two.

Tuesday. "That's the door. I'll go."
Gemma looked as if I'd brought a wasp's nest in.
"You'd better open it."
Her expression wasn't inviting comment. I slit the tape; bubble wrap, then another carton.
"What's this, a game of 'pass the parcel'?" I asked.
She gave me a stern look.
Rough stones pressed into foam. Diamonds, some fifty carats, at a guess. I looked at Gemma and waited.
It took a minute while she sniffed, then frowned at me. "You remember my Aqua-Club?"
I nodded. Gemma flew to Upington every month. She bought carvings for the next container, then drove to the Orange River, near Augrabies. Photographing giant catfish, so she said.
That had a limited appeal to me. They have enormous mouths, and they eat each other. I prefer my fish with chips and vinegar.
"At first, it seemed we irritated the locals," said Gemma.
"The second time, one guy came from the river as we arrived. He had a bag tied around his waist. We were curious, waiting to see what was in it. Jacques, the other photographer, brought a couple of frostier from our icebox.
"He joked with them until they showed us what they'd found.
"I know a rough diamond when I see one. It scared Jacques - possession of uncut diamonds carries a heavy penalty in South Africa. I told him not to be a wimp, but he sat in the car and sulked."
Gemma looked guilty. She crossed her legs, shooting a glance at me.
"Jacques had coveted a fancy camera for months. I bought one from the first packet proceeds, but he never came again. I told him I'd cut off his balls and feed them to the catfish if he said a word to anyone. He believed me."
I caught the flicker of a smile as she studied her fingernails. Perhaps castrating Jacques tickled her imagination.

"The syndicate started with me and three Orange River locals. Now we're eleven, including packers in South Africa and the drivers here.

"One packer collects from Augrabies every month. I've not seen an uncut diamond for a year until today."

Gemma gave me a furtive look.

I couldn't hide my admiration.

She crossed her legs the other way. The frown had gone.

"Our driver finds the diamonds in each container. He delivers to Hatton Garden.

"The syndicate's a mish-mash of people's colour and religion, or lack of it. We share wealth beyond a monopoly. Selling uncut stones is legal here. In South Africa -." She shrugged.

I had one reservation. "All the diamonds are from Augrabies?"

"Every one. We've agreed; the syndicate ends when we've taken everything we can from the river. Everyone has plenty stashed away. By then -." Gemma shrugged again.

"No conflict diamonds?"

"Never."

We were comfortable from my consultancy in South Africa, but the years had aged me. Officials harassed us to invoice through a minister's niece - the payments discounted if we got paid at all. Everything we achieved came from my skills. The intermediary added no value. I'm happy back in England.

Sure, we have a pleasant property and some money in the bank. Our perpetual student daughter is polishing my dissertation for her doctorate in engineering. The younger one has her stable. All from the sweat of my brow, so I thought.

"What about HMRC?" I said.

"The company pays its taxes."

"On the diamonds?"

Defiance crept into Gemma's expression.

"Some. Without the diamond business, there's no profit. Anyway, the National Lottery is my tax. It finances charities that wouldn't get funding otherwise; I buy tickets daily."

"And you won. Is that how Lizzie got her stables? Otherwise, someone might see a disparity between our income and the family's lifestyle?"

"Dad's retired," said Gemma. "But he's still a respected CA. I asked him what would happen if someone digs. He said five years - suspended sentence, but he's giving me a hand to keep things straight."

I was sure Gemma's Dad would use both hands for a share of box seventy-two. "How much is in the bank?"

"Here, or the Cayman Islands?"
Well, that does it. I'm not too proud to live off a lady - time she was Mrs Smith. I'll be a full-time writer. Maybe someone will read my scribblings and 'discover' me.
The guy in Hatton Garden has a workshop in Clerkenwell. They make necklaces and stuff when bits don't fit in his accounts.
I've sketched a catfish for him. It's curled into a ring, with a big stone in its mouth.
It thrills the girls. They've booked our venue for a week on Saturday.

Sunday. Six weeks later.
"That belongs in a museum, Dad."
He studied Gemma's digging-stick over his designer spectacles. My son-in-law knows everything, but my grandson's got more nous than him.
"Maybe, but it's on my wall," I said. "And I'm not your Dad."
Young Matt, he's another matter. Every time they visit, the little lad climbs on a chair and finds the rock. I superglued the halves together.
He rolls it around the floor, rumbling like a volcano. He has a feeling for stones, like his Gramma Gemma. Odd how that skipped a generation.
"Mum told me that stick saved your lives. That was the last time she spoke to me. I'm not sure what Mum meant, and now she's gone." Lizzie gazed into the dying embers in the fireplace, remembering.
Her partner stared in expectation. I don't trust him, but my daughters knew little about their family's fortune.
"It's all recorded with our solicitor with an instruction to open the envelope when I kick the bucket. Better that way."
The know-all snorted. "I'm going for a pint. Coming, Lizzie?"
She shook her head. "You go. Some of Mum's things need sorting."
Lizzie waited until the engine started. "Are you okay, Dad?"
"I'm managing, but your sister took it hard. At least you've got Matt and that man of yours."
"He tries too much to make you like him. Won't you give him a bit of slack, for me?"
"I'll try. Now it's just us, I'll tell you how we found the stick and the stone if you put the kettle on."
Even Matt looked interested.

Gemma wanted to see the Okavango again. July - a lot of water in the Delta. I asked about her malaria.
Gemma shrugged. "I'll use repellent. We can't give up everything we like."
She always had the last word.

We hired a Land Rover, two days' rental left, Gemma said we should drive north, sleep under the stars, where there's only sand and sky.
Lizzie smiled, stroking Matt's hair. "That's Gramma."

The Land-Rover had long-range tanks, and two fifty-litre cans; one for diesel, one for water.
"Drive until dark," Gemma said.
I thought I saw a flicker from a warning light, but we'd left the tar-road long ago. It took some concentration, negotiating the deeper sand.
By the time we stopped, the desert night was bitter.
We wore every stitch of clothing with us. Huddled together, Gemma kept waking, rubbing the mist from a window to see the dazzling Milky Way - until the condensation froze.
Ice crystals sparkling in a glimmer of morning light, I braved the cold and found the keys. The diesel clattered into life, no warning light.
"We'll get moving," I said. "When it's warmer, we'll stop and make some coffee."
"I have to pee," Gemma said.
"Can't you wait? The dawn comes quickly here."
"Not." She'd gone longer than expected.
I opened the door. Without a wind, the cold doesn't hit you right away.
I found her scratching around with a stick, fifty metres away.
"Got it," she said, holding up the broken halves.
"Great. Can we go?" The frost had seeped into me.
"In a moment."
I climbed into the Land-Rover. Gemma seemed impervious to the cold.
"What were you looking for?" I asked.
She fitted two halves together. It had been a single shaft, belled at one end.
"Someone made a hole in the banjo end. It's a digging stick. Quite old. I'd hoped to find the insert."
It seemed clear to me; the owner discarded the broken shaft. He cut another handle and fitted the obsidian blade to the new one.
I was showing off. I'd read about indigenous people's implements.
Gemma's eyelids drooped; it was warm inside the car. The cold finally got to her, or maybe boredom from my discourse.
There was no road, just sand. The sun climbed, threatening; so too the warning light.
The Land-Rover coasted to a halt. I heard the creak of hot metal and a menacing hiss.
Gemma stirred. "Whassup?"

"I don't know," I said, unlatching the bonnet. Outside, the heat was building. "We'll need the air con when we move again."
Wisps of steam wafted up. I propped the hood and waited.
Gemma yawned. "That's not good, is it?"
"No, it isn't, but I'm not putting my hands in there until it cools. I'll bet there are no tools."
My stupidity, not checking before a trip like that.
"I'll get the gas bottle, make some coffee," said Gemma. "There's biltong and eggs. Bacon is vrot."

Funny how you lapse back to South Africa speak.

Gemma showed no concern, studying her digging stick while the kettle boiled.
It was a split radiator hose.
"Can you fix it?" she asked.
"No. I'll bodge something. We'll travel further before it overheats again, but we've lost a lot of coolant. I'm scared to use much from the drinking water. Look at the map. It seems there's little chance to get a refill. There's no signal on my mobile. How is yours?"
"Nothing. What are we going to do?"
"Get your pants off," I said.
"Now? Will that help you think of something?"
"It will. Have you got more in the wash bag? And the bacon wrapper. What other packing is there?"
Wraps of plastic, six pairs of briefs tied around the hose; I filled the expansion tank. The coolant gurgled and bubbled, then rumbled through the engine - lots of drinking water. I held my breath as the motor turned. It started in a waft of smoke.
"Let's get going," I said.
"Where to?" asked Gemma.
"North," I said.
The four-wheel-drive hauled us from the sand; Gemma grinned. After thirty years, her fortitude still amazed me.
"My compass isn't working," said Gemma.
"Mine seems okay. If we keep heading north, we'll cross into Namibia and find the river."
It wasn't to be. The bacon wrapper and panties disappeared in a blast of steam.
Red light menacing, I felt the engine tighten. We rolled to a halt before it seized.

"What now?" asked Gemma.

"I'll look, but it'll take a while to cool."

"Okay." She studied her stick again. "You know, I might be the first to touch this implement for centuries."

We'd finished a lot of water, the biltong, and warm beer before I could put my hands near the engine block. The sun sank through the haze as I straightened up.

"The hose has gone."

"That's all my panties, anyway. Drop the bonnet; let's sleep. We'll think of something in the morning."

I didn't share her optimism, but as the daylight faded, rest was wise. She left her digging-stick on the hood.

It was daylight when Gemma prodded me.

"Something's moving," she whispered.

I tried to remember where we were. Gemma sat bolt upright.

"They've got my stick."

Wrapped in a blanket, she was outside in an instant, confronting four San people alarmed at an Englishwoman hopping about in my socks.

It's politically incorrect to call these amazing people bushmen. In my experience, the San don't give a shit. They saved our lives.

We had no words in common. I held Gemma, pointing to the implements they carried. Little bows and arrows, ostrich shells for water, and a digging stick. I smiled and bowed my head to each, the only greeting I could offer. Honey-coloured faces creased in grins.

Amid clicking tongues and laughter, we told of our predicament using hand signs and contorted faces.

Gemma learned how to use a digging stick. Rolled eyes and gestures of passing years confirmed the antiquity of her broken handle.

Not twenty metres from where we stood, they started delving. Water; without it, we would have died.

They understood our predicament. In the sand, they drew another broken vehicle, about a day away.

Gemma wanted to come with us. They smiled, shaking heads, convincing her to stay.

We rested while the daylight lasted, then trotted into the sunset. It took longer than it should - I couldn't match their pace.

I do not know how the San navigate, but there it was; an old Chevrolet, up to its wheel-arches in drifted sand.

What happened there? Nothing good, I feared.

We propped the bonnet revealing more blown sand - no evidence of overheating.

The hoses looked possible; but how to undo them?
Those patient people grinned, watching. Their conversation reminded me of crickets in the English countryside.
Water from half the ostrich shells had gone, yet the San were generous with my share.
Hopeful, I lifted the boot lid. Empty cans lay open - evidence of deep sand's deadly fuel thirst.
In desperation, I folded back a carpet, revealing a recess in the floor. Tools.
In minutes I'd released the hoses - serviceable, more or less. My San friends distributed the tools between them.
We drained two ostrich shells, waiting for the sunset, snoozing, then loped back slower with the heavy tool packs.
I shortened a hose from the Chevrolet; not ideal. I prayed to any deity who might be listening. Maybe the San's mantis-god took pity.
Money means nothing to the bushmen. How to show our thanks? I unbolted a wing mirror and gave it to them. They hugged themselves with laughter at their reflections.

We took the marked route for back through the Caprivi, changing the hose for a proper one. Returning our vehicle, I left the tools - except for one pack. Inside were two ugly stones - once a single piece, like Gemma's digging stick.
In the Sandton Hotel, we ordered breakfast in our room. Odd for Gemma; usually, she was up, impatient to talk to guests.
"It's the excitement," she said. "I'll sleep for a while; it's a long flight back to Heathrow."
"I'm going down to The Square, maybe find presents for the girls. Can I bring you something?"
She smiled. "Some panties please."
I packed her suitcase, one half-stone inside each of Gemma's shoes.

She woke only once on the flight.
You girls were there to meet us. I saw your smiles fade.
"Lovely to see you both," she said. "I'll be all right in the morning. I just need sleep." Gemma's eyes closed the moment the car moved off. We couldn't wake her when the car stopped in our driveway.
I rode with the paramedics in the ambulance. At midnight in the ward, they revived her. I held Gemma close and told her about the stone's two halves, just like the digging stick.
"All seven hundred carats for you," I said.

She smiled. "Give it to the girls. You're my rock. Keep my digging stick."
"Her hand went limp in mine. I felt the spirit fly."
"There'll be an autopsy," they said. "Probably cerebral malaria. Get it checked if you show symptoms."

Lizzie phoned. "I'm with my sister and your favourite son-in-law. Mum told us there'd be an inheritance." She paused. "That rock Matt plays with, it's a diamond, isn't it?"
"We've agreed," Lizzie continued. "We don't need the money. Mum would want a trust for malaria research."

I gave her the Hatton Garden number. He sold our stone at a nine-figure bid.

George McAlear - Small Change

Sitting in my spot, asking strangers if they can spare some small change, while most hurry past, avert their eyes, or regard me with disgust, I feel I'm the lowest of the low, dirt on the sole of society. Some do look at me, though, screaming in my face to get a job, to stop stinking up the street, while a pair of constables always move me on. Wind cuts through me, cold permeates every square centimetre of flesh and bone, rain soaks through to my very soul. On miserable winter days, I give up after a couple of hours, hurrying down to the embankment, finding shelter, spending the day being dispensed soup, sandwiches, tea and sympathy by cheerfully charitable folks. If it becomes too cold, I seek warmth in the day centre, obtain clean socks and pants, perhaps have a shower, but not a shave, the grizzled look good for business. I play cards and drink coffee, before setting out on the long weary trudge to the almost derelict squat I call home.

At other times, particularly when the summer sun has risen above the office building opposite, I feel like Leo on the Titanic, king of the blooming world. My spot is one of the best in the city; on the right is a still open bank, with a still functioning ATM, where some folk, brimming with largesse, drop a guilty coin into my cup; on the left is a burger joint, where enough coins in the cup buy me a burger, or where I use the toilet when the need arises, and one teenage member of staff will bring me out a free cup of tea, beseeching her God to bless me. I'd prefer coffee, but years of experience has taught me the correct response to Christian charity should always be, "thank you very much." Three doors further on is the food and wine store, where a cupful of coins will purchase tobacco, a bit of food, or a bottle, perhaps even all three. Another pair of bobbies tolerate me, sometimes engaging in a bit of friendly banter.

I'm up early most mornings, as other member of the homeless fraternity may attempt to acquire this prime position for themselves, and I forego free breakfast at the convent I pass on the long walk to staking my claim.

No matter the season, or the weather, I stay on through the evening on Fridays, to benefit from the generosity of mostly young folk joyfully released from the tedium of their nine to five treadmill. I could be insulted, or spat upon, or pissed upon, and there's always the threat of drunken violence, but more small change than usual is dropped into the cup, and there may be a note or two from the ATM. I pack up before the store closes, purchasing enough food, tobacco and alcohol to sustain me through the weekend, and journey back to the squat by bus.

Most weekends are lost in an alcoholic haze, but I sometimes keep myself together, having a shower and shave, and acquiring clean clothes, at the Saturday morning day centre, shedding the skin of my weekday begging existence, then wandering the city streets, visiting pubs, shops and cafes, exhibiting to the world the persona of the guy next door. I ponder this, wondering if I could ever throw off the hopeless drunk, and become the apparently solid citizen others see on these rare weekends.

Then there is the woman. I notice her, striding purposefully along the pavement opposite, then stopping and looking over towards me, before entering the office building. After a few days, as I'm looking out for her, she appears from the right, gives me a long quizzical look, drops a pound coin in the cup, turns, crosses the road, and enters the building. This behaviour continues, and I study her as she studies me. I would say she's in her mid forties, and she reminds me somewhat of my ex-wife, who threw me out after ten years of tolerating my alcoholic excesses. She's roughly the same height and build, and her hair looks naturally blonde, where my wife's colour came from a bottle. The woman's hair is always immaculately coiffed, almost understated make up and lipstick accentuating a natural beauty, her moderately expensive clothes stylish but businesslike. As she strides away from me, I look at her legs. I freely admit I have fantasies about her, fantasies always being part and parcel of my psyche in years of enforced celibacy, living as I do.

Our morning ritual evolves, as she inserts a "good morning" between the look and the dropping of the coin, and I add my own "good morning.". This continues until a particular Friday morning, where she looks me straight in the eye, pauses, the coin suspended above the cup, and she asks, "Can I buy you breakfast?"

The younger members of the fraternity get this kind of offer on a regular basis, but they come from middle-aged men as a rule. Her offer confuses me, as she says, "come on then, I don't have a lot of time."

I trot after her, as she passes the burger joint, walks on and enters a cafe. I've been in it once, finding the food well cooked but exp, the service slow compared to the fast food convenience of my usual haunt.

Seated at a table, a waitress swoops, asks what we would like.

"I'll just have a cup of tea," the woman replies.

Resolutely avoiding eye contact, the waitress turns to me, "And for you, sir?"

I know exactly what I want, "I'll have the full English, please, with toast and coffee."

I look at the woman, she looks at me, her eyes darting around my face. I can't take the silence for too long and state, "my name's Ian, by the way."

"Oh yes, sorry," she replies hoarsely, placing a polite hand in front of her mouth as she clears her throat, "I'm Helen."

I puncture more silence with, "Can I ask what this is about?"

While the waitress brings her tea, and my coffee and toast, silence reigns once more, till we're alone.

Finally maintaining eye contact, Helen hesitates, then blurts out, "I have a proposition for you."

I munch a bite of toast, wash it down with coffee, then ask, "well, you said you don't have much time, so what is this proposition?"

"I'd like you to be my husband."

The statement is so unexpected, seems so preposterous, I drop the slice of toast I'm holding, but I smile, verbalising the thought that strikes me, "sounds more like a proposal than a proposition."

"No," she continues, "let me explain. My husband left me six weeks ago. He's a real walking talking midlife crisis, having an affair with a younger woman, and announcing he wants to set up a new life with her. I helped him pack. The thing is, I've kept up the facade of a happy marriage with people at work, and there's a function coming up."

She clams up when the waitress brings my breakfast, then continues when we're alone again, "this function will be a big affair, with awards and speeches and suchlike, and they expect us to bring spouses."

Between mouthfuls, I ask, "let me get this straight, you want me to stand in for your husband at this thing, do you?"

"Well, yes."

As I drop my knife and fork, and throw my hands up, shake my head, thinking I've never heard anything so ridiculous in my life, she carries on, "no, no, hear me out, please. Only one person at work has ever met

Geoff, and that was years ago. Then, the first time I saw you sitting there, I had to take a long look at you, as you're so like him, you could actually be identical twins. With the do fast approaching, I was starting to panic, and this crazy idea formed, to ask you to be Geoff for a few hours."

"I can't see it working, but what would be in it for me if I agreed?"

"Whatever you wanted, if it was in my power."

"What I could really do with is a place to live, and maybe a job."

Looking at her watch, she replies, "I'm going to be late for work, but I will say I have thought about that, and I may be able to help you. I work in property management, we always need caretakers for empty properties, and some of them have accommodation provided. I could look out for something. Look, I'm getting off to work now, so I'll leave it with you to think about."

As she gets up to leave, I ask, "when is this function?"

"Next Friday evening. Think about it over the weekend, let me know on Monday morning. If you don't want to do it, I'll understand, and I'll try to come up with something else."

She leaves, and I watch till she's out of sight, then go back to my breakfast. My heart isn't in it for the rest of the day, and I sit in the day centre, contemplating the craziness of the situation. Usurped from my Friday evening slot, I sit waiting for handouts, then begin the long trek to the squat.

I have an unusually sober weekend, and my spot taken again on what could have been a lucrative Saturday morning, I join the ragged queues for the day. The more I think about her proposition, the more ludicrous it seems, though my fantasies concerning her intensify.

Come Monday morning, I'm up extra early, staking my claim, though it's a dreary, grey, wet, misty morning. Helen's early too, and we march to the cafe, she telling the waitress to bring a full English, toast, tea and coffee.

Once we're alone, she asks, "well, what's your decision?"

"Let me ask you first, why did you feel to had to do something so incredibly stupid? Why didn't you just tell people at work the truth, or come up with an excuse for him not being with you?"

"I've lied to them for years, going on and on about my perfect marriage, while I knew it was falling apart, and I kept up the lie after he left. They're all expecting this man who doesn't actually exist."

"I don't know if I can do it."

She reaches over, touches my arm, looks into my eyes, "please, do this for me. I've made tentative enquiries about something for you."

"Are you trying to entice me with a job and a house?"

"No, well yes, actually, I'm desperate."

As my breakfast arrives, and I start to eat, I think about it. Between mouthfuls, I decide, "okay, I'll do it."

"Oh, thank you, Ian. Now, don't take this the wrong way, but one evening this week, I want you to come home with me. There's still some of his clothes there, and I think they'd fit, but you can try on a suit, and I can coach you a bit."

She chatters away nervously before leaving for work, and I finish my breakfast, go back to my spot. The following day, she smiles with her 'good morning,' then the next, she waits till nobody is close, kneels down, and says, "I'll pick you up in my car here after I finish work at five," then I watch her cross the street.

That evening, she drives past the squat, all the while chattering away, telling me Geoff can be unbearable at times, pontificating on anything and everything, but she's painted him as shy and introverted, a man of few words, so I don't have to say a lot, finally quiet as she parks in front of a solid suburban semi.

The house is surprisingly minimalistic, as I was expecting fussy. She shows me the bathroom upstairs, asks me to have a shower, then try on the clothes in the bedroom next door, before returning downstairs. I've already had a shower at the day centre, but I acquiesce. There's a dark blue suit, a white shirt, socks, pants, and a fairly new pair of black shoes. There's also a tie, an item of clothing I haven't worn for years. I stand looking at my naked body in the mirror before trying on the clothes. The trousers pinch a bit at the waist, but I think they'll do. Knotting the the tie proves difficult, though I did it thousands of times in a previous life.

In the front room, I stand before her asking if I'll do.

"My god," she answers, "it's like seeing him standing there, let me just," and she walks towards me, adjusts the tie, as I look into her eyes.

"You're taking a big chance here, Helen," I tell her, "I could be a rapist or a serial killer, and you've invited me into your home, and into your life."

"Believe me, it's crossed my mind, but a tissue of lies forced me into desperate action."

She cooks us a meal, I change back into my own clothes, then she drives me to the squat, still keeping up a nervous stream of chatter, telling me more about Geoff. Dropping me off, she strokes my arm and thanks me again.

Friday arrives, she's finished work early, picks me up in the car, drives me to the house again, and I shed the skin of homeless Ian, renewed as bank manager Geoff. The function goes a lot better than I'd expected. Her workmates and their spouses take up two tables, she introduces me, but I don't remember many names. I don't say much to anybody, telling a few I work as a bank branch manager, and I'm worried that I won't have a job, with so many branches closing down. I dance with Helen, and I feel her body against mine, her hair brushing my cheek, her breath on my neck, I smell her perfume, and I'm aroused. Frustration tells me to get drunk, but I'm careful not to drink too much. Finally, it's over, and we're back in the car. She tells me, "I'll take you back to get your stuff. Keep the suit, it looks better on you than it ever did on him," then is silent till we're back at the house. She asks me where I want her to drop me, but still doesn't utter a word as she drives. Before I get out of the car, she reaches over, kisses me on the cheek, saying, "thank you, Ian, thank you so much."

I put my hand on her arm, say, "I'm glad I could help, Helen."

We look into each other's eyes, and I have an overwhelming desire to kiss her, but I open the door, walk away, hear her drive off. There's a jar full of small change in the squat, so I buy a bottle of cheap wine at the all night grocers, sit in another man's suit, and drink it greedily.

Life carries on till Helen comes out at lunchtime one day, buys me lunch, and tells me she's held up her part of the bargain, she's got me an interview for a job. She sets it up fur her to interview me herself, and I sit opposite her in the suit and tie she gave me, while we chat for ten minutes.

I begin the job two weeks later, as caretaker in an office block. The first three floors are occupied, then twelve empty floors further up, I have a small but comfortable flat, my penthouse. Three months later, out on my balcony with a coffee and a smoke, I see the first snow of winter fall on the city.

Helen and I meet twice a week, have a meal and a drink. I still feel the strain of restricting my alcohol intake when I'm with her, and in the rest of my life, but, day by day, the strain eases. Despite my resemblance to the dastardly Geoff, Helen seems to like me, and hugs me, kisses me on the cheek. She's taken off her wedding ring, telling her workmates Geoff is gone from her life.

In town to buy Helen a Christmas present, I see a young woman in my spot. Getting some small change from my pocket, I look at her face, ravaged by addiction, or the elements, or by the life she leads. I drop the coins in the cup, walk on. That night, having wrapped the present, the most expensive ring I can afford, I take coffee out to the balcony, light a cigarette, look out on the snow covered city, think about how my life has changed, due to my resemblance to another man, and to the desperation of a woman painting herself into a corner with lies.

Georgina Beasley - Rollies, Docs, and Beanie Babies

Dave pats his cheeks with the heels of his hands and whispers to his reflection, "You ungrateful piece of *shit*!"

He has washed his luscious strawberry hair, groomed and oiled his beard immaculately, and put on his favourite pair of glasses. Everything is on point for his hipster aesthetic, but none of it can detract from his deeply saddened eyes, held up by pockets of puffy skin.

Dave pleads with himself, "Just snap the fuck out of it!" He drops his head to stare at a splodge of blue toothpaste on the otherwise immaculate porcelain sink. It's his girlfriend Molly's voice that breaks his dull concentration.

She sings out from the other side of the bathroom door, "Davey bye! I gotta run to get the 7 o'clocker! And baby? Good luck at your appointment. I am so, *so* proud of you."

He holds onto the sink to support himself as he unfurls his spine to come up to standing, "Yep, yep, thanks Molls." He waits until he hears the front door slam before leaving the bathroom.

Dave sits on his therapist's sofa holding onto a linen cushion. He looks down at the bobbles sewn around the outer hem rather than into her eyes or at her mouth. 1-2-3-4 bobbles are missing. He counts to four over and over again in his head, quickening the pace and then slowing it down. He nods at the same time, feigning involvement in the session - the same way he does at team meetings. He knows his work would contribute to his therapy under their new wellness scheme if he told them about his little issue - then he'd be able to afford to go to a therapist whose cushions weren't missing bobbles. But he trusts this woman now, even though he's yet to see results, and he would rather be fired than tell any of the HR team what's going on for him. He stops counting and tunes back in. His therapist, as always, tells him panic attacks are normal and preventable. She starts to talk him through a new theory, one about finding access to an emotional middle ground.

Dave continues to nod, "ah hah" he says, "yeah that *does* make sense." It doesn't. 1-2-3-4, 1-2-3-4, 1-2-3-4.

When Dave finally gets off the tube, the sun has established itself nicely and is lighting up the pavement in front of him. He tries not to think about what excuse he will use when he walks into work an hour later than normal. An excuse like Molly having a stomach ache… no, that would raise too many questions, maybe he could say… *Dave. Stop. Deal with the problem when it hits. Relax. Find that emotional middle ground.* He sucks in the col, crisp air and actually gets a sort of fluttery feeling in his belly, right in deep under his sweater, flannel shirt and layers of craft beer podge. The changing seasons give him a sense of anticipation.

Anticipation = good emotion. Good work.

A well projected voice snaps him out of his nice little think, "Evening Standard! Free, Evening Standard!"

Dave sees her shoes before her face. They look sort of like the ones he had to wear at secondary school. She must have picked them up second hand and spent a decent amount of time cleaning them up. Their shininess is what makes them catch his eye. She must have polished them that day, especially for her shift. He looks up. Her smile is one of the most genuine he has seen. Her eyes tell him that she thinks it might all be okay.

He has never polished his Dr. Martins, other than one time he tried to get some mud off them with some organic face-wipe of Molly's. He just waits until they look plain messy rather than disheveled in a cool kind of way, and replaces them without a second thought. He *can* just replace them; he's never thought about whether he should. And he doesn't even get an ounce of pleasure from a new pair - it's just a bit of a faff to order them and wear them in. God forbid a new pair would make him smile. In fact, he hasn't smiled properly all day, not even when Molly thought he was asleep and put his coffee on his bedside table so he would wake up to the aroma. He can't get this Standard Issue Girl's smile out of his head– and her shiny shoes. And god dammit, now he's too far away from her to give her some cash. *Selfish, pathetic, privileged, guilty…* he feels his balance go, his periphery vision blurs, his breath become clunky, his fingers tingle.

"Mate, you okay?" he doesn't look up to see who the voice belongs to, but instead clambers down to the side of the pavement, his feet in the gutter, head in hands. He finally gasps, only for the breath to leave him again almost immediately. This gasp and release repeats, over and over.

"Mate you're too close to the road, here–" the stranger hooks his arms under Dave's armpits and pulls him back away from the gutter. Dave can see fast moving legs working their way around him but can't feel his own.

"Talk to me, is there someone I can call?" The stranger is reaching into his jacket pocket. "You've got to enter in your code man– do you have a partner? A friend?" Dave offers his thumb to unlock his phone, and a moment later Molly is on speaker.

"Oh baby, just breathe, real deep. I'll do it with you." He still can't look beyond the hand which is holding the phone for him. Dave knows that if he looks into the stranger's eyes he will just enter into their story, how they are going to be late to wherever they are headed because of him - maybe their daughters' birthday, maybe he's always late for her, maybe the candles in her cake are melting into the icing as she waits. Gasp in, release.

"Dave, in for four, and out for four." He focuses on Molly's voice for a moment, then disappears back into his head. At first all the thoughts are moving quickly. He's thinking of himself, of Molly, together, their story. Then his thoughts contort into slow and heavy ones.

Slumped over on the payment he just knows he and Molly must be in their last chapter. Soon she will be free of him, and he will become a story she will tell over dinners with her happy, fun, easy going friends. He scrunches his face, then releases it, his mind flirts with the idea that it could almost be a relief not to worry about what she must think of this man he's become, the man he always was.

*

Dave met Molly three years ago at the specialty organics store on his street. He was going through a vegetarian phase at the time, and the store had the freshest produce he could find. He didn't want any nasty pesticides if he was making so much ethical effort. His reading of ingredient labels had become somewhat excessive, he would grasp for produce and products in a compulsive manner, as if he were reaching for a medicine that would ease all his discomfort. He caught sight of Molly while trying to read the back of a kombucha bottle. *Purified water, cane sugar…* she reached into the yogurt fridge beneath him. He stepped back slightly to make room for her and looked down to see a very straight parting separating her chestnut hair. *Tarte cherry juice, organic black tea...* she appeared beneath him again, putting the yogurt back from where it came from, this time he noticed her sage-like scent. *Bacillus coagulans...* He couldn't keep his focus with all her toing and froing - she must have reached, walked, and returned about three times. Dave finally turned to look directly at the culprit who was disrupting his flow. She was taller than him, and strong. She potentially might be able to beat him in a fight. He liked the look of her.

"What's wrong with the poor yogurt?" he asked. He was always pretty smooth at the beginning, the angst only became visible later.

She looked a little taken back but smiled. He smiled too - her lipstick matched the omega plums in her basket.

"I just can't decide what to cook for this dinner party I'm hosting. Yogurt, almond and blueberry cake - or a brownie ice cream situation, what do you reckon?"

"The cake, definitely the cake." Dave reached for a tub of coconut yogurt and handed it to her, "It's a dollar more, but it's definitely worth it - and it'll go with those blueberries." He turned his back on her slowly and walked away.

"Hey!" She called after him, "Hey. So the dinner party isn't 'til tomorrow - and I haven't got plans right now. Are you down for a drink? Or are you one of those guys who can't stray from his schedule."

They had taken their groceries with them across the road to a small wine bar Dave had always liked the look of but had never gone into. At that stage his friends were more of the beer drinking lad type. He looked like them, but found their banter claustrophobic.

She seemed impressed with his suggestion to go there, "My favourite! You better have tried the gorgonzola - it is *so* delicious," she had said loudly.

They were seated outside after she had admitted she loved a cigarette with her red wine. This confession didn't stop her from a stream of health-related questioning. She had seemed so much nicer amongst the organics. First she asked about his drinking habits (apparently not good - she had looked very judgy despite pouring herself a *much* larger glass than him from their bottle of red); then she asked about the quality and quantity of sleep (too little of the bad stuff apparently - she went on to ask whether he snored throughout the short window of poor sleep he did get);

then she was onto dietary requirements (he told her that his eczema flared up a little with dairy, but was a non-event since he had switched to the oat milk - although he still had a flat white from time to time! She looked grossed out and moved the cheese board towards her); then sexual preferences and kinks (Jesus - women? No kinks that he was willing to share, even if he risked coming across as vanilla. Her large sigh signaled he had). She eventually paused. Thank fuck.

But then, "Can you roll? I need the bathroom."

Dave was left outside alone, with a handful of tobacco and papers in front of him. How hard could it be? Line the threads down the middle and roll it right on up, little lick of the paper, et voila! But no. No, it was not that simple. On his third attempt the fruits of his labour were all moist, droopy and crooked. She would be back from the bathroom any second, and would be able to see that in fact he could not roll a cigarette to save himself. He considered abandoning his brown paper bags filled with the goods for his weeklong meal plan, and fleeing the scene.

Molly's shop suggested she would be able to pick up the bill no problem. But he just didn't want to leave the soggy cigarette behind, nor take it with him as a reminder of this moment. So he stayed, knowing that when Molly got back to their table, she would look at him in a way that will make his masculinity shrivel up inside of him. It was at that moment he realised who Molly reminded him of - his cousin Sarah.

When Dave was a child, he used to collect beanie baby toys. They were little round people filled with rice or something. He couldn't go to sleep unless he had them all lined up across his chest. All eighteen of them. There was an order he liked the most, but that wasn't essential. He just needed the weight on his chest and all their faces looking outward. He loved those beanie babies.

One day Sarah came over. She was a couple years older than him and used to call him 'weirdo loser boy'. It was raining that day. The two of them had been sent off to play nicely together, but she had other ideas. She shut him out in the courtyard, and then, instead of locking the door, being the sadist she was, she rested one of his beanie babies on the inside door handle and put a bucket of water underneath the handle. This way, if he opened the door to get inside, the beanie baby would fall in the water. He was in that courtyard until his mother came looking for him over an hour later. He was shivering so much she made him have a bath, and all his relatives kept on coming into the bathroom and laughing about what happened, and then laughing some more when he tried to cover himself with bubbles. The next time he saw her, she told him she'd give him two pounds, which she had stolen from her mum, to tidy up her bedroom. When he had her room looking immaculate, she had given him an extra pound. This swirling of hate and love felt good to him even as a young boy. Cruelty validated his anxiety, a chaser of kindness made him feel looked after. He once told Molly about Sarah and the beanie babies. Her reply was that "She didn't cut your fingers off or kill your kitten, so maybe let that one go babe." Bitch.

As he drank his wine and let the gorgonzola inch its way down his throat he decided yes, Molly and Sarah were both sociopaths. Sarah with his beanie babies, Molly with her fucking cigarettes. Perhaps all women were.

*

Dave knows that Molly isn't *that* woman anymore. She's not the bully, she's the carer. Perhaps he is the bully, with his emotional withdrawal and his angst. Molly keeps his breath going, his heart beating.

He watches at the wheels of the cars, buses, taxis, speeding around the roundabout in front of the pavement he has surrendered to. Over the loud and erratic noise of the traffic, he can hear the dedication coming through the phone, "Dave, what happened? And where are you? I'm leaving work now, I can be anywhere in like 20. Dave?"

He pauses, takes a moment to focus on how he got here, and leans in towards the phone, "Molls? Her shoes were just so shiny."

Hazel Whitehead - The Tow Rope and the Chair

The weight of Dominic's long-buried but never forgotten secret hung heavily over his life. It disturbed his mind, his body and his soul. Sometimes, his heart felt as though it was being squeezed by a giant gorilla or that the winner of the World's Strongest Man – the one with an unpronounceable Scandinavian name and muscles the size of a small child – was jumping up and down on his stomach; especially in the early hours of the morning.

At heart, he knew he was a good man. He knew it because people told him so with monotonous regularity. He even believed it himself because he'd spent so long making amends, making a difference to all the people in his care, bringing them closer to one another and to God. But then, they didn't know about his secret or see the fear which plumbed the depths of his being. Right now, he was fine. Monday morning. A new week. Sunday services had gone well. The youth group had been lively last night, leaving the floury evidence of their pizza-making behind them. To Dominic's amazement, five of them wanted to be confirmed so it had been something of a celebration. He smiled to himself as he jammed casserole dishes into the oven. The old gas cooker had a mind of its own and the seals were hanging on by a thread so, as usual, he ignored instructions about timings and hoped for the best.

Dominic loved nothing more than a crowd of parishioners squashing round the scratched, refectory table sharing food and bonhomie. His kitchen cupboards were full of mismatched tumblers and what his father called *church hall-green* crockery. Being unfashionable, living with ill-fitting curtains and failing to modernise was all part of his traditionalist style. Unconsciously, or was it consciously, he was making a statement about sacrificial poverty.

He cleared the table, knowing there would be precious little time later. Swan Meadows assembly at 9.15. The flower festival committee at 11.30, closely followed by a Trustee meeting; then there were two wedding couples to fit in before Evening Prayer and finally, the Oberammergau planning meeting – with casserole! Never a dull moment, being a vicar. So much good to be done and so little time to do it.

He moved the ladies' group bibles and swept aside a week's correspondence. He replied to just one email, signing on for the final safeguarding module which, the Archdeacon said, he must do on pain of death. One day, he told himself, when the old and the young, the sick and the depressed didn't need his urgent attention, he would have a good spring clean and strip off the horrible, swirly wallpaper in the living room. He would organise himself and his Rectory properly, get rid of outdated papers, take the vestments to the dry cleaners and hang them up on proper hangers. Maybe he'd even clear the garage and the garden shed.

'Could be a dead body in here and we'd never know,' his wardens had quipped as they hunted for the tombola drum last summer.

One day he would do all that; but not this morning. He unscrewed the lid of his fountain pen. Eighteen parishioners wanted to come to the 2021 Passion Play and it was never too soon to plan. A five-and-a-half-hour performance in German – even with a three-hour interval – wasn't for the fainthearted. He wanted to be sure they knew exactly what to expect, including the dramatic and all too realistic crucifixion scene. He knew his attention to detail rattled his friends and colleagues but he also knew they trusted him implicitly.

Satisfied with his preparations, he put on his signature cream fedora and picked up his keys. Today's assembly was about forgiveness. Not seven times must you forgive your friend, he would say, but seventy times seven, even if they've taken your best football stickers or broken your I-phone. And who can tell me what seventy times seven makes? That's an awful lot of forgiveness!

The sound of the doorbell disturbed his mental rehearsal. Dominic liked interruptions. They made him feel needed and being needed was seductive. It gave him a warm glow of humble superiority. Whether it was a hesitant, single mother looking for a baptism and wondering what response she would get, a member of the finance committee or a drifter down on his luck and looking for a bowl of soup, they would all receive the same friendly welcome. He would deal with *this* caller as though he had all the time in the world, however inconvenient, and still be in time for assembly.

'Good morning, Sir,' said the older man in the grey raincoat. 'Revd Lane, is it?'

'*Father* Dominic Lane, to be precise. Or *Canon* Lane if you prefer. How can I help?'

'I'm D.I. Buckley and this is my colleague, D.S. Hall. All right if we come in, sir, rather than standing on the doorstep?' ID was shown but Dominic's eyes would not focus.

His hands became clammy, his heart pounded, his stomach churned. He tried to organise his face to conceal what was going on inside him. Was it Dad? They wouldn't send a Detective Inspector. Was it the burglary? He hoped not; they had already claimed and spent the insurance money. The eagle-shaped lectern would have been on its way to the States before they reported it missing, the officer had said so it was unlikely … or was it, finally, God forbid, was the oppressive burden about to crush him for good? Was this the knock he had dreaded for so long?

'Well – er – yes, of course – but I'm off to school. Year five. Forgiveness. Starts in fifteen minutes. Meet you back here in an hour?' Dominic knew he was rambling.

'Afraid year five will have to manage without you this morning, sir. They'll have to think about forgiveness another time. Give me the details and D.S. Hall will phone them; say you've been unavoidably detained.' The search warrant was produced and two more officers appeared from nowhere.

And, so, the long-awaited nightmare began. They sat him down in the kitchen and told him he was under arrest. He'd be taken to a station in London to be interviewed under caution. They had informed his Bishop and – no, he couldn't make a phone call – not yet – maybe later. They confiscated his passport, personal and parish mobile phones, bagged the computer and asked him if he'd like to tell them about anything else he had hidden away; because, make no mistake, they would find it if it was there.

'There must be some mistake,' he said, his voice unrecognisable even to him.

Dominic felt sick. He had been as good as gold in this parish, not so much as *looking* at a boy let alone touching one, always careful to have other adults present whenever he was with them. But there was incriminating evidence he wouldn't want them to see on the other mobile. He glanced surreptitiously up to the shelf where the undertaker's brown, plastic urn perched. It contained, ostensibly, the mortal remains of Joseph Bennett, a name he'd stolen from a gravestone. Surely, they wouldn't be so disrespectful as to look there.

To distract them, he asked about a lawyer and they said they'd sort that at the station. He pictured his family and the crap they would have to go through. He wouldn't be the only one to be crucified. As they left, he slipped the dog collar out of his black, clergy shirt with the frayed neck and turned off the oven.

Sitting in silence in the back of the police car, Dominic looked back at his life. The Church had threatened to ruin everything, back in the nineties. Women were going to be priests! Of course, women would never be *real* priests and, as his friend had said, ordaining a woman was as ridiculous as ordaining a boiled egg but ordinary people wouldn't know that. It was the thin end of the wedge. Who knew where it might end? Women bishops? And being gay didn't help, either. It was tacitly allowed provided you didn't admit it, flaunt it or get caught in the act. He and his chums had closed ranks and met in carefully chosen pubs.

There had been three young men, acolytes all poised to carry the candle for the Lord, literally and metaphorically, all under age. At least they were when it started. Three fledgling, impressionable lads ripe for the taking. Within six months, the shame of what he had done to them had led him to resign his post and leave the capital. For more than twenty years he had got away with it, never for one moment thinking those teenage boys would ever breathe a word. They would be too afraid, too ashamed.

He was betting they thought nobody would believe it of 'the wonderful Father Dominic' as Geoff's dad had described him at his leaving party. They were teenagers. Nobody listened to teenagers – not back then. Warning bells had clanged loudly in his head when the Jimmy Savile debacle changed the landscape but nobody had knocked on his door. The most recent crisis had occurred only a couple of months ago when Sam's dad had rung to congratulate him on being made an honorary Canon of the Cathedral – a kind of gold Blue Peter badge for long service and good behaviour.

'Saw it in the parish mag,' he'd said. 'Read it out over Sunday lunch. Not before time, Father, and richly deserved. Everybody was over the moon – well, nearly everybody. Sam would have been, normally, but he was a bit below par – had to rush out before he was sick all over the roast lamb. Some kind of bug.'

Dominic could just imagine it. Sam didn't have a bug. The sickness which had lain dormant for twenty years was now erupting, finally free after being kept down for so long. He could picture it. Sam would have rung Geoff who would have rung Oliver and they would have gone together to the police or the bishop.

He pictured them, the three of them, Geoff, Sam and Oliver, being told Father Dominic had been arrested as promised and was being questioned under caution. Geoff would be relieved but not in a crowing way. He had always been a kind lad and a bit diffident. Sam, the needy one, would have run off crying to a counsellor. And Oliver would tell his besotted wife exactly what had happened to him in the back room of a sleazy pub.

And here was Dominic now with a duty lawyer and three police officers in an anonymous interview room in an unknown police station somewhere in London. They'd said he could make one phone call but not on his own mobile so he struggled to remember his dad's number.

'Dad. There's no easy way to say this. I've been arrested.'

'Where are you?'

'London somewhere.'

'Is it serious?'

'Very.'

'OK, son. Call us when you can speak.'

The lawyer's advice was clear. 'Admit to nothing, give no names or contacts, make no comment. It's twenty years ago and it's your word against theirs.'

Dominic followed the advice.

'No comment. No comment. No comment.'

All the while, he wanted to release the words which were screaming inside him. He yearned to get it over with and to shout from the rooftops.

'Yes, I did it. I did it. I'm guilty. Guilty as sin.'

But he didn't because the lawyer told him not to and because it was obvious what would happen if he did. He would be locked up. He knew what they did to people like him, especially hypocrites who hid behind a veneer of respectability. His ministry would be over, his priesthood would be meaningless and there would be no way back. Ever.

Even if he made it out of prison alive, he'd be over seventy by then. Parents would keep their children away from him, old colleagues would look askance with contempt and pity and God would cast him into outer darkness. He would never learn to live with his own self-loathing. Ironic really, he thought. He'd been pronouncing absolution and God's forgiveness on all manner of sinners all his adult life but he would never forgive himself.

They let him out just after midnight in a strange suburb with no phone. Across the road was a shabby motel with garish neon lights and grey, net curtains across the door. It was a cheap dive but he was in no position to be choosy. He needed a shower and a bed, not Egyptian cotton sheets. The young receptionist's hair was pulled back tightly with a scrunchy and she wore a sweatshirt that hadn't seen the inside of a washing machine for some time.

'Need anything else?' she said, with a smirk, as she handed him the entry card.

'No,' he said, fiercely. Thank goodness he wasn't wearing his dog collar.

He pulled the door firmly shut. The room was barely adequate but he didn't care, was grateful to be out of that oppressive, brown interview room. He slumped on the bed with his head in his hands, rolled under the duvet, tears streaming down his face. His head was spinning, the officer's words ringing in his ears together with the echo of his own voice 'No comment. No comment. No comment.'

Leaving before anybody else was up, he asked his way to the nearest train station and drew out some cash at a machine. At least they had left him with one card. By lunch time, he was sitting in the Bishop's study hearing her say, as kindly as she could, that Dominic was suspended from all duties on full pay and should not make contact with any of his parishioners or the press. Suspension was a neutral act, she said. Derek, a retired clergyman, would be a listening ear and would make contact soon.

Dominic went through the motions. He knew the score and responded robotically. He neither confirmed nor denied what had happened, thanked the Bishop for her time and drove home like a Learner driver for fear of having an accident. It was like being a bad actor in a second-rate play with a predictable plot.

He knew what would be going on in the parish now because word would get out like water dripping from a leaky hose. You didn't have to be paranoid to imagine what people were saying. And he was right.

'Lock him up and throw away the key, the bastard.'

'Poor Father Dominic. Who's made this up?'

'If he's laid a finger on my grandchildren, I'll kill him myself.'

'He couldn't have been kinder to my dying Mam. He hasn't got a bad bone in his body.'

'A man's innocent until proven guilty – but you have to wonder.'

Dominic wasn't party to any of these conversations but he'd heard them all before in different places. Human nature didn't change. To some, he would always be an archangel and to others the devil incarnate. Back home, he wandered from room to room, examining at the things which made up his life, as though by touching them, he could commit them to memory before they were taken away. He emailed Tony, the church warden, saying he would be leaving important papers – wedding applications, accounts, rotas and a list of hymns for the next month – in a box on the Rectory doorstep and could he please collect them after dark but not call in.

He gathered up all the washing, including the sheets from his bed, and left it piled in the utility room. He cleared the fridge – an open packet of ham, half a quiche, some egg whites waiting to become meringues – and washed up the pile of crockery. He took the casseroles out of the oven and dumped the contents at the end of the garden for the foxes. He worked his way through the pile of correspondence, filing most in the bin. He wrote cheques to pay the bills, birthday cards for his twin nephews and a letter to the travel firm cancelling the Oberammergau tickets. He left the small pile of stamped envelopes on the hall table. Somebody would find them.

Every time the doorbell rang, he remained motionless, hardly daring to breathe until the innocent caller gave up. Every time the phone rang, he let the voice speak before deciding whether to answer. He ignored them all except Derek's – the poor sod designated to be kind to him - because he knew if he didn't, Derek would be round breaking the door down, in a caring kind of way. After a brief and monosyllabic conversation lasting all of sixty seconds, he agreed to meet Derek on Thursday, an appointment he had no intention of keeping.

Finally, he piled all his diaries, thirty years' worth of sermons, Lent course material, artwork – anything which represented his ministry - into the wheelbarrow by the back door. He added the DVDs, mobile phone and USB sticks the police hadn't found. He struggled to push the barrow across the uneven grass – never had got around to having that path laid – and half tipped, half threw the contents on to a bare patch of earth. He splashed a liberal dose of lawnmower fuel over the pile and struck a match, hoping no neighbour would be looking out of a window at this time of night.

There was nothing to live for now it had come to this. The 'much-loved' parish priest who 'had served the Church of England so well' – words the bishop had used at his installation – sounded empty, fatuous and hollow. He shut the back door, fought his way into the garage, stumbling over the tombola drum. He took the tow rope from the boot of his car and an old kitchen chair and went back into the garden.

Helen Rana - Topless

'He's not coming out,' the passing focus puller told Dawn.

She scowled in frustration, irked by the lack of activity. Although the camera, sound and lighting equipment were all set up around her, the crew had wandered off, mostly towards the catering van nearby or outside the studio for a chat or a cigarette. This was the third series of the gripping TV series, *Righteous Killer*, and she prided herself on having brought the character of hapless police detective Tanya skilfully to life. She enjoyed working on the high-profile drama, even though her male co-star garnered the best lines, the most time onscreen and attention off-screen as the much-adored eponymous assassin, Simon Severin. This morning they should be filming Episode 2, Scene 7, watched by a group of investors. Instead, she was waiting in the fake bedroom while he was hiding inside his caravan. She picked up a cheap magazine that someone had left on a kit box and started glancing through it. She was in for a long wait.

The director, Grainne, barrelled forcefully by, heading straight for the 1950s pastel caravan with the name *'Marc Rasmussen'* stuck on its door. 'I'll get him out.'

Inside, Marc was adamant. 'I'm not coming out.'

He had worked as the lead actor on this programme right from the start, and considered himself both professional and reasonable. In this instance, he thought it was reasonable to ask for a rewrite. In fact, he had convinced himself it was so reasonable that he had decided not to leave his undersized sanctuary until they did so. It would be a simple rewrite, just to change the direction *'Tanya snuggles into Simon's bare chest'* to something along the lines of *'Tanya and Simon cuddle on the sofa'*. It really was eminently reasonable. He sat inside his tiny caravan, drew the thick bathrobe around him more tightly and settled down for the impasse. He had recently played a supporting role as a hippy student involved in political protest during the late 1960s. He stated a line from that film. 'I'm staging a sit-in.'

Outside, Grainne groaned.

It had been a strange morning. He had arrived on time, gone through hair and makeup, changed into his costume – well, stripped down to his joggers and comfy slippers – memorised his lines and movements. He had scrolled through his social media, scrutinising his body in the mirror to see how warranted the criticisms were, and stepped inside his tiny on-set trailer, shrouded in a fug. He had skimmed through the latest print publications, news and entertainment websites to read about himself, then locked the door, cocooned but feeling undervalued and trivialised. Then it had struck him that one very simple, straightforward rewrite would solve the dilemma and change his main purpose in this scene from dressing the set to driving the plot.

There was a violent banging on the flimsy door, then Grainne rattled the handle and yelled through the plywood. 'Marc, don't do this – not today of all days. I'm begging you, come out!' Although she said that she was begging, it sounded like a command. There was a sharpness in her voice as she fought to regain control over the situation.

Marc wondered whether the door would hold against her onslaught. The television studio was nothing more than a large empty warehouse, this corner of it populated by tiny vintage caravans which someone must have bought as a job lot in a fit of whimsy. The area was decked out with fake grass and bunting around a catering van, a sort of ersatz village green. He would have preferred a more practical set-up with comfortable modern amenities. But nobody cares what actors want.

He answered the director. 'Not until you change the scene.' He was beginning to feel exhilarated by the unfamiliar sensation of having some power at work. As an actor, he was usually at the mercy of everyone else.

Grainne hammered on the door again, pleading. 'Please, Marc. Just do the scene.'

'No,' he replied. 'I'm not prepared to be treated like a bimbo any more!' He eyed his script with disdain.

Scene 7. Interior. Tanya's bedroom. Night.

Simon and Tanya are cuddling in the bed after making love. The duvet covers them waist down.
Tanya snuggles into Simon's bare chest.

TANYA
Don't go. I feel so nervous with that maniac on the loose.

SIMON
You're supposed to be a tough cop!

TANYA
That's what worries me. He's targeting cops. I could be next.

SIMON *(stroking her hair)*
Not you.

TANYA
And we're no closer to catching him, he never leaves any clues. He could be anybody.

SIMON
Well, you're safe with me.

Marc vehemently scored out the words *'bare chest'*.

Grainne talked through the locked door, agitated. 'The investors will be here any minute now and we need to impress them. We need their money. We're in dire financial straits – we won't be able to finish shooting without some extra cash. I'm not even exaggerating.'

He weighed up this new information. If the shoot folded he would still have fulfilled his contract and would be free to have a holiday. Since he was enjoying a moment of popularity, he had been endlessly working punishing hours in frequently gruelling conditions. Some time off might be nice. 'Not my problem,' he said, unconcerned.

He heard a thud, followed by silence. Marc, comfortable on his cushioned seat, stared at the back of the door with its fire escape diagram. He said nothing, revelling in the reversal of dynamics. Grainne had won one industry award and been shortlisted to work on a very prestigious series on the back of this drama. She owed much of her success to Marc's efforts.

He pondered the possibility of deliberately flunking his next audition, so that he could have a break. He could probably manage that just by speaking in his actual Welsh accent – nobody wanted a Welshman as their leading man.

Grainne spoke desperately again. 'Come on, Marc.'

'I'll gladly do the scene, as long as I can keep my top on.'

He heard a long sigh, then the director spoke in a calm, measured tone. 'It is critical for the artistic and narrative integrity of this scene that you take your top off. You know I wouldn't ask you otherwise.'

'Yes, you would! Virtually every scene I'm in has me flaunting my chest or my arse. You treat me like a tart!'

'Don't be ridiculous.'

Marc folded his arms belligerently. 'Change it then. Change this one little scene to prove that you're not just using me as a sex object.'

'We can't rewrite it now, it's too late. Anyway, we need to see the erotic intensity between you and Tanya. We've got to see the intimate physical connection as she confides in you, with no idea that you're the killer. It's the pivotal scene of the entire series. It needs to be body to body, straight after sex, a visible closeness.'

Marc was unmoved. 'I'm not doing it. I'm not going topless one more time in this episode.'

'Oh, for crying out loud! I might understand if you were a woman…'

'Yeah, you wouldn't want to sexually objectify a woman, would you?'

'But, as you're a man, I really can't see what the problem is. Your chest isn't private. You see men walking round with their tops off all the time.'

'It's not about my chest, it's why I have to keep displaying it. I don't want people to just gawp at my body. I want them to see me act.'

'Oh god, Marc. All actors are commodities, you know that!' She was exasperated. 'Same as directors and everybody else. Same as any employee anywhere in the world. Your only choice is whether you want to be a sought-after commodity or a throwaway one.'

Marc heard a second voice outside his trailer door. He scrambled over to the window and peered out around the twee gingham curtains. He could see Jasmine, the assistant director, whispering urgently to Grainne. 'The investors are here.'

Grainne thumped the door furiously. 'Bloody hell. Marc, come out before I sue you for breach of contract! *I* am the director here. You need to take my direction. Right, I'm off to greet the investors. I'll give them a little welcome drink and speech and you'd better be ready on set by the time I bring them back!'

He hunched down out of sight as she strode off towards the reception area. Grainne was right. He knew he had to sell his best asset – his good looks and manly physique – while his value was temporarily inflated. He also realised that many of the investors were probably only looking to put their money into the production so that they could claim proximity to him. It was so irritating. Despite having spent years training for this career, working hard at short-term, badly-paid jobs, now that he was successful he had to spend more time focusing on his appearance than on his work, to keep looking the way his fans imagined him to be.

Still, he mused, there was inevitably disappointment when anyone met him in real life. The first thing they normally said to him was, 'you're much shorter than I thought you were'. The second thing (often asked with a sneer) was, 'is that accent real?' The profession of acting was full of disillusionment. Peeking out of his little window, seeing the people dawdling outside, all relying on him to come out and let them do their jobs, he started to tire of his self-imposed lonely exile. He wanted to get back to work, contribute to the creative and commercial endeavour.

Derek, the series writer, was ambling towards his caravan, carrying a drink and a notepad, at a loss for what to do. He didn't notice Marc observing from the small window as he greeted Jasmine. 'All right?'

'Not really. His Nibs won't come out. He doesn't want to take his top off – he says we're treating him like a prostitute!'

Marc was appalled by her lack of respect as she spoke dismissively about him. Derek rolled his eyes at the absurd suggestion.

Jasmine continued. 'He wants you to rewrite the scene so he can be fully clothed.'

'That won't work.'

'That's what Grainne said. She said it needs to be when they're naked after they've had sex, for artistic and narrative reasons.'

'Yeah, and the more he gets his kit off, the higher the audience figures will be. That means we'll get recommissioned for another series and I'll still be working. My entire career depends on his bare chest right now.'

This was too much for Marc. He rapped on the window, 'I can hear you, you know'.

Jasmine knocked on his caravan door. 'Hey Marc, Grainne's gone. Can I come in?'

Marc opened the door. Jasmine stepped up to the entryway but no further, noting the messy interior – carelessly strewn clothes, the table covered in paperwork, tabloid newspapers and celebrity magazines.

'Are you OK?' she asked, genuinely concerned. Anxious about delays to the running schedule and disappointments to the business people's visit, not about his feelings.

He slid back down onto his bench seat, his dressing gown falling open. He noticed the effort it was taking her not to look at his body. He rapidly scrolled through messages on his mobile phone, growing more irascible with each comment he read.

'Why are we shooting *this* scene the day the backers are on set?' he demanded.

She looked slightly sheepish, her eyes flickering down to his toned legs. 'What do you mean?'

'Why *this* particular scene at the exact time they're here?'

She pretended not to catch his inference. 'Because we're in the studio this week…' She tailed off, not even convincing herself.

'But why a bed scene? Why not a conversation in the kitchen scene?'

She couldn't meet his eyes, stabbing at her sheaf of papers. 'It's just the scene that's scheduled on the call sheet.'

'Are you sure it's not because they want to get an eyeful of me?' Marc continued tetchily, 'because that's what they're investing in? They want a piece of me?'

'You're being paranoid. They invest in *Killer* because they get a good return on their money. Plus, it's a great show – great writing, great story, great characters.'

'Characters?' he scoffed. 'My character is mainly my appearance.' He turned the screen to show her an online post. 'Have you seen this? I'm a joke in the acting community. They're calling me "a leading male torso".'

Jasmine inadvertently glanced at his muscular chest. 'It's just social media. Ignore it.'

Marc glared. 'This is not the great unwashed. It's my peers. Fellow thesps.'

She shrugged. 'Jealous, probably.'

There was an awkward knock on the open door.

Jasmine backed out of the caravan, relieved by the interruption. 'Gotta go.'

Dawn barged into the caravan to confront him. 'Why are you being so unprofessional? We're already an hour behind schedule and the investors are on their way. You're ruining everyone's day.'

Marc answered steadily, 'I'm not taking my top off any more'.

'Your top *is* off!'

He realised that his robe was wide open, so pulled the sides together to cover his chest. 'I'm not taking my top off *on screen*.'

'Why not? I'm taking *my* top off!'

'Yeah but, no offence, nobody cares about you taking your top off.'

'That is very offensive! I've got a great body!'

'But your whole career doesn't revolve around it, does it?'

'Well, neither does yours.'

'Really? Did you read the reviews of the docudrama, *Flawed FC*?'

'Of course not.'

Marc quoted from memory. 'Marc Rasmussen plays damaged footballer Emet Lewis with brio and verve, providing enough on-pitch drama for male viewers and more than enough changing room nudity to satisfy his female admirers.'

'What's brio?'

'That's not important! And what did the critics say about my character in *Freaked Out*?' He recited another quote learnt by heart. 'The pill-popping party fiend played by Rasmussen spends all of his time wearing just a pair of tiny white underpants. Set to record.'

'They're good reviews! I've had a lot worse.' She tossed the crumpled magazine at him. 'You'd better be outside in five.'

Dawn stormed off. Marc flipped through the pages of glossy celebrity gossip, stopping at a full-page colour picture of himself lying on the bed in the studio, completely naked, face down, captioned: *'PHWOAR! We can't wait to see more of hot-bod Marc when series 3 of "Righteous Kille hits our screens this autumn!'*

He was perking up. All the attention was making him feel a lot better.

A third actor, Glen, walked in and loitered by the table. He was middle aged and stout, decked out in a loud three-piece suit, with complicated facial hair and swathes of tasteless gold jewellery. He spoke in a thick Birmingham accent. 'Come on, fella, you're holding everyone up. I would like to get home to my wife tonight.'

'Sorry mate, but this is important. I'm making a stand for our craft over commercialisation.'

'How d'you mean?'

'I'm not going to play any more scenes topless, and that's final.'

'Why not?' Glen was taken aback. 'Everybody loves you with your top off.'

'Yeah, but it's getting silly. Every part I'm offered includes me taking my clothes off. I'm getting typecast.'

'Hah! I've built a successful career on being typecast,' Glen retorted. 'I look like a dodgy copper and I get paid to act like a dodgy copper. As long as I put on a London accent I keep getting work. There's no shame in it, you've just got to play to your strengths. Anyway, we're only here to entertain, what does it matter?'

'Well, *I* think it matters. I'm sick of being ogled.'

'That can be the title of your autobiography then, *Sick of Being Ogled* by Marc Rasmussen!' He slapped Marc heartily on the shoulder and squeezed outside, jauntily rapping on the side of the caravan as he left.

Rasmussen wasn't even his real name, Marc brooded. He had changed it because there were already too many actors called Marc Williams.

Jasmine ran breathlessly to the doorway. 'Grainne's right behind me with the investors. Are you coming out to do the scene?'

'Yeah, of course. Close the door so I can make a dramatic entrance.'

Jasmine slammed it shut.

He heard the outsiders approaching, thrilled at being on a TV set, Grainne guiding them. 'I know this is what you've all been hoping for,' she was saying, 'the chance to meet our superstar, Marc.' Their enthusiastic murmurings grew louder. 'Well, this is his trailer and he's inside there now, ready to do his next scene.' She paused for effect. 'So he should be with us in a moment.' She raised her voice on the last sentence in the hope of encouraging him out.

Time to go to work, Marc decided. He would give them what they wanted. By relinquishing control over the scene, he had regained his power over the entire production. Everything here – creativity, money, jobs, reputations – depended on his ability to act. To portray actions, emotions, a person and a story. To look the way he was paid to look.

He flung open the caravan door. The potential financiers cheered and wolf-whistled, delighted by his sudden appearance, filming him on their cameras and phones. He held his pose for a moment.

At last, he spoke. 'Welcome to the set. We're just about to film Episode 2, Scene 7.'

The backers' eyes gleamed expectantly, basking in his presence.

'This is a bedroom scene.'

Some of the group gasped.

'So I'll need to take my top off.'

The tension was agonising.

Marc slowly untied his robe and let it drop to the ground.

Helen Sewell - Prayer for My Daughter

Walking. I'm walking, an endless trudge as if I have been doing this my whole life. I am not really near anywhere, but at the same time, not so far away. I left home this morning, but what time, exactly? I'm not sure. All I know is something in my soul was unsettled.

Trudge.

There's a wooded hillside on the skyline, the slope scattered with whitewashed houses. Sungleamed turrets nestle among coteries of trees, each home's snug, sylvan berth patchworked like lichen in the distance, each blazed face rearing from an envelope of greens. The flat tops of tall oaks form an eyrie, pierced at the centre by the pale needle of a spire.

You are on my mind.

I trudge on, past a small stream, where reeds fringe the water. One bends down, genuflecting to the tide, the current jerking it back and forth, back and forth, like a pen endlessly ticking items off a list. I turn down a path where the recent rainfall tumbles in an impromptu river-dance over the stones. Its ripples flash in the sunlight like a train of digital data – on, off, on, off – a million miles a second. I glance up. A triangle of birds soar against the now lowering light. Their backs glint aircraft silver, drawing a milky pulse through the watery blue. I watch them recede to become another fleet of binary-blink, their pixels undimming with distance. I muse that had I not realised their avian origins, I would be persuaded a fleet of UFOs were passing by.

As I climb the hill, I stop to look out over the next valley. The sun tumbles on its journey down. The white blaze covers me like a wedding veil, as I stand, drinking in its photon soup, saturating myself in its pale light, glugging like a vitamin D junkie trying to hold onto the last fix before a drug famine. I watch the orb sink down, turn to orange, its tangerine yolk falling into the cup of the mountains above the scrambling valley beyond.

I rub my arms. I didn't dress for cold. A pattern of evening birdsong bounces among the ancient foliage as I wind upwards along a small path. The moon appears – a white tick on denim – its glow dinted to semi-silence behind a latticework of branches. Here's the gate of the church, cloistered under a small archway. I lift the rectangular clasp and go through. The stone-fronted building looms in the twilight, the only thing to distinguish the warmth within a subdued light from the stained glass windows. I try the door – its heavy lock bends, cold beneath my hand. The solid oak panel opens to the familiar smell of sacred interior: must, ancient stone, incense, polish from pews with patches scarred yellow by the faithful. Old wood and worm mix their smell with the dropped pollen and petals of white lilies – a sweet, faintly uric odour.

I make my way to the front. The altar bears cushions either side, cross stitched by generations of diligent women. On the metal candle stand (20p per candle), one tealight prayer burns on, others are dead. Absentmindedly, I light one. My grasp shakes a little as I drop it into the waiting holder with a small clonk. I don't have 20p. I'm sure God doesn't mind.

Next to the stand hang three rosaries, with a notice. *Please help yourself for prayer and return after use.* I choose a black one. Wooden beads. Small.

I grasp the beads in my hand, each one bruised by the fingers of a thousand penitents, each one rounded by a million heart cries for mercy. I sit, waiting. What next?

Hail Mary… My lips round like the beads, shaping around the words that I draw in a whisper from the fusty, dust laden cupboards at the back of my mind. They freeze into the still, cool air.

Full of Grace…

She was beautiful. I see her in the sunlight, running towards me, her hands outstretched.

"Mummy! Look at this!" She uncurls her little fingers. It's a shell! Exquisite as her tiny hand, beautiful in its completeness and design. Her hair is golden, like mine, shining in the sun, the frizz looking like a halo.

The Lord is with thee…

The Lord is with everyone, but I pray so much more that he was with you… that you are with Him…

Blessed art thou among women…

You never had the chance to become a woman. Here you are, in the chicken run, chasing the hens, throwing them tiny handfuls of corn as they cluck around your legs, giggling in your red wellies. Blessed by never fully knowing the pain of this world… Never feeling it all … Never knowing much about love… nor its concomitant pain… I hope so anyway. You never met my three cats, my beautiful collie, as she snakes in and out of the chickens, trying to herd, but, too impractical to get it right, instead sending them flying against the fence, squawking.

What next?

And blessed is the fruit of your womb…

You were the fruit of my womb, and, in my mind and my heart, you shall forever be called blessed.

You're laughing as we get in the car, full of jokes and giggles. I tickle your tummy as you wriggle in the backseat. Sit tight, baby.

Pray for us sinners…

We should have been married, they said. It was wrong. I was the first one in my family to have a child out of wedlock. What was the alternative? Abortion? They didn't approve of that, either. Pete and I were happy, for a while. We were living the good life, trying to abide by nature's laws in the middle of a generation that didn't care. We were always considered alternative, with our garden full of sunflowers, vegetables, chickens and, to make the round, a goat, in the middle of a small town in Kent, where the neighbours were telly-loving Ford Fiesta owners with the latest gadgets, food processors, dishwashers, washing machines – where we even washed our clothes by hand, making a rod for our own backs out of pointless eco-righteousness. Needless to say, we were shunned by most, but happy, in our own world of telly-free wholesomeness. Our entertainment was books, digging, made up games, long discussions about politics and philosophy. Neither Pete nor I were bothered about marriage, and, even if I had been, I suspect any gentle push would have sent him the other way; like when you are trying to pump up a car tyre, and instead, the pressured air hightails away in a slippery hiss, never to be seen again, leaving you with a flat.

Will God forgive me, for my sin? Though I trust He has, I can never forgive myself. It's not the kind of thing you just scrub out. Thirty years have passed, but I will never, ever forget you.

You were my first child, and my only one. You were, in common parlance, an accident. I didn't really want to get pregnant at that time, I felt I had a life to live. Pete and I were trying to make a difference, change the world, from our little house in Kent. We were setting up campaign groups, joining political movements. We needed our energy. It wasn't that I didn't like children, but I wasn't planning on having one, just yet. We didn't have much room, after all, with the goat, the chickens, your father's views that tidiness and order indoors was next to godlessness. But when I announced to Pete that I was pregnant, he smiled, and his blue eyes sparkled. Even so, after you were born, I took extra precautions. One surprise was enough, though you were the best surprise I could ever have hoped for.

It wasn't far, that we drove that day. I had noticed the flabby rubber the day before, asked Pete to pump the tyres of our "woody" VW beetle, but he was preoccupied with something else. I don't remember what. Pete, turned off by the practicalities of life, could not be relied upon to care about such unenlightened necessities as shopping, preferring to sustain himself on the skinny courgettes and paltry potatoes gleaned from our garden, along with his heights of erudite thought. He would get obsessed. It was sometimes practical, at least in theory, (such as when he tried to get a hydro system, complete with self-built water mill, flowing round our garden that had no natural source of water). But normally it was some head in the clouds intellectual issue that he had to resolve to his own satisfaction before the realities of life could be attended to, by which time, the sun was falling in the sky and it was too late to do what normal families needed to do – paying bills at the bank, buying essential supplies. OK, I confess. I forgot too, or maybe it was a devil-may-care attitude that made me step on the accelerator without checking if the tyres were tight. When the car began to wobble, I did consider stopping. But we *needed* things. I had asked Pete to do it – that was good enough.

Except it wasn't.

Later, the driver had said he was lost, trying to find West Street.

I drop the beads on the floor. They make a small clatter against the polished wood, as a tear squeezes from my eye.

Now, and at the hour of our death.

The car had wobbled along the road. I had to pay that bill, it was well overdue, they cut your electric off in those days. With a toddler, I couldn't let that happen. I know that I should have been paying attention, not mentally grumbling about your father, arguing the toss in my head over whether to turn back because of the tyre. The wobbling increased, along with a clonking noise. I pulled up, in front of the turning to North Street. The road was quiet. I swear it was quiet. With my logical mind, I know, there was no way I could have seen what was coming. But if only I had just got the pump out of the garage and done it myself … if only I hadn't been relying on a man who wasn't like OTHER women's husbands – those who did odd jobs and didn't sit about dreaming of a better world (not that a man like that would have suited me).

I heard the noise too late. A truck, barrelling along North Street towards us. I took off the handbrake, forced down the accelerator. I thought I'd time to get out of the way, but the car bumped forward, painfully slowly, the flabby rubber anchoring the tyres to the tarmac. I heard the discordant wail of brakes as the truck's speed diminished, painfully slowly. Too slowly.

If only I hadn't been faffing about all day long with things that didn't really matter, I could have left earlier; if only I'd turned off and taken the short cut, instead of deciding to drive along by the sea … But why did I stop there? In front of a junction …

all these ifs and buts they all add up to one thing –

I miss you like life itself.

It was too late for you, my baby. My beautiful girl. I, in the front of the trundling car, did not get the full impact. I suffered some cuts and bruises, that is all. I deserved much more. Pete left shortly after you died. He said he couldn't manage any more, couldn't manage his little project. I never knew I was a project, but there it was. I suspect he couldn't cope with the grief. That's why I moved away to Wales, started again, started my own project, with a life as hollow as a bone.

I'll leave it here. Yes, this is where I'll leave it, here, with God, in this little church on this little hillside. This is where I'll leave you, my baby, until the hour of my death. Until, if God is merciful, we meet again.

Amen

I turn from the dots of candlelight and step out into the night.

I'm surprised by the magnificence, the majesty of creation, looming like awe against the dark. Trees plume up to greet the star-scattered sky, their filigreed crowns cascading inky twigs into the denim night. Constellations hang from the criss-cross tangle of branches, balanced there like celestial fairy lights. Its a free Christmas; there's a Christmas night here for the taking, every clear Welsh night. And there's another birth, celebrated once by angels' song, now by gifts and choirs and pretty decorations, that ended in a tragic death, too soon, a death in exchange for mercy, for those that believe. We all make mistakes, don't we? My family's disapproval didn't make me bitter. I cling to what I know to be good.

In my heart, I thank God silently again, for His mercy, and begin my long walk home.

J W Voyce - Sometimes Snowflakes Shimmer

Attraction is a funny thing.

From childhood we start to behave according to the way our appearance is perceived by others. Beauty breeds an array of reactions: from self-assurance and pride, to a sense of entitlement and conceit. Some are able to disregard the notion, while others revel in the positivity it manifests around them. Conversely, ugliness often spawns feelings of inadequacy and denial, of shame and jealousy. Again, there are those who choose to ignore it, those who decide not to let such superficiality define them and learn to focus their attention elsewhere.

Whatever an individual's take on the matter, there is one thing it is not: inconsequential. As we get older the topic doesn't disappear. Like it or not it's the basis of relationships, the argument for hiring someone, the reason why one person's opinion should be heard over others. I defy anyone to try and claim that the thought has never even crossed their mind, to tilt their head back and chuckle about ever giving such trivialities the time of day. Most of us are dissuaded of its importance, are comforted with proverbs of beauty being only skin deep. Ah, 'But ugliness goes clean to the bone', declares the famous retort. Beauty is ascribed to many things, from art to nature, from a song to the condition of someone's soul. Ugliness is reserved exclusively for the adverse: an ugly exchange is one better not repeated. Ugly weather is usually best avoided. A protest can be described as beautiful, until it turns ugly. It is not without irony that those who place too much emphasis on physical beauty can be described as having an ugly personality.

But what is it to avoid allocation to either camp? To be neither attractive nor unattractive? Now we enter my domain, the world of the ordinary. As I walk through the supermarket I receive no prolonged gazes or double-takes. In my mind these are responses reserved for the devastatingly attractive and unattractive. My ordinariness is surely consistent with the general lack of attention my existence generates here. Even wearing masks, it's easy to tell who's good-looking and who isn't. I fill my trolley and approach the checkout. Now a clear recognition of my existence is required. I lock eyes with the girl. 'Hiya,' she says. I'm paid the vaguest and most fleeting of smiles before she swiftly starts scanning my items. The briefness of the acknowledgment is a perfect indicator of exactly how unremarkable I am—in my mind at least.

Even my name is ordinary. David Smith. I used to curse my parents for it (granted, Smith couldn't be helped, but there exists a world of options beyond dull old '*Dave*').

In a society where uniqueness is idealised—though not necessarily promoted—I'm often saddened to consider how tediously normal I am. Like a lot of people I work a forgettable nine to five job for a faceless company. My haircut (short back and sides) is a commonplace affliction. I listen to chart music, drive a small and ubiquitous hatchback, and the shows I watch on Netflix are always in the 'most watched' list. If I was forced to fill a string of surveys for my age demographic, I'd probably find that my behaviour and preferences are about as typical as one could find. I feel like a pigeon who longs to be a peacock, or a sheep who's envious of the Border Collie ushering him into his pen.

Since the start of the pandemic I find that the diverse activities one might partake in to establish their quirkiness have all but disappeared—not that I ever graced such groups before March. As gyms are back open, I head to mine after I've put my shopping away.

It's the peak period (between 17:30-19:30), and the place is packed. The application on my phone logs my attendance, and it informs me that I'm currently an 'average user' (3-5 times a week). I find one of few vacant stationary bikes at the end of one row and start peddling. The woman beside me is taking it seriously, huffing and panting as she cycles to nowhere. She hops off her bike twenty minutes later and wipes the machine down. Something glimmers at me from the console. I look closer and notice it's a ring. I dismount to pick the item up and find her on a nearby cross-trainer.

'I think you left this,' I say, holding it out.

She places a hand on her chest. 'Oh god… Thank you so much.'

Two days later I return to the gym, and the trusty bike section. The woman is here again, busy peddling and panting away. I return the smile she pays me and start my workout.

The following week it happens again: I join her on the same row and we share the same small beam of recognition. It's not until I return on Thursday that she acknowledges the unlikely recurrence. 'You again,' she says with a smile.

'Great minds think alike,' I say—what a miserably ordinary aphorism.

After three full weeks of sharing this routine, I start to wonder if one of us is repeating it on purpose. It can't be me, I think; I've always started my gym sessions on the bike. The occurrence is so common by this point though that it's almost reassuring, and our immobile rides are now accompanied with conversation. Her name is Fatima, I learn, and we're the same age. She asks me my interests. 'Oh, I dunno, the usual,' I say, 'listening to music, watching films…' She's particularly easy to talk to. In another environment I may have felt nervous. But this is a gym workout, not a date.

Her life sounds far more exciting. She's a licensed hypnotherapist, which I didn't even know was a thing—the licensed part, that is.

'Mostly I help people with addictions,' she says. 'Smoking, drinking, etcetera.' She tells me her hobbies include free-solo climbing and taxidermy.

'What, like dogs?' I say.

'Dogs, rabbits. Anything I can get my hands on.'

There is nothing ordinary about Fatima. Her skin is dark and she has one blue eye, one green. She only listens to music with foreign lyrics ('I prefer it when I have no idea what they're singing about') and reads novels I've never heard of ('I favour indies'). She hasn't watched a single film that came out in the last two decades. At first I thought her interests were affectations—the kinds of things people profess to liking when they want to appear edgy or different. I've since learned that she's simply odd, in the best possible way.

Discovering how my new acquaintance utilises her free time highlights how much of mine is wasted. At home I trawl senselessly through social media. It appears that even during a lockdown everyone is 'living their best life'. I see sculpted physiques and beautiful faces, and witness bursts of creativity in a seemingly endless reel of art of music projects.

I turn to Netflix and let the algorithm decide what I should watch before bed.

It probably sounds silly to worry about living too normal a life, but lately I've been having trouble sleeping. Whiling away the hours with such unvarying repetition—understanding that all my activities and aspirations are shared by so many other people—seems to stir a kind of listlessness. What's the point? I think to myself as I toss and turn in bed. If I die tomorrow, what distinct impression would I leave behind? If you're only purpose is to occupy a space that so many other people could fill for you, why bother?

In primary school I remember a teacher saying that people were like snowflakes. Although the term now means delicate or easily offended, back then it was a metaphor for individuality: no two snowflakes are identical, and the same could be said for us. I remember marvelling at the observation; being informed that these tiny crystals each had their own minor variations instilled me with a sense of soothing optimism. That sense has faded now. Who cares if snowflakes differ somewhat on the micro level? They basically all look alike. And when they accumulate into a big heap of snow all those differences are invalidated completely. I'm a snowflake, and my ordinary world is that big heap of snow: consistent, homogenous, and indecipherably samey.

I start to look forward to my gym sessions with Fatima more than I care to admit; on days without her, my bike rides seem to last far longer.

When I emerge from the changing rooms this evening and spot her in the usual place, I feel a little twinge of excitement.

I've noticed how we've gradually grown more comfortable with each other, and our chats have become less restrained. But whenever the topics turn personal, I can't help but distinguish how different we are. My resounding conclusion is that *she* is a delightful anomaly.

'I bet you look at me sometimes and think, "Wow, what a boring sod".'

She sighs. 'Have you heard of confirmation bias, David?' I nod. 'Well… don't you think you're actively seeking out ways in which you're ordinary?'

I raise my voice despite the smile on my face. 'It's easy for you to say… you're interesting!' She senses my defensiveness and pays me a mocking smile of her own. I frown, simply wanting her to admit that I'm right so we can move on. 'Look, people like you live exciting lives …and normies like me simply watch in jealous admiration.'

Infuriatingly, she shrugs. 'I don't believe there's such a thing as normal.'

'Nonsense,' I say. 'I'm living proof.'

She slows her peddling and turns to lock eyes with me. 'Have you heard the story about cockpit design in the US Airforce?'

Fatima likes telling stories, I've learned. 'I think I'm about to…'

She grins, clearly eager to elaborate. 'Well, in the 40's, the American Airforce had a serious problem: their pilots kept crashing and they couldn't understand why. Eventually they realised the issue was the unsuitability of the cockpit. So, in 1950, they measured thousands of pilots, on well over a hundred dimensions of size, from thumb length to crotch height.'

'Kinky.'

'Be serious!' She giggles. 'Then they then calculated the average of all these measurements… surely from this they'd be able to design a better fitting cockpit for everyone, right?'

'I want to say yes, but I'm certain you're going somewhere with this.'

'You know what they figured out? There's no such thing as 'one size fits all'. From the thousands of people they measured, no one was average. Some had longer arms than the norm but shorter legs, or a large chest but small hips. They realised that if you try to make something fit the *average* person, funny enough, you've made sure it fits *nobody*.'

'Hmm,' I say, stopping my peddling entirely. I have nothing further to offer and she walks away looking thoroughly pleased with herself. For the second time in a month, I notice she's left a ring (a different one from before) on her bike, and again she's moved over to the cross-trainers. I climb onto the one beside her and I wave the ring in the air.

She takes it from me and groans. 'I need to start leaving these on,' she says. She slides it onto her finger, which is already rather occupied with similar adornments. 'Thanks… again.'

'Big fan of gold jewellery, eh?'

'I'm Arab. Arab women love yellow gold.'

Still not quite over our previous disagreement, I ask, 'Is it common for Arab women to have blue or green eyes?'

'Well actually in Martil, in Morocco, where I was born, it is fairly common.'

I raise an eyebrow. 'How about one of each?'

She smirks. 'Ah, you noticed that.'

'Why are you so keen to prove me wrong? I'm ordinary. You're not. Enjoy your uniqueness!'

Fatima laughs. 'Being different isn't always a good thing.' She pauses contemplatively. 'When I first started school in the UK, all I wanted to do was fit in with the other kids. But I was teased constantly. For *everything*. The way I looked, the lunches my parents packed for me…'

'Kids are vile.'

'Did you ever have that issue?'

'The complete opposite,' I say with mild vindication. 'I faded into the background. Sometimes I used to wonder if anyone even knew I was there.'

Once out, the admission feels mildly painful. I reflect on it later at home and scold myself for being such a downer. I have bizarre urge to impress Fatima—although I scarcely know what I could do to achieve this.

My cycling friend now entirely dispenses with small-talk when I join her on the bike. I say hello and await whatever interesting comment she's about to hit me with. She's yet to disappoint. This time she turns to stare at me for a moment.

'You have a very symmetrical face, David.'

'Do I?'

'Yes. I've noticed that whichever side I look at you from, your profiles are identical. Your eyes, your ears, your mouth—they're all uniform and perfectly level.'

'Sounds like another way to say that my face is boring,' I say.

'Why does your mind instantly go there? I think it's a particularly attractive quality.'

'Attractive?'

'Yes. Compare it to mine…' Fatima turns side on and touches her brow. 'Even forgetting the difference in colour, you see how this eye is slightly higher than the other one?' She points to her nose and faces the other way. 'This nostril is more rounded. And this cheekbone is more pronounced.'

I shake my head. 'I don't see it.'

'Come on! I'm so uneven. Depending on which side you approach me from it's like two different people.'

'You're just fishing for compliments.'

'Not at all,' she says. 'I'm simply making an observation.'

'I think it sounds like you're forcing me to point out how striking you are—not that you don't know that already.' I feel my heartrate increase as I say this. Am I flirting? It's too embarrassing to contemplate; she's out of my league. 'Fatima, *my* eyes are a mundane brown, while yours practically leap out from your face.'

'There's much beauty in symmetry, David.'

I feel myself blushing. 'Well, I'm glad you think so.'

When I return home that night I have friend requests from her on Instagram and Facebook. I immediately compare our pages: she has considerably more friends and followers, and her photographs show her in a range of interesting settings. My most impressive pictures are from humdrum holidays—Paris, Marbella, Ibiza. Fatima is tagged in weird and unfamiliar festivals, snapped snowboarding and climbing mountains in God knows where. Once again I'm forced to reflect on my banality.

'*Fatima has commented on your photo*,' I'm notified. I check the picture.

It's a face-on shot of me beside a friend. She's uploaded a photo in the comments section—it's a cropped version showing only my face. The caption says 'Facial Symmetry Breakdown' and overlapping the image is a cross-section. It intersects my face, apparently to express the balance. I chuckle to myself. I don't know who else would have left such a comment. It's unashamedly Fatima; anyone else might have been self-conscious, but I realise she probably couldn't care less about how it could be publicly perceived.

I receive a text from the friend in the photo. 'Who's that Fatima babe?' it says. 'Sounds like she's got the hots for you!'

I ignore the message.

I'm imbued with confidence as I find her on the bikes two days later.

'This lockdown must have killed dating,' I say, attempting to sound casual.

'You think?'

'I mean, it's pretty hard to ask someone to go for a drink when all the pubs are closed…'

'Maybe you're just being unimaginative,' she says.

'Well, what would you suggest?'

Fatima pauses. 'Have you ever given blood?'

Now I'm truly lost.

'Um… I have, actually. Last year a van came to our offices. Why?'

'Oh good. The centre I use is in the library at the end of the street.'

'O.K.?'

'How about instead of coming here one night, we meet there?'

'Are you asking me out?'

'Why yes, David, I do believe I am.' I try not to blush as she opens her phone. 'They have appointments available next week…'

'It's a date,' I say. 'A really weird date.'

I open the app and it brings up my information. My blood type is O, the most common—no surprises there.

Both a pint of blood lighter, we're sat several feet apart in the refreshment area a week later. 'A free coffee and a chocolate bar', I say. 'I can't believe I've never thought about this as a date idea before'.

Fatima laughs. She tells me her blood group is AB positive, the rarest type.

'Figures', I say.

'What are you?'

'O… O for ordinary—'

She rolls her eyes and interrupts me. 'Positive or negative?'

'Negative.'

'Negative is way less common! And you're lucky; your blood can be used for everyone'.

Our next few dates are virtual. We cook meals together via video link, sink up movies and simply talk late into the night. Although our interests differ greatly, I find that most of our views on life are strangely similar.

I feel my horizons broadening because of her. While I'm still not sold on the taxidermy, I read the novels she recommends and we discuss them at great length; I find that haven't looked at social media in weeks. I make her laugh. She gives me insight. Most of all though she makes me feel far from ordinary.

I'm still just one snowflake in a big heap of snow. But now and then, if you pay close enough attention, and the light lands in just the right way …you'll notice a sparkle.

Sometimes snowflakes shimmer; there will always be someone who finds you far from ordinary.

James Rose - The Doughnut of Destiny

I suppose it all began … Are you taking this down? Of course. It's being recorded. Yeah, I think the trigger was Klaus coming into our office and saying, 'Good God, what are you doing here?' I didn't realise that what he meant was 'what are *you* doing *here?'* So I just replied, 'Same old, same old,' and didn't even look up from my screen.

'But I saw you just two minutes ago down in the tunnel, checking the power settings,' he insisted.

I still didn't look round.

'I was going to do that,' I said.

I'd thought about doing it but I'd thought about not doing it even more. I hate it down there. It's stuffy and cramped. After a run you really should check the settings on the actual machine but you can check them remotely. So I had come to the office instead.

'That Dutch mathematician, what's his name? Stefan. He looks like me from a distance,' I said.

'No, it was you,' Klaus insisted.

I spun my chair round for him to see my face, just in case he too had got mixed up. Admittedly unlikely, as we'd shared the same office for two years.

'Couldn't have been. I came straight from the canteen at least ten minutes ago,' I said.

'You must have a doppelgänger,' he said, as if that finished the argument.

'Yeah, right!' I said swinging my chair back. Great scientist, Klaus, but suffused with German Romanticism. The Goethe of CERN they used to call him when he worked there. But it bothered me, because I *had* been going to go to the tunnel to check the power settings. In my mind's eye I'd even seen myself doing it. But then I changed my mind.

I should fill you in about the facility. Not many outsiders know what we do and even fewer can understand it. Sometimes I think there's quite a few on the inside who don't either, but that's another story. Remember when the journalists thought up the God particle? That really helped the public get a handle on what the Large Hadron Collider, the LHC, was about. But our work will, I suspect, prove a stretch too far for most. You'll remember how everyone got ridiculously bothered about creating black holes in the LHC? What would they make of multiverses?

At the quantum level, the theory of multiple universes is entirely respectable, if difficult to digest. Our machine is trying to prove that however hard you hit matter, there are no more tiny particles. Which is why it's so big and powerful. If there aren't any more particles, 'the multiverse hypothesis will stride into the limelight', as someone once said. I could explain but I think that's not what you came to talk to me about.

Trying to prove a hard-to-understand hypothesis by not finding something, how exciting is that? Yes, I see you've managed to suppress your excitement very well. So that sketches in the background for you. Anyway, we haven't broadcast our activities much. We leave that to Brian Cox and Jim Al Khalili. It's what they're paid for. I just keep my head down and collect the data.

Klaus stayed for a few minutes, muttered one of his absent-minded departure grunts and left, probably to meet up with Axel to discuss Bayern München's Saturday result. We are human, you know. I'm an Aston Villa man, myself, which tells you something about my ability to bear disappointment.

There's a well-known scientific quote, so well-known I can't quite bring it to mind immediately. Under the circumstances, you will no doubt forgive this lapse. But it's something to the effect that you must always be open to any observation that seems odd and contrary to the prevailing paradigm. Well, if I allow that Klaus is a good observer and that the girl in Stefan's office, who told me he was on annual leave, was right, we seemed to have something odd, at the very least, and undoubtedly contrary to the current paradigm.

I gazed at my icons of scientific inspiration hanging on the wall: Marie Curie for persistence and self-sacrifice; Karl Jung for being scientific and spiritual; and on the shelf my lucky mascot, a basalt statue of Thoth in his baboon form, the Egyptian god who invented science. I focussed on these icons, especially Thoth and let my imagination off its leash. I went to the chalk board and laid down some particle trajectories, energies and masses. My hand paused. I dropped the chalk and sat down.

'So what do you think, Klaus?' I asked him later. He wasn't as much a Goethe as I had hoped. He'd used the standard response to something inexplicable and tried to discredit the observation - even his own. I braced myself for denial and anger, which usually follow. They didn't.

'That sort of nonsense will do your career no good.,' he said slowly and earnestly.

I was probably safe from the rack and the stake but not from the rejected grant applications and the dead-end junior lectureship in a minor university. I decided to back pedal.

'Yeah! Just floating an idea. Best forgotten. Thanks,' I said giving in gracefully.

But I had no intention of forgetting it. If I could provide proof of multiverses on a larger scale than the quantum, I would have by-passed all that 'if there are no more particles, there must be multiverses' stuff. That's Nobel Prize territory.

Could my doppelgänger be a tantalizing image of another universe, in which I did decide to check the power settings instead of reviewing the data in the office? That was the hypothesis I'd put to Klaus. Perhaps the high levels of energy generated by the torus temporarily slowed their separation. I did mention the torus, didn't I? No? I didn't think I had. Nothing to do with bulls. That's a different spelling. Well it's the machine at the hub of our experimental set up. An enormous subterranean doughnut designed to smash the tiniest bits of matter into tinier bits. Although if you're a multiverse fan you hope not to find any. The Doughnut of Destiny, as one of the canteen wits had dubbed it. The DoD. We love our acronyms!

Not your sort of stuff this, is it? The details aren't relevant to my present circumstances but it was down in the tunnel alongside the torus that I had been 'seen' or was it *an* 'I', who had been seen.

I'm an experimental physicist, so all that theory was a bit of a push for me but constructing an experiment was right up my street. What I needed to do was prove Observed Simultaneous Bilocality – being seen in two places at the same time. I prefer OSB to BSITPATST. Latin over English for gravitas and credibility every time.

Waiting for data to emerge after the runs is an occupational hazard and we normally use the time to write papers and grant applications, play video games and try to beat on-line gaming sites. Instead I developed an experiment. First, I hacked into the security CCTV network to feed the camera outputs to my computer. It was important to have a record with timer markings.

Then I gave the computer some times when I would be free to perform a number of equally likely personal activities in sight of the security cameras: office work, walking along different corridors, waiting in the main lobby, trying to find my car in the car park, reading in the library, eating in the canteen, checking the power settings in the tunnels by the DoD and so on. Then it chose two of these activities for me to think about and after a defined period of time randomly instructed me to perform one of them, providing me with a hard copy printout. And off I went, ensuring that I passed in front of the cameras. The idea was that the computer's random decision would create separate universes, in which I would perform different activities with a chance they might both be caught on camera.

You will never believe what happened. Well, I suppose it depends on how sceptical you are. You're right. Nothing. I checked and rechecked the data and eventually twigged that the randomly chosen activities had always been well away from the DoD. The first observation was, as you will remember, right next to it. So I reprogrammed the experiment to include a bias towards having activities near the DoD. I ran the experiments again and this time stored the camera outputs for a big review session rather than check each one.

To be honest, I was getting bored and I should have been doing other work. If I get a Nobel prize, it will be just reward for tedious hours watching empty corridors and the nerve-wracking highs and lows before recognizing that it was a colleague and not me in the corridor while 'I' sat drinking coffee.

In fact, I almost missed it. I was half looking at a magazine and half looking at the screen, when a sudden shudder ran through me. I hit the Pause button and rewound. The timers synchronized and there I was, or at least a faint shadow of me, going reluctantly down the stairs towards the DD tunnel while simultaneously sitting in the library making some notes from a journal. I checked it several times, backed up the images to my account on the facility's main frame, and the cloud. Then I sat back, feeling more weak than jubilant. I knew this wasn't enough. Why had I produced a doppelgänger on that occasion and not others?

If proximity to the torus was a factor then what about its power? I trawled through the data and found the DoD had been charging up to near maximum power. With these two factors now nailed down, I could increase the number of positive observations.

Curiously, I never saw a version of me disappear. The figure would move out of the line of sight of the camera or become hidden from view but in each case I did not reappear. The duration of the phenomenon was also related to its proximity to the DoD, probably by an inverse square law but I didn't have sufficient data. Luckily, our office was just close enough to have a reasonable chance to get some hits. I was beginning to perceive, albeit briefly, the separation of the universes, the path the other me had taken, which under normal circumstances was imperceptible.

Then I had a real blow. A sock in the solar plexus blow. When I reviewed all that backed up information showing OSB, the image wasn't there. It had gone. I told you I was an Aston Villa fan, so you'll know that we can take setbacks. Don't worry, it's a Birmingham club. I mention it just so you understand that I was devastated but plugged on. Oddly, that overwhelming despair was a breakthrough.

When I couldn't find the images, I thought, 'I want out of here. Away. Into the sunshine. Have a drink.' But I stayed on and did a few more runs and to my surprise saw myself sitting head in hands in the office *and* walking out. And that image didn't fade. I wondered whether a third factor that allowed the stored dual images to persist was my emotional state. Ghosts remaining at sites of high emotion came to mind.

With a theory, an experimental method and hard to falsify objective data recordings, I had cracked it but now what? A scientific paper would simply be rejected. I needed a demonstration that showed how OSB linked to the factors I had identified.

I asked Klaus. 'Do you think that for a really good experiment, they would boost the collider right up and turn it off again soon after?'

He wasn't impressed. 'What and postpone all our other experiments? For that completely off the wall theory of yours, I bet. However, you might have a chance at the next service. You'll get an on, off and a power up to max but it's not scheduled for some weeks.' He consulted the facility's calendar. 'About three weeks.'

'Thanks Klaus! I think I'll take a fortnight off,' I said.

I needed a break. I had leave coming, so I decided to drive down to the Med. and return in time to set up the experiment. I'd show them! I let admin. know and packed my things that night. Early next morning I drove to work to pick up bits and pieces from our office. Klaus was there, unusually early for him.

'I thought you'd gone,' he said glancing up from his computer.

'No, just going now,' I said as I put a few notebooks and my statue of Thoth into my rucksack and checked I'd switched off all my electronic stuff.

'Have a good time!' he said without looking up again.

On the way out along the corridor I checked my pocket for my keys, which weren't there. Typical! I must have put them down in the lab and picked up the rucksack without them. I sighed and went back, irritated with myself. I wanted away.

The door to our office, which was usually left ajar, was pushed to and I opened it quietly so as not to disturb Klaus. As the door swung open, I could see he was no longer at his desk but at my computer, a memory stick in its port and screens of data scrolling up.

'You bastard!' I shouted advancing towards him.

He recovered rapidly from the shock of seeing me. 'We could work on this tog- '

My rucksack hitting him on the side of his head gave a low thud that surprised me. He fell, stunned. As if I were really in a parallel, slower moving universe, I mused on the irony of his being knocked out by the Egyptian god of Time and Mediation. Serves him right, I thought until I saw in slow motion his head hit the protruding metal foot of the desk. He lay completely still.

I broke out in a sweat. This couldn't be happening. I knelt down and felt for his carotid pulse. Nothing. Mine raced. I rolled him over, thumped his chest, checked his pupils. Dilated even looking directly up at the LEDs. I'd killed him. I never meant to. You'll have to believe me. I never …

I got up and locked the door. I checked his stick. He had been stealing my theory and my data. I wished I were in the universe where I'd picked up my keys and left. I checked the CCTV images, which showed me heading out of building. I checked our office CCTV download and there I was coming through the door. And Klaus looking up. And being hit on the head. Falling from view. And I disappeared as I knelt down to tend to him. I checked the two timers. 8:02:46. 8.02:46 and 8:02:47. 8:02:47. Both clocks. In the corridor and in the office. Perfect pictures and perfect proof. The door handle rattled. There was a knock and Axel shouted, 'Klaus! Are you in there?'

I realized then that I wouldn't have to write a paper that would be rejected by journal after journal. The prosecution and your defence will prove the correctness of my theory. In open court for all the world to see. At some cost to my liberty, of course.

Had not Marie Curie lost fingers and shortened her life and many other scientists been persecuted and risked their lives for science? Was Klaus's life and my own long-term incarceration not worth the understanding and the fame this will bring me? Mine will be a story every schoolchild shall know, more interesting than Newton and his apocryphal apple, as scandalous as Burke and Hare, more self-sacrificing than Galileo.

I'll plead guilty to manslaughter and be convicted by the same evidence that proves the multiverse theory. It will be for all to see. Guilty but vindicated in the light of the history.

Herr Advocat? I insist you use all the data as testimony.

No. Oh, no! Not that.

Not 'Innocent but Insane.'

Jayden Whitehouse - One for Malice

One for Malice

It wasn't my fault. I knew this. No matter what anyone else told me. I wasn't the one who had held the knife to his throat; it wasn't me who cut sliced through his skin with practiced ease. No, it wasn't me who had committed that heinous act, but I did witness it and that made me a suspect.

I didn't ask for him to be killed in front of me, I just wished for the pain to stop; for him to leave me alone and let me live my life the way I had wanted to. In peace, comfortable in my own skin despite my many 'disappointing' traits.

He had never been all for my actions. I was his daughter. His cute, precious little princess who he needed to protect and smother and keep all to himself because they world was full of 'dangerous people who wouldn't think twice about hurting me'. Can you believe that? Even though he was the only one who had ever hurt me, disregarded my thoughts and feelings as if they meant nothing. As I was nothing more than a trophy daughter to show off when it suited him.

That all changed though. When I came out to him; when I had told him that I didn't want to be his daughter anymore, that I wasn't comfortable in the body I was in and wanted to change it. He shouted at me, swearing and screaming. It got so bad that the neighbours called the police on suspicion of domestic violence. He denied it all of course, claiming to have a disobedient and thug of a child.

I didn't let his opinion deter me though, it would never deter me. Not from something I wanted so bad that I was willing to do anything to get what I wanted. I stopped wearing what he wanted me to wear. Donated all my dresses, skirts and frilly, floaty, floral t-shirts to a charity shop; if I wasn't going to wear them someone less fortunate might just be interested. I used the allowance I had been saving up to purchase clothes that I like for a change, clothes that made me feel more comfortable to step outside.

Two for Mirth

It was exhilarating, that first day. No one knew it was me at first, they couldn't tell by looking at my face that I was the same person they had all knew. I introduced myself with a new name, a name that I like and one that sent a small burst of warmth through my chest whenever someone called me by it. It was freeing to be able to play football with the lads without them trying to 'go easy on me' because I was a female.

It was funny. This group of friends, my guys friends who had known me since we were thirteen couldn't recognise me by my face, nor by my voice. Both of which I was sad to admit looked exactly the same as the day before. Maybe they just didn't want to acknowledge what was right in front of them? Maybe they could see it was me but didn't want their thoughts to go down that way of thinking just yet. I was holding back my laughter when Brian, my closest friend as a girl had started spilling his feelings for my 'female self' to the new me. I was biting my lip so desperate not to laugh in his face and end this little game I had going too soon; it was bringing me much too much enjoyment for me to want to stop now.

It sort of got worse after that, however. My dad thought it was his right and his privilege to inform all my friends, the school board, my family and anyone else in our small town who would give him the time of day about my 'rebellious phase. They all knew suddenly. They stopped calling me Jay and referred back to calling me by my dead name, a name I refused to acknowledge in any form.

I tried to explain myself to everyone I knew; anyone who asked me or tried to set me back on the right path that I wasn't at all comfortable being called 'Jade' or she/her. It made my insides squirm uncomfortably and I just wanted to haul up in my room and cry for days. It wasn't a phase that I was going through, nor was it a rebellious act. I didn't want to be a girl anymore, nor did I want to ever be associated with that version of me. The version of me that had never really been me.

Three for a funeral

He called me a murderer. Told me that if I go through with the hormone treatment and the operations then I would no longer be his child, that he would have nothing to do with me anymore and I would have to fend for myself. It was hard to hear. My dad, the one person in the world who was supposed to support me and love me unconditionally was turning his back on me. It was heart-breaking but I couldn't give up. Not now that I had come so far. He didn't get that I hated the body I was born in, that every time I caught a sight of my physical features my dysphoria would consume my mind.

He threw me out just a week later and I ended up living on the streets for a week. It was the hardest thing I had ever had to do, especially when he told me that he would allow me to come home if I just stopped all this nonsense at once. I couldn't do it though. I couldn't go back to living a lie; not now I had gotten a little taste of freedom. I refused. He disowned me.

I hated myself for a while after that. I thought that I was being selfish, that I should just give up on my dream of becoming the real me and go back to living in the mould everyone expected me to live in but I knew I couldn't. Maybe it was a little selfish of me. Maybe I was being an ungrateful, hurtful git for wanting something so bad; for putting through my friends and family through so much hardship. I couldn't stop though. The constant dysphoria; the deliberate misgendering and deadnaming were slowly killing me. Blood congeals on my wrists as another one of my ex-friends shouts the wrong name at me in the street and I run.

Four for a birth

Then he found me. A complete stranger that I had never seen before walks up to me and puts his arm around my shoulders. He smiles down at me and for some reason I feel myself relaxing, it was the most comforting and disconcerting thing I had ever dealt with before. 'Jay, I think I know a way that you can be happy,' we his first words to me. Those words disarmed me completely and I knew that I would be alright. That this stranger would help me.

I accepted his offer. Spending the next few weeks, months in his home and he protected me from my old friends, from my family and stuck by me when I went to my first appointment. He was brilliant, supportive of my choices, I just didn't know why. He had apparently been looking for me since my dad had threw me out but I had never seen him before, never even heard of him, but I didn't care. He saved me. He helped me.

His name was Lucifer and I couldn't help but snort at that. He was named after the Devil and was helping a Transmale make it through their transition. The irony of the situation wasn't lost on me at all. Nor was it lost on him when I explained my mirth to him. His only response was to smirk down at me, ruffle a hand through my hair and brush a kiss to my forehead. I didn't understand the flutter in my stomach.

Five for Silver
Six for Gold

I did it. The doctors gave me my first dose of Testosterone today and even though it hurt to have a needle that size inserted in a place I really didn't want it to be, I could never have been happier. Lucifer took us out to dinner to celebrate the official beginning of my journey and I will be honest; I was almost in tears. Everything was beginning to fall into place.

My old friends still made their snide comments if they walked past me in the street and my dad still refused to acknowledge that I even existed. In fact, I had heard him telling people that his daughter had been killed by a sociopath just a few months ago. The story made me roll my eyes, especially when people would recognise me as I walked beside Lucifer down the street. He was really playing up the whole victim stance on the matter and it irritated me to no end.

There he was playing the victim when he was the one who threw his own child out into the streets without so much as a scrap of money or means to survive. He had disregarded me simply because I wouldn't cave to his ideologies; because I refused to let myself be slowly killed by their suppression and preconceived notions of social normative behaviours. I broke away from their ignorant teachings and became the person I was meant to be.

Seven for a story
That should never be told

I learnt to never tell people of what I used to be, that I wasn't born as a male because they would take it as some strange sort of permission to misgender me. So, I soon learnt to keep my past to myself, nothing from before my transition came to the surface, except when I was alone with Lucifer or having one of my scheduled meetings with my counsellor. I wasn't allowed to dwell on how low I had sunk emotionally before I had been saved, I wouldn't allow the ghosts of my past the satisfaction because I had finally managed it. I had broken free of their chains and let myself be me. I was comfortable with myself for the first time in a while and I couldn't be happier.

Well, I didn't think I could ever be happier than when I got the all clear for my surgeries. I was finally going to become the male I always thought myself to be and no one could ever doubt me again, not with this physical proof of my gender. It was exhilarating.

Though it wasn't as exhilarating as the events transpiring when I was released from the hospital to continue my recovery at home. My chest was tender, and my entire body was aching, scars slowly fading into light pink lines as they begin to heal. Lucifer had promised to look after me, help me with things I couldn't quite yet do on my own until I was well enough to do them again.

It was during one of these times, when he was assisting me in walking from my bedroom to the living room so I could settle onto the sofa and watch a bit of tv when he did something I wasn't expecting. He brushed his hands through my hair, trailing his fingers down my cheek before he brushed a sweet, chaste kiss to my lips. Just a second of contact, nothing to intimate but my breath caught all the same. A grin stretches across my lips at his nervous expression and I brush my lips against his in return, just another light caress but he gets the message.

Eight for Heaven

We were officially dating, and Lucifer wasn't at all put out by the fact that I used to be a girl. Well, I kinda already knew that from before but it is still a comforting feeling to know that there are some people out there who would accept me for who I am and for who I used to be. The weeks we are together fly by and I can't keep the smile off my face when he comes home or whenever I see him pottering around the house.

It is like I had died and gone to heaven. I may have lost my friends and family, but I had gained something more. Something more precious then even my physical body. I had found that special someone and I was never going to let him go.

My aches we finally beginning to dissipate as well so I was able to get up from the sofa and help Lucifer with the housework and running errands just like we used to do. It was magical. I had never felt so at peace with my life and I couldn't think of anything better than right now. Life was perfect and I prayed to God that it stayed this way.

Nine for Hell

Then he showed up. I didn't know why he had decided to turn up on our doorstep after so many years but he was there and I made the mistake of allowing him into our home. He was soaked from the rain pouring and once he stepped into the light of the hallway I knew something was terribly wrong. His eyes were shadowed, there was no life in him whatsoever. He reached a hand into his pocket and slowly pulled out a knife which glittered in the artificial light.

I screamed.

Lucifer came running into the hallway and immediately grabbed for me. He tugged me backwards just as my dad leaped forward. He cried out, face contorting in rage and Lucifer and I run through the house heading for the back garden where we hope to escape through the alleyway. It was asking for a lot but we were not going to trap ourselves in our own home where dad had the perfect opportunity to kill us.

I was terrified as Dad came crashing through the kitchen behind us, arms swinging widely as he tries to strike us down for whatever reason. He was deranged, I concluded. Something must have happened for him to lose it like this and I didn't want to be around when he came to his senses. I shove my hand in my back pocket and hurriedly dial the police, screaming down the phone for them to send help, that my dad was trying to kill me and my boyfriend.

We made it to the back garden and were just heading for the gate when my ankle caught, and I went crashing to the ground. Dad advanced on me, knife raised, the sharp edge glinting menacingly in the moonlight but just before he could bring it down Lucifer grabs his wrist. He twists it sharply and I wince when a crack echoes through the night. He grabs the knife and raises his own arm, slashing downwards in less than a second.

Dad falls to the floor, chest darkening as blood flows freely from the open wound. Lucifer drops the knife to the ground turns to me and hugs me tightly assured that our attacker was in no real state to continue his assault for the time being. We sit there for a second, until the sounds of sirens can be heard in the background.

It wasn't my fault. I knew this. No matter what anyone else told me. I wasn't the one who had held the knife to his throat; it wasn't me who cut sliced through his skin with practiced ease. No, it wasn't me who had committed that heinous act, but I did witness it and that made me a suspect. I didn't ask for him to be killed in front of me, I just wished for the pain to stop; for him to leave me alone and let me live my life the way I had wanted to. In peace, comfortable in my own skin despite my many 'disappointing' traits.

Ten to the Devil wherever he may dwell.

Jessica Emery - Round of Applause

I can hear her doing it again. Every morning before school, Mum claps at the birds. She stands on the balcony which looks out over the canal and she claps and claps. I'm warm in bed right now; even my head is warm, under the duvet. It's a bit dark, too; my eyes are closed, the duvet is high over me like a fortress, the curtains are drawn. But outside my room, down the corridor, I know that Mum is standing on the balcony in the bright light. Clapping at the birds.

My alarm is squawking at me, *get up get up get up*. I stick my hand out from under the duvet and bash the clock until it shuts up. Then I get out of bed and stick my feet into my slippers, which are giant and shaped like R2D2. I pull apart the curtains. Mum always used to open them for me but since she started clapping in the morning as well as the night, she hasn't had time. Outside, the sky is as blue as the walls in Miss Jatt's Year Two classroom.

Next, I open my door and shuffle down the corridor in my bit-too-big slippers. The lights are off. The door to the balcony is open a little though, so I can see all the way down. I follow the light coming from outside.

I peer around the balcony door quietly. Mum is wearing her pink fluffy dressing gown with the little white love hearts all over it. I know this is her favourite outfit because she wears it all the time. A cigarette is burning in her left hand. She is leaning against the metal barrier that stops us from falling all the way off, into the canal.

Then the magic happens: a seagull flies up close to Mum. She starts clapping, three times, five times, loudly. Mum has mastered her clap so that it makes a great slapping noise; she doesn't have to put down her cigarette, either.

'Will you *be quiet?!*' I hear one of our neighbours yell, probably at their dog.

I move from the doorway, taking a seat on the little plastic crate. The balcony is just one small, metal platform, so my crate is right next to Mum, which I like. I can see the dry skin on her ankles. I hold onto the metal railings and peer through, braving a peep down, feeling dizzy. I'm looking out from between the bars on the window of a pirate ship. I'm a stowaway, surveying the waters below. Sometimes I'm the captain too, or the baddie who has taken over the ship, looking for gold. It's a great adventure, up here. I'm not really supposed to play out here alone but sometimes I do when Mum is watching tele. She doesn't notice.

After a few minutes I stand up. Even though the sun is shining it's chilly in just my blue stripy jim-jams, and anyway I need to get ready for school.

'Shall we have breakfast now, Mum?'

A pigeon swoops suddenly. Mum begins her clapping, so loud that it almost hurts my ears. The man down the way starts yelling at his dog to be quiet again.

'Mum?'

'You start without me, I just need to--' she says, clapping.

I go downstairs and get the coco-pops, pouring two big bowls. I put the milk into my bowl, then I stare at the clock until three minutes has passed. Three minutes is the perfect amount of time for the milk to go chocolaty. Often when I get home from school, Mum's cereal is still in the bowl. It's worse when there is milk in it. It goes soft, looks like Brucey Cat's sick.

Once I've washed my face, brushed my teeth for two and a half minutes and put on my school uniform, I go back to the balcony.

'It's time for school.'

'It is,' Mum agrees, checking the time on her phone.

She takes one last look at the canal, a brilliant queen watching out over her land, then she follows me down the stairs. Me and Mum have matching trainers, the Nike Airs with the big padded soles. Mine flash. Mum puts hers on now, but I have to wear my school shoes, which are boring black and do up with Velcro instead of laces. We walk to school together, but I stop holding her hand when we turn onto the road that school is on. That's one of the things that the boys in my class don't like: hand holding. Not girls, not the teachers, but especially not Mums, I've learnt.

Whilst I'm waiting for the bell to go, four boys come up to me. They're much taller than me; I guess they must be in Year Five or even Year Six.

'Was that your *Mum?*' One of them asks. His hair is gelled down on the top but spiked up at the front like he is wearing a cap.

'Yes,' I reply. 'Is she *okay?*'

'She's fine, thank you.'

'Then why was she wearing her *dressing gown?'*

All the boys laugh at this, they shriek and hoot, so I guess it must be funny. I laugh too. 'What are *you* laughing at, gayboy?' Another one asks. He has the arms of his green school jumper tied around his neck like a cape. This isn't one of the ways you are allowed to wear your jumper.

I don't know why I was laughing, so I shrug. By this point all of them have stopped laughing. I stop too. Then the bell goes, just like my alarm clock but louder, *schools starting schools starting schools starting.*

'We'll see you at lunch, then.'

In the classroom I am thinking about the boys. The way they said *dressing gown* made it seem like it was a bad thing. But everyone wears dressing gowns. I have one, it's fire truck red. Craig, Mum's ex-boyfriend, he used to wear one which was really short, and his legs were all hairy, way hairier than mine. When I went to stay with Gran and Gramps last year, when Mum was ill, I saw their dressing gowns too. And besides, what's the difference between a dressing gown and a coat? I've seen the other Mum's wearing pink coats and coats with big fluffy hoods and coats which are so wide and puffy that they look like they're stuffed with cushions. What's the difference?

The boy I sit next to, Kim, is nudging me with his elbow. I look up and see that the teacher is staring at me with an angry sort of face. The whole class is staring at me. Miss Jatt repeats my name, and I say that I'm present, even though she can see that.

During maths, I whisper to Kim, 'do you have a dressing gown?' 'Shut up,' he whispers back.

At lunch time I decide that I don't want to see the boys from this morning. They said that they would see me, but they said it in a way that didn't make me want to see them. I calculate where best to go. The canteen is too risky: everyone eats lunch, every day, especially boys as tall as them. Lunch will have to wait — good job I had coco-pops this morning. I can't hide in the toilets, either. I've tried that one before. It really annoys the people who are desperate for a wee. They bang on the door over and over which reminds me of when Craig used to stay. If I say I'm doing a poo, to get them off my case, they say things like *eww* and *gross*. Which is weird, because everybody does poos — I suppose, anyway.

If I can't go to the canteen or the toilets and I definitely can't go to the playground, that leaves only one place. I wind down the corridors which are covered in all sorts of important information about school and life, such as the anatomy of a stick insect and the eight times table. I make it safely to the library, feeling like a spy who has just completed the first part of their secret mission.

The librarian is a nice lady who reminds me of Gran because her hair is short, curly and white, and she's a little bit fat.

'Hello, dear,' the librarian says. 'Shouldn't you be outside?' 'I have a pass,' I tell her.

'You do?' She looks at me from over her glasses, which are shaped like half the moon. I nod. She doesn't ask to see it.

'Could you tell me where to find a book about clapping at birds?' 'Pardon?' She frowns.

I repeat what I said but slowly. She can't hear very well, like Gran.

'I don't think we have a book about… *clapping*… at birds. But we have lots and lots of books about birds, in the nature section. Follow me.'

The nature section is right at the back, so if the boys did come into the library, they wouldn't see me straight away. There is even a bean bag; I pick a few books off the shelf and take a seat. Now I'm an explorer of new lands, discovering new birds. They will name the new birds after me, so even after I'm dead people will remember me.

The bell goes, *back to class back to class back to class,* like a parrot cawing the same phrase over and over again without ever thinking what it means. Leaving the other books in a pile on the floor, I grab my two favourite books. 'Best of Birds: A-Z' has all the fun birds in it, like flamingos and toucans and dodos which are dead. But I hope the second book, 'British Birds', will tell me what I need to know.

'No books about clapping, then?' The librarian smiles as she stamps my books. 'No,' I say sadly.

I dash down the corridors with my books like precious cargo. In my head I can see the look Miss. Jatt will give me because I'm late. When I open the classroom door, she gives me that exact look, and I think for a second that I am a fortune teller, but then I remember to apologise. Miss. Jatt tells me to see her after class. She also tells me to wear my uniform properly; I undo the arms of my jumper-cape and stick my head into the head-hole. I figure only the big boys are allowed capes.

As I'm sitting down, Miss. Jatt reminds the class that tomorrow is not only Friday, but it is also Sports Day. She says that all the parents are invited, that we must remember to remind then. It would make more sense if she just reminds them herself, instead of reminding us to remind them. But as I am already in trouble, I don't suggest this.

After school, I try to slip past Miss. Jatt with the rest of the boys and girls but she says my name.

'Yes, Miss?'

'Wait there a minute.'

I stand by her desk as she smiles at the final children who leave the classroom. Now it is just me and Miss. Jatt and all the empty desks and chairs which are lined up in front of us like soldiers standing to attention. I like being at the front of the classroom, in front of the huge white board. I make a note to add 'teacher' to my list of possible jobs for when I'm a grownup.

'Today is the fourth time this month you've been late.' 'I was in the library.'

'Did you not hear the bell?'

I consider lying, but then I remember that lying is not good, and I've already done it once today.

'I heard it. The librarian made me late. She was slow at stamping my books.' 'Why were you in the library? You should have been outside.'

'I needed a book. About clapping at birds.'

Miss. Jatt frowns, opens her mouth, closes it. Then her face softens like a big knife of butter on toast, a Sunday treat.

'I see you're signed up for the egg and spoon race tomorrow. Will your parents be coming?'

'I'll remind Mum.'

When I get home, I eat the second bowl of coco-pops really quickly. Thankfully there was no milk in the bowl, so the pops aren't all in a mush. I tell Mum about my day, speaking loudly so that she can hear me over the tele. I remind her about Sports Day. When she doesn't respond I remind her again. I don't want to be in trouble with Miss. Jatt if Mum forgets. Then I go to my bedroom and I study my books all evening, before and after fish finger dinner. I read every word, look at every picture, but I can't find what I need to know. I decide to just ask her.

I head down the corridor to the balcony, guided by the sound of Mum's clapping. I sit down on the plastic crate next to Mum, who is standing and smoking. I think I prefer the balcony at night. The lights in the houses opposite us look like stars. I like to pretend up lives for the people in the houses. The best is when I can see a silhouette of somebody in their window, like Peter Pan's shadow.

Mum claps two loud, sharp claps. I look around for the birds but can't see any. Then I wrap my hands around the railings and peer through, looking down into the canal. I see some ducks swimming; they are lit up by the lights in the garden opposite us, which we could get to if only we weren't so high up, and there wasn't the River Lea between us. I look closer at the ducks, then correct myself: they are coots. They have red beaks and are smaller than ducks. I tell Mum this.

'They're all the same, birds. Beaks, feathers. Shitting everywhere, always noisy.'

'Ducks are not the same as coots,' I correct her. 'Birds are birds.'

'Why do you clap at the birds, Mum?'

Mum stops watching out over her land and turns to look down at me. I wrap my arms around my knees.

'I'm keeping them away. I clap because I *hate* them.'

I stand, leave, get into bed without brushing my teeth. Once the duvet is over my head, heavy and soft, everything is quiet. I am the only person in the world. What is there to hate about birds? My books are full of brilliant birds, clever and pretty. Some birds even help *pollinate,* which helps us breath! I think about the birds' feelings - the ducks, swans, coots and pigeons - what they'd think if they knew Mum hated them. Luckily, they don't realise. They just think they're getting a round of applause.

The day is perfect, with warm sun, a soft breeze like kisses, and not a single cloud. Everyone's Mum has packed them sun cream. Miss. Jatt gives me some from the drawer in her desk. Then we pile outside with all of us laughing, whooping and chirping happily.

Nobody can stay in the line we're supposed to be walking in, but Miss. Jatt doesn't seem to care for once. Other years come out too, so that we are all flocking across the playground together in the direction of the school field. Everyone is joyful because everybody is together, nobody is in lessons and we are all wearing our P.E. kit, which is almost as good as non- uniform.

I spot the big boys from yesterday across the way, near the netball hoop. I make myself smaller and camouflage myself within the group, which is something many birds do, I learnt.

Mums and Dads and Grans and Gramps are already gathering around the outside of the field. I can't spot Mum yet, but I wrote her a note which I left next to her coco-pops. I'm sure she'll be here.

I am in House Red and I shout for everyone in House Red, cheering them on. There is the relay, the sprint, the three-legged, everything. I feel fizzy with excitement and happiness.

Mum's still not here even after the sack race, but she will be here soon, I know. She probably forgot to feed Bruce and had to turn back. She's always forgetting to feed Bruce.

I'm enjoying the day so much that I almost forget about the egg and spoon race, but then somebody announces, 'egg and spoon!' and then they call my name. I've been practising at home, up and down the stairs, so I know I'm good. I'm not nervous, except a small bit.

As I walk to the start line, I look around for Mum again and finally I spot her. She is making her way to her seat now; she has just made it in time to see me win. I am grateful that it is too hot for her to wear her dressing gown.

First they give us our spoons, then our eggs. My hand is steady. I put my right foot on the starting line but not over it; I don't want to cheat. Then I wait as they count down 'three… two… one… GO!'

Without needing to look around, I can tell that I am winning. Nobody is in front of me.

My arm is straight, my legs are going *back and forth back and forth back and forth.* The finish line approaches, and though I know I shouldn't take my eyes off the course, I want to see Mum's face as I win. I spot her easily in the crowd. She is standing, yelling. Her hands are slapping against one another in the air. She is clapping. *Clap clap clap clap clap.*

My egg falls from my spoon, rolls. I stand on it. The yolk is hard; it crumbles into the grass and soil.

John Buckley - How I Knew Mrs Pymer Did Not Own a Dog

When Uncle Aubrey took me on his milk round I'd have been four-years-old. My older brother wasn't about and neither was Dad, so it wasn't holidays or weekends and yet I was at home, just me and Mum, so I had not started school and that's how I know I'd be four. Therefore, it was 1956, the month doesn't matter.

He wasn't a real uncle, just someone Mum had landed with the title as she did with a lot of family friends, who found themselves aunts and uncles to me. I watched for him to arrive on his cart - we never called it a float - which was pulled by his horse, Rupert.

Out of the bedroom window mostly I could see countryside, a few houses, electricity pylons marching off over the horizon and tall ICI chimneys at its soda ash plant where steam and smoke rose continuously: when the wind was in our direction the smell of ammonia was so strong it was like burying your face in a baby's nappy would drift over our house. Cutting across the view was the Trent and Mersey Canal which still carried colourful, chugging narrowboats to and from ICI. Nothing bigger than sticklebacks survived in the canal's coffee-coloured depths, but swans and narrowboats gave it life.

Our road was unadopted and made of packed earth. If potholes ever appeared in the surface residents of the nine terraced cottages would fill them with ash and cinders from their coal fires It saw little traffic, farm vehicles mainly, because, at the end of the road was Uncle Aubrey and Aunty Amy's farm. It was laid out the way farms are in Ladybird picture books and nothing better than mucky and ramshackle. Wet or dry our road led to an estuary of mud that was the farmyard. Ducks and chickens were truly free range and there were rats because I once saw Uncle Aubrey's dog catch one and shake it dead.

Our house was number sixteen, a two-up two-down with no bathroom and a loo in the back yard. Only occasionally would strangers stray our way, people with something to sell or a job to perform. Once a large man in a turban and carrying a suitcase was spotted by Mum knocking on each door in turn. We hid under the stairs and then I went and spoiled it by waving to him through the window and she felt obliged then to invite him in and see what he had to sell. His case was full of ties and we bought one. I knew she *had* to buy from a gypsy selling pegs because it was bad luck not to. Once she opened the front door to a tramp, as dirty and hairy as you'd want a tramp to be, and she filled his enamel billy can with hot tea, but wouldn't let him in.

Behind the houses Uncle Aubrey's cows grazed in fields that bordered a council estate where most of his customers lived and they could see the cows whose milk they were drinking. The cows occasionally bit clumps out of their hedges or nibbled on other plants they fancied and could reach.

Below my window Rupert brought the cart to a gentle halt. They'd have been out once already: "I do me churns first, then me bottles," Uncle Aubrey said. It was a small cart and customers who preferred their milk straight from the churn were served, while Aunty Amy filled the bottles for the second run.

Mum said Rupert knew the round better than Uncle Aubrey and would stop and start without being whoa'd or geed up. The crates were made of metal, the bottles were glass, tall and silver topped. I clambered aboard and felt important sat up there. Uncle Aubrey had a weathered face and instead of a white coat milkman's uniform he wore a battered black blazer and carried about him a warm smell that was probably a distillation of the dung from cows, pigs, ducks, chickens and Rupert, that he sloshed through for much of the day. Some time later Uncle Aubrey was taken poorly - a word reserved for the seriously ill - and one night his bull terrier Bonzo howled terribly and Mum said that would be because Uncle Aubrey had died. That's how I knew when you were dying your dog howled and I wondered what it would be like lying in bed listening to your dog howling for your death. What if he howled and you didn't even know you were ill?

We made a start, rattling and shaking our way to the main road and then Rupert pulled us to into a left turn into a long straight avenue on the estate of semi-detached houses all with large gardens front and back, separated from each other and the footpath by privet hedges, well clipped and uninterrupted for the length of the avenue. Another avenue ran parallel and the two were joined by similar but shorter roads all called Drives. The front doors had been painted alternately brown and black by the council and there were lime trees and grass verges alongside the road. Often you could look from one end to the other and not see a single motor car. There would be smoke from the chimney pots because there usually was: coal fires were how a family boiled the kettle, heated water and the adjacent oven for cooking and getting the clothes iron hot.

Rupert worked on a system of the garden gates and he would stop directly opposite each one and Uncle Aubrey would jump down, grab what milk he needed and head off up the path briskly, leaving the bottles on the doorstep and bringing back the empties. He said at number seventeen he'd leave me for ten minutes because he had eggs to deliver to the lady there and I was to wait on the cart. That's how I knew eggs had to be taken into the house and took much longer to deliver than milk. I wondered when he would need my help.

He had just put two pints down on fifteen's step when the door flew open and out burst a large woman. Momentarily she seemed to fill the doorway. I noticed her hair was tight and wet in metal curlers and she had no handbag and women always carried handbags. She was in such a rush she kicked one of the bottles into the air and it smashed on a flagstone into lots of sharp pieces. What seemed to be far more milk than could ever have been in the bottle flooded on to the path and into the garden border. Uncle Aubrey just stared at the milk as if surprised by what the bottle had contained. The woman didn't pay it any mind though. She started off up the path at a march and the sight of her approach alarmed me. She was wearing a pinnie aprons were always pinnies then - over a floral dress which reached her shins. I could see one side of her face was very red and her eye on the same side was half-closed and swollen. She seemed to be bearing down on me and I was frightened, but at the gate she came to a sudden stop and clutched at her chest with one arm and the gate with the other to hold herself steady. It seemed to spur on Uncle Aubrey and he dashed to her. He put his arm around her; I remember thinking it wasn't what men normally did unless they loved the woman, so I was surprised. He leaned forward to look her in the face, like someone peering around an open door. He said something and she took a deep breath, but it seemed to hurt her.

Right then a crashing noise came from within the house where the door remained open and a furious voice was shouting words so angrily and fast I couldn't make out what they were. But then what followed was: "You stupid cow!" Which is how I knew one of Uncle Aubrey's herd must have been chewing clumps out of the back hedge but I didn't understand what it had to do with the woman and Uncle Aubrey didn't defend his cows at all. Instead, he glanced back, made his mind up about something and quickly ushered her to the cart.

"Shift up Leslie," he ordered, "Mrs Pymer's coming with us."

I shuffled along the seat so I'd be in the middle and looked at Mrs Pymer as she tried to climb up but she seemed unable to find the effort she needed and Uncle Aubrey heaved on her buttocks with his shoulder to help her up and eventually she flopped on to the seat next to me. There was another crash inside the house and Mrs Pymer flinched and then leaned back and breathed out a long blow of air only to gulp down another huge breath and repeat the process.

"Are you coming with us to deliver the milk, Mrs Pymer?" I asked, wishing to be polite but at the same time I knew I had got something wrong. Anyway, I hoped she wasn't because I might never get to hold Rupert's reins.

She looked at me and almost smiled, but something was stopping her speaking and she just nodded once. I thought her face looked strange and grey but didn't say anything.

Uncle Aubrey climbed aboard at the other side in a hurry. "Seventeen's eggs'll have to wait," he muttered and I saw a woman's face at the window as Rupert launched himself into a surprised trot. I remember thinking she was still wearing a nightie and she frowned and stepped back from the window as we clip-clopped on. Her door was open.

I felt scared but didn't understand why. I didn't look at either adult, I kept my eyes on Rupert's ears and the avenue ahead. Uncle Aubrey scutched Rupert's behind with the reins and seemed too excited to even say gee-up, which everybody knew was the way to get horses going. Instead he made a sort of strangulated sound in his throat and when Rupert wanted to stop at twenty-one, Uncle Aubrey scutched him again. Rupert tried to look round as if to see what was wrong.

Uncle Aubrey yanked the reins to make him take a right turn, along one of the Drives into the other avenue. A car rolled by at the junction and followed by a red double-decker bus and faces seemed to press against the windows to stare at us, as if they somehow knew Uncle Aubrey was behaving differently.

Soon we were at the shops. They were just known as *The Shops*, even though I knew there were other shops in other places. There were five in the row including Ibbotson's fruit and veg where every morning Mr

Ibbotson in his brown overall brought out all his goods laid them out in front of his window and Winnie Stenton's wool shop, which is still the cosiest shop I have ever known and had a smell all its own. Then came the chip shop, Hill's newsagent's and lastly Lambert's post office, which had nothing in its double windows bar a big picture of a stamp bearing the Queen's head. I had been inside with Mum and all its business was conducted over the counter, behind which stood a small bony woman, Mrs Lambert, protected by a wire grill. Outside was a red telephone box and Uncle Aubrey leapt down from the cart and pulled the heavy door open fiercely.

"Uncle Aubrey has gone to make a telephone call," I informed Mrs Pymer, who sort of grunted slowly in response. Both her eyes were closed tight now and her face screwed up in a curious way so I turned my attention back to Uncle Aubrey and watched him through the small windows of the phone box pick up the shiny black receiver and hold it to his ear. He began to dial and then stopped. He tried again, stopped and started hitting the silver coloured rest violently with his fingers and listening to the receiver again. He said something - I've no idea what - then threw open the door, leaving the phone dangling by its chord and strode into the post office.

I didn't know what to do. Certainly I couldn't see how Mrs Pymer could possibly help deliver the milk. Uncle Aubrey burst out of the post office.

"Bloody Fred Karno's," he said loudly, and I imagined he had been trying to ring someone called Fred Karno, who had somehow let him down.

"Her phone's not working either. You wouldn't believe it's the post office that owns them," he shouted, to Mrs Pymer rather than to me. She didn't take much notice but that is how I knew all telephones belonged to Mrs Lambert.

Uncle Aubrey had now disappeared inside Hill's and I continued to not look at Mrs Pymer and not say any more, because she obviously didn't want to talk.

She just sat there, erect, both eyes open again now, like the paintings in my picture bible at Sunday school, the way people looked when they have seen Jesus or a ghost.

Slowly she bent forward in the way trees do when you chop them down with an axe and almost toppled entirely over the front board. For a second I thought she was trying to climb on Rupert's back. But she stayed where she was, almost folded in half and making a little noises in her throat so I thought maybe she was being sick. I knew I should do something, tell someone. I climbed down, slowly because it wasn't easy, and ran into Hill's, a shop I loved visiting because its sweets and, oddly, Uncle Aubrey was behind the counter with Mrs Hill, who was talking urgently into the telephone mouthpiece. Her phone was working. Maybe it was Mr Karno. Uncle Aubrey spotted me.

"I think Mrs Pymer's being sick. She's falling off the cart," I said and saw a look of concern come over his face. He ran outside, muttering to himself, chunnering we used to call it.

I didn't want to follow Uncle Aubrey to Mrs Pymer, I think I'd had enough of both of them. Mrs Hill appeared by my side and put her hand on my head in a kindly way and said. "Well done," but I didn't know what I'd done well. She asked me if I'd like a comic and I picked one though I was too young to read and she gave me a Sherbet Fountain and I kept quiet because I hadn't any money and didn't know if she would ask for some but she didn't.

Some time must have passed before I heard the bell, the incessantly urgent ringing of an ambulance and we went to the door to look. When you heard such a bell you knew something exciting was happening and people came out of their houses to see what was going on.

Uncle Aubrey was aboard the cart again and he must have pulled Mrs Pymer back into a sitting position because they were side by side although neither spoke. Mrs Pymer still looked grey and, strangely, her arms were now folded as if she was just waiting for something.

Two men in black uniforms and silver buttons with peaked hats jumped out of the ambulance. One strode directly to the cart, the other opened the back doors of the ambulance and brought out a stretcher. The first ambulance man pulled one of Mrs Pymer's arms free from the other and held it lightly by the wrist. She didn't object. Didn't even look. The ambulance man shook his head and placed her hand gently on to her lap.

He spoke to Uncle Aubrey while the other one took out a notebook from his breast pocket and wrote down what he said, very official. They weren't in a hurry now. Mrs Pymer didn't move a muscle. I thought it strange how none of it seemed to interest her.

Then I realised. "Is she dead?" I asked.

"I think we should go inside again," said Mrs Hill.

"She was going to help us with the milk," I said.

But we didn't go inside straight away. Mrs Hill couldn't stop watching the ambulance men struggling to get Mrs Pymer off the cart. They tried all sorts of ways, with a lot of puffing and chunnering, but eventually one tipped her up by the ankles and the other caught her shoulders and they managed to lay her flat on the canvas stretcher on the road. One of the ambulance men pulled a blanket over her. Which is how I knew, when you died they covered your face, I supposed because no one should see you dead. I was still eating my Sherbet Fountain.

Uncle Aubrey looked at me in a kindly way. "Leslie, I've got to go see Mr Pymer first..."

I didn't want to go with him, not there.

"To clear up the milk?"

"To tell him Mrs Pymer's been taken to hospital and don't forget I still have to take the eggs to the lady at number seventeen..."

"I know and that takes ten minutes."

I'd have said it with a whine in my voice, thinking of all that hanging round waiting.

Mrs Hill had one of those smiles that isn't a proper smile and said she would take me home and there was a waft of cow muck as Uncle Aubrey quickly left to rejoin Rupert outside. When Uncle Aubrey died and Bonzo took on so and I remembered what happened I realised I'd heard no howling so Mrs Pymer had not owned a dog.

John Roberts - Chimneys I Sweep and In Soot I Sleep

Alfred Powell, thirteen years old, lay on the cold concrete floor, his head on a bag of soot, stunted bug bitten body covered with empty hessian sacks, he dreams, every night, and conjures visions of hefty chunks of roast beef, pints of hot 'Birds' custard trickling over jam rolly polly puddings, numerous assortments of potatoes, chipped-boiled-roasted, over generous portions of Chickens stuffed with chestnuts orange peel, sizzling sausages oozing with fat gigantic pork pies, large chunks of good bread trickled with inch thick dripping and fulsome plates of exotic fruits and nuts.

Alfie, salivating, rolls over and trembles nuzzling his shivering thin body closer, wrapping his arms around himself as he desperately thwarts off the unforgiving freezing wind which blows relentlessly down Grunt Alley in Digbeth. Grunt Alley is a shoddy squalid yard built from the remaining unused materials after Milk and River Street's jerry built 'back to backs' were completed. In the centre is the foul backyard where putrefying rubbish is stored in Miskins, beside communal washrooms, lavatories, and an illicit brewery. The stench is overwhelming. In this brutal slum neighbourhood, the residents do not survive for long.

The fearsome wind wreaks havoc upon the ramshackle wooden windows and doors, sending roof slates slithering to the dirt strewn cobbles below. Outside the house of Bernard Hemming, master chimneysweep, the tempest rocks the clumsily painted sign relentlessly as it hangs down from a listing wooden pole insecurely tied to the crumbling external brick wall. The buffeted sign's musical squeak reverberates throughout the grimy Building, rickety staircase, kitchens and down into the basement.

Yawning loudly Bernard turns over grinning lecherously, cupping Meg's left voluptuous bosom in the palm of his callused dirt engrained hand. Her bleary eyes suddenly opened wide, flushed face she briefly faked a seductive smile whilst pulling the tattered aged woollen bed coverings over most of her fulsome chest. Inwardly wincing, in one swift movement she rolled out of bed, shivering, assailed by blasts of cold unforgiving wind gusting through the cracks in the window, she began to hastily dress.

Hemming scratches his poxed face vigorously and sat upon the side of the bed as he pulled on his threadbare trousers. Leaning forward he pressed his hands in his front pockets searching for cash. Bernard's grimy fingers clasped around his coins, slyly allowing most to slip back unheard into his pocket. Grasping a single penny, he flung it at Meg furiously growling unheard expletives, staring daggers at her through angry sunken, gunmetal grey eyes. Megan Malone watched it spin and twirl upon the wooden floorboards gripping it as soon as the spinning coin dropped, and then, business done, left the house in just a few moments without a backward look.

Banging his heavy cudgel against the flaky damp green stained crumbling thin spider webbed stair walls, Bernard, face full of thunder, and a pain between his eyes, staggered down the narrow gloomy flight of steps swaying side to side like a sailor in a storm as it spiralled down to the basement where all the young chimney sweeps slept.

It's still dark outside, dark, like Bernard's mood. Hemming shoulders sagged, he put his face in his hands, "Alfie, Alfred, George, Jacob… wake up," he said between his fingers. His harsh voice becoming increasingly louder, "Harold, get up, William, up-up-up… now, breakfast an' work… hurry. Awake, Edward, Arthur, Jack, awake, at once… Wake up your lazy toe rags, we have jobs to do, customers to see, chimneys to clean.

As Alfie stirs, his first sensation pain, agony, discomfort. Eyes inflamed and sore, knees and elbows throb from grazes irritated by soot and ashes. Emerging from the various corners and nookey holes of the damp rat infested basement appear many young chimney sweeps, dressed in an assortment of hessian sacks, shabby ragged cast-off clothes, mufflers, and flat caps. All gasping for breath wheezing noisily with dirty hungry faces, skeletal thin weak rib protruding bodies. In the centre of the room, a wooden table leaning lopsided, having been struck by Hemming's cosh in a fit of rage, in the middle is a single large, cracked plate holding odd sized slightly green slices of bread besides which are chipped cast-off mugs of sugared tea.

*

The early morning sun is a mere thin slit with barely enough strength to pierce the grey, purple coloured smog awash with foul smelling acrid ash, embers, and dirt. Alfred, George Wesley, and Jacob Pagett walk along Digbeth High Street, to the accompaniment of the discordant threatening blare of a thousand Factory whistles echoing around, and the voluminous street noises and unpleasant throat gagging odours. Dodging past hawkers and vendors peddling their wares, weaving to avoid pickpockets, Policemen, prostitutes, drunks, beggars, honest workers, and the many unwashed vagabonds.

Digbeth's busy main roads and cobbled streets are crammed full with line after line of heavily loaded wagons pulled by tired old nags, overfull omnibuses, here and there, window curtain drawn Hansom cabs conveying snuff pinching Businessmen and finely dressed Ladies. Very reminiscent of white African explorers amongst the deserving poor and pagan natives.

Digbeth is a heaving tumultuous flooding stream of dirt-stained cowering wretched figures rushing hither thither. All headed for furnaces, workshops, abattoirs, and countless manufacturers. Some, heads bowed and anxious, many cold, threadbare, starving, shoeless or foot sore. Their faces streaked with poverty and despair. And yet, like strutting suited Peacocks, here and there, the top hatted Bosses, displaying red, rosy faces and fulsome beards, moustaches, and sideburns.

This workshop of the world is one long continual display of perpetual fire and brimstone. A blackening dense place of machinery and tall chimneys, brick buildings, steam engines, factories and factories and more factories, giant gas holders and the throat sticking stench of Vinegar and Brewers oats, it's rivers and canals the colour of black with foul streaks of filthy green, brown, and red, smelling putrid. From everywhere, every place, without exception, day, and night, is the constant flow of traffic and the endless clanging of wood and metals being shaped, unrelentingly punched, hammered, and bent, and clothing tanned, woven, and dyed.

*

The day began badly, it was a Tuesday, the sweeps delayed when Bradford street was blocked by an omnibus colliding with a heavy wagon overloaded with pig iron. Thirty-five minutes later, Alfred and his posse stood on the doorstep of number of Thirty-five Grosvenor Street, soot bags and brushes dangling from Alfie's wrist, besides him is hunch shouldered George Wesley, one of the older Sweeps and Jacob Pagett, a new apprentice, just six years old and shivering cold. It is the new home of Mr. and Mrs. Bullock and their two daughters, Adele, and Victoria, both Daughters of marriageable age and looking for husbands, very Jayne Austen. Mr. Aristotle Bullock Assistant Director of the Birmingham Municipal bank, Corporation Street branch, is a man very much on the up.

His wife Charlotte, eldest Daughter of the Vicar of Wimbourton, and pillar of the community.

The new Harborne estate, with its servants, imposing front doors with stone steps and architectural iron balustrades, double fronted bow white windows, large fireplaces, gas lighting and long rear gardens, had recently been built to accommodate the fast-expanding middle class, full of merchants and senior clerks, University Professors and Bankers. The house is a shrine to Liberties of London, Wedgewood ceramics, Hepplewhite furniture, Sheffield cutlery and the Empire.

Greeting them a yawning unkempt dressed Servant, mumbling haughtily under his breath, with reluctance he showed them into the house and together entered a grand upholstered drawing room. Alfred's eyes roamed it enviously. The fireplace is tiled, the latest fashion, with a solid oak surround, richly carved, standing upon its mantelpiece, two silver candles, at either end, flanked by an assortment of Staffordshire porcelain figures. Pride of place in the centre is a gold embossed clock that chimes on the quarter, besides it a Chinese vase containing fragrant fresh flowers. The only flowers any of the Chimney sweeps know are weeds growing abundantly wild between the cracked cobblestones of Grunt alley.

Placing a cloth to cover the mantelshelf Alfie shoved his head up the flue and turning to stare at George, with a stare deepening into a fierce and terrible, he said through thin quivering lips, "it's too narrow… too small for me ".

George, sighed with spiritless impatience leant into the fireplace and nodding his head in agreement said in a rough sore throat hoarse voice, "Okay Alfie, you sure?"

George coughed and gobed a mouthful of coal soot into a dirty rag. Turning towards the perspiring nervous Apprentice he said, "Jacob, it's time you began to earn your keep, young un,' up you go."

He grinned at Jacob and spoke in a sympathetic tone, "Jacob, I want you to climb up …okay lad, get up that chimney, remove yer 'shoes an' clothes… quick lad."

Little Jacob, forehead creased, hesitantly does as he was told and doffing a cap and holding the black-bristle brush over his head with a shiver he slowly squirmed inside the flue, putting one hand by his side, pressing his palm against the wall, he raised the other hand high above his head, palm against the opposite wall. Twisting himself body keeping the lower half rigid, he inched his way into the blackness, held only by the pressure of his body against the chimney's sides defining gravity. Abruptly he felt frightened, his easy movements curtly halted as he finds himself squeezed between the walls, waggling sideways Jacob tried to climb a little further.

Pagett opened and closed his eyes repeatedly fast, checkmated by this predicament, worsened by the terrible darkness. Dirty soot rains down, falling past him pitter-patter, pitter-patter to the grate below. George and Alfie yell words of praise and optimism which Jacob, entrapped and terrified, ignores, neither hearing nor understanding.

Lips pursed, sweat flooding his eyes he stopped overcome by fear Jacob thought to himself,' I can't see a fing,' can't breathe. Can't go up. It's so grim. The chimney is narrowing, twisting… I'm suffocating. I want to come down. More pain! Pain like needles in my feet, needles in my legs.'

Jacob's face is one of perfect misery. He leant out trying to edge higher but stopped as the flue tapered, unable to move, frozen still, as still as a Michelangelo sculpture. The young sweep's heart hammered in his pigeon chest, his eyes wide open as his silent cries give way to tears, thinking to himself,' they will send George to stab me, or worse.'

George below turns to Alfred saying in a brittle worried voice "Alfie, the Boy's stuck, light a fire, now."

Alfie, startled, replied blinking," Yow' sure, really. I don't wanna'…yow' sure, really, "then he grinned, "I don't wanna'…ok," his grin faded, and he started to look frightened.

George, eyes narrowed saying in a thin reedy voice, "We aint' no choice Alfred, just do it."

Alfred stepped back and shrugged, "Naaa' we don't need ter' does' we, not yet anywoy,' soy' yow' gid' me yaw' noyf ', wull' prick the soles of his feet, that wull' mek' him cloyme,' or fall."

George, hands shaking answered through clenched teeth, "Okay, but if it goes wrong, I'll tell the ol' man it was your fault… okey dokey." His mouth snapped shut.

Alfred, knife between his yellowing teeth, scrambled up the flue writhing and swaying, legs akimbo until he saw through the black sooted obscurity the Apprentice's feet. Gently he reached up and pushed the point of the knife deep into the Apprentice's feet until like a ferret Jacob scrambled upwards fast, crying, snivelling and eventually he reached the roof top and the grey smoke-filled sky.

*

A few hours later, after lunch, a cup of weak tea, meagre single sausage, and thin sliver of mouldy crust, they arrived at Alderbrook House. It's a huge Estate which includes five tenant Farmer's cottages, brick outbuildings and acres of land. Lord Alderbrook absent, as usual, now spending most of his time in London, gambling.

Standing at the top of the double fronted flight of marble steps between white Palladian columns, George turned to face the two Sweeps, and says bossily," Mister Hemmings as' axed' me to mek' sure Silas Melbourne… the Estate manager, buys more soot from us."

"Well, I aint' climbing up any bloody tall black chimneys today, "Jacob, grimacing, said fiercely, "No."

Alfred chuckled. George said with a dismissive gesture, "Okay Jacob, go an' clean the smaller chimneys in the Farmers cottages, they're a doddle… you won't get stuck again," Jacob nodded and smiled thinly.

George turned to Alfie, "Alfie, do the main Room. "Alfie's nose flared, and he inhaled a sharp breath. "Oh… look Alfie," said George, "Look here, comes the servant, he'll show you to the room, once I've done with Melbourne, I will come and see you're okay, ".

Alfie closed his eyes and thought,' yes George …you're a smarmy bastard.'

The footman, tall, and thin with a furrowed brow, in 'civilian' mufti, wearing a dirty grey vest, black trousers with braces, off white shirt, big rip across the elbow. He looked about twenty-five years old. Irritation writ large across his ferret face, with hardly a word spoken he gestured to Alfie pointing towards the room.

Alfred was bought up short seeing the grand stairwell and its stained-glass windows. Entering the main room alone, Alfred stepped back to admire the yellow sienna marble fireplace and the portrait hung above it.

Alfred entered the cavernous fireplace. Although he would never let on, he was terrified whenever working on his own with no one below and conversed to himself.

"Right here goes, "Alfred muttered aloud lightly, sounding braver than he felt. "Gotta' watch out for the long sharp-angled flues."

In the stygian darkness he caressed the old and crumbling bricks which drip, drip, dripped soot to the grate below. The higher he climbed the tighter the chimney. Wriggling up along the quickly closing shaft he hunched his thin shoulders and pushed his top half through the narrowing gap, but the rest stayed trapped, stuck fast. But Alfred was not browbeaten, well not yet, and, elbowing and shuffling began to kick away the blockage but moved not an inch.

Alfred shuddered and said in a confidence absent voice, "I can't go forward or back, "he replied, "If I climb up… or down, I'm imprisoned, jammed. "He trembled and brushed his cheeks lightly.

Pausing, lips closed, eyes wide open but blind. He continued talking to himself, "Alfred don't do anything silly… oh god, I'm in a right fix. "His unseeing eyes in the darkness seeing nothing. Emptying his lungs, torso twisted stretching out in desperation, straining every sinew, his flailing hands seeking, but not finding any finger or foot hold, every attempt was unsuccessful.

"I'm caught in a spiders web," he said out loud, "I can't see anything …damn and blast." He again extended his hands exploring the flue walls blind, finding no hold his lips set in a grim line.

Brow puckered with anguish, Alfred let out a loud heartfelt groan in a dark frightened angry voice, "George, "he yelled, "You there, help, please… George." No reply was heard from below.

Suddenly there was a fearful grumbling noise, Alfie was engulfed by an avalanche of black soot. His coal dust coated body shook, in a voice raw and scared he pleaded," I can't see a damn bloody thing, "Alf shook his face and spine tingled with fear, "Oh help… help, George, "his voice went rough and croaky, "Err, you there, "he grunted, "Get me out, I can't move."

Tears ran down Alfie's soot-stained cheeks. In a terrified tone he cried, "I'm stuck, damn, damn." Alfie frantically wriggled and twisted, arms flailing, his hat fell into the grating below, his legs kicked out frantically, "I'm stuck, he said, "Help, "Wincing he tasted bile at the back of his throat.

"Help, I can't move one way or the other, get me out, please George… you there… Alfred you there." His courage faltered and a horrified expression crossed his face.

"George, "Alfred bellowed in a distinct thick nasal tone," I'm trapped, lord av' mercy on me, if I don't get help in a few minutes I wull' be ded'." With a sigh he covers his head in the palm of his hands. Then he frowned, made a disapproving noise with his tongue and lips.

Alfie slipped as the time aged mortar crumbled to dust. He forced back a scream, and nose flared, sweating uncontrollably, legs bent hard against the black sooty chimney wall. Between coughs and stutters he bawled, "Help, ployz' Georgie… you the'er, help, ployz' get me out." Alfie shrank back, scared stiff.

Poor Alfred, he screwed his wet eyes tight then it dawned on him the narrow chimney is totally impassable. Can't move up," Alfred said aloud, with a panicky expression across his face, "Up, down or sideways." Then he mouthed a few almost forgotten prayers, proof Sunday School meant something after all.

He rubbed his eye with a sharp knuckle, "Help! I can feel mi' strength is failing, "his mouth felt suddenly dry, "Oh lord above help me… George, help," he screamed.

Luckily, Georgie heard him and swung himself up into the flue. He leant out as far as he could until his hand gripped Alfie's foot. Then with a heave George pushed him with a huge painful surge levered him upwards inch by painful inch. Writhing and squirming Alfie, followed by George skidded down to the grate, and safety, Alfie's hands blooded and bruised.

Much later in the evening Alfred lay in his cellar again. It's dark, he's cold and hungry, no change there. He dozed fitfully, then without warning dreams he is staring into a brick chimneys Whitby jet blackness, believing he is trapped, stuck fast in the flue again. He feels soot filling his throat, his hands claw and scrape his feet kick away the sacks covering him, he awakens suddenly, and, exhausted, drifts into sleep knowing tomorrow and the following tomorrow will be the same as today.

Joseph Andriano - Love Me Tenderstem

"I can still hear screams." Tony hugged his potato-like figure and rocked back and forth on the squeaky chair in Isla's office. "They were screeching and gargling and gurgling," he said, scratching at his chunky-chip arms fretfully. "But I still don't understand why. Or how?! How could they even scream?" Flakes of skin from his eczema floated in the air like puffs of salt, and stuck to his straining, red face. "But it's also never happened before, so why now? I've cut tenderstems a thousand times and they've never screamed at me."

Isla looked up from her notepad. "Tenderstems?" she asked. "Yes."

"Broccoli?"

"Well," Tony blew his nose into his elbow, "tenderstem broccoli isn't *just* broccoli, is it? It's a way of life. It lasts forever. In sickness and in health, till death cuts us in half. It's not like the fat broccoli that looks like trees, you know that one?"

"Yes, I know what broccoli is, Tony." Isla placed the notepad on her desk facedown, so as to cover the little doodles of her ideal self; long and thin with short spiky hair, holding hands with a man in uniform. "You remember it screaming?"

"Yep. It's such a distinct scream. Like a beached whale gasping for air," Tony nodded. The chair squeaked in agreement. "I remember it like it was yesterday."

"When did it happen?" "Last night."

"Ok," Isla leaned back and eyed the walls of her office. She smiled at the replica painting of Manet's Asparagus, which hung next to her law degree. "I've always loved your painting," she said.

Tony turned to the asparagus.

"Verda loved it too," he said, hanging his crusty head over his plump belly. "But I don't do it anymore. Well, unless I'm confused."

Isla closed her blueberry eyes and breathed softly through her nose.

"Tony," she sighed, "it's not right for you to be here, but…" She lifted her notepad and eyed a gold fork on her desk. It read:

Congratulations Isla Sprigs Best Fork'n Lawyer.

Love, DC.

It always made her smile, even if his name didn't flash across her phone anymore. "Tell me what happened," she said.

"It's all hazy now," Tony began. "I rushed home and the front door was open, so I was already on edge. I walked down the hallway, which was covered in shoes. It was a mess, but I didn't want to get angry with Verda. So, I went into the kitchen to start cooking and I saw the tenderstems on the table. I couldn't believe it. First the door, then the shoes, and then the tenderstems on the table for everyone to see. I just saw red. I remember hacking away at them with the giant steak knife Verda got me for Christmas. And then," he burst into a grating screech, "they started wailing!"

"The broccoli?"

"The tenderstems. They were saying, *'why, oh why!'* and stuff. *'Please don't do this Tony!'* and *'we're sorry Tony!'* and then one said, *'I love him'* in this really little voice, like a thin, kind-hearted woman with an accent. And the other said, *'oh god, I'm sorry god!'* with this deep voice, like a muscly philanderer, but also with an accent. Have you ever heard a tenderstem do that?"

"What?"

"Call out to god." "No."

"With an accent." "No."

"It's horrible!"

"Then what happened?" asked Isla, scribbling the words between love-heart doodles and little verses: *'he loves me, he loves me not'*.

"I started eating them! They were very salty. I didn't use garlic and olive oil though like I usually would. I just used tears: salty, salty tears. But, I was so shaken that I dropped the knife and it fell straight into my big toe. See?" Tony leaned over his belly and tugged off his boot.

"Tony, I don't need to see your - oh!" Isla gasped, lifting the notepad to her face. "You left the knife in your toe?"

Tony's toes were fantastic: fat and pointy, and a blood-red orangey colour like sweet potatoes, but with freshly polished toenails. The pointy end of a silver steak knife was wedged neatly into his big-toenail.

"I had to leave the knife in my toe," he said, panting and sweating and rocking, while his chair squeaked spiritedly. "How else would you believe me about the tenderstems if you didn't see the knife in my toe?"

"Tony," Isla paused, cocking her head and admiring his French tips, "sometimes when we experience trauma, our mind will reframe a memory so that we can accept it. Are you sure this isn't all in your head?"

"It's in my toe!"

"No, as in, the broccoli screams."

"I thought that straight away. But then how can I think *'this is in my head'*, while still hearing their screams, which are also in my head? I remember everything, apart from the things I don't. You know how it is with memory; everything is so certain and then someone tells you there were no tenderstems to begin with. But the parts I do remember re-emerge vividly when I'm doing other things like sitting on the bus or painting with blood on the floor."

"Painting with blood on the floor?"

"Yes, or sitting on the bus. I know it's bizarre. But I don't want to lose Verda. I think she's in love with that German doctor from work. Gruenstiel is his name. He's staunch and muscly and has the hair of a thousand florets. I hate Gruenstiel. He's one of those half-men. He probably does push-ups and drinks green milk. He's never committed a true, unforgettable wrong like cutting the ends of screaming tenderstem or drinking blue milk. Gruenstiel: The half-man."

"Tony, why have you come here?"

"You're my lawyer. If I can't tell you I cut the ends off screaming tenderstems and am now walking around with a knife in my toe, who can I tell?"

"I'm not your lawyer anymore," she said, "but if I was, I'd advise you go to the hospital. You have a knife in your toe."

"Ahh!" Tony tensed his fists so hard they browned like overcooked dauphinois. "I can't go to the hospital. Verda works there! They'll probably just take the knife out and ask where she is. No one will believe me. I'm the victim here!" Tony pounded Isla's desk angrily and it sent the gold fork spinning into the air. It spiralled downwards and fell straight into his second toe.

"Tony, are you ok?!" asked Isla, standing up. "Oh god, we *need* to get you to a hospital." "We can't go to a hospital!" he winced; the veins on his forehead bubbled and pulsed like vibrating squiggly fries. "We can't!"

"Ok, then let me call Verda," Isla lifted her phone. "She is a doctor after all." "No, you can't call Verda either," moaned Tony. "Her phone's gone." "Tony, Verda called me yesterday. She obviously has a phone."

"Why'd she call you yesterday?" Tony's face dripped with sweat like a crisp caught in the rain. "Why?!"

"It doesn't matter why she called me," said Isla, "where's her phone?" "The – the Thames," grunted Tony.

"The Thames?"

"Yeah, you know the river?"

"Yes, I know the River Thames. Why is it there?"

"I'm not sure," Tony screeched, "I just remember watching it fly into the Thames this morning. I was on the bus here. It was in my hand, and then, all of a sudden, it leapt from my hand and spun into the river. You know these phones; it was probably an app."

"You threw her phone into the river?"

"No!" he said, his face folded into a sneer and he spoke with a dribbly spit, "it was probably an app! I thought we were friends, Isla Sprigs, that's why I painted that asparagus for you."

He turned to the asparagus on the wall. "I hate asparagus. It has no cool Chinese kale backstory. Have you ever heard an asparagus scream?"

"No."

"Yeah, me either."

Isla scrunched her face, and her insides grumbled anxiously.

"Tony," she said, rubbing her stomach to muffle its moans, "Verda called me yesterday to ask if I could represent her in your divorce."

Tony stopped rocking. The chair stopped squeaking.

"I saw it on her phone," he said, widening his eyes excitedly, "so that's why you're not my lawyer anymore?"

"Yes."

"Are you gonna turn on me too? Like the tenderstems? Like Verda?" "Where is Verda?"

Tony eyed the fork in his toe.

"Love, DC? Where is DC?" he asked.

"Why won't you remove the knife?" asked Isla. "Was the door actually left open?"

"Why won't you go to the hospital?" "Was the floor covered in shoes?"

"Why is your wife's phone in the Thames?" "Were there ever tenderstems?"

"Why would you cut the ends of tenderstems?" she asked, "They're edible."

"Ahh!" Tony's roar shook the office, rattling the painting on the wall. "You don't know what its like, do you?! To get a call from your wife saying she wants to leave you. And then to rush home and see your favourite vegetable naked and kissing some chunky bastion of green milk. I'll kill 'em!"

Tony yanked the knife and fork from his toes and lunged at the painting. He chopped at it desperately then lowered his face to the canvas and tore bits off with his mouth. "Is this what you want?" he asked, slurping and sucking and choking it down.

Isla's phone rang.

"Is that your phone?" Tony asked, nibbling on the canvas like a cat nibbling leftover mash. Isla looked at the screen. The letters *DC* flashed across it.

"Go on," said Tony, his eyes yellowed like mozzarella on a jacket potato. Isla answered.

"Hello?"

"Isla, sorry to call like this," said a flustered man, "I know it's been a while." "What's up, DC?"

"The team were called to Tony and Verda's place; the neighbours said they heard these crazy screams, like a whale gasping for air. It's a mess, there's blood and shoes and vegetables and green milk. Lots of green milk actually. Verda and that doctor Gruenstiel have been…"

Isla gasped. Tony smiled, revealing his chaotic French-fry teeth.

"Two officers are on the way to yours now, we think you're in danger. There's a painting on the floor like the one in your office."

Tony crept towards Isla.

"An asparagus, painted in blood."

Josephine Galvin - Second Person

Sunrise slices through the vertical linen blinds, forming stripes across charcoal cotton bedding. Outside, a steady hum of city traffic fails to build into weekday frenzy and a dislocated church bell rings in melancholic nostalgia. The blinds are always one quarter inch open, day and night. When you first came here you corrected what you imagined to be an oversight, only to find they had been moved back, quietly and without comment.

He is in the kitchen area preparing your muesli. You always begin the day with muesli and he always assembles it by hand. A complexity of naturally dried ingredients are kept in labelled glass cylinders on the marble work surface. Not one oat or raisin is spilled or wasted. Once, in the beginning, you'd asked for toast. We don't eat bread, he had said. You were happy to acquiesce; you were now a 'we'.

He brings in the breakfast with oat milk and a glass of filtered water, and places the items on the white rattan bedside table. Without meeting your eye, he hands you the grey tea towel that you are expected to tuck around the edge of the duvet. The emphasised precision of his action is designed to remind you to be careful. Some months earlier, you had carelessly gestured at something on the television and had knocked the bowl, spilling its contents over the unsteady woven top. Since then he had ordered, and fitted, made-to-measure glass shields to protect the tables. He has also removed the television.

He doesn't join you for breakfast, he never does, preferring to eat standing up, whilst checking his emails in the open-plan kitchen/living space. As you eat in silence, forcing fragments of goodness past the lump that seems to have developed in your oesophagus, you can hear sounds of running water. This flat boast designer facilities: power shower, infinity sink and wet room style floor. You are trying not to miss lying in a bath.

Through the now open bathroom window, more bells herald the end of early morning mass and the sounds of a radio, and of laughter, mingle with a fragrance of frying bacon in a synaesthesia of other lives. In the flat next door, Jared is opening the door to his two children. He has them every other Sunday and for a week at half-terms. Jared seems very pleasant: sad eyes, easily flustered. He always asks how you are and, although your conversations are limited, they always leave a positive imprint. He will probably pack a picnic and then hurry them out of this expensive confinement, seeking activities to fill his allotted father time. He is mindful that their exuberance may annoy neighbours. Like Alex.

The bathroom door opens and Alex returns to the bedroom wrapped in the dressing gown you bought him at Christmas. You had got it right the second time. You now know not to buy man-made fabrics.

'Shower's free.'

His eyes travel to the remnants of your meal and you both move to lift the dish.

'No, you get your shower. Oh… you've left some…' He frowns at the white bowl.

'Too much? It's exactly the same amount you always have?'

Your face tries to assemble an apologetic look but you imagine you just look vague.

'Ok I'll give you less. It's pointless wasting it. Sticks to the bowls unless you wipe it immediately.'

'Sorry…'

When you come out of the shower, Alex is already working. The double desk arrangement is filled on one half by his large flat screen computer and on the other, by files and documents stacked in orderly, almost co-ordinated, columns. A partner in an accountancy firm, he uses the weekends to catch up in the calm of the flat. You move silently around him, making yourself inconspicuous, checking your own emails on your phone.

Sounds of laughter and two sets of excited feet running, breaks in from the communal landing. Voices shout for 'Daddy'. An insistent knocking of small fists indicate that the flat's automatic closing door may have shut behind them. You suppress a desire to help, to be involved.

'Grief, get them under control', Alex mutters under his breath.

You listen as Jared opens the door, shushing whilst ushering them downstairs to planned adventures. Moving to the window you wait to see them bouncing out through the building foyer into the early spring morning. Little hands swinging rhythmically, cupped in large protective ones. You're not sure which of them you envy most.

You venture a question, 'are we doing anything later', whilst despising the echo of neediness and the way your voice cracks before you finish a sentence.

'Maybe … food, film?' I just need to finish these first.' He indicates the screen with a nod of his head. It is not an invitation to look.

Back in the bedroom you open the wardrobe in which you have a small allocated section. You were delighted when he first showed you the cleared space. It was sufficient for the Friday to Monday time you had begun to spend here and more importantly; he was making room for you. Your own house, back in Levenshulme, is nearer your workplace. You're a part-time physio. Everything in your life is now compartmentalised. Selecting jeans and jumper from limited choices, you briefly consider visiting your dad to give Alex some space. But you'd have to get the metro. The flat has an underground car park with a single allocation; your mini remains at your house.

When you'd first started staying over, one night had swiftly become two. It took another six months, and a Sunday night accountancy firm dinner, for a three-night pattern to become established. You'd imagined it was part of a natural progression. But the routine became fixed, with no variation expected or welcomed. Any traces you leave are wiped away in the week by paid domestic services. You seem unable to make a mark on your surroundings. In trying to be ideal, low maintenance, you are careful not to crayon outside your designated space, and you don't bleed over the lines.

Nor could you alter the arrangement he had deemed established. If events (largely fictional) brought you into town on a Tuesday or Wednesday, it was never convenient to stay here. He may work late; he may go to bed early. His duplicate door key remained in his wallet.

Four months into your relationship, a weekend coincided with your mum's first anniversary. You'd brought photograph of her in a small brass frame, and placed it on the single, still-empty cabinet in the lounge area. Alex had made no comment, but had appeared to listen patiently whilst claret unravelled memories. It was the first time you had not made love; instead you'd sobbed yourself to sleep whilst he lay quietly alongside you. In the morning you'd been headachy, ashamed, but he'd dismissed your concerns. You were grateful that he seemed unfazed by these excesses.

You began to relax, to imagine. On Monday when you'd unpacked your holdall back in your neglected terrace, you found her picture layered in bubble wrap, placed carefully under your unwashed laundry.

This arrangement has lasted almost two years. You are thirty-one next birthday; Alex is forty-five, and divorced.

You know nothing about Claire, other than she was an accountant also. No confidences shared; no clues provided. You lack the guidance that admittance to his past would have afforded you. You need to know what went wrong, so that you can do it differently.

You had questioned him in the darkness before sleep. When he appeared softened, receptive.

'Has there been… er… have you had many other girlfriends?'

'A few'

'Anyone in particular?'

'I don't know what you mean, exactly?'

'Apart from Claire, was there anyone serious… anyone that you loved?'

He withdrew his hand from under hers.

'I don't ask you this sort of thing, Lucy. It's the past, let it go.'

But you can't, so you giggle and dance and entertain on the side-lines. You fit in, merge, hush as appropriate. But you are shut out from the centre, the place where the grown-ups dwell. You're an apprentice, a trainee and you have no guidelines. The space for explanations remains unfilled.

There are no clues in this beautiful, clean, empty living space. No pictures of Claire. No pictures of anyone. Where intimacy could build on pillow talk regrets or sadness, there was just a gap. An untallied set of figures.

'Do you love me, Alex? 'Was that little-girl whine really you?

'Yes. Of course.'

'Why don't you tell me?'

'I just did.'

'Why don't you ever say it first.'

'Don't be silly, Lucy.'

You are not secure in what you offer. You like to cook, but Alex doesn't like cooking smells in the flat. He is irritated by evidence of neighbours' culinary endeavours, closing windows, turning on air-conditioning. It was probably lucky that he has never chosen to spend a night at your house in Levenshulme; the air is rich with delicious concoctions. You used to cook a lot for your dad and also for friends, but that all seems to have faded away. Any spare time at home is hollow, yet full of Alex, of missing Alex, of trying to fathom him. He hovers out of reach, dominating your perspective, like an exam to be taken on poor research, with insufficient revision.

Another morning passed: sitting on the bed to appear relaxed; checking emails that were mainly retail enticements; staring at the magazine you'd picked up on Friday and some leaflets from the station. Maybe you needed a job that enabled you to bring work home. You'd look more important, professional, more like Claire. She would have undoubtedly worked at the weekends; would she have thought you trivial?

Sounds percolated in from the street below; people emerging from lazy morning lie-ins to source some Sunday lunch. You show your face round the door to the lounge.

'Shall I get us some food?'

'I'll go'. He is smiling. 'Good timing, it's a natural break.'

You are disproportionality pleased with this success. You pass him his jacket as he heads for the door. He doesn't ask what you would like.

The afternoon passes companionably. After the bento box debris had been taken out to the communal bin, leaving no evidence and no scent, you are leaning into him on the leather sofa. These moments are your reward; breathing in the clean musky smell of him, his arm around you. Whilst he fast-forwards though the options menu, your mind weaves ties of permanency around your bodies and your future assumes his shape.

He has a substantial DVD collection, filed alphabetically within grey leatherette storage boxes and, as it's easier to be relaxed if he is happy, you always leave the choice to him. As the adventure movie's plot becomes more frenzied, less credible, you drift further into dreaming. You have watched this one alongside him many times. There is a part at the end when the hero is reunited with his family, a little boy clinging to his neck. You look sideways at his face, still creased with vicarious intensity. You know it's the wrong time. You know it will spoil the atmosphere, but you do it anyway.

'I bet you were cute at that age'. The margins of a smile encourage you. You carry on.

'I can imagine you with a little boy like that'.

He stiffens. He knows what's coming. But you've started now.

'I think you'd be surprised how much your feelings would change if you had your own.'

'No. Absolutely not. No.'

'Why though. You never say why?' Your voice raises. You are losing something here.

'Don't try to analyse me, Lucy. I've answered your question. Many times.'

Although your bodies are still touching, the air between them is splintered with ice and disappointment. If you move you will be forced to choose one side of this unbridgeable chasm.

He never asks your feelings on this, and you lack the courage to explain your growing need. It would serve no purpose. A pervasive image of this unconceived child is no longer confined to dreams, he is always with you. His outline occupies a booster seat in the restaurants you go to; he is excited by trains. He skips alongside you at the market near your house, and you buy strawberries to eat on the walk home. He plays around your feet even now, as you sit on Alex's cream leather sofa. An only child yourself, you envisaged a large Italian-style family, rambunctious, messy, loving. But now you'd be happy with one. Self-preservation leaves this unsaid, and shame makes you mute. Further conversations would only hasten a finality you are ill prepared for.

You have another evening left before tomorrow's return train journey; a journey weighted by transitory belongings and forensic analysis. Is it the end of one more romantic weekend or a recurring rejection, another failure?

He chooses the restaurant, a noodle bar, he selects the wine, and he pays. You insist on getting the bill roughly once in every four times to keep your dignity; he allows it if he judges the place reasonable enough. The disparity of your earnings makes this forgivable. He is animated tonight, complimentary even, and you would normally shine in response, ensuring your last night makes a positive impression. For once you fail to perform as expected. You are not sure he actually notices.

And tomorrow, after the repeated breakfast routine, the kiss and his early departure, you have the space to yourself for the couple of hours before your train. An empty time, a disconnect. A time when the lack of you is reflected more strongly. Without Alex here, there is no one here.

As always, you repack your clothing from its allocated space: watching as his clothes swell and expand into the area vacated. You take your small washbag from the pristine bathroom with no bath, and you complete a cursory, and unnecessary, check to ensure you leave nothing behind. You do not need to pull the door behind you; its automated mechanism ensures that it begins to shut slowly as you pass through. A soft creak heralds the beginning of this closure. You stand facing outwards, listening for the click as the metals meet, and finally the harsh dead clank of bolts engaging. You are now locked out. As you have always been.

And when your train is called and you manoeuvre yourself and your holdall through the turnstiles on the platform, treading lightly in the footsteps marking almost two years, you will wonder how long it will take him to fill the tiny gap that you leave behind.

Josephine Nolan - The Things We Do for Love

When she heard the news, she wondered if he was trying to punish her. Amanda lay back on her bed. The tears had dried on her face. As she stared at the ceiling, she tried to remember the signs along the way. They must have been there, but she chose to ignore them.

Amanda had met Oliver at a dance. She had watched him dancing with other girls, saw them smiling up at him. He had them twirling this way and that, showing off their net petticoats fashionable at the time. He was very handsome, his black curls shining under the lights. 'She Wore a Red Dress' was being sung, and the violin and bass guitar held her attention. She turned sharply as someone tapped her shoulder.

Oliver stood over her, all six feet of him. 'Would you like to dance?' he said.

She could not believe her luck. With his arm around her, gliding around the floor, she felt like Ginger Rogers.

On her birthday, eight months after they met, he took her to a Greek restaurant. It looked like a Victorian house from the outside.

'Nice to see you again sir' the waiter said to Oliver and guided them to a table near the window.

That night Oliver proposed to Amanda.

Amanda's father was a quiet man and didn't stand on ceremony. Her mother was delighted that her eldest daughter was getting married. She said,

'Who wouldn't love such a gorgeous boy. You're a lucky girl Amanda. I just want you to be happy'. That was enough for Amanda. She couldn't wait to show her sister the ring.

At work, the girls gathered around as Amanda extended her left hand. She was the first to get engaged in her small group, and they were all a bit envious, though genuinely happy for Amanda.

'When is the big day? Have you decided yet?'

Paula worked beside Amanda and wanted to have another look at the ring.

'It's gorgeous Amanda. It must have cost a fortune'.

Amanda looked down at the beautiful solitaire. She had no idea how much Oliver had paid, as he had gone into another room with his cheque book.

'Have you met his mother yet?' Paula enquired.

'He's taking me over to meet her next weekend. I've no idea what she's like'.

'I'll find out soon enough', she thought.

To Amanda's delight, her mother offered to make her wedding dress. They arranged a weekend to go shopping for the material. It was a bit soon to book the venue, but she had her heart set on a smart hotel just outside the city. The gardens would be beautiful for a June wedding.

Oliver had worked his way up through his company and was now the top car salesman. He had bought a new car, a dark blue Ford Zodiac, straight from the showroom, 'perks of the job', he told Amanda. He sometimes did promotions at weekends that took him all over the country. Oliver was an only child. His father had passed away a few years previously. He lived with his mother in Swords.

Amanda was introduced to Mrs. Hill a few weeks after the engagement.

'How lovely' she said with a tight smile. 'I'm so happy for you both. Don't be in too much of a hurry to get married' she said. 'You're still young. Enjoy yourselves for a while'.

Oliver helped his mother bring in the tray of cups and saucers, and a plate of biscuits. His mother followed behind with a pot of tea and left it carefully on the table. She sat down beside Amanda, while Oliver poured the tea and passed the cups around. It was a very formal room, good mahogany dining table and chairs. Dark mustard velvet curtains. The brown carpet had a floral design with a hint of gold. There were a few landscapes here and there, with a large gold framed mirror over the open fireplace. There was a piano to one side of the room, displaying two photographs. One was a black and white wedding photograph, Oliver's mother, dressed in a two-piece suit and hat, standing beside her husband. Neither were smiling. There was one of Oliver, dressed in his cap and gown. He had never mentioned going to college.

Oliver's mother wasn't at all what she had imagined. A good-looking woman but quite austere. She sat straight backed on the chair. Their grey tabby cat weaved its way around the legs of the chairs. Amanda bent to stroke it. The cat leapt up on Amanda's lap, purring away happily. After talking about the cat, things got more comfortable. Oliver was relaxed and a lot of the time the conversation was between him and his mother. Amanda was happy to sit and listen. When he was happy, she was happy.

Trying to get information from Oliver was difficult at the best of times. There were things about the wedding plans she wanted to discuss, but he would say,

'It's all about the bride, so do what you think is best'.

She pinned him down a few times, but it created an atmosphere between them. She was annoyed at his lack of interest.

One evening they met for a cup of coffee in town. He seemed distant. She wanted to talk about how many people were coming to the wedding. His lack of interest was the last straw.

'Look, if you don't want to get married, just say so. I really don't care' and with that, she picked up her handbag and headed out onto the street.

It was raining. She put her scarf over her hair and headed for the bus stop. She looked behind her as the bus came along, sure he would have followed her. The bus stopped and she hopped on.

A few days passed and there was no word from Oliver. Amanda was sure he would have phoned her at work. By the middle of the following week, she decided to phone him. She was told he was out sick and, no, they didn't know when he would be back. She confided in Paula.

'Let him stew', Paula said.

'How can I if he's sick?' Amanda said.

She could not get him out of her mind. Her boss piled the work on all day. When she had finished one tape, there was another waiting to be done. It took her mind off Oliver for a while. By Friday, there was still no word. She decided to get the bus over to his house in Swords.

The weather had turned cold. Sleet had been forecast. Amanda wrapped up well with a hat and a thick scarf. Her fur lined boots would keep her feet warm. When the bus eventually came along, the conductor would only allow two people on board. Amanda was glad she was at the front of the queue. Even though she had boots on, her feet were freezing. The windows had steamed up. It was hard to see where the bus was going. When she saw the church by the traffic lights, she knew where she was. The conductor called out 'Swords Town Centre' and Amanda made her way down the bus.

Oliver lived about a fifteen-minute walk from the bus stop. The path was slippery. She nearly lost her balance a few times. Amanda looked up at the house as she opened the front gate. She stood in the porch and knocked twice. She could see a shadow inside the glass panels. The door opened. Oliver's mother stood there.

'May I come in?' Amanda said.

She was frozen through at this stage.

'Come into the kitchen Amanda, its warmer there'.

'Take your coat off. Sit down and I'll make some tea. She pointed to an armchair beside the range. 'You must be frozen' Mrs. Hill said, as she busied herself putting the kettle on and settling a few cups.

Amanda looked around the kitchen. The window over the sink looked out to the garden. She could see a few tall trees standing like skeletons, waiting for the spring. There was a small table with four chairs. An old dresser stood by one wall, with matching blue plates and saucers, cups hanging on hooks. Everything was neat and in its place. Amanda could feel herself beginning to thaw. She wrapped her hands around the cup of tea. Oliver's mother left a plate of Madera slices on a table beside her.

'How is Oliver, Mrs. Hall?' Amanda asked.

'Well, I haven't heard from him since he left, but he was very excited about the new position'.

Amanda's mouth dropped. 'What' she said, 'What new position? I thought he was sick!'

'I thought you knew', Mrs. Hall said.

She was numb as she sat on the bus on her way home, but not from the cold. Amanda had asked Oliver's mother for his address, but Mrs. Hall didn't have one, yet. It was all so vague, and incredible. According to his mother, he had been offered a promotion, in London, and had to take it up straight away.

Amanda knew his mother took no pleasure being the bearer of such news. As the bus took her home, Amanda tried to remember the details of the conversation, but her mind was going blank. What would she tell her family? Should she just come out with it the way she had heard it from Oliver's mother? Should she tell a different story to save her embarrassment and humiliation?

Her mother was putting some groceries away when Amanda walked into the kitchen.

'Hi love. Put the kettle on', her mother said. 'I think it will freeze again tonight'.

She looked around for a moment, then continued emptying out the groceries. Amanda filled the kettle and put two cups and saucers on the table.

'Are you alright Amanda?' her mother said. Amanda continued making the tea.

'He's gone, mum!' she said.

Amanda's mother stopped what she was doing. She said,

'Sit down love' and drew out a chair for her. Amanda told her mother everything.

On Monday morning, Amanda phoned in sick. She decided to ring Oliver's place of work. The receptionist asked who she was.

'Oh' the receptionist said, 'I'll put you through to Mr. Clarke'.

Amanda had to get to the truth of what was going on. Mr. Clarke came on the phone, and he too, asked who she was.

'Have you got an address for him', he asked. Amanda explained that she had only just heard he had moved to London.

'Well, when you do, you can let me know, before I get a warrant out for his arrest'. Amanda was in shock.

'Why would you do that?' she asked.

'I'll have him in court for fraud' he bellowed down the phone. 'I took him under my wing like a son, and that's the way he repays me'.

Amanda put the phone down. Her own family were bewildered. Oliver seemed like such a nice, straightforward boy.

'There was something about him' her father said one day. Amanda turned on the spot.

'What do you mean? I thought you liked him!' After a moment, his father said,

'There was something Amanda. I couldn't put my finger on it. Where does a young man get money for an engagement ring and a new car within a few weeks?'

'If he was still here, you wouldn't even think like that' Amanda said, storming out of the kitchen.

'I'm sorry love" her father said, but he knew Amanda hadn't heard.

It was coming into Spring. You could feel the warmth in the sun. The cherry tree in the front garden was showing off its pink blossoms, branches cascading delicately. Little shoots were peering through the earth, willing the sun to spread its warmth. Life was coming back in the park opposite the house, as clumps of snowdrops and crocus appeared. At home, things seemed to go on as normal. The family got up and made their way to work each morning. Her mother thought Amanda was losing weight. Amanda responded with

'Mum, I'm fine'.

At work she side-tracked the questions about the wedding as best she could, or just spoofed when she had to. Paula was her only confidante. Sometimes they went out for lunch together. It was the only place safe from twitching ears. Paula never pressed her but was always there if Amanda wanted to talk. Sometimes she thought she would explode. There were so many unanswered questions. And, despite the hurt, she still loved Oliver.

Amanda still wore her ring, but now it was only for show and to stop questions at work. She was sure Oliver would walk through the door one day and explain away the accusations. Coming up to Easter, she decided to visit Oliver's mother.

Amanda bought a bunch of daffodils at the shop beside the bus stop. No matter how the visit went, she felt sure his mother would appreciate the bright yellow trumpets. The bus flew along. She was in Swords before she knew it. As she walked up the road towards Oliver's home, doubts began to fill her mind.

'I've come this far' Amanda thought, 'there's no point in turning back'.

She was getting more nervous by the minute. 'I'll just write a note and leave it with the flowers in the porch' she thought. She even hoped

Oliver's mother was out.

'Hello Amanda, you'd better come in'.

Oliver's mother didn't seem surprised by her visit. She held the door open and gestured for Amanda to go on down the hall, to the kitchen. The house was warm, she could feel the heat making her cheeks tingle. When she pushed the kitchen door open, she was stuck to the spot. Oliver was sitting down at the kitchen table. It was set for two, and he had made a start on his fried eggs, sausages and bacon. There was toast in a rack in front of him. Words failed her for a few minutes. Mrs. Hall came in behind her and pulled out a chair.

'Sit down Amanda and I'll make you some tea'.

She took Amanda's coat and switched on the electric kettle.

'What the hell are you doing here? I thought you were in London'.

Amanda was still standing, staring at a very relaxed looking Oliver. He didn't get up and come towards her. Amanda was staring at him, waiting for an explanation.

'You heard about the bit of trouble I had at work then', he said.

'I was told you had taken money. How could you have just left without telling me'.

Amanda was beside herself. She couldn't get over his casual attitude.

'And all the time you've been away, not one phone call? I was at my wits end', she said.

At last, he got up and stood behind her, his hands on her shoulders. Instinctively, she stood up, and was in his arms. The tears fell, in spite of herself.

'I've missed you so much' she sobbed. Oliver's mother left the room.

'I have to go back Amanda. Mam has already paid back the money I owed. It was either that or prison. I can't work here again Amanda. They wouldn't touch me with a barge pole in this industry'.

They were facing each other beside the kitchen table. Oliver explained that he owed a lot of money, living on the '*never*-*never*', as her own mother would say. Things just piled up.

'I took some money each time I did a cash sale. It all mounted up and got out of control. I was out of my depth until finally, I knew judgement day wasn't far off. I couldn't think straight Amanda, couldn't see a way out'.

'Why didn't you tell me what was going on?' she said.

'I couldn't tell anyone. I just had to get out', he said. There was a pause. 'Would you come back with me Amanda? We could make a go of it in London. I don't have a proper place right now, but in a few months, we could get a flat together'.

Amanda wanted so much to say 'Yes, of course she would go, anywhere he asked'. Her heart was yearning to be with him, to make a life with him. She looked into his appealing blue eyes, touched his beautiful thick black curls. She wanted to kiss his lips at that very moment, but there was something nagging her. She wasn't sure what it was.

'Where are you staying over there?' she asked. 'Why couldn't you send me your address?'

'It took me a while to find a place Amanda. It wasn't easy'. He hesitated for a few minutes before continuing.

'I met someone and I'm sharing. It's only temporary'. Her heart seemed to drop at the words *'I met someone'*. She watched him. She could see his lips moving, but he seemed to be far away. She put her hand on the table to steady herself.

'You've met someone Oliver?'

'She's just putting me up for a while. There's nothing in it' he said.

Amanda felt like lurching at him, giving him a slap.

Mrs. Hall was putting the vase of daffodils on the telephone table. Amanda couldn't remember there being a telephone there on her last visit. The fading light was coming through the panes of glass on the front door. Amanda felt a chill going through her.

Mrs. Hall said 'Thank you for the lovely flowers. Look after yourself, Amanda'.

She opened the door and stood there as Amanda made her way down the path to the gate, and down the road. Amanda didn't look back. Oliver didn't come after her. Thankfully, the bus soon came along. As she sat there, Amanda twisted the engagement ring a few times on her finger. Then she slipped it off and put it into her pocket.

Julie Wiltshire - Web of Deceit

A wizened old man sips his beer. His fingers trace a migratory scar trailing through his wispy hair. He peers blindly into the police office window opposite the pub, deep in thought.

Frank, a morose bugger, straddles the corner of his pockmarked cluttered desk, swinging his scuffed right carbon boot. He takes a long drag on his cigarette, leans his head back and menacingly blows a smoky halo. "You don't need a halo where you're going Frank," Linda mocks.

Frank and Linda duck their darts, with flights of loathing. Linda squealed on Frank five years previously, misconduct concerning hit and run case. Frank bristles at the hard hearted, blonde haired Linda. She flirts in her mourning suit, her inviting ample bust gushes over the top of her starched white blouse showing a hint of a hooker. Most fancy their chances, but Linda knows the testosterone office is just a junkie's vein, full of pricks. She is married, but that ranks low in her life.

"Here run your eyes over this lot." She scatters the breadcrumbs of paper over Frank's desk, feeding her bird of prey on dregs of death. With a defiant death rattle Frank clears his throat. He hopes for chunks of succulent flesh he can sink his teeth into, not tiny morsels. Linda who always had a grudging respect for Frank ponders on what he will do after his retirement in a few weeks. His clothes reek of loneliness, faded shirt, worn out collar. The top button swings like a fallen trapeze artist hanging by a thread in his safety harness. A kedge-belly peeps from his shirt, forty years of fast foods and fat sugared doughnuts, oozing blood. "We have to be seen going through the motions with this case Frank, but it's only an old bloke." The paragon of virtue, the pretender dispassionately drifts through the door of the CID room. I'm an old codger now, he ponders.

Frank slides his small wiry frame off the desk. He fingers inside his pocket and retrieves his worn snapshot of Rosie, taken from him three years into their marriage. Effervescent eyes gaze towards him, dark ringlets coil around a pallid face, pouting lips, too delicate to kiss. Road kill Rosie, pickings on a tarmac platter for a murder of crows. Frank crumples into the weary weather beaten leather chair, replacing the photo. Defeated he thumbs through the post-mortem paperwork.

October 2010. William deceased, 85 years of age, discovered on bedroom floor. Second wife says he fell out of bed, stepson says he fell down the stairs. A coroner's report states unnatural causes.

Examination

Elderly white male of small build. Abrasion over lower right flank 20 x 10mm. Abrasion on lateral right buttock/upper right thigh 20 x 20mm. Bruise on the posterior right forearm 90 x 70mm also laceration. The right clavicle fractured 7cm from the sternoclavicular joint. Right third and sixth ribs both fractured posteriorly. Intrathoracic haemorrhage.

Frank lurches forward and reads on. Poor Bill smashed to pieces like a china plate on a kitchen floor.

Frank makes some fleeting calls. The stale fug is buzzing with the hum of heartless homicides. A round faced clinging clock mocks the hours, peering from the peppermint dappled walls. Nobody works on his beat. A brown wasted Wilton paws the floor, a mishmash of pounded mesh trails to the door. A hanging fluorescent corpse with an impediment blinks his eye. Frank heaves himself up flattening his dishevelled grey polyester suit which he had thrown himself into. He uses the dog and bone.

Frank arrives at the scene of the crime. A three bedroomed ticky-tacky terraced house, which the council knocked up in the fifties. He plods down the concrete cancerous path pointing to a green peeling door. The alabaster lace twitches. The croupier enters holding up his ace warrant card with pride. The brittle Barbara Cartland of 80 years, dressed in pinks and pearls sits silently, not showing her hand. Her manacled sons, still attached by their umbilical cords hover around their mum with no sign of emotion. Gladys cocks her head to one side. Her left lower lip droops for effect. She dribbles drivel about finding Bill dead in the morning by his bed. Frank clocks the sons, one a slim shifty silent type, the other a bumbling guy with startled bleached hair and baby blue eyes. Both poorly dressed, which ring alarm bells. They are playing their parts of being the devoted sons but knew what was in it for them as the mother had succeeded their stepfather. Frank has seen strange stories play out before him where money is concerned. "Which one of you is Ian?" Frank asks. "I am, replies the obese of the two. "Why did you give a statement to the police officer. It should have just been your mother?" "The young police officer took two statements, I tried to help mum to remember as she was confused. Firstly she told me Bill, who wasn't well, had fallen out of the bed, and then she said he had fallen down the stairs" quivers Ian. Frank scribbles frantically in his dog eared notebook. Without raising his eyes, he makes a call to collect more information from other family members, and retreats.

Frank lights up another fag in his car. He reclines surrounded by discarded food wrappings and empty open mouthed fag packets screaming "Smoking Kills." He slowly draws on his cigarette, savouring the second, and exhales. The grey smog crawls up his face. The gasping engine of the car splutters to life and Frank speeds away in his Cortina. Next stop to see the dead man's offspring.

The door of the grand Cotswold home is opened by a smart woman called Jenny. Not short of a bob or two here thinks Frank. Sprawled in the lounge on the Regency striped sofa is Dave, the younger sibling. Frank notes his frayed jeans, jaded t/shirt emblazoned with "Ark at Ee." The marionette Dave cracks his fingers and fidgets. His legs twitch uncontrollably on their invisible strings. Frank realises a slug of booze would dampen Dave's nerves. Frank spots that Dumpy Dave looks worn out mentally. Bound to be controlling wife problems ponders Frank, it usually is. Frank notices Dave's wedding ring which he fiddles with and assesses that another poor sod is probably drowning at the bottom of a beer bottle.

Veiled in domesticity, Jenny fluffs in her nesting box, and makes Frank a cup of tea (he desperately wants another cigarette but dare not smoke in her lounge). He asks Dave for his recollections.

Frank listens intently to Dave's tale of events. "I got a call from Gladys 8 o'clock on Sunday morning saying she couldn't wake up dad who was on the floor. I told her to phone 999. I arrived at dad's house fifteen minutes later. Gladys hadn't bothered to call the ambulance or the police. I did, but it was too late." Frank slides his nicotine stained fingers through his thinning hair, and clears his throat. Jenny's façade crumbles, her eyes cup the silent tears, her upper lip quivers slightly. "Dad was stiff, his open mouth frozen with shock. The police hid the rest of his body from me with a blanket before I was allowed to go into the bedroom. He was like the painting of "The Scream, except with false teeth in." Frank is welded to the conversation. "His whistler was in his ear as well," wheezes Dave. "He lived across the road from the White Lion and was glad he couldn't hear chucking out time when he took his aid out to sleep. It was odd he still had it in and his teeth?" In unison Frank and Dave clear their choking phlegm. Frank's eyes ping pong across the room. "Shall I carry on?" asks Jenny. Frank nods. "Gladys and dad were rowing the night before dad's death. I heard them on my answerphone. I wish I hadn't deleted the call. They were leaving a message saying they weren't coming in the morning for their usual coffee, and Glady's was yelling at dad to put the phone down." "Does your father drive to your house?" "Yes." Jenny continues. "When I arrived at the house the following morning Dave told me dad was dead. I rushed to comfort Gladys who looked surprisingly silent and sat and dressed. To let Dave in she must have stood on a chair to unbolt the top lock. She supposedly couldn't walk and was unstable without her heavy sticks so this was strange. The lounge was sprayed with blood. Gladys needed the toilet, I helped her upstairs. I noticed blood up the stairs and spots on the lounge door, also there were pools of blood on the window sills. Nothing made sense. Gladys's emotionally retarded sons appeared and stood in silence not attempting to comfort their mother or help to clear up the blood." "I busied around with cloth in hand to wipe as much of dad's blood from the surfaces checking with the police if it was alright to do so. Frank pricks his ears up. He clears his throat once again and reaches into his pocket for his putcher to catch his mucus eels. "I want the telephone calls checked the night before dad's death from their land line," Jenny begs. "Fine," replies Frank.

Frank makes his way back to the office, which is a grey stone affair covered in snatches and grabs of graffiti (not Banksy's) just off Nelson Street, in the heart of Bristol. He eases himself out of the car. The magnetic force of the Red Bull opposite draws him in through the cheerless rays of the afternoon sun. He pauses in the doorway and lights up another fix, a few heavy desperate drags and carelessly flicks the butt away.

The pub has seen better days. A stagnant musty stench of stale beer and damp mingle with the acrid aroma of toilets. Sticky tables covered in faecal ringed mats, and back breaking chairs rest on a gloopy Axminster, which delights in sucking the squelching shoes. Rows of pewter tankards droop dejectedly from the ceiling staring through a mist of dust. "Hi Frank," says creepy Colin. The slightly sweating, middle aged primate poser stalks the bar. His rolled shirt sleeves hug his elbows, exposing his hirsute tattooed dragging arms. "Starting early today Frank, what's your poison?" "A pint of Courage Best, please mate. Alcohol makes the world a kinder place." Frank downs the frothing pint, with a chalked isogloss mapping the upper lip, to the piped music "Won't Go Quietly" by Example, and scuttles off to the office.

Frank's hunch pays off. After an hour he finds a file on the thin shifty hound from Hades. He ran a massage parlour and brothel near a secondary school in the East End of London. He has done time. That's why John could not make eye contact, he had history.

The phone rings, Jenny is flustered. "This might be irrelevant Inspector, but a few months before dad died, he arrived at my house and was in pain retrieving his arm from his jacket. He told me he'd taken a tumble in the garden. Two weeks later he had two black eyes and a small scar across the bridge of his nose. He said he had bumped into a door." "What's this leading to?" "I don't know," says Linda, "Sorry I bothered you," and hangs up, too worried to reveal the horror that is keeping her awake at night.

Days later Frank, who feeds on facts not predetermined guesses, was following up on all leads. The land lines in Glady's house were checked, but did she have a mobile? Jenny's daughter swore she had? Gladys snapped no. The funeral was allowed to take place and the inquest would be held in due course.

All were summoned to Jenny and Dave's childhood home in Oak Drive, Avonmouth for the funeral arrangements.

"What favourite suit would you like the deceased to be buried in," innocently asks the vicar. Gladys replies "Bury him in a shroud, they are blue, blue was his favourite colour." "Did I hear you right?" snaps Dave. Gladys's eyes flash with danger, the room closes in. Jenny and Dave immediately knew they were going to be stamped out on the decision making as Glady's was his wife and didn't want to pay for any service sheets for the funeral with Bill's photo on.

The funeral was a stark affair. A few loyal stragglers from Bill's Bowling Club showed their faces. The flittermouse arrived in a wheelchair, flanked by her black vampires who hung by her side. The rancid reel, wrapped up in herself, had never used a wheelchair before. She wanted the sympathy vote. Everyone at the funeral was fooled by Gladys's fabricated flimflam of frailty. Jenny waited with baited breath for flashes of lightning to strike Gladys, and the church crosses to spin. Jenny and Dave clung to each other, the blood ties stronger than ever.

Jenny and Dave met Frank again. Jenny told him "We went to see Gladys. We were told dad hadn't left a will. Although dad lived frugally with Gladys for 35 years after mum left him, he recently received considerable inheritance money from his cousin. We asked if we could have one last look in his bedroom. There were drawers choked with paperwork, sealed in clear plastic bags. I found a framed photo of dad and I discarded on top of his wardrobe. Why? "Was it Glady's who threw it up there in her jealousy or had dad thrown it up there so the witch was happy." A woman always knows the whiles of a woman better than any man.

"I wanted his bowling bag" mumbles Dave wanting any little memento of his dad. His palms sweat. A rash snakes across his neck. Panting he reaches into his pocket for his blue plastic asthma inhaler, and takes two puffs. Dave wishes he could have a swift drink. Jenny jogs her memory and recalls what Ian's wife said quietly at the funeral to Dave "Whatever has she done this time to her third husband?"

Dave realizes after receiving nothing from his dad there is one thing he has, revenge. He has his dad's ashes. He was the one who signed the papers at the funeral directors. He is the only one who can remove them. Frank tells him to take control of his dead father's ashes, man up and do what he needs to do. After all Glady's can scream and shout for a few weeks but it will all be over.

"What the hell are we doing here?" "Don't blaspheme in the graveyard," Jenny replies. She reaches into her handbag and retrieves a sheet of paper. Sobs explode through a plethora of words "Do not stand at my grave and weep…" On a bleak December morning in Dunster two leaded soldiers stand to attention, swallowed up in grief. The sympathetic needles of rain the polished face of the Bristol Channel with tears. Jenny and Dave scatter the blanket of ashes of their father over the sodden granite graves of their grandmother and grandfather, knowing in their hearts that's where their dad would want to rest. His sister was also in the next grave.

Only Jenny, Dave and Jenny's daughter turn up at the Coroner's Court for the inquest. The contradictory statements were read out. "We do not have sufficient evidence to prosecute therefore the verdict is Accidental Death," announces the Coroner. The assistant shakes his head in disbelief. The Coroner apologises to the three family members after the court case but apparently there was not enough evidence to prosecute, and we would never know what really happened that night.

On his final day at the grubby office Frank lights up another cigarette. He remembers Ian said Bill was not a well man. Ian was lying. Frank had done his paperwork. Bill's doctor told him William had a medical two weeks before he died and was healthy for his age, bowling three times a week. Frank knew he was still driving his car over to Jenny's every week for coffee. Bill was unbelievably incredible fit, but where did he get all his bruising over several weeks and what happened on the night of his death to produce all that amount of blood left all over the house. Nothing made sense.

Did the young police office being his first week at work take all the necessary information down correctly when taking the wife and stepson's statements. Frank thought he should have been in short trousers he was so young.

The tough old weather-beaten cop feels niggled. He taps his desk over and over again. Something is missing. Bill might have been old but Frank won't dismiss him because of his age. Undeterred Frank makes one last phone call and like a Jack Russell that has spotted a rabbit makes a dash.

He rings the rusty doorbell of the old lady's house and Gladys calls out "The door is ajar, come on in dear." She is sat centre stage, still playing the frail old lady leading role with her hands hugging her head. "Sorry to bother you madam but I have a few questions I want clarified, as I am still not happy about your husband's death." "First of all my dear," Gladys trills, "Could you pass me my glasses on the floor I think they're by the side of my armchair as I'm finding it difficult to get up at my age. Frank's not much older than her creaks his knees as he bends down to feel around the chair.

In the corner of the room destiny awaits. With pin prick eyes the heartless black widow looks down on her prey caught in the spun web of her salivated lies. She silently slides her crooked claw under the settee and grasps her weighty blood stained walking stick.

Frank could remember no more.

Kay Inckle - The Virgin Mothers

"I'm not a virgin; I just don't have sex with men."

Eve looked at me and a bead of sweat formed at the nape of my neck and trickled down my back. I cleared my throat and attempted to meet her huge dark eyes with an assuredness that equalled hers but that was quite a challenge. Not just because of the certainty of her gaze, but also because I desperately trying not to let my eyes drop to the naked, brown breast that her baby daughter was suckling from. I wished she hadn't mentioned sex. I was already struggling to keep my mind from contemplating my own mouth working that nipple, and now that was pretty much all I could think about. I knew I was flailing, at risk of making a complete bollocks of this interview and of myself. Of course I've seen women breastfeeding before and I don't usually pay much attention. I don't know why she affected me so much. She was a weird combination of things, this Eve. She had a kind of uber-femininity about her, but not the usual type. She wasn't all dolled up and coy with big flirty eyelashes or anything like that. She wasn't even wearing make-up so far as I could tell, and she was dressed in a simple loose white shirt and slim fitting purple pants that showed her curves. But there was this vibe about her, like she had an extra dose of femaleness or something. Whatever it was, it was powerful, and it was making a total mess of me. I could see why they picked her to be the spokeswoman for them, the virgin mothers, or The Gynarchists as she pointedly reminded me.

"Gynarchist," she explained, as if she was talking to an educationally sub-normal ten-year-old, "It's an amalgamation of 'gyn' as in genecology, the female reproductive system, and anarchist as in the complete eradication of all current structures of power."

I nodded, trying to rein in my thoughts and get things back on track. Initially I had thought that being picked for the big interview was a major coup, but now I had my doubts. Surely it would have been better if a woman did this? It was a bit unfair to expect me to sit here and look at her with one boob out and talk about sex and keep myself from melting into a drivelling wreck. I began to wonder if this was actually some kind of set up and if Maria had something to do with it. I know she doesn't like me. She's one of those bitter old career women who was so desperate to succeed that she forgot to have any fun in her life and now she resents anyone, especially men, who manage to do well *and* have a good time. Maybe she signed me up for this deliberately knowing that Eve would make a complete dick of me. Well, I would just have to prove her wrong.

Even so, I was desperate to loosen my tie and ease my collar, but I knew how that would look. Who was it that decided men should always wear suits for the TV news anyway? It's barbaric under all these lights. Eve, in contrast, looked incredibly cool and solid: unshakeable, as if she really did have access to some kind of hidden source of knowledge rather than just being the leader of a gang of bonkers lesbians.

"So," I replied, introducing a hint of condescension but keeping it friendly at the same time, "You've found a new way to make babies that doesn't involve men?"

"It doesn't involve men, their sperm or any of their biological matter," Eve confirmed matter-of-factly, as if it was as unremarkable as stating that the sun gave off heat and light. I expected her to keep talking but she didn't say anything else.

"So how do you do it then?" I probed, putting on the kind of smile and tone that I would use to coax a shy pre-schooler into showing me their painting.

Her eyes bored into me and I could feel myself rapidly losing control of the entire interview. It was no good trying to play power games with her, she made all my tactics pathetically transparent. She kept her eyes fixed on me and took her time deciding whether and how she was going to answer. She knew that millions of viewers were hanging on her every word, assured of their interest in her and not me. She had all the power; I was just the annoying prick who kept getting in the way. I thought about saying something else; trying to provoke her into an answer by being a bit confrontational. I could have said that we all know it isn't possible to make a baby without any sperm, that's human biology one-o-one. But I decided to keep my mouth shut, gambling that if I gave her some space she would talk. And she did.

"The ovum; *the egg,*" she explained as if I was too thick to know what an ovum was, "Always carries an x chromosome. The sperm carries an x or a y. All males have the female x chromosome and are effectively part female."

I worked on keeping an interested but neutral face. I was wondering if she was going to get on to the tosh about how the y chromosome is just a deformed x, a biological anomaly. I'd read a bit about that in the briefing for the interview. They think that males originated as an aberration in nature and have only managed to survive through violent oppression of other living things.

Eve carried on with the biology lesson: "When the sperm enters the egg, the egg starts dividing and develops into an embryo which carries its own x chromosome and either an x or a y from the sperm."

I wondered if I should hurry her to the point since none of this explained how they were supposedly making babies without sperm. But I kept quiet, it seemed to be my best tactic so far.

"In nature there are some very rare instances where an egg will begin to divide and form itself into an embryo without the introduction of a sperm. The baby always has x chromosomes and is therefore always female."

I kept holding back, she was finally opening up and any interruption from me would only have closed her down again. Penetration, I thought to myself with a smile deep inside, any penetration from me would stop her talking.

Eve continued, "We have found that a combination of plant extracts which have progesterone-mimicking properties can be used to stimulate the ovum into self-division when consumed immediately prior to and during ovulation."

I seized my opportunity to interject a moment of clarity for the viewers, "So you are using plant extracts to stimulate unfertilised eggs to develop into babies?"

"That's right," she smiled at me and for the first time since we had been introduced it looked genuine. "We are creating a community of women. Women who live sustainably, without causing harm to any living things, human or non-human. We live in complete harmony with the earth, and not only without depleting natural resources, but also by restoring what has been harmed by *man*."

She said "man" like it was a swear word and I could feel myself starting to tune out. My mind kept wandering to what it would be like to make a baby with her in the good old-fashioned way. I don't know why she was having this effect on me. I'm not normally attracted to black women, or mixed race, or women of colour, or whatever the correct word is. It's not that I'm racist or anything, I'm not. It's just more natural to be attracted to people of the same race. I'm sure there is a sound evolutionary reason for it. I forced myself to return my attention to what she was saying, I needed to get in with some good challenges and it looked like she was going to give me some easy wins pretty soon.

"We, The Gynarchists, are the only possibility for the continuation of life on earth," she stated with the clam assuredness of a scientist. "If current structures continue the planet will be uninhabitable in less than fifty years. We don't have time to develop technological solutions or to work towards becoming carbon neutral, we have to find a way of living that both honours and restores life *now*."

"But why does that not involve men?" I asked, posing the question that I knew the viewers would want her to answer.

"It's men who kill each other, fight wars, trade in human and non-human lives. It's men who cause most of the violence, pain and destruction on this planet. If you think about it rationally, less men equals less violence and destruction, it's very simple. The Global North has long been calling for population control in the Global South in order to alleviate human suffering and environmental degradation. What we are proposing is just as logical – even more so given that the Global North is having the most deleterious impact on the planet. We have to be rational about it: most of the current problems on earth would not exist without men." She looked at me, a challenge in her eyes, "It's a simple fact."

"So it's true that you hate men?" I interjected, glad to have finally regained control.

She looked at me and exhaled in three short puffs through her nose, smiling slightly with a quizzical expression as if I was some kind of semi-amusing imbecile. "Hatred?" she asked, raising her eyebrows at me, "That's a very interesting way to define a group of vegan women who want to live equally and sustainably, without causing harm to any living thing."

I opened my mouth, but she carried on before I could say anything.

"It's men who batter, rape and murder women every day. It's men who kill animals for sport and butcher them in abattoirs. It's men who physically and sexually assault children. It's men who massacre people in wars about race, religion and nation. All of that feels a lot more like hatred to me." She stroked her baby's fuzzy dark head and a look of pure love crossed her face that was so intense it could have sunk a battle ship. Then, thank God, she finally put her boob away.

I got in whilst I had a chance, "Not all men," I pointed out as she buttoned up her shirt.

She sighed, "I don't see men out on the streets demanding an end to violence against women. I don't see men challenging the structures of masculinity that give them so much power. It's true that not all men directly harm women, but most men are complicit, and all men certainly benefit from it."

I think that was when she really lost everyone. You can't go round blaming men for everything that's wrong in the world. It's as stupid as it is unfair. It also made it patently obvious that despite what she had said earlier, they did hate men. It probably wasn't even true about how they made the babies. They had most likely found a way to simply identify the sperm that carried an x chromosome and then inseminated themselves with that.

In the weeks that followed I often wondered if she felt responsible for what happened after the interview. Did she feel guilty? Did she realise that if she hadn't spouted all that stuff about men it would never have spiralled out of control like it did? There was an avalanche of complaints about hate speech before the interview had even finished and an angry crowd had gathered outside the building by the time she left. She had to slip out of a side door with her baby swaddled against her when one of her gang arrived to collect her in an old bio-fuel van.

There were huge demonstrations across the country. The Gynarchists were listed as a banned organisation and Eve was arrested. Emergency "gender terrorism" legislation was implemented to criminalise any attempt to undermine or threaten the existence of one gender. But even the new laws couldn't quell the outrage. The Gynarchists had stirred up a deep, primal fear that wasn't easily allayed. Vigilante groups formed to defend men's rights and that's when it started to get really nasty. Yet, despite everything that they said about living peacefully, The Gynarchists didn't do anything about it. They could have stopped it all if they had wanted to. They could have renounced their agenda and disbanded if they truly believed in living peacefully and protecting life. But they didn't, they only fuelled the fire. They released a statement claiming that a female-only, life-centric human collective was the only prospect for the continuation of life on earth, and so, for the sake of the entire planet they could never abandon their path. That's when the vigilante groups started attacking pregnant women or mothers with young babies, fearing they were part of the male-eradication movement. Women were advised not to go out alone if they were visibly pregnant or had a young baby.

Throughout it all I couldn't get my head round the fact that Eve was letting all letting all of this happen. She provoked all of this anger and violence and then did nothing about it.

I was on my way to the airport to collect Jeanine when I saw her. She was not anyone that I knew or even the kind of woman I would normally notice. It was just that she was walking in a very peculiar way, hunched over and almost waddling. As I drew alongside her, I realised what it was. She was pregnant and trying to hide her bump. No mean feat given that she looked about to drop. She shouldn't have been out on her own like that. She'd be an instant target. I felt a bit sick and looked away. I suppose I could have offered her a lift, but I didn't. Afterall, if she made the choice to go out in that state what could I do about it? I've never pretended to be any kind of superhero and it's really not my responsibility if she decides to put herself at risk. I kept driving, breathing against the familiar nausea that stirs in the pit of my stomach every time I hear about a pregnant woman or a new mother and her baby getting battered. It's gross, all of it.

I turned my thoughts to Jeanine instead. That was her last three-month sojourn in the States until after our wedding. I already knew how good it would feel to have her back. As usual, I'd missed her more than I had expected to. Despite the freedom her absence gives me, I always find myself longing for her return; her and her soft yielding body. I pulled into a parking bay, anticipating a long night of reunion sex.

As soon as I reached the arrivals hall the monitor told me that her flight had already landed so I took my place directly at the barrier. Minutes later Jeanine emerged through the smoky glass doors pulling a stack of suitcases behind her. I felt an unprompted smile spread across my face. But, as she approached, I could see that there was something different about her. Nothing obvious. Her hair was the same as always and she hadn't had a radical change of wardrobe or anything like that. It was something deeper, in the way she moved, like she knew something. I was sure it couldn't be anything that I'd done, besides, we have a tacit agreement that what happens when she's away doesn't count.

She met my eyes without smiling. I returned her gaze, perplexed. With her eyes still locked on mine she ran her free hand slowly over her belly. I followed the line of her fingers and noticed an almost imperceptible swelling below her waist. She walked towards me, fearless. I swallowed.

The nausea in my stomach told me that was not my baby, nor any other man's child, that she was carrying.

Martina Biavati - August

In the moments right before dawn, the sea seems to rise within itself, like the sun is fighting beyond the horizon to burst through and shine its light on the Eastern coast.

We used to have this tradition, Julian and I, that when July turned into August we would welcome our last month of freedom by staying up all night and waiting for dawn to break.We used to have all sorts of useless traditions, in the way that you have with people you've known all your life, like how we used to go to the circus whenever it came to our small town, and we always said hello on the first Monday of June, and goodbye on the 31st of August. The three months in between were spent together, and we would play in the sand, and give half-heart attacks to our parents when we swam too far into the sea.

The summer Julian turned eleven and I was ten, we were finally allowed to go by ourselves to the town ten minutes away by bike. Even though we were still kids, the road was safe, and both towns were so small that we knew them like the back of our hands. Julian had promised he wouldn't let anything happen to me, because those ten months of age difference always became years when we were out on our own. That was also the first year that our parents allowed us to see the first dawn in August, even though we weren't alone: our dads were there, sleeping on the beach chairs they brought, and we both were barely keeping our eyes open. Then, the sun rose above the horizon and Julian shook me awake, and that moment became ours.

The truth is simple: I don't remember a time in my life when Julian wasn't there to say hello at the beginning of summer, but I do remember the moment when our traditions stopped. Everyone said it was inevitable, and some part of me, a deep, hidden part, somewhere near my stomach, knew they were right. But I didn't listen, because I never do, and so I willingly set myself up for heartbreak.

At some point, when we were no longer children but not teenagers yet, we grew up. He grew up first, maybe, and I was a few years late, but the fact remains that one summer 'hello' and 'goodbye' were the only things he said. He had his friends, and I had mine, but I never made any new traditions, and the town was small enough that I know he didn't either. There was something sacred, I think, about the ones we had already made.

So, I was still going to the beach on the nights between July 31st and August 1st, first with my dad and then by myself, and he would always come as well. We never talked. Just sat next to each other, in silence, and stared alternatively at our phones and at the sky. The night would stretch between us, dark and cold, and we would wait for the sun to come up so we could go back to our lives. It was a hard silence to fill, the kind that feels heavy and thick like the winter fog. We both had things to say, and we didn't know how to say them, and it became clear that neither of us knew what we were doing there. But each year we still showed up, and we sat in silence, and we saw to our rites. Then, high school was over, and that year, for the first time, I welcomed August alone.

Human brains are funny. Forget about a date enough times and, as the years go by, you won't be able to remember why your eyes get drawn to the calendar, or what the google notification you set up even meant. Eventually, the remains of a tradition will only consist of that weird second in which you *know* you are forgetting something. Even that, however, won't bring more than a tilt of the head: then, you'll check your pockets, find everything you need, and you'll let it go. The sun will rise, and the calendar will turn, and you'll have moved on.

I was never good at moving on.

My therapist tells me I have abandonment issues. And commitment issues; but apparently the latter stems from the former, so the reason why I can never have a stable relationship is that I am so afraid of being left behind that I am always the one who does the leaving. I told her that was bullshit and that you can't have commitment issues if you've never had a relationship in the first place. She just shook her head and set up the next session.

But now it's barely gone three in the morning, on August 1st, and I specifically took time off my job to fly all the way back to this godforsaken town and sit in the sand. I'm waiting for dawn, and I think she might have had a point. Maybe I can't hold down a relationship because some part of me thinks I already am in one, and that I have been in one since before I even knew what a relationship was.

This stretch of the beach is empty, like it always is, but further north I can hear the music coming from one of the few beach bars that won't be closing for another hour or so. There's little sticks and broken shells all around me, and less than five feet ahead of me, in the darkness, the waves crash into the shore with a rumble. It's a clear night, and I can see the stars with a clarity that I hadn't realized I missed: I am twenty-five and still observing my rites.

A stick breaks somewhere behind me, and I turn around. I should be scared, or worried, but, even after three years, I recognize his shape without even seeing his face; a weird sort of relief settles deep into my stomach. This year, my vigil won't be lonely. Julian says nothing as he sits next to me. It's been three years, and it feels like it's been a lifetime and like it was only yesterday at the same time.

We sit cross-legged on the sand, watch the sea, and listen to the beat coming from the bar, to the noise coming from everyone that is laughing and drinking, and living. Every once in a while, someone walks on the beach in front of us, either yelling a slurred *Hey* or saying nothing at all: we ignore them all. The silence isn't heavy like it usually is; it's this fragile thing between us, and it feels like one wrong breath will be enough to shatter it into a thousand pieces, and, at that point, it will be another three years before we can be in the same place at the same time again.

I don't know how long we've been silent for, but the wind has picked up to the point that I am cold even though I am wearing a winter sweater, and the bar has long gone silent. The sky is pitch black, and the only light comes from the stars: I feel Julian shifting next to me.

"You weren't here last year," he says.

"I couldn't get time off work." I reply. "But you weren't here the year before."

He nods. "I was on holiday with some friends."

The silence falls once more, and I still know him well enough that I know the hitch in his breath, that half-second of consideration when he's gearing up to say something important.

"My grandma died last week." He whispers it like a secret, and it hits me like a slap.

I remember his grandma, Mary Jo, with her short white hair, and her bright one-piece bathing suits and even brighter clothes, always in shades of pink and purple. She always said getting old meant being able to wear whatever one wanted so long as it fit, and then she always proceeded to organize fashion shows where Julian and I would take turns wearing her strangest clothes as we were waiting for the hot midday hours to pass. I remember the way she would take the two of us out for breakfast when we were kids, how she would push both of us in the swings when we couldn't decide who got to go first. That she's gone hits like a punch in the gut, even though it's been almost a decade since she was well enough to come to the beach.

I whip my head around, staring at his solid shape. "Julian… I am so, *so*, sorry."

He shakes his head. "We saw it coming, so it…"

"Don't say it wasn't *bad*."

"It wasn't as bad as it could have been," he says. "She was… she was happy, in the end, I think."

I want to reach out, to bring him into me, to hug him, because, despite everything that was going on, he was still there the summer my grandad died, when I was sixteen. I know that now it's my turn to be the one that brings comfort. "How are you feeling?"

"Empty," he says. He doesn't look at me, but keeps staring at the sea. Every once in a while, his chest gives a small hitch, like he's fighting against himself, waiting to give himself permission to break.

"I know," I say.

The inches between us seem like an ocean, and he gives a watery laugh: he's been on the verge of crying probably since he arrived, and it won't take long for the dam to break. Not now that he's talking.

"I never even wanted to show up," he confesses. "Was sure you wouldn't be here."

I knew that, but it's amazing how things you know are still capable of hurting. "Then why did you?"

"'Cause… 'Cause you know what one of the last things she said to me was?"

"What?"

"She asked about you."

My nose starts burning, and I have to swallow a couple of times to be able to speak without starting to cry. My voice comes out as a whisper, one that is almost swallowed by the waves. "I didn't know she even remembered."

"Most of the time she didn't," he confirms, his voice breaking on the last word. He clears his throat. "But that one was a good day, and she asked me what happened to you."

I blink, choke on what could become a sob. He's cutting me open, and digging in to find all of the big questions, the same ones I always asked and the ones that I never could find an answer to. I want to reach out, to hug him, but I also want to fold in on myself, to protect what little piece of me is left from him. I try to get my mouth to form words. "What did you say?"

"What my mom told me," he said. "That you moved halfway across the world and work, now."

"And was she happy with that?"

"Yes, but she also took great pleasure in informing me that I was an idiot, and that she wanted to know what happened between us."

I feel a small smile fight to stretch itself over my lips. That sounds like Mary Jo, with her bluntness that almost became rudeness, and that Southern accent that grew stronger whenever she was excited about something. But also there's that old worry, that *what if I did something wrong*, that rears its ugly head back up from where I buried it all those years ago, when I was twelve and I had felt like something important had slipped me by and I hadn't even noticed. "What did you say?"

He turns towards me, finally. His voice is raw and rough. Like a wave, it feels as though he's moving closer. "I told her we'd grown up too much."

And now he's moved away again, back towards the open sea. So low I'm not sure he even hears me, hidden below all the old hurt those words bring up again, I say, "I suppose we did."

"She said we both had to stop being idiots," he says, talking over me.

In the darkness, I can feel his eyes flickering all over me, like he can't decide on where to look. "She said that we have been stubborn for thirteen years now, and we have run out of excuses."

Mary Jo's words ring in my head, chasing each other: she's right, like always. And we do need to talk about it, but I know him well enough to know that he's not being completely honest with me. "Julian," I say. "Why are you here?"

"'Cause my grandma died," he repeats. This time, I can feel his eyes locked on mine, a brown so dark and rich that you can hardly separate it from its iris even in the daylight. He needs something else, I know. A little push, something he can cling to and use as an excuse to take what he needs.

"And what do you need?"

He's silent for a while, but I know his mind is working a mile a minute, coming up with a hundred different answers that will be perfectly acceptable and that will completely shatter this new truce we created. "I need us," he says.

After that, it's the easiest thing in the world to move closer. I throw my legs over his, and he shifts towards me as well. I bring my arms around his neck, and bring his head down, until it's resting above my clavicle. His hands grip my shoulders so tight I can feel his fingers digging into my skin even through the sweater. His breath is hot against my neck, and I can feel his tears falling down. I breathe in, and let myself feel just like he is.

This is not the first time we hug, and it's not the first time one of us is crying into the other's shoulder either. The sky is pitch black, and I don't know what time it is anymore, and none of it matters, because Julian needs me, and now we're both crying.

Through the tears, half-hidden between hiccups, he says: "I don't know why I did that."

"It's okay," I say in a whisper, "it's okay."

He shakes his head, but doesn't lift it. Some things are easier said in the dark. "It's not."

There's nothing I can say to that, nothing I can do to make everything better, so I just sit there and let him cry. I hold on to him, and move my hand through his hair, up and down, following the rocking of the waves. His shoulders shake, and he is crying himself ragged, and I slowly let the night slip away.

In the moments right before dawn, the sea seems to rise within itself. The sky is pink and violet and blue, and the sun will break through any minute now. Julian is still hanging on to me, and my legs are still over his, and his head is still on my shoulder. He's breathing, low and ragged, against my neck, and sometimes a hiccup escapes him. Neither of us has anything left to give by now, and if I believed in anything I could almost see Mary Jo and her bright clothes in the way the sky's colours fade one into the other. But I don't, so, when I look past the horizon, I only see the sun, about to win his daily war with the sea.

I can feel the moment Julian decides he doesn't need comfort anymore. Above us, the stars blink once more, and Julian sits back, wiping his eyes clean with the sleeve of his sweater. I sit back, crossing my legs, and return to my space.

The sea rumbles, and he speaks: "I loved you, you know?"

My heart misses a beat or two, but those words don't feel warm and promising like they should. Or like they would have all those years ago.

He brings his knees up to his chest, and crosses his arms above them, resting his chin on them. He doesn't offer anything else, and I don't either. We both know we are several years too late. The sun shines beyond the horizon: dawn breaks. The sky turns orange and pink, and the stars blink out of existence. The waves crash on the shore, and silently, we welcome August.

Patricia Dunkley - The Golfers

THE CREEK lay across the fields and beyond that was the golf course. Jim and Tom humping their golf sticks over their shoulders were flabbergasted when they realised, they had to cross the creek to reach the course.

"Come on Tom, you're not frightened of getting wet, are you?" Jim bluffed. He wasn't going to be the one to welch.

"Of course not," replied Tom, "a bit of water never worried me." He waded into the creek with his bag of clubs held high in the air.

Jim stared gob-smacked and quickly followed suit. The water peaked at their shoulders before they reached the other side. "Very refreshing," said Tom." The only thing is that posh club won't let us play looking like this, you know."

Tom stared down at his drenched trousers and shirt with a forlorn grin. "I suggest we strip off and lay our gear in the sun for a while. With the heat today they could be dry in ten minutes." He threw his clubs on the ground and started to pull off his trousers.

With a hasty look around Jim hurriedly followed suit. He was no prude and if it was good enough for Tom to stand there looking like a right Charlie, it was good enough for him.

The two friends had started school together at the tender age of six and had barely been apart since. Now, at the splendid age of twenty-six, they knew each other's every move and disposition. There had always been a keen sense of rivalry between them, but with real friendship that only comes from growing up together sharing intimate secrets, smoking the first cigarette and discovering sex.

All that "puberty blues" stuff with girls had now turned into "woman trouble". To make matters worse they were both now madly in love with the same female.

Platinum blonde, with a delicious body that curved in and out at the right places, Virginia Elliot was a delectable sight to behold. Not only did she look good, she was a real sportswoman and could play a mean game of golf. On top of that she was heiress to a fortune left by a doting grandmother, or so it was rumoured. Not that the fellows had known this when they had met her at a local hot spot wriggling her hips with the best of them. Her ample bosom was barely refrained from popping out of the scanty top she was wearing. Needless to say, Tom and Jim had both fallen hard, like meteorites from outer-space. Her ready smile and saucy blue eyes had had them sizzling like sausages on a barbecue.

Each of them taking turns to chat her up on the packed dance floor. Night after night at the popular clubs. The two fellows were neck to neck in the race for Virginia's attention. Or so they thought.

Now standing bare chested, in their coloured boxer shorts, they gawked at each other with foolish grins.

"I didn't know you wore Bombay Bloomers," Tom said, eyeing Jim up and down with a smirk on his face.

"I never used to," Jim readily replied, "but Virginia said they were good for you and it was the way to go." He gave a grin. "So just in case, I changed over to them."

"Just in case?" Tom queried, staring at his mate, his eyes bright with merriment.

"You know," Jim beamed, "first base and all that. I wanted to show her that I'd listened to what she had said, and taken her advice." He looked down at Tom's boxers and made a funny face. "At least mine are not covered with black spiders." He eyed Tom off inquiringly. "Did Virginia give you the same spiel?"

The two friends exchanged grins.

"Absolutely! The subject came up when I kissed her goodnight." he said, roguishly.

"I bet it did," Jim grinned at his mate, "the same thing happened to me."

The two men threw their heads back and laughed heartily. They had a sneaking feeling they had been taken for a ride, but neither was going to say anything about that.

"Come on. We'd better hurry up and get this stuff dry," Tom said, laying out his trousers and shirt. "Why didn't you tell me the creek was that deep?" He glowered at Jim.

"It was your bright idea." Jim replied, spreading his clothing out alongside Tom's. He looked down at his boxers. "What about these? Shall we take them off too?"

"Are you crazy? Tom blurted out. "Do you want to get us arrested for indecent exposure? We'll have to lie in the sun back and front. Dry out as best we can." He added, dropping to the ground and making himself as comfortable as he could. "Life is always complicated whenever I'm around you Jim Riches. Sometimes I wish you would join the Navy and run away to sea." he added, cheerfully, staring up at the bright blue sky.

"And I wish you would stop playing Alpha male all the time and let me get a word in first." Jim glowered. "I happen to know there is a perfectly good bridge near the clubhouse. We could have crossed that and not had any of this angst." He dropped down alongside his friend.

Tom gave him a withering look. "Why the hell didn't you say so?" he questioned. "Typical of you. Act first and think later. Well, it's too late now. We might as well have a snooze." He closed his eyes, stretching out in the sun. "A little nap will do me a power of good. It was another late night and all that jumping around on the dance floor makes a man tired."

"You're not joking. It's harder than playing football. My legs fair ache." Jim rolled over onto his stomach. "Wake me in half an hour. There's a good fellow."

The warm sun streamed down on their muscular bodies and it wasn't long before the two of them were fast asleep, each dreaming of Virginia and wondering how long it would take to get her into the cot? Ah! Virginia with her platinum blonde hair and her Doctor's degree. Brains and beauty. They both snored deeply.

Meanwhile the two young boys hiding in the bush, after collecting lost golf balls poked each other with a snigger. They had watched the whole thing - Men wading across the creek with golf clubs held above their heads like weapons, going into battle. Grown-ups were crazy! They did the weirdest things. Now they were fast asleep in only their undies! Two adult men in the middle of day asleep like babes in the woods, with their gear laid out just begging to be pinched.

They giggled together and like silent soldiers, sneaked forward and gathered up the clothing, making off as fast as their legs would take them. If it was good enough for grown-ups to behave in a foolish fashion, it was good enough for a couple of kids to teach them a lesson. They had been told a thousand times and more, never to take their clothing off outside the house, in broad daylight, and never to go into the creek! These two had broken all the rules, so serve them right. This was the best fun they'd had for ages.

Tom was the first to wake. He sat up and looked around, he'd forgotten for the moment where he was. Then he saw his mate lying alongside him with arms stretched out, just like he'd done as a kid when they'd gone camping together. Gawd! He thought. The two of them sure went back a long way. It was then he noticed their clothes were missing. Wait until he told Jim this latest drama in their on-going saga. He'd probably spit his dummy out and blame him. Tom bent over and gave Jim a hearty slap on his backside.

"Wake up. Wake up," he prodded Jim. "We've been done like a dinner."

Jim struggled to sit up. "Where am I? What's going on?" He stared across at Tom. "What's the idea of slapping me like that? I was just in the middle of a very productive dream," he said irritably.

"Well, dream on sunshine. Some buggers gone off with our gear," Tom replied brusquely. "All we've got is our shoes and golf clubs and what we're wearing." He looked down at his boxers and pulled the wallet out of his waistband. "Thank God we kept these safe. At least we learnt something from boy-scout days." He shot Jim a woe-begone smile. "We'll have to get to the pro shop and buy some more gear, new duds and a T. shirt. Let's hope there are not too many people on the golf course. This is turning into a disaster of a day."

"Bloody hell!" Jim exclaimed. "You've got to be joking! How do you think we're going to walk up the fairway in just our underwear, with golf clubs over our shoulders? We'll have every head turning our way. That's if we don't get run in," Jim moaned. "We haven't even got any socks. You know long socks are an absolute must with shorts on members day!"

"Socks! That's the least of our worries. They've got a very mean-spirited Course Ranger here and if he sets eyes on us. We are dead meat. Believe me!"

"Bloody hell!" Jim groaned. "If only we'd brought the car. All this 'walking and get fit campaign", baggy under-pants, no beer and vegetarian food. I'm fast going off Virginia. And what's more I'm starving."

The two men clambered to their feet, put their shoes on and picked up their golf clubs, swinging them onto their naked shoulders. They eyed each other off and gave a bit of a laugh.

"Bloody hell! We must have rocks in our heads to be humping these clubs instead of using a buggy!" Jim exclaimed. "It's the last time I'll ever listen to a woman spouting on about tradition and all that carry on. And as for air circulating around my now not so private bits- I'm sure getting plenty of that," he wailed as he limped forward. "I just hope I don't see anyone I know."

"Stop whingeing," Tom whispered, as they reached the course proper and started to make their way up the fairway, ducking in and out of the bushes that delineated the first and second holes. "Just hope we can make it to the first tee without being seen. The pro shop is a stone's throw from there." They slowly crept forward and were soon halfway up the fairway.

"Bloody hell!" Jim moaned. "I can see a golf cart heading this way. What are we going to do now?"

"There's nothing we can do." Tom deliberated for a moment. "I suppose we'll just have to tell them what happened and hope for the best."

"Bloody hell!" Jim croaked. "We'll be the laughing stock of the club. I wish we'd never agreed to have a game with Virginia. If she sees us looking like this it will be curtains."

"Now hear this. Now hear this," a man's voice boomed out over the airways. "Stand perfectly still. Repeat. Perfectly still. This is the Course Ranger. The Course Ranger. Stop where you are right now!" The golf cart zoomed towards them, lights flashing, bells ringing.

"Bloody hell," Jim proclaimed. "Who does he think we are? A couple of terrorists?"

"I told you he was zealous." Tom said, moving closer to his friend. "He has the reputation of a dragon. I think he was a Sergeant in the SAS before he took this job."

"I believe you," Jim said, propping his golf clubs up in front of him, preparing for the onslaught.

The Course Ranger stopped his buggy right in front of them and jumped out.

"What the hell do you two think you're doing? Sneaking around dressed like that?" He glared at the two men, waiting for them to answer. "I'll have you know our dress regulations are strict here. We don't have any riff-raff on this golf course- and as for no socks! Show me your golf cards." He thrust his hand forward. "Woe betide you if you haven't got any. There's a new regulation for non-paying players. Your name goes in the book and you are banned from the course for six months."

Jim looked at Tom. "Go on, you tell him," he whispered, and for gawd's sake make it sound good.

"Well, it's like this," Tom said, looking the ranger straight in the eye. "We've been held up on your golf course. Stripped of everything except our clubs. Two fellows are dressed to kill in our gear and probably signing your visitor's book as we talk. No doubt they intend to do the place over. I just hope your insurance will cover us for the treatment we've received."

Tom took breath and glowered at the ranger. The man was huge, with Viking legs and massive shoulders. Standing rigid in front of them he was dressed to perfection.

"Where did this assault take place?" he asked suspiciously, eyeing the men over. It sure seemed strange that these two were walking around half-naked. Perhaps they had been set upon, but they might also be a couple of odd-bods from the nudist colony that was just beyond the golf course at the beach. You could never tell these days what people got up to. He waited for their answer.

"We were in the bunker on the second, when out of the blue. Boom! Boom! We were both knocked out and woke up like this." Tom explained. "How would you feel if you were playing golf and got mugged?" he complained. "We didn't expect this sort of thing to happen; not at this club."

Jim's eyes filled with admiration. You had to hand it to Tom, he sure had a quick wit ready for any contingency. He nodded his head in agreement at Tom's words.

"We need some clothes, and quickly", he blurted. He was getting fed up with being looked at by the passing golfers. Besides which, Virginia was supposed to be meeting them here and it was very nearly time to hit off.

The Ranger stared at the men in wonder, his mind ticking over at their story. If they had been mugged the Club could be in for a hefty insurance claim. On the other hand they could be spinning him a yarn; it sounded a bit fishy. He made a quick decision to take them to the Pro shop and get them fitted out. Perhaps that would keep them happy and if it did, he knew they were having him on.

"Okay. I'll take you to the shop and you can get some gear. We'll see how things develop after that." He waved his hand toward the vehicle. "Hop into the buggy."

Tom and Jim threw their clubs into the rear and squeezed into the golf-cart.

"That's more like it," Tom said chirpily, prodding Jim in the ribs and giving him a wink.

Jim didn't say a word. He was terrified in case anything went wrong and the two of them were flung out for all to see in their funny underwear. He just hoped Virginia wasn't anywhere near the Pro shop.

The Ranger quickly reached his destination. "Okay, out you get the pair of you." He wasn't really happy about this, but had decided to string them along.

Tom and Jim quickly jumped out of the vehicle and as they did so their wallets fell to the ground.

The Ranger watched with satisfaction as the two of them grovelled to retrieve the items. "Robbed and left you your wallets? He snorted. "I don't think so!" he exclaimed moving forward. Just as he did so a lively voice rang across the airwaves.

"Daddy. What are you doing with Tom and James?"

"Daddy!" Tom and Jim exclaimed in unison and stared at each other.

The Ranger watched as the woman advanced and stood in front of them. He eyed her with admiration. She certainly was a good looker this daughter of his, but she sure could be a handful at times. "Know these two, do you?"

he asked with speculation, waiting for her reply. Goodness only knows where she found these odd-bods she went out with he thought. He had no intention of letting these two out of his sight.

"Of course, I know them," she exclaimed crossly, "I'm supposed to be having a game with them." She flashed them a dazzling look of fury.

"Not today, Virginia," the Ranger said with satisfaction and ushered them forward. "As soon as they get kitted out, these two are over to the Captain and into the book," he said tersely. He had no intention of letting Virginia wheedle her way out of this one.

Jim and Tom eyed each other knowingly, as love for Virginia melted like snow in summer.

Bloody hell, Jim muttered, as they moved forward to face the music. "What a lucky escape." He grinned at Tom. "I think it's time we took up fishing. How about it old friend?"

You're on," Tom replied. I'll organise a boat that can go out to sea," he faced his friend, "and don't tell me you get sea-sick or else."

Who me? Never!

Paul Rennie - Parking Problems

She pulled aside the lace curtains of her front room, peered suspiciously out over the low privet hedge to the road, and tutted through thin lips to herself. Yes, as she thought, there was another one. A red Ford Focus was reversing slowly into the parking space directly outside her house. Hilda Dibden had lived in the red brick semi-detached house in Town End Street, Godalming, for 53 years. She had moved there with her parents in her twenties, and after they died she had stayed put, living alone in the virtually unchanged two bedroom house. It still had the original layout, with a kitchen at the back and a front living room with a casement window overlooking the street. It was once a quiet residential road within walking distance of the shops and bright lights of the town, but with the advent of new housing development, multiple car ownership, double yellow lines, and the threat of traffic wardens and wheel clampers in other parts of the town, it had become congested with cars and a favourite free parking spot for people going shopping, or commuters heading to the station. The problem was that the Edwardian houses in Town End Street were built in days when there were few motorized vehicles, and when there was no need for garages or driveways to park private cars. Consequently space was now at a premium. Mrs Dibden had never owned a car, but she considered that the kerb and road outside her house belonged to her, and woe betide anyone who had the temerity to occupy it.

She banged on the window to attract the car owner's attention, but he didn't hear her. She needed to act quickly. She tore off her apron and rushed outside to remonstrate with the driver, but he was too quick for her. By the time she got to the street, the smartly dressed grey haired man in his fifties had walked briskly away towards the town centre, and was already turning the corner. She went back inside, and every so often twitched the curtains to see if he was coming back, getting herself into her usual state of indignant anger. How dare he steal what was hers. This happened many times a day, and she was doggedly territorial about the space. She would rant at those who parked there, explaining that she needed that parking space for her visitors, although truth be told, she never had any, because the way she glared out of the window with such a sour expression encouraged people to give her a wide berth. Even people on foot were subjected to her glare, in case they might be eyeing up the parking space for future use.

Hilda didn't have much chance of making new friends, because she rarely went out in case someone should sneak into the parking space when she wasn't watching. She needed to be on permanent guard against trespassers. She told those motorists who were prepared to argue with her that she had high blood pressure and needed the space kept clear in case there was an emergency, although, ironically, it was her obsession with the parking space that contributed to her hypertension. But still people continued to park outside her house, and her days were spent peering out and checking for space invaders. She was well known to Waverley Council, as she had called many times to complain about cars parking in her street, but the Civil Enforcement Officer had patiently told her that nothing could be done. It was a public road and people had a right to park there, and the other residents needed somewhere to leave their cars. She wasn't even allowed to put up a no parking sign. A few times in the past she had put plastic garden chairs in the space to deter parkers, but they were always moved, or once, disappeared completely. Now she resorted to direct challenges if she could catch intruders in time, or if not, leaving rude notes tucked under their windscreen wipers. As often as not, the notes were ignored, and she would find them crumpled up on the ground in the space where the owner's car had been.

She looked out of the curtains again. It was still there, the red car that seemed to be mocking her, saying, 'look at me I'm in your space'. A vein throbbed behind her eye. This was too much. The car had been there for at least an hour and a half. Perhaps the man had left it there while he went up to London on the train, and wouldn't be back until the evening. Maybe he had gone on holiday and the car could be there for weeks. She worked herself into a frenzy. This was the last straw. If he wasn't coming back, she would have to take action, and it wasn't going to be just a note this time. She would teach the driver not to park in her spot. She went to the sideboard and took out her sewing basket. In it was the bradawl she used for making holes in leather. She took off the cork that protected its tip, revealing a sharp point on a spike fixed into a polished beech wood handle and a brass ferrule. She ran her finger over the point. Yes, this would do the job very nicely. She put the cork back on, dropped the tool into her apron pocket and marched out of the front door, and stood beside the offending car. There was a sudden gust of wind and her front door slammed shut behind her, but she wasn't worried because this always happened and she kept a spare key underneath a flowerpot under the window. She gave a furtive look both ways along the street. As usual it was empty at this time of day, apart from the line of cars. She took out the bradawl, pulled off the cork, bent down and in one quick motion plunged the spike into the wall of the front tyre. There was a bit of resistance, but the point pierced the rubber quite easily. There was a satisfying hiss of air escaping as the tyre started to deflate. She could feel her heart pounding and the vein throbbing, but the elation she felt was therapeutic. She moved to the rear of the car and jabbed the needle into the other tyre. Again there was a hiss, and the car did a little lurch as it leaned over onto its wheel rims. As Hilda straightened up, she felt a slight pop somewhere inside her head, followed by a dizzy feeling. Her vision closed in, her legs gave way and she fell to the ground. The bradawl, she was still holding, dropped from her hand and rolled away somewhere underneath the car. There she lay in a crumpled heap on the damp pavement.

A few minutes later, the red car owner with the grey hair came back from his dental appointment, gingerly probing the new filling in his lower molar with his tongue. He saw the elderly lady lying beside his car and rushed over to help her. He knew enough first aid to realize immediately from the dilated pupil of her left eye and the way that side of her face drooped that she had had a stroke. He also knew that time was critical in getting a stroke patient treated to have the best chances of them making a full recovery and avoiding permanent disablement or worse. He reached into his pocket for his mobile to call an ambulance, but then realized he had left it at home on the kitchen table, in case it fell out of his pocket while he was in the Dentist's chair. He looked to see if there was anybody else around who might help, but the street was deserted. Ah, perhaps he could ask the person in the nearest house if he could use their phone. He went to the door and rang the bell, but there was no reply, not surprising really, since Mrs Dibden was on the same side of the front door as he was. He then had a thought. The lady was wearing an apron, and had no handbag, so maybe it was her house he had just tried. He searched her person as much as he dared, to see if she had a key, but all he could find was a cork in her apron pocket.

He would have to find another neighbour. He tried a few more houses along the street, but no-one seemed to be in. The street was still deserted. The lady was in the same position as he'd left her, obviously unconscious but at least breathing normally. There was nothing for it, he couldn't leave her there any longer on the cold pavement. Time was of the essence, so he would have to drive her to casualty himself. He opened the passenger door and tried as gently as possible to lift Mrs Dibden into the seat. She was quite a large lady, and it took a lot of time and effort to pull her up off the ground in her unconscious state and bundle her into the seat, and even longer to reach over her and connect the seat belt. He jumped into the driver's seat, turned on the engine and started to drive off. The steering felt oddly heavy and there was a flapping grinding noise from the passenger side. He jumped out again and went to look, and for the first time saw that both tyres were completely flat. The car wasn't going anywhere. In desperation he looked up and down the road again. Surely someone must come by, it was so close to a busy town and lunchtime was almost over. Eventually, round the corner came a man on a bicycle, wearing a bright yellow jacket and black helmet. The car owner waved frantically to him to attract his attention. The cyclist cheerfully waved back, then turned up Carlos Street, never to be seen again. The road was deserted again. A few more minutes went by and he checked on his passenger. She was still breathing, so no CPR was needed, but she was making slurred sounds. She needed treatment immediately. A young schoolgirl with a ponytail suddenly appeared near the car, peering alternately at her mobile phone and at the unconscious lady in the front seat.

"What's the matter wiv 'er, 'ad too much to drink?" she asked unsympathetically.

"No, I think she's had stroke, we need an ambulance," said the driver. "Can I use your mobile to call 999?"

"No battery," said the girl, in a surly manner, and walked quickly away before he could ask her anything else.

The driver was getting increasing worried. Out of the corner of his eye, he noticed another figure turning the corner and coming towards him. He could make out a frail elderly lady in a long black coat, blue hat and surgical stockings, using a shopping trolley as a walking frame. He waited for her to reach the car, but she didn't seem to be getting any closer. Had she stopped? Then, just as he was giving up, there was slight movement again. She moved the trolley forward a couple of feet, and after a long pause, moved her legs to catch up, then, after another pause, repeated the process. She was definitely heading his way, but she was going to take an eternity to reach him. He raced towards her to ask if she lived nearby. After all, she couldn't have travelled far from home. After more precious time while he convinced her that he wasn't trying to steal her shopping, he established that she lived two doors down from the first house he had called on. He explained that there was a lady that had had a stroke and could he use her mobile phone to call for an ambulance. "I don't get on with mobile phones. My son bought me one and the buttons were too small, and I couldn't work out how to charge it, so I gave it back."

"How about a house phone? Do you have one that I could use to make an emergency call?" he asked her. She agreed and they continued to edge slowly towards her house.

"I think we need to go a bit quicker", said the man. "Could you give me the keys, so that I can dash in?"

"I need to see your photo ID card," said the elderly lady, "You hear about those villains who trick their way into people's houses and steal their savings."

He didn't have anything on him that she would accept, so they continued their snail-like progress along the pavement. After about five minutes they reached the car, with Hilda still in the passenger seat.

"That's Hilda Dibden," said the elderly lady. "She and I fell out twenty years ago over parking in the street, when I used to own a car. Never speak to each other now."

After a few more agonizingly slow minutes they reached the house and the elderly lady, after fumbling for ages in her bag for her keys, went inside, shutting the door. After five more minutes, and just as he was considering ringing the doorbell, he heard a toilet flush, and she eventually passed the phone out to him on its cord. He was finally able to call 999, and to give them their due, the ambulance service arrived just inside its target time.

Lured by the flashing blue lights, a surprising number of residents appeared from their houses to watch the spectacle. Mrs Dibden was given an injection of clot buster drug by the paramedics, placed on a stretcher, and loaded into the ambulance. But that wasn't the end of the drama. As the ambulance started to drive off with the siren blasting, it stopped again abruptly and the driver got out. Something was wrong with the tyre. The bystanders watched the paramedic as he checked the front nearside tyre, swore, and then extracted a bradawl that some careless person had discarded in the street, and had become embedded in the tyre when driven over as the ambulance arrived. There was another long delay as the crew changed the tyre. As the ambulance left for the second time on its journey to the Royal Surrey, the car owner trudged wearily into town to find a garage to replace his own tyres.

Six weeks later, Hilda was back at her home, but the stroke she had suffered and the delay in initial treatment had left their mark. The hospital had done all they could, but now she was discharged into the social care sector. Noreen, her kindly carer, brought over a plastic cup with a fixed straw, and held it up to Mrs Dibden's lips.

"Here you are, Hilda, a nice cup of tea. It must be hard being stuck indoors all of the time, with no change of scenery. I tell you what, why don't I move your wheelchair over to the front window so that you can watch the comings and goings outside? I'm sure you'll enjoy that. I'll pull the net curtains back."

The patient made a gurgling sound that Noreen mistakenly took to be approval. From her new position Hilda stared out of the window through the one eye that she could focus.

A silver Audi was manoeuvring slowly into the parking space outside.

Paula Conway - Fata Morgana

"I saw France!" Hanna ran from the gate that led down to the beach, up the crazy paving pathway back to the house. "I saw France," she shouted again, bursting through the back door into the kitchen.

"Hanna, you haven't been down to the beach by yourself, have you?" asked her mother, turning briefly from the stove to face the child. In her hand she held a clump of fish and mashed potato, glued together.

"You've got to come and see. And Dad. Quick." Hanna ran from the kitchen to the hallway, momentarily confused about the layout of the rented holiday house. "Dad," she yelled, "come, quick." Then she darted upstairs to pull her brother by the arm away from his precious game-thing. "I saw France," she panted for the third time, "please come and see. It's beautiful."

Finally, all three of them followed her back down the path, through the gap in the tangled bramble bushes at the bottom of the garden, where the little picket gate led down steep steps to the beach that Hanna wasn't allowed to go to by herself. Here, at the top of the cliff was a clear view of the sea. On the first day of the holiday, when they'd all stood together in this same spot, the tide was out and they'd seen rock pools and hundreds of strange wooden posts, worn by the sea into all different shapes and sizes. Her Dad said they were the remains of an ancient forest that stretched far out to sea, and beyond the horizon, he told them, was France. Now, she had seen France with her own eyes – floating in the sky, just above the ocean. Buildings with slanting red roofs, a tower with smoke rising and a castle, or perhaps it was a church, had all emerged from the clouds and hovered above the sea like magic.

Hanna's mouth had literally fallen open in wonder and she started laughing with excitement and joy. Then, glancing along the cliff, she saw the old man. He was standing at the bottom of his garden also looking out at the water, through binoculars. When he lowered the binoculars to pick up a sketch pad, he noticed Hanna and waved.

"Is it France?" shouted Hanna into the strong afternoon breeze.

"D'you know," the man's words floated back to her, "I think it is.

What a clever girl you are, knowing that." And then, Hanna ran to find her family, to show them the wondrous sight.

Now, here they were, clustered together, just like on the first day of the holiday, except today, the tide was in, and all they saw ahead of them was the vast, blue ocean and a few low clouds, streaked pink with the beginning of a slow, August sunset.

"I told you she's mental," said her brother, Matt, as he walked back to the house, his hands flapping impatiently by his sides.

"But it was here," said Hanna, "just a few minutes ago. It was there across the water. See that boat?" Hanna pointed to a small sail boat gliding about a mile out to sea. "Just there, and the man said it was France."

"What man?" asked her mother sharply. "You mustn't talk to strange men. How many times have I told you that?"

"What did you see, Hanna?" asked her father.

"She didn't see anything, Donald. Don't indulge her." Hanna's mother wiped her hands on her apron and bent down to look into Hanna's face. "You mustn't lie, Hanna, do you understand?" She squeezed the flesh at the top of Hanna's arm, "and don't ever talk to strange men," she said, before striding back to the house. Hanna felt the burn of her mother's fingers on her naked arm and tears pricked the corners of her eyes. She stared through them across the water. Where had it gone?

"There were buildings, a tower and a church. And the man said I was clever for knowing it was France. He had binoculars and then he was drawing it," she said, still staring at the rippling, glittering water. She turned to her father. "He was over there in the garden, not next door, the one after that." She pointed to where the man had stood, and the tears rolled down her face. "He said I was clever, for knowing it was France."

"Come on, Han," said her father, putting an arm around her shoulder, "it's dinner time, and your mother's made fishcakes, your favourite." But Hanna shook off his arm.

"Let's go to the man's house and ask him," she said, filled with new hope. "It's just two doors away. Then you'll believe me."

"That's enough, Hanna. We're not disturbing anyone. It's dinner time. You've got a vivid imagination and that's the end of it."

But that wasn't the end of it, Hanna recalled. She was sitting now in the kitchen of her mother's flat, waiting for Matt. Their mother had died six weeks ago, and today they were to start packing up her belongings and clearing the flat. Sipping coffee from a take-away cup and flicking through a pile of newspapers, a vivid colour sketch had caught Hanna's eye and transported her back to the family holiday nearly thirty years ago. She stared at the paper, and a small laugh escaped from her open lips. She wished she could show the picture to her mother. Not just show it, but thrust it into her face and say, *see, I was right. You should have believed me and then it could have been different.* Well, it was too late for that, and, she hesitated, what exactly would have been different? She tried to read the article below the picture, but the rest of that summer evening danced in front of the words on the page.

"Please," she'd begged her father. "Please can we go tomorrow and ask the man to see his picture." By now, they were back at the house and her father's face was closed and blank as a garage door. Hanna could feel frustration and a creeping confusion rub at her skin like sand.

In the kitchen, her mother was standing at the sink washing the pots and pans used to cook the dinner, even though they hadn't yet eaten. She didn't turn around when Hanna walked in, and it might have ended there, Hanna mused now, if it wasn't for Matt, who sauntered in at that moment.

"Here comes the nutter. Here comes the nutter," he sing-songed into her face. "What have you seen now? Italy? Belgium?"

"Stop it," Matt, "said their father as he dried up a frying pan. But Matt didn't stop.

"I know, I bet you've seen America," he jeered.

"Shut up," shouted Hanna, "shut up, shut up, shut up."

"Stop it, Hanna," shouted their mother over Hanna's voice. "Leave Matt alone."

"Why don't you believe me?" Hanna turned to her mother. "Why do you always take his side?"

"I've had enough, Hanna, of your lies and make-believe." Her mother's face was flushed, and beads of sweat stuck to her hairline. One dribbled down her forehead. She was a big, solid woman with huge bosoms. Hanna could never really get close to her because of those bosoms, which stood between them like a shelf. "Go to your room, Hanna." Her mother's voice rose in exasperation above the fishy steam in the over-heated kitchen.

"Leave her be, Myra," sighed their father, as he walked out of the room. Matt leant against the table, smirking.

"I said, GO-TO-YOUR-ROOM." Hanna's mother pointed a finger in the direction of the stairs and her hand looked huge and monstrous in the bright yellow washing up glove.

"No," said Hanna. Her legs wobbled but she made herself big by squaring her shoulders and bunching her fists. She had never before defied her mother. They locked eyes, or rather, Hanna locked eyes with the yellow finger.

"I saw France," she said, "and my real mother would have believed me." A pungent silence filled the small room. The yellow hand with the pointy finger trembled. It was the only thing moving.

"I didn't hear that," her mother gasped. "You didn't say it." A monster filled Hanna's heart and stomach. A steely grey monster, like a Dalek in Dr Who.

"You heard," said the monster in a horrible, gravelly voice. "*She* would have believed me."

The yellow finger fell, then her mother's body landed heavily against the corner of the table and the whole platter of warm, soft fishcakes flew across the kitchen in all directions.

Before that day, Hanna couldn't remember thinking much about where she came from. The story was always the same – that her mother had died giving birth to her, that Myra and Don had been waiting for a sister for Matt, and finally found their perfect baby girl. But after that day, Hanna now realised, she had carried two mothers with her throughout the rest of her childhood and into adult life. One, until six weeks ago, ever present and corporeal; the other, like the shimmering city in the sky, floating somewhere close by, visible only to her. She looked back down at the paper, blinking away sudden tears. She wasn't sure which mother she was crying for.

"Castles in the sky! Rare Fata Morgana mirage caused by hot and cold air, seen off the coast of Hastings," said the headline. In an old council filing cabinet, the article continued, a letter had been discovered, sent thirty years ago. It described the mirage an eighty-one-year-old man had seen from his home on the coast just outside Hastings. He believed it was a projection of Le Touquet, the French holiday resort more than forty miles away, and he'd included a drawing. There, on the kitchen table, were the buildings, the tower and the church which Hanna had seen on the same day, standing by the picket gate, staring out to sea.

Hanna stood up, leaving the article open on the table. She wandered through the flat, feeling the presence of her mother's absence, and behind it the more distant loss of her father, covered now in a layer of dust. From the lounge, with its heavy carpet and dated furniture, she walked slowly into the glass conservatory at the back of the flat, which opened onto a small garden. The garden looked bleak and limp on this grey Saturday morning in January. In one corner of the conservatory was another old filing cabinet – black metal with four drawers, in which her mother kept all her important papers. Hanna stared at the filing cabinet. Her mother had been an organised person, and in that cabinet, there could be a file with Hanna's name on it. A file she'd never asked to see. She took a step towards it, but then heard keys in the door and her brother stamping his feet on the doormat.

"Hey," he called out, "you there, Hanna?"

"Here," she called. She walked back down the hall to meet him.

"It's freezing," Matt said. He didn't kiss or hug her. They were not a touchy-feely family. "Why didn't you put on the heating?" He reached for the thermostat, then put the kettle on in the kitchen. "I've brought a stack of boxes," he said, glancing down at the open paper, then glancing away.

"Matt," said Hanna, "do you remember that ghastly holiday in East Sussex, when Mum and I had a huge fight because I'd seen a city in the sky and none of you believed me?"

"Oh, Han, don't drag up all that ancient history," said Matt, opening cupboards. "Where's the coffee?" He turned to face Hanna, a big man turning forty that year. His nose was red from the cold, his hair receding. "It's weird being here without her, isn't it?"

"Are you missing her terribly?" Hanna asked. Matt had always been closer to their mother.

"You know… I just…" Matt's face twisted and a snorting noise came from his nose. It was the closest he could get to crying. Hanna tentatively patted his arm. His jumper had bobbles on it and she had an urge to pick them off one by one.

"I'm okay," he said. "The kettles boiled. You look tired, Han. Do you want a fresh cup?"

Hanna was about to show Matt the picture in the paper and the article. "It was all true," she was going to say, "everything I saw, the man drew, and here it is. You should have believed me." She felt the old grievance rise to her throat, then suddenly fall away. She and Matt were doing something new, something different. They were being kind to each other. She put down the paper.

"Right," said Matt, holding out a mug of coffee for her, and picking up his own. "where shall we start?" He wandered out of the kitchen and Hanna heard him unfolding carboard, then pulling strips of tape to create boxes. She sipped the fresh, hot coffee and leant against the fridge, always full, now empty. Their mother had been such a big woman in every way, yet Hanna had never again dared to mention her birth mother, the circumstances of her birth. Then, one afternoon in her late teens, Hanna saw another mirage.

She'd been on the tube and had sat down opposite a woman in her thirties. The woman looked up and briefly held Hanna's gaze, before looking back down at her book. She had large, dark brown eyes and long red-brown hair with a widow's peak just like Hanna's, the same straight, blunt features. Hanna's stomach contracted in excitement. The woman got off the tube at Euston and crossed over to the Victoria line. Just before the doors closed, Hanna leapt out of the carriage and followed the woman onto the southbound train. At Victoria, Hanna followed her to the bus station, then suddenly came to her senses and wondered what on earth she was doing. She watched the woman climb onto a bus and felt strangely ashamed of herself. She had been surprised to find tears on her face.

Hanna was thirty-seven now, with no partner, no children and a job that she pretended was a career, but in which, she knew, she was treading water. Standing there with her back against the fridge, she recalled again the shimmering city and her overwhelming excitement and joy at seeing it. If whole cities, with towers and churches and sloping roofs could appear through the clouds and hover above the sea, then anything could happen, but somehow nothing had.

"Where shall we start?" called her brother again.

Hanna followed his voice into the lounge, and together they surveyed the clutter and debris of their mother's life.

"I'll start in the conservatory," she said, picking up a box.

Peter Hankins - Birth of a Punk

'It's called "punk rock",' said Robert, an enormous grin on his face. He was practically jigging in his seat with the excitement. He loved it when he knew about something we didn't.

'I had no idea you enjoyed that kind of thing, dear boy,' said Stevie, 'I had you down as a late quartets man. Not that you'd make a fuss about it of course,' but he raised one eyebrow to show he was ready to listen to an explanation. We liked explanations, the four of us; giving them, learning them, critiquing them – that sort of thing was our bag. We were the top pseuds of our generation; the four of us were all off to Oxbridge when term started, and we were enjoying the sunlit interregnum of hope fulfilled and labours recognised before we entered into our kingdom and began enjoying our happy ever afters.

We sat in the Trafalgar, where we used to go after evening debates or public speaking competitions at school. It was a dreary little place, but it was the only pub in town that could be relied on to serve us - though the grey-haired old barman glowered and frowned at us as if to say he knew what we were up to and we'd better not get any younger. He needn't worry; we'd soon be gone. I couldn't imagine we'd ever come back to this place once we were all old enough to go to a decent pub.

'They're called the *Ramones*,' said Robert, a light in his eye, 'they each take "Ramone" as their second name, you see, as if they were brothers. And they play badly *deliberately*. They call it "punk rock". Get it? That's the point; that they're terrible. It's fantastic!'

I could see at once why he liked the idea. It sounded like rock music had finally got irony, and we loved irony. Irony was safe. You never looked stupid or out of things; you never got *wrong-footed,* if you were being ironic.

'How very exciting,' said Stevie, 'Surely, Bobby, it's just one band, though?'

'No!' said Robert, 'There are going to be lots of them. Lots. Seriously. This is the next big thing. It's a new era. It's inevitable, because it's part of the historical cycle of rock.'

'Go on then, Hari Seldon,' said Brian, 'Was the advent of punk rock inevitable, and if so, why? Write on one side of the paper only.'

'You see,' said Robert, 'Popular music always starts simple. Folk tunes, you know, country dances. It gradually becomes more complex and sophisticated, but at the same time it gets more artificial and more inaccessible. It becomes decadent and out of touch with its roots. Then there's a revolution and a period when any idiot with a guitar who can sing a simple tune has a chance of breaking through. It's a cycle that repeats every couple of decades or so.'

'Provide two examples,' said Brian, holding his mug of Harp lager without using the handle, like a real man would.

'Skiffle, for one,' said Robert. None of us actually knew what skiffle was – I'm pretty sure that even Robert had just read about it in the NME and automatically memorised the word. 'Rock and Roll itself, for that matter. Anyway, that's what's happening now. The revolution. Glam Rock was the last decadent knockings of the *Ancien Régime*. Now, instead of needing glittery platform shoes, a million-pound synthesiser, and a symphony orchestra, all you need is a ripped t-shirt and a crap guitar. Anyone can do it. *We* could do it.'

'No,' said Brian, 'I'm sorry, but I think you'll find you're allowing yourself to be carried away by the exuberance of your own verbosity there. *We*, the select few here, *we* in particular, could *not* do it.'

'*Yes, we could!*' said Robert, 'You don't even have to be able to play the instruments!

'I *can* play the guitar,' said Stevie, 'tolerably well, in fact. Acoustic, of course – I worship Julian Bream - but electric is easier, actually.'

'That's OK,' said Robert, 'We'll put you on drums.'

We exchanged glances around the table with a wild surmise.

'Wait,'said Brian, 'Are you *serious* about this?'

'I wasn't,' admitted Robert, 'But now I'm thinking, well, why not? Why shouldn't we get in on this?'

I think we all felt the mad attraction of the idea. We felt powerful. This was our time. Throughout the long years of school, we pseuds had accepted the status of a powerless minority. We got the best marks, but we were never Captain of anything but chess: we were not prefects, and no-one gave us three hearty cheers in Morning Assembly. Our nicknames were not the respectful ones that rugby players got, though not too rude either. (Around the pub table: Robert was 'Beeper' – I don't really know why, but it actually suited him; Brian was 'MiniWoof' because his surname was Barker and he had a sportier older brother. Stevie was 'Tissues', not because he used a lot but because of the way he pronounced the word, sounding each 's' separately. I was Veg, the vegetable, ie brain-dead; I believe it was an ironic reference to my perfect exam marks.) We were not oppressed or bullied, exactly, but we were not in charge either, not the way the beefy, sporty Hearties were. But after nine or ten years, school had finally run its course for all of us, and all of that was about to change. The meek were about to inherit. The Hearties would go to provincial universities or none; they would be branch managers or senior administrative officers at best. We were going to be top barristers, merchant bankers, Cabinet Ministers, or have our own comedy sketch shows on the telly. We would rule the country, and they would supply us with services. They would be very polite to us, and we would be nice to them about it.

This was the way the world worked so far as I knew, and our triumph was especially heady for me, given the unmentioned fact that I lived in a council house with my widowed mother, while the others were the sons of accountants and doctors, people whose main houses had at least five bedrooms. The idea that the crest of this wave could carry us on further, to actual rock star status, well…

'It might look good on our CVs,' I said, 'mine's a bit weak on the "team player" thing, to be honest.'

'Are you quite sure you've got this right, though?' said Stevie, frowning at Robert, 'This punk rock - all it amounts to is playing badly on purpose? Isn't that a rather thin premise?'

'Oh, no, I haven't explained it all,' said Robert, 'there's a lot more to it than that. It's nihilist, to start with.'

That one word pretty much sold it, as far as we were concerned. Nihilist! Who in Bedford but us knew about nihilism? Who else could even pronounce it correctly? We agreed to read up about punk rock and discuss the details when we met again. Reading up on things – that was our bag.

It should have been foreseeable that our chief difficulty would not be instruments, clothes, or music, but what to call ourselves. Robert borrowed a bass guitar from his brother and lent it to me on condition I would support his ambition to be lead vocalist. On reflection, it wasn't much of a deal, but I was enchanted by the glamour of the guitar. Robert also owned a junior drum kit, which he lent to Stevie.

'"Junior"?' said Stevie, mortified.

'It's a real drum kit,' said Robert, 'Not a toy. Look, it's that or a Stylophone. Or get your own instrument.' Brian *had* got his own, simply by telling his parents he wanted an electric guitar as a reward for getting top grades.

Clothes we frankly agreed to defer until we had an actual performance booked. There was no way any of us was walking around town covered in safety pins. Stevie provided music.

'It's an atonal piece I wrote for the clarinet,' he said, 'It's very nihilistic.' I didn't think he had quite got the hang of punk, but Robert made us play it at triple speed, inaccurately, and shouted obscenities over the resulting noise. He was pretty pleased with the result.

But what were we to be called? It should be rude, ideally, and some wordplay would be good. Our problem was that we were indeed pseuds; much more comfortable criticising other people's ideas than proposing our own. We kept drifting into the pretentious intellectual territory which was our natural home. Robert suggested 'The Spheroids' for example; I thought that if that was where we were going it should clearly be 'The Bollocks', but I was too embarrassed to say so. Finally, Stevie waved his hands and said it *simply must* be a magnificent phrase he had come across in *Brief Lives.*

'Sir Thomas Browne is walking through Axe Yard one day when a cart runs over his foot. So he shouts out: "God's glistening turds!". A lady passing by tells him not to blaspheme, but he replies "Madam, there's no blasphemy in't. Our Lord lived thirty years on Earth: think you that he never shat? Had I called them 'stinking', why then you might have arraigned me, perhaps."'

'I've read *Brief Lives,*' said Robert, 'but I don't remember that one.'

'You haven't read the unedited version, dear boy,' said Stevie, 'listen, if we can be *God's Glistening Turds,* you can be lead singer. Now I really can't say fairer than that, can I?'

'It's too pseudish,' I objected, but I was over-ruled.

None of us had any idea how to get a gig, and none of us actually enjoyed our own music – though I began to find a cathartic pleasure in thrashing away at my bass, pretty much ignoring Stevie's atonal composition – so chances are, the whole thing would have fizzled out in a couple of weeks. But Robert came across a sort of Open Night, at a place called 'The Garage' in Luton. Anyone could sign up and play a single number, to see whether they lived or died in front of a real punk audience.

That put us under pressure. For one thing, we only had one song. At the Open Night you were basically only invited to play one, so that shouldn't be a problem. But if you went down really well, you might get an encore.

'If that happens, we'll just play the same thing and I'll improvise some different words,' said Robert. I didn't think the difference would be noticeable; nobody could make out what he was shouting anyway. That, in itself, was probably for the best. Stevie had wanted him to sing some John Donne *(To His Coy Mistress)*, but Robert had freely rewritten it in a punk style: 'The fuckin' graveyards fuckin' suck, the fuckers there don't fuckin' fuck…'

We met up on the day at Brian's house; he was borrowing his sister's van to take us to Luton. We looked a mixed bag, it has to be said.

'I think we should have had a dress rehearsal,' said Brian. He had been to London to buy clothes and was wearing a leather jumpsuit with many zips; but he had done nothing about his hair. Robert and I had spiked up our hair, and he had sprayed pink on his. We both had ripped t-shirts, but he had leather trousers, while I only had jeans with safety pins. We looked like we were in fancy dress. Stevie had had his hair dyed platinum blond, and wore some pastel slacks with a very nice shirt. Unfortunately Gary Numan would not be invented for several years yet, so he looked as if he was ready for tea with granny.

'It doesn't matter,' said Robert.

Luton is a seedy city, and the Garage was its sleaziest venue. Perfect for early punk rock, but I was terrified. At that stage I had actually never been to a live gig before; I had listened to a total of three punk records, twice each; yet here I was about to play at what might well be the most authentic punk venue outside of London. It was not a garage, and never had been; it was the basement floor of a decaying office block. The bare concrete pillars did give it the feeling of a multi-storey car park, though. Posters plastered over the bare concrete and a long bar at the back which served lager in plastic glasses provided some sense of its being an entertainment venue. The stages, two of them, were small and low and presented no barrier to interaction between the bands and the crowd.

Robert took us to the back where the MC, who seemed to be doing all the organising on his own, checked us off a list. He was an amiable, laid-back bloke, in a biker jacket, smoking a roll-up.

'"God's Glistening Turds"?' he read, and laughed, not unkindly, 'So you're shit hot, are you, lads? Don't worry, you'll be OK.'

We stood around in the thundering racket of the other bands. I'd never really had exam nerves, but now I wanted to be sick.

'Hey, Terry!' said somebody. I looked at him in fear; it was the big, beefy lead singer of the band who were next after us, called 'the Bastards'. His eyes were ringed with black make-up. 'Geoff,' he said, 'it's Geoff. Didn't know you was a punk, eh?'

'Oh yeah,' I said, 'hi, Geoff!' Geoff was my next-door neighbour; we had been at school together until I passed the eleven plus. In fact, I remembered guiltily, we had been pretty good friends once. Stevie looked at me enquiringly.

'This is Geoff,' I said. 'I know him…' Geoff and Stevie looked at each other with a certain wary interest.

'Awright,' said the MC to Robert, 'Yer on when this lot come off. Get set up.'

'Speak to you after,' said Geoff.

'Who on earth was that wonderfully uncouth vulgarian?' asked Stevie.

'He's my next-door neighbour,' I said.

'*Really*?'

We started setting up. In what seemed like a few seconds, the MC ran out on to the front of the stage.

'And next!' he shouted, 'The Turds! They're crap!' And then we were on. There was a short, terrible interval while we got ourselves ready, and then we started, out of synch but what did it matter? My throat was tight and all I could do was whine faintly. I thought Robert did well. Three cans of piss were thrown at us, but really it was just sympathy urine. Hardly anyone spat on us. I'd been afraid we'd be booed or even attacked, but it was worse than that; at the end we slunk off in something close to silence.

It wasn't as if they hated us, more as if they had lost interest.

'Sorry, guys,' said the MC, passing us on his way to introduce the Bastards, 'Don't give up, eh?'

We stood and watched Geoff and his mates in dazed silence. They launched themselves into the music with wild abandon, Geoff shouting the words in a strangled voice quite unlike his normal, mild one. As Robert listened, a look of outrage came over his face.

'What the fuck is that?' he demanded, 'how is *that* punk?' The Bastards were delivering an energetic version of the theme tune from the *Banana Splits*, a kid's TV show. But it was three times as fast as the original and five times as loud as we had been, with a lot of rhythmic shouting. Geoff bounced around like a ball, screaming at the top of his new voice.

'Makin' up a *mess*! Makin' up a *mess*! MAKIN' UP A MESS! AAAAAAAAAH!' And then back to the chorus, 'La la la, la-la la la! La la la, la-la la la!'

They were getting a very different reception from ours. The crowd were leaping up and down, there was a rain of cans, and a torrent of spitting. One bloke leapt on stage and grabbed the lead guitarist by the neck, but nothing stopped the music. It was overwhelming, crushing, electrifying, hoarse, rough, loud; like being charged by Satan's cavalry.

'I think it's ironic,' said Stevie.

'Wow,' said the MC, 'those guys, eh?' He ran out on stage.

'He's telling them to do an encore,' said Robert.

They did the tune from *The Magic Roundabout* with more rhythmic shouting. It went down a storm, and they finished in triumph, clearly the favourite band of the whole event.

And then, as Geoff was coming towards me with a broad smile on his sweaty face, I had a sudden epiphany. We were not going to inherit the earth after all, we pseuds. Oh sure, we would get big houses in Surrey. Expensive, comfortable cars. But we would never be cool, or get real respect. We would go on being a slightly scared, tolerated minority. More than that, I now realised that we would get our worthless rewards because we had always done what teacher said, and we would go on doing what teacher approved of. For life. We were boxed in, tamed and emasculated. We would do as we were told and when at last we came to die, we should find that we had never lived.

'Everything is shit,' I said, in sudden wonderment – how had I never noticed? '*Everything!* Complete shit. University, books, money, music; *shit, shit, shit.* We've been cheated. Scammed. Even this. *Especially* this. This is the shittest thing of all. The whole world is a gigantic fucking conspiracy of shit. Turds? Christ, we had no idea.'

Geoff, approaching with a grin of triumph on his face, heard what I said. He pointed a meaty finger at me as if to say, 'this guy gets it'. Then, like a baptism, he gobbed on me.

Peter Latham - Big Dipper 1972

I am Pip Bridge. This is what they tell me. They say they want me to remember, but the drugs fog my mind, leave vague ghostly outlines of memories, chemical chimeras, as insubstantial as dream images fading on waking. Yet my dreams I do remember, though only fragments, vivid and violent, jolting me awake, my body taut and tense. At first, and for a long time, I dreamt rarely, remembering very little, but recently the dreams have become more frequent, and more vivid. Last night I dreamt of two skull and crossbones signs, flashing past me, with red flags waving next to them. Then I was walking down some kind of steep steps, an incline. I looked down and saw that the ground beneath me was dark red. In another dream I am looking at my hands, scarlet and shaking. The staff here are wary of me, walk on eggshells, thinking I will crack and they will have to clean up the mess. What do they know that I don't? The arrival of the psychiatrist who comes to see me every week is announced by the ponderous clanging shut of the first door (with three locks) and the boom of the heavier second door (with two locks) closing, a ritual he performs each time with apparent equanimity, gaining him access to the febrile world of the tormented, deluded, persecuted, a world he traverses with calm detachment, shielded from it through psychoanalytic abstraction, a neutralizing of our pain. The psychiatrist, like all the staff here, regularly asks me about my name, if I remember it, if it triggers associations. I tell them: I don't know where my name, or I, come from. No triggers. No associations. They also make comments about the healing that will be so much harder than that from my physical injuries, the broken legs, the elbow fracture, cuts stitched, bruises faded. I ask them what they mean. They refuse to answer, or says things like, "You will remember in your own good time." Now that I have recovered fully they make such comments less often.

I don't know how long I have been here, and the staff won't tell me. Years I think. Months merge, weeks wash over me, days drift and disappear. When I ask, they say, "What's important is that you feel better." I know that that is called a non-sequitur, but all conversations here are full of non-sequiturs, random exchanges by people locked in private conversations that no-one else is privy to. I also know, from the pristine library copy of *The Penguin Dictionary of Philosophy* (unmarked apart from the

'St. John's Library' stamp on the first page), what that sealed-off state is called: solipsism. I have read all the library books here, many twice, three times: *The Agony and the Ecstasy*, *A Burnt-Out Case*, *Ship of Fools*, *Linda Goodman's Sun Signs*, *Sex and the Single Girl*, *In Cold Blood*, *Better Homes and Gardens New Cook Book*, *Stranger in a Strange Land*, *The Naked Ape*, *Phyllis Diller's Marriage Manual*, *The Concise Oxford English Dictionary*, *You Only Live Twice*. A few others. Here we are all solipsists. But we couldn't, even if we wanted to, share our worlds with others, those of us, that is, who don't see the people in the hospital as just more teeming and tormenting phantoms of the mind. None of us can form the fragments of ourselves into a whole that can be articulated, or even give them a shape that is not blurred and ill-defined. We are ill because we are undefined.

They say I am an orphan. I remember a name though: John Cunningham. Was he my father? There is a man here also called John, he is the only happy person in this place. I've heard from one of the other patients that he has had ECT twenty times. John is on repeat, every time he passes by with the library trolley of books, he asks, to no-one and everyone, "Ain't it marvelous? Ain't it marvelous?" It's a rhetorical question, but none of us could answer it, least of all John. I like him, he's found a way to be here, to live in the endlessly repeated loop of pointlessness. He has embraced it, even if he doesn't know it. Others are hostile to John, resent him, his upbeat insanity. But I think they are jealous – who wouldn't be? Arturo is the opposite of John. He is seething. He tells me, "I am physically and mentally incapable of doing anything. This is what they have done not *for* but *to* me." He has a naïve belief that he has been betrayed, that the doctors and nurses are here to do for, not to, him. He could probably learn a lot from John. "Ain't it marvelous?" I made the mistake of laughing at Arturo one time, his earnest outrage. He put both his hands round my throat and squeezed hard. Two of the staff rushed in, the first pulled Arturo's left arm free of my throat and shoved it through the hatch of the door just behind us, the other grabbed his right arm and administered the injection of a sedative. A very temporary respite that will not alleviate Arturo's suffering for more than a few hours – and he has hundreds of thousands more to get through. If he does.

Not all of my dreams are disturbing. I occasionally wake up laughing. My laugh is an echo of the laughter of the other girls I am with, who must be my friends. We are on some steps, hugging and squeezing each other, teasing, poking, giggling, there is a sign just above us with an arrow and the word 'Station'. A smiling woman is taking a Polaroid of us. This dream recurs but does not change. I am always on the steps with these girls, but we never move, though I can see the bridge at the top of the steps and a 'Trains to London' sign at the end. Sometimes I just dream of the bridge, a frozen image, and I wake up with my heart thumping, in a cold sweat.

Arturo tells me his dreams, but they are like his waking life. Even in dreams his anger and despair give him no respite. He awakes more furious than when he went to bed. Sleep destroys, instead of restoring, any possibility of calm, let alone sanity. Arturo will surely not survive this place and I don't want to be here when he is gone. He is in an odd way a beacon of hope, as the cliché has it, and the hope is that we refuse our incarceration – but where would we be then?

Jane is the closest thing I have to a friend here. Why do I say 'thing'? Perhaps because we are problems to be solved, objects to be expelled from the system as soon as possible, numbers that determine the success or failure of the hospital. Hence John's twenty ECT 'treatments'. Did I mention that John used to be a chef? Very highly regarded apparently, not that you – or he – would know it (now, you wouldn't trust John to cook an egg, he'd boil it to a husk with everything congealed and dried up inside). Jane, though, is only too aware of her past – it's what got her here. She worked in a library, not the best place to hide the shakes and twitches, the flood of paralyzing and unstoppable anxiety, borrowers' dismay at her sudden disappearances from the counter. The other staff had been warned, notified of her previous incarceration, that they should be on the lookout. No-one talked to Jane, they just called St. Clare's. Staff were dispatched. Most of the books in the library are from her former employers, a salve no doubt for their guilty conscience. Apparently they didn't see the irony - dumping their unwanted, ignored books and their unwanted, ignored employee here. Jane tells me that her husband is sadistic, had been sticking pins in her while she slept, some kind of black magic. I believe her.

Dr Olufsen raised his eyebrows (something he does with irritating frequency) when I made that joke about John boiling an egg. "A husk with everything congealed and dried up inside?" he asked, repeating what I had said back to me as a question (something else he does with irritating frequency). He is, predictably, interested in my dreams and talks about 'dream distortion', which means the dreams I have are not about what they seem to be about. I disagree – my dreams are about exactly the things I dream about. When I say this Dr Olufsen places his hands together, as if in prayer, and places his chin meditatively on his fingers, smiling benignly. He keeps returning to one of my recurring dreams, in which a girl who is next to me in some kind of carriage high above the ground falls screaming, even though I reach out to grab her. "Who do you think this girl might be?" he asks me. I tell him I don't know her. "Don't know her or don't want to know her?" he asks. I look him in the eye, stare unblinking at his crinkly smile. "I. Don't. Know. Her." He makes notes on his pad, no doubt about me being 'resistant', though he is the one who is resisting, refusing to see or listen, trying to make my dreams fit into his theories.

In a recent dream I saw my name on a sign. White neon letters were flashing on and off, my name alternating with other letters, words, I couldn't understand, like this: PIP BRIDGE, REPPID GIB, PIP BRIDGE, REPPID GIB, PIP BRIDGE, REPPID GIB, PIP BRIDGE, REPPID GIB, PIP BRIDGE, REPPID GIB.

I don't know what this means. One thing I do know though: I'm not telling Dr Olufsen about the dream.

I have started to have strange intrusions into my waking hours - psychic disturbances I believe they are called, mental jolts, shocking me into immobility, stopping me in my tracks. A few days ago I heard a voice shouting 'Ruth! Hall of Mirrors!' as I was walking with my lunch tray in the canteen, dropping it as I swung round to hear who'd said it. No-one had. Later in my room I saw a sign above the mirror, 'Pay to Be Scared', flashing on and off. That night I dreamt of the bridge again, but this time I was walking with my friends across it, and we went down the steps to the platform, just as the train came into the station. Then we were on the train, swaying and laughing where we stood near the doors, and I heard an announcement, 'Battersea Park. Alight here for Battersea Fun Fair'.

This morning I was talking to Arturo and he said, apropos of nothing, "Mr. Cunningham, are you responsible?" "What did you say?" I asked him. "I didn't say anything," he replied. I think he's getting worse.

I had a another dream about my name last night, but this time the words were in red, and I saw my fingers writing them, on some steps below a sign that said 'Dodgem Cars'. In an uneven, jagged scrawl I wrote: PIP BRIDGE. I could hear loud voices behind me, shouts, crying, fairground noises, and I ran, past huge spinning wheels with lights, carriages gyrating high in the air, and into the road. Then blackness.

***

The queue snakes around the dodgem cars, the Octopus, the Ferris Wheel, the Carousel, the 15p they each will pay for the 'Thrill-a-Minute Joy-Ride Where You Pay to Be Scared' held in clammy, expectant hands. They are queuing for 'John Cunningham's Big Dipper'. She is near the front, impatient, watching the Big Dipper ride come to a standstill in slow motion, the letters in the neon sign above flashing on and off, her friends just behind, not even watching, cackling over a joke about a boy one of them had sex with. One of the girls shouts 'Hall of Mirrors!' and they all run across to the entrance, one calling back to her, 'Ruth! Hall of Mirrors!' but she doesn't pay attention because the gate has now opened, the carriages are ready. She takes her place in one of those at the front, looks about her, confused at not seeing her friends. A woman behind her says, "Go on Pip, sit with the nice young lady, Daddy and me want to sit together." She smiles at being called a nice young lady, her friends would laugh if they heard, make jokes. The girl looks at her warily. She smiles, "Hello Pip, I'm Ruth". Pip looks down shyly, "Hello." Pip asks if she can have her seat, on the outside, wants to be able to look down, look up, during the ride, so she gets up and takes the other seat. The yellow metal clamp locks them in their seats. The cars begin to move to the bottom of the wheel, above them a sign, 'FINAL WARNING. DO NOT STAND UP', *flashing pale green then white, and they ascend slowly up the enormous wheel. People are clapping as the ride starts, whooping, hands held high. As they reach the top of the wheel there is another sign overhead in red,* NO STANDING, *red flags waving above the sign, two skull and crossbones signs, one before* NO *one after* STANDING. *The descent is steep and fast, people are screaming with thrilled fear, thrown about in their seats like rabbits in a fox's mouth, the yellow metal clamps the only protection from falling out. They plunge and ascend at ever greater speeds, the breath ripped from their lungs, the world turns upside down, then is righted, then turns upside down again, hair pressed back, features bulging in the pressure of speed. The 'Please keep seated' notice repeats itself as they go round and round, up and down, the string of light bulbs in the crisscross lattice borders flashing by in a blur. 'Stay in car to ride again' rises up and falls away, rises up and falls away. Those at the front look down and see spiraling slats in the rails, look up and see the pearl necklace of bulbs threaded around the framework of the Big Dipper, and another sign,* 'KEEP HANDS AND ARMS INSIDE CAR'.

The three-car wooden train that she is in suddenly detaches from the steel drive train holding it on the wooden track. The cars start to slip backwards, hit a tight turn, and the last carriage derails. The brake man is frantically trying to put the brake on but it isn't working. The derailed carriage flies around the next dipping bend, and hurls off the side of the Big Dipper through a wooden hoarding, smashing into the sign above the entrance booth. People are hanging over the edge, some groaning in pain, some silent, bodies are sprawled on the ground by the entrance to the Big Dipper. The other carriages are stranded, rocking back and forth, the passengers who had unlocked the yellow metal clamps thrown by the initial jolting impact out and into the slats, bloodied contortions of limbs, others thrown over the side of the Big Dipper. The girl next to her screams that she wants to get off, and leans on a wooden barrier, which immediately collapses. She tries to grab the girl, cries "Pip!", but watches as Pip falls screaming to the ground far below. As she walks one hour later falteringly down the tracks of the Big Dipper she realizes that she is walking on blood. She feels something click inside her, a switch is flipped. She grows suddenly burningly cold, as something beyond fear and anger floods through her.

She is on the ground but does not remember how she got there. She has a shard of glass from the smashed entrance booth to the Big Dipper in her hand. She sees flashing lights in the dusk, hears voices talking over each other. "Mr. Cunningham, are you responsible for the Big Dipper accident tonight? What have you got to say to the families of those who died and are seriously injured?" John Cunningham says there will be a full investigation, employee negligence will be not be tolerated, safety is paramount. She walks up unnoticed, but vaguely sensed, behind him. "You." He turns, the shard behind her back flies round and upwards, right to left across his throat, the arterial spray of blood arcing and then falling, arcing and then falling, spattering then splattering her face and chest and her hands. Her vision is blurred red, she drops the shard and walks pasts the still spinning, flashing fairground rides. She stops and then walks to the steps below the 'Dodgem Cars' sign, writes with the blood on her hands PIP BRIDGE *on the top step. She walks, somnambulant, out to the dark street. Another click, the switch inside her head flips as she crosses the road, stopping still in confusion. There is a dull thud as the car hits her, and she is thrown across the road, sprawled limbs on the pavement. The last thing she sees is the red pulsing from the gash in her arm, as John Cunningham's blood drips silently from her face, mingling with her own, a binding and unbreakable covenant. Until.*

Philip Charter - Marbles and Memories

"The mind is a complicated thing, Mrs Spenmore."

"Mine's a bloomin' mystery," I said. "That's the only thing I'm certain of."

Mary didn't laugh. She was an unusually serious woman.

I'd been particularly concerned about misplacing things. A few weeks before, I'd found a red-lettered gas bill in the kitchen, a cheese and tomato sandwich going green in the conservatory, and a pair of Gerald's socks (red *and* green) hiding in the television cabinet. At least those things had turned up. I'd lost the keepsake I bought on our honeymoon — a little glass lighthouse filled with patterned sand from the Isle of Wight.

Mary peered over her sharp nose. Gerald called her 'the memory bird'. He wasn't wrong. She looked just like a bird — not Big Bird from Sesame Street, more like a startled crane. But, she was patient, and according to the classified section of the *Falmouth Packet*, she was the only qualified expert in the area.

"Stick to the process, Mrs Spenmore. I've seen you make steady progress since we started."

"I've told you, call me Maggie." Honestly, a 'memory retention consultant' should remember to call her clients by their first names. The whole 'Mr and Mrs' thing reminded me of my twenty-five years spent as secretary to a prickly lawyer, Herbert Blake. After a quarter of a century of service, he deemed it proper to send me a plain red Christmas card. *Dear Margaret, happy Christmas, Mr Blake.*

"Here's the list," she said, "household objects, numbered. I'll give you a minute to create your narrative." She'd conveniently forgotten the question about whether my memory was deteriorating.

Mary came once a week and we did mental exercises, recounting dreams and excavating details of life events big and small. I could barely follow the reruns of Time Team that Gerald watched. What hope did I have of unearthing finds in my muddied memory?

That particular session, I wanted to better my record for memorising objects in order. One time I managed thirteen. No danger of getting past that unlucky number, let alone worrying the current world record holder Prejish Merlin, who had listed four hundred and seventy objects in order. Practise, practise, practise, Mary said, but she dodged my question about how many *she* could remember.

"The trick is to rhyme the number and include the object as part of the image in your mind's eye," she said. Rhymes never came easy to me. My literature form tutor once described my poems as infantile, which I personally thought was harsh criticism for a twelve-year-old.

Try again. "Number one. Daz washing powder."

One rhymes with son. I imagined Nicholas all those years ago before he moved to New Zealand with his boyfriend. He wore brilliant white underpants, not when he moved, but when I pictured him as a toddler. I'd always been loyal to the brand, even when *Which?* Magazine downgraded it to fourth best for stain removal. Nicholas's boyfriend is called Darren, but he isn't a Daz. Gerald turned a certain shade of beetroot when our son came out. Of course, I'd known for years. Mothers find things in their children's bedrooms, while fathers are organising the tool shed or shouting at rugby matches on the telly.

"Two. A bowl of *potpourri*."

Two rhymes with new, as in 'new house'. We'd wanted to move for some time, but the market never worked in our favour. Gerald said viewings interrupted his circadian rhythms. At first, I thought he meant his six o'clock ablutions, but he said it means sleep patterns. The young families saw our place as old-fashioned. What did they expect from a pair of pensioners, strobe lights in the kitchen and a solar-powered toilet? The estate agent sprayed an awful fragrance of baked cookies for that 'authentic homely smell'. Nothing beats the tried and tested scents. I love the smell of *potpourri* in the morning.

Mary reached down and brought the items onto the table as I identified them, like The Generation Game only in reverse. She's too young to have watched it in its heyday. Now, what was—?

"Three?" she said, interrupting my daydream about a young Bruce Forsyth.

Three sounds like tree, or at least an Irish person saying three. "Ah yes," I said, "the Tai chi book." I'd put the book up a cherry tree in my mental picture. Lionel Blair sat on the lowest branch, legs swinging, flicking through the book. He'd been at the opening of some assisted-living flats I viewed in Bridport, but I'd been too embarrassed to meet him. The follow-up sales call confused Gerald. "We're not even seventy yet, Maggie," he stammered. "Those places are for fruitcakes and crones."

Four was easy. Pussy Galore, the only woman I'd ever fancied. "Playing cards." Goldfinger was a nasty cheat, wasn't he?

Mary placed the cards with the other items.

By that point, I was ready for a cup of t— that was it! "Tea leaves," I almost shouted. Onwards to five. What rhymes with five. Jive? Beehive? Nosedive? External hard-drive? It didn't matter any more. The system had gone. I got lucky with 'tea', and thirteen was a long way off.

While I certainly didn't miss Mr Blake, I did miss work. Watching Eggheads on BBC Two every day didn't really count as an accomplishment. I'd even applied to go on the show with the ladies from Yoga. Mind, Body and Seoul we were called. Jessie was actually from Tai Wan, but she said she'd pretend to be Korean so we could use our clever team name. We would donate the prize to Dementia UK. Gerald and I had seen what the disease did to his mother.

Back in my kitchen, Mary sensed my struggle. The hour ticked down, and she was about to do that thing where she slapped her legs and said 'right,' before upping and leaving.

"Six. Car keys," I blurted, putting a stop to any thigh slapping. Six rhymes with Weetabix. The keys were hidden inside one of Gerald's bloody cereal boxes in my image. Two packets a week he got through. More than a thousand per year. We could have built a second home out of all of those wheaty bricks he's put away over the course of our marriage. He brought them with him on holiday, even on domestic trips. Even on our honeymoon in Ventnor. They say marriage is about sacrifice, well, I'd sacrificed plenty of space in the suitcase to his immoveable concept of breakfast over the years. Such a shame we hadn't been back to the Isle of Wight.

A hand touched my arm. "Mrs Spenmore? Maggie? Where've you gone?" It must have been a full thirty seconds since my last word.

"Sorry … just thinking about breakfast." I must've sounded ridiculous.

"Everybody's thought patterns are different," she said, wearing the same sympathetic look as the doctor who admitted a three-year-old me to A&E after I ate plasticine. "Sorry, our time is up."

Something about those words pressed a button that shouldn't be pressed — a big red button with a protective case over it. I was alarmed. My time was up. Before long, I'd forget the stories behind all of these objects. My mind would become a rusty law-office filing cabinet, pushed off a cliff by a maniacally laughing Mr Blake. Lionel Blair would watch and laugh from his tree.

Mary gathered her things. "Now," she said, "I'll be away for the next two weeks. Remember I'm off to Ireland for a conference. Tipperary." It might as well have been Timbuktu.

As soon as the door closed, my lost key fob sprang to mind. I was normally so careful with things. We had an organisation system for my tea towels even though we only had three. My time was up. The well inside me rose. I sat on the stairs and sobbed. That was the first time I'd cried since Nadiya won the Bake-Off finale, and no one can begrudge tears for such an emotional moment. Blobs of salty water squeezed through the gaps in my fingers, over my hands and onto the carpet.

Gerald found me a few minutes later. "What's that memory bird said to you, love?"

His face was blurry through the tears. His hair slicked into a side parting like he was a child off to a birthday party. He stood back a foot or two, calculating the severity of my latest 'Maggie moment'.

"Oh, don't worry, love. Just losing my marbles is all."

"Just as long as you've not lost your marbles," he said, pretending not to hear me. He always could cheer me up with his silliness. "Memory class not go well?" he asked, sitting next to me on the bottom step of the stairs.

I dried my eyes. "Can't think where I could have lost that key fob. You know, the one with—"

"You mean this?" He held up the glass lighthouse.

I gasped. "But it's empty."

"Mary got you doing observation as well? Nothing gets past you."

"Where did you find it?"

"Well, I've got a confession to make, love." Now he definitely looked like a naughty schoolboy. "You know I misplace my car keys on occasion?"

I did know. I'd threatened to get him one of those elastic keychains to clip to his jeans.

"I err … borrowed yours last week, dropped them in the supermarket car park and it—, well, the sand came out. Tried to catch it with my foot to cushion the impact, but I just ended up drop-kicking it into this woman's trolley."

I didn't know whether to feel relieved or angry. At least I'd stopped crying.

"She was asking the trolley-collector bloke for help and didn't see it go into her shopping. Let me tell you, she did not appreciate me rummaging through her groceries. The poor thing was eighty-odd and rammed me with her trolley to get me to stop. Must have thought I was after her fondant fancies or something." Gerald continued without taking a breath as I listened in amazement. "I had to explain to the trolley warden why there was coloured sand leaking into this woman's shopping. I told him to be careful, but he plunged his hand in and cut himself on the thing."

That made me wince.

"Luckily, the woman had bought some plasters for her granddaughter and patched him up with a pink Hello Kitty bandaid."

I was crying again, but this time with laughter. He chuckled and said it was a wonder the police weren't called. It took me a good minute to compose myself before I could speak. "I can just imagine it, you daft sod."

"I'm sorry. It's important to you, so …" Gerald handed me the glass trinket. "I wanted to fix it first."

The glue held it together so well, you'd never know it was broken. "Shame it's empty," I said.

He said we could fill it up when we go.

"Go where?"

He smiled. "The Needles of course. I've booked us some WightLink ferry tickets and a couple of nights in a B&B in Ventnor."

There I was cursing his Weetabix, and he'd gone and done something so romantic. "Is it the same one?"

"God no," he said, "health inspectors closed it down years ago."

Gerald got to his feet, but he was two steps further up, so when I went in for a kiss my head met the level of his bulging stomach.

"That's not all," continued the belly. "I've booked an appointment with an estate agent. You've always loved it there, and we might get more for our money."

Views out into the English Channel, the breeze in my hair, walking along the cliffs. "Marvellous," I said. "Better than those retirement flats." I went into the kitchen, put the key fob on the kitchen table along with the other items, and switched the kettle on. "What about your rugby club, love?"

He shrugged. He'd find another one. We need a change of scenery.

"And I won't miss any classes with Mary. She's off to Tipperary. Probably come back a nun."

"Sister Mary Magpie?"

We laughed.

The kettle boiled and Gerald poured the tea. "Now you've learned her secrets, you could fly the nest, set out on your own."

We sat at the table and an item brushed against my foot. There were still a good few objects under there. Gerald reached down to clear the space for our legs but I stopped him. "Wait." I looked around the room, with its 1980s tiles, pine chairs and oversized radio. We'd been in the place forty years, but the thought of a new house excited me. "Let me try and finish my list."

Gerald nodded. "Go on then."

"Seven … pen. Eight … err, thimble. Nine … pine … our framed photo."

Gerald rummaged under the table and pulled out the corresponding items. Like shooting ducks in a barrel. No, wait. Ducks in a row. *Fish* in a barrel.

"Ten, now that's *um*, a baseball cap. Eleven … Radio Times Magazine. That's it. Now, twelve … Banana!" How had I done that? The images in my mind lined like a very respectful set of suspected criminals. "Thirteen, green … plants. Oh, packet of tomato seeds."

Gerald grinned and held up a finger. "One more, love."

Was the curse of thirteen about to be lifted? Fourteen … Mr Bean, Vaseline, amphetamine, Mary Magdalene, dialysis machine, poly-tetra-fluoroethylene? I was in one of those spirals again, trapped in a cycle of rhyming memories. Gerald got up to busy himself in the kitchen. Then it hit me. "A pack of glass marbles." (Well, they were decorative glass beads really, but Gerald would appreciate the joke.)

"*Yes*. Well done, my love."

Fourteen in a row. I mean, Prejish Merlin had absolutely nothing to worry about, but my memory was improving, not fading.

"You did it," said Gerald triumphantly, putting the dish of glass beads onto the table.

I sat back like the cat that got the cream. And I *did* get the cream because Gerald plated up two chocolate eclairs from the fridge while I *ummed* and *ahhed* over the last item.

"You'll be setting up shop in Ventnor next."

"What do you mean?"

"Could be a good way to meet people. Take what you've learned from Mary, and offer some free classes. Nursing homes and the like."

The idea of it. Me, the ageing memory mistress. Sipping my tea, I considered it all, a new place, and a new job. We might even run into elderly celebrities like Lionel Blair.

"Come on," said Gerald, pointing to the telly. 'Eggheads is about to start."

Richard Hooton - Dreamsnatcher

IT was a scream to shatter dreams. As a ghostly white moon hung overthe castle, the bloodcurdling noise reverberated. It reached the building's bowels where a servant, Hera, was scrubbing pots in the grimy kitchen. Her heart froze as her head jolted upwards. *Change is coming,* she thought. Hera smiled but it flickered out like a candle. She recognised the rumbling above of chambermaids bolting from their beds. Hera shivered. Not because of the cold, that horrid sound or the stench of rotting food. Something else chilled her blood. *Can I trust him?*

Hera scoured goblets and plates while in her mind she wandered as freely as the wind, exploring corridors and rooms to marvel at opulent tapestries and treasures, roaming gardens vibrant with blossoming flowers and speaking openly with anyone.

'Orphan girl.' The head cook banged on a table. 'Get your head out the clouds.'

Hera cowered. They'd called her that since she'd arrived fifteen years ago. It'd stuck like the grease to the bowl in her hand. She blinked back a tear.

'Too much needs doing for you to be daydreaming. Get up there and help.'

Hera trudged up a circular staircase to the Royal rooms. A door opened and King Henry, his cheeks aflame and eyes bulging, emerged. Shoving past her, his huge girth shook as he stomped to another bedroom. Hera followed, hovering in the doorway. She glimpsed Prince Edward quaking in his bed, servants bowing at his side. A slither of guilt coiled in her empty stomach.

'Three nights running you've awoken me,' snarled the King.

'It was horrible.' The Prince gripped his sweat-soaked sheets, knuckles white.

'You're not a child.' King Henry's lip curled. 'Dreams can't hurt you.'

'I was old and fat.' The Prince was as pale as a moonflower. 'My worst nightmare.'

His father frowned. 'That's all?'

'This isn't normal. I'm cursed.' Prince Edward's head sank into plush pillows. 'If you loved me you'd do something to stop them.'

'You're weak and pathetic.' The King spat out the words. 'Brought to tears by a fantasy.' He stroked his beard. 'But I like a challenge. I'll find a way to stop these nightmares.' Turning, he muttered: 'If only for some rest.'

Hera stepped from his path as he left.

*

As the sun rose, Hera was already carrying out her duties, a whirlwind of activity in the kitchen. Hearing a quiet sob, she searched for the cause and found a small girl hiding beneath a table. Though her arms ached, she lifted the infant onto it so they were face-to-face.

'What's wrong?' Hera's voice was as gentle as a breeze.

'I've been sent here to work.' Tears streamed down the child's cheeks. 'The King says I have to pay off my parents' debts.'

The girl was a mirror reflecting Hera's past. *She looks just as I did when I arrived.*

'Don't worry.' Her tone dropped to almost stillness. 'I've a secret. Things will change. Soon we'll be free.'

The girl gazed at Hera's pallid features, at rough skin that made her seem older than her years, and into eyes that appeared worn by experience. Her tears abated. Hera found the girl some leftovers.

'Never be afraid to dream,' she said. But her heart pounded. *Will he come back?*

*

While the sun progressed its journey through the sky, the kitchen became full of chatter that buzzed like wasps in Hera's ears.

'Edward's handsome,' giggled a servant. Hera blushed at the mention of the Prince.

'The King made an announcement,' exclaimed another. 'Whoever cures Prince Edward of his nightmares will be rich.'

Hera dropped some plates with a clatter.

'Clot.' The head cook whacked her around the head. That guilt inside her stung more than the blow. As she cleaned the mess, Hera listened intently to the gossip.

'But the King hates his son,' whispered the servant. 'They say he thinks the Prince is too soft to be a worthy heir. He had the Queen killed for not providing him another child. He wants to be rid of the Prince, then find a new Queen to bear him a better successor.'

The guilt gnawed at Hera like the rats scurrying around her feet. *What have I done?*

*

The castle became a cauldron of intrigue as sorcerers and physicians arrived to chance their spells. Hera watched their weak efforts with unease. One foul witch bubbled up a potion that turned her own hair pure white. A muddled magician flourished his wand but cast out the castle's candles rather than the dark dreams.

'Charlatans,' boomed King Henry. He had them beheaded. It put off other attempts. The nightmares continued, the castle quivering around the King's black mood. Fear shadowed Hera. She knew failure mixed with sleeplessness was a dangerous concoction. Her mind spun when an unusual creature swaggered into the castle. Wearing a black cloak with huge sleeves like wings, and with an arched nose and thin lips above a weak chin, he resembled a crow. A fascinated crowd gathered, Hera hidden among them, trying not to catch the crow's eye.

'You think you can stop my son's nightmares?' The King stared at him, his nose wrinkling.

'I know I can,' cawed the stranger.

'How?'

'A simple spell.' His clawlike fingers withdrew a wand from his cloak. 'But a word of caution.'

King Henry stiffened.

'Every medicine has side effects.' The stranger smiled but his green eyes remained cold. 'I can rid the Kingdom of nightmares forever.' He paused, the wand held aloft. 'But all dreams will vanish with them.'

Hera's mouth ran dry. She wanted to cry out but restrained herself.

'That's all?' King Henry's belly wobbled with mirth. 'Who'd miss dreams? They serve no purpose, no function.' He wafted a hand. 'They're just clouds so high in the sky they're invisible. No-one would notice.'

'Then I can begin?'

'Anything for a good night's sleep.'

The stranger flourished his wand, uttering a torrent of incantations. Face contorted, his eyes screwed into tight slits, his movements growing wild like a possessed conductor. Then he stopped stone still.

'It's done.' He casually replaced the wand in his cloak. 'Where's my reward?'

'Wait.' The King scratched his head. 'I don't even know if it's worked.'

'I'll return in three days. After three undisturbed nights you'll pay.'

King Henry agreed. Hera slipped away, avoiding the King's roving eyes. *Would it work?*

*

The sun shone fiery bright to wake the castle. Hera was among the trembling maids at the King's bedside as he awoke. *Both Prince and King slept soundly.* A smile as broad as his waist stretched across King Henry's face.

'I succeeded,' he told them.

After two more nights of snoring, the stranger returned, collecting as many bags of gold as he could carry. He departed with a swish of his cloak and that strange smile that made Hera shudder.

Then it began.

At first no-one missed their dreams.

But the people grew lazy. Comfortable, they no longer strived to achieve anything. There were no new ideas, no inventions, no innovation. Desire drained, drive departed. Maintenance went undone, the Kingdom deteriorating into ruin. The harvest wasn't reaped: fruit withered on the trees, vegetables rotted in the ground. Livestock perished where it stood.

'Why toil when we have plenty of food?' said the people.

Stocks ran out.

'We can survive,' said the people.

Starvation took over.

'We're not that hungry,' said the people, for apathy had only ruined them.

They descended into a deep depression. Death rates increased as the elderly gave up on life. Birth rates declined as couples stopped procreating. The Kingdom was dying.

King Henry issued another proclamation, calling for the wisest men in the Kingdom to advise him. They didn't have the energy to respond. So he called for the wisest men in the neighbouring Kingdom.

Gazing through a window, Hera surveyed the decay. She couldn't stand to be without her dreams. With no hope of a better life she was bereft. *I shouldn't have trusted him. This wasn't what he promised.*

She saw an elderly man approaching the castle, kicking through tangled weeds and brushing aside rope-thick cobwebs. Hera was sent to escort the old soul, called Klevert, to the King. As they made their way, he studied his surroundings, sniffing and tasting the air. A knowing smile lit his face.

They entered the throne room, where King Henry was slumped in his seat.

'Can you lift this curse?' The King's voice was weary.

'It's not a curse.' Klevert shook his head. 'You've been tricked.' Hera's stomach lurched.

The King clenched a fist. 'Who could trick me?'

'I've dealt with this cloaked fellow before.' Klevert ran a hand through his flowing white hair. 'His name is Vangance. If I remember right, he's long held a grudge after you drowned his mother for being a witch.' King Henry shrugged. 'He must have poisoned your son to cause the regular nightmares. It was a trap.' Hera's head dropped.

'The spell wasn't a cure,' Klevert continued. 'He needed your permission to allow him to banish the Kingdom's dreams.' Creases erupted on the King's brow. 'So he created the nightmares in order to destroy the dreams. One can't exist without the other.' The King drummed his fingers. 'You see, opposites balance. For example, you have to experience fear to be brave.'

King Henry thumped his throne. 'How's this led to our ruin?'

'Dreams are our subconscious desires and fears. Banish them and you rid the mind of all aspirations and yearning. And without hope people are nothing.'

King Henry arose and paced the room. 'How do we reverse it?' he growled.

'I don't know,' admitted Klevert. 'I'm not a magician.'

'You've no solutions,' bellowed King Henry. 'Only riddles. You're banished.'

Klevert looked happy to leave. Hera could take no more.

'You murdered dreams.' She clutched her head, glaring at the King. Rage erupted across his face as the guilt inside Hera consumed her. She fell to her knees. 'I poisoned the prince,' she cried. Two guards seized her. 'I slipped a potion in his food every night.'

King Henry cracked his knuckles. 'Why?'

Hera looked him in the eye. 'Vangance said if I carried out his orders my dreams of freedom would come true. I was desperate.'

The King drew his face so close to Hera's that his beard's whiskers jabbed her.

'Tricked as well.' His breath made Hera hold hers. 'You'll rot in the dungeons.'

*

As above, down below: the dungeon smelt as rancid as the King's halitosis. The gloom strained Hera's eyes and she heard rats scamper. *Be careful what you dream of.* She gave a hollow laugh. She'd wanted freedom from her relentless job. *That stale kitchen seems heavenly now.* She remembered the little girl's face: despair turning to hope, now dashed. Her heart sank.

A guard entered. 'They're building your gallows,' he told Hera. She exhaled. *There's no escape.* At least she'd be put out of her misery. *Let it come.* 'But first you have a visitor.'

A cloaked figure shuffled in. Lowered his hood. *Vangance.*

'Why've you returned?'

Beneath his beak, Vangance's lips curved upwards. 'What's the point of a victory you can't experience? I came to admire my handiwork.' He sniffed. 'And the fools here will never catch me.'

'You deceived me. You said your potion for the Prince would allow you to return to make the King kind and grant everyone freedom.' Hera stared at his features, which were gnarled by hatred. *How could I have believed him?*

Vangance flapped his arms. 'You're just a means to an end.'

'You've destroyed everybody, when your quarrel was with one man.' Hera's aching arms strained against her shackles.

'One is all.'

From the courtyard came the sound of nails being hammered into wood.

'Nothing can save me,' sighed Hera. Her mind whirled like a hurricane. 'No one will believe anything I say now. So tell me, can the curse be lifted?'

Vangance's eyes glowed. 'I'm the only person who knows how.' He stuck out his pigeon chest. 'It can only be lifted if the weakest in the Kingdom overcomes their worst nightmare. They'll be rewarded with the prize of their dreams.'

Hera's lips trembled. *The weakest?*

A commotion outside grew louder. King Henry, Prince Edward and their men burst into the dungeon. Vangance slunk into the shadows.

'Your time's up.' King Henry's voice brooked no argument. But the dream hadn't completely died in Hera.

'I can save the Kingdom.' Her hoarse voice was loud.

'I won't fall for more tricks.' King Henry thumped a fist into a cupped hand.

'It's not a trick.' Her assuredness made the King hesitate. 'The real villain's over there.' Hera nodded towards Vangance. 'And I must face my fears to reverse his witchcraft.'

Vangance stepped forward. 'Foolish,' he croaked. 'It would've been better for you to go quietly.'

King Henry looked at Vangance in horror. 'How dare you return so brazenly? You'll die alongside her.'

'Then your Kingdom dies with me.'

'Wait,' said Hera. 'I'll defeat him and lift the curse if my life is spared and I'm granted one wish.'

'I'll let you try.' The King was known to enjoy sport. 'Release the girl.' The guards unlocked Hera's shackles. She dropped to her knees, rubbing her shoulders.

More people gathered. 'What can a mere girl do?' they asked in unison.

'What are you most scared of?' crowed Vangance. 'The largest of spiders?'

He pulled the wand from his cloak, slashing it through the air like a knight would a sword. A tarantula as large and hairy as a bear appeared, poison dripping from its fangs. The growing crowd shrieked.

Hera took a step back, then stood firm and glared at the spider. It scurried away.

Vangance thrust his wand forward as straight as an arrow from an archer. It turned into a thirty-foot Boa Constrictor.

'How about a giant serpent?' he smirked. Prince Edward fainted as it slithered towards Hera. It reared in front of her with venomous eyes. She didn't even tremble. The snake slid away.

'Then what *do* you most fear?' asked Vangance.

'Not achieving my potential.' Hera stretched tall. 'But I've proved myself by standing up to you.'

'Nonsense. You're not brave enough to survive this change.'

Vangance swirled faster and faster until he transformed into a scorpion. Hera felt hypnotised as it scuttled closer. Its deadly tail twitched. And drew back.

Hera breathed deeply. Summoned all her energy. Sensed her spirit thunder through her.

'I am change.' Her voice was a gale. She felt released. Quicker than a tempest, she stamped down, crushing the creature. Black blood and grey guts oozed from underneath her foot.

'I was never afraid of you.' She glanced at the mess and laughed. 'Men have such limited imaginations.'

'Is the curse lifted?' asked King Henry.

Hera felt a surge of ambition. 'We can dream on,' she declared with gusto to cheers that swept hope through the Kingdom. A little girl in the crowd gave the loudest roar of all.

The farmers gathered their tools to work the fields, the maids rushed to milk the remaining cows and carpenters took the wood of the gallows to use for repairs.

The King turned to Hera. 'Whatever you desire is yours.'

She saw Prince Edward being helped to his feet. *He's vain.* She faltered. *But he's generous and sensitive. He'll support me and allow me to control the Kingdom for the better.* 'I want to marry the Prince.'

The Prince beamed as brightly as a sunflower.

The King snorted. 'You were born a peasant, not royalty.'

Hera studied the Prince and saw a loyal puppy gaze back. *Together, we'll bring freedom and prosperity for all.* The crowd watched the trio, transfixed.

'I dare to dream.' Hera's voice wasn't wavering. 'So the wedding is our reward.'

The King faced a sea of imploring eyes reminding him of his promise.

Silence lingered. King Henry smoothed his golden robes. No-one dared speak.

'Very well,' the King said finally. The crowd's repeated cheers flowed as freely as fresh air.

As the sun sank over the horizon, a new moon rose heralding sleep full of dreams of a royal wedding. Hera and the King's eyes locked. They nodded warily. Hera knew that even more turbulent times lay ahead.

Siobhan Flynn - The Advantage of Shadows

I

I flew home from London to finalize the sale of my parents' house, which had been on the market for over two years. I booked a room at the new Travelodge in the town, ten miles from where I had grown up, arriving late on a Sunday night, for my Monday morning appointment. On the advice of my real estate agent I had dropped the market price to encourage a sale: the imminent construction of the new road through the area, could, he had warned, significantly devalue my property.

Early the following morning, I visited the graveyard, my garage-court bouquets flimsy and insubstantial in the bitter February wind. Numbly, I recalled my parents' deaths, my mother's, slow and painful, my father's, sudden and shocking. I remembered how my grief had been under-pinned by relief: relief that they were at last protected, safe in their Heaven. On a whim I decided to take a last look at our house, negotiating the once-familiar back roads in my shiny rental car, and pulling in tightly next to the overgrown privet hedge.

I didn't get out.

It was the year 2000, a clean slate, a new tab. I loved the look of all those zero's, wide-open and receptive, unlike the huddled digits of the 1980's and 90's, closed, and coiled in on themselves. I was thirty four years old. I had a successful career, in the administration section of a prestigious engineering company. The proceeds of the house sale would put a welcome dent in the substantial mortgage I had on my apartment in Kensington.

I wouldn't ever be back here again.

As I prepared to leave, a car approached me from behind – one of those big old rust-buckets, layered with mud and farmyard manure – slowed as it passed me, then, disappeared in a roar of diesel, up the winding Hill Road. With a shock I recognised its driver as Martin Flanagan, older, greyer, surlier, and I froze.

Part of me wanted to leap from the car, to wave frantically, to race up that road, as I had done so many countless times in the past, to follow him, to face him, to shout, to scream, to demand that he tell me the truth. The truth of what had really happened to his sister, Mo, my best friend. But I remained motionless in the car, getting colder and colder, until I realized that if I didn't move, I would miss my appointment with the solicitor.

A young secretary chattily admired my coat, and offered tea, which I politely declined. Philip Cullen, a local man, middle-aged and affable, took my icy hand in his fleshy one, assuring me he had everything in order. Some cursory chat followed – he had known my parents – but he quickly realized that I wasn't one for small talk, as he spread out the necessary documents for my attention.

"It's a good time to sell," he mused, idly, as I perused my contracts. "The new road coming through will bring changes." I nodded, while he continued, "Though I believe there's a bit of controversy, over the felling of Flanagan's wood."

The pen slipped from my grasp and rolled across his desk.

"They're felling the wood?" My voice was high, strangulated squeak. He handed me back the pen.

"Yes, well, a part of it anyhow, along there by Marty Flanagan's land. Some crowd are objecting, but I'd say they're wasting their time!"

He unfolded a copy of the local paper, pointing out a headline,

"Environmentalist Group up in arms over proposed destruction of local woodland."

I steadied myself on the edge of the desk. With a supreme effort of will I managed to conduct the business at hand, thank the solicitor and take my leave.

Back in the privacy of my hotel room, I knew I should shower, have something to eat, prepare for my return flight in the morning, but I crept fully clothed under the duvet and let the familiar darkness wash over me.

It was nineteen years since I had set foot in Flanagan's wood.

For nineteen years, I, alone, had carried and concealed Mo Flanagan's terrible secret.

And now, this.

II

We had been friends since junior infants, myself and Maureen Flanagan - whom I had never heard referred to as anything other than Mo. Growing up, in a rural backwater, a quarter of a mile apart, most of our leisure time was spent, largely unsupervised, in the Flanagan's rambling old farmhouse. It's various barns, surrounding fields and woodlands, provided us with a variety of diverse entertainment throughout all four seasons of the year and as the only child of middle-aged parents, I revelled in the freedom afforded to me there.

Mo had no recollection of her mother, who had died before she was a year old. Her family now comprised her father, two brothers, Martin and Gerard, eight and ten years older respectively, and her father's brother, her Uncle Arthur.

Despite the considerable time I spent at Mo's, the lives of these men, these two sets of brothers remained a mystery to me. They were collectively taciturn, mostly absorbed in the workings of the farm, I came and went unannounced and they registered my presence with no more than a passing comment, if at all. Except for Martin, I had rarely exchanged more than a few words with any of them.

Since the farm work took precedent over the housekeeping, domestic chores were executed to a minimum standard. Aside from dinner, all other meals were taken at random, comprising whatever food happened to be on hand at the time.

As the sole female member of the household, Mo inherited at a relatively tender age, the bulk of the daily chores, assisted, with some resistance, by Martin.

Her school uniforms grew shrunken, or baggy, faded and frayed from careless laundering, her shoes scuffed and tattered, her mane of tumbling black hair hung rakishly to her waist.

Six months my senior, she seemed infinitely smarter and wiser. She was brave, kind and strong, and knowing no different way of life, moved through childhood and adolescence with ease and resilience, a confident, cheerful, smiling girl.

In secondary school we were an invincible double act, taking the bus each morning from the cross above Flanagan's to the Convent of Mercy in town. As often as not, we did our homework together: my mother had returned to part-time work and my father was rarely home before six thirty: the prospect of spending a couple of hours in the splendid disarray of Mo's living room was infinitely more attractive than returning to the pristine emptiness of my own home.

The change in Mo manifested itself gradually. I would catch a stray glance, notice a vacant look in her eye, a sudden falling away of her concentration, sense a vague despondency about her.

There were days when she wasn't at the bus stop, when I travelled alone, and oddly bereft, to school. Times when I didn't see or hear from her for days - the farmhouse didn't have a phone.

Then, one Friday night, as we sprawled across her great, sagging bed, pouring through our magazines, she broke down without warning, and told me she was pregnant.

My initial feeling was one of stunned disbelief: her declaration was scarcely more of a shock to me than the realization that she had been with a boy – *gone the whole way* – with a boy and hadn't told me. We were fifteen - over the past year, boys had formed the basis for a great many of our conversations, although neither of us had had an actual boyfriend.

"Sure, you can't be, Mo," I shook my head. "It's impossible!"

But when she wordlessly raised her shapeless, sagging jumper, there was no mistaking the taut, uplifted bulge of her abdomen, which the dual combination of her pleated school gymslip and the thick woollen jumper had, so far, successfully concealed. I stared, and stared.

"But, Mo, I mean - how? I mean, how could you not have told me?" Hurt, indignation, incomprehension, words choked out.

Mo drew a great, shuddering breath.

"Remember when I stayed with my cousins in Galway last summer? Well, there was this friend of my cousin, John Joe. Eddie Connelly, his name was.

"Oh, Laurie, it was terrible! He gave me cider to drink – I was so sick afterwards. I hardly knew what I was doing. And it really was awful – and oh, God, I so, *so* wanted to tell you but I just couldn't. Oh, Laurie, what am I going to do now?"

I had the oddest sense that she wasn't telling the truth – and yet, and yet. Had she been with a local boy, I surely would have known.

"When is it…?" I eventually enquired.

"Around the middle of April, I think."

"Jesus, Mo, that's less than three months away!" I cried, aghast, as she collapsed, weeping, into her pillow.

I huddled, immobile on the end of her bed, as long minutes dragged.

Finally, I heard my own voice, low and hurried, but speaking with surprising conviction, unveiling my hastily construed plan. I was an avid reader of romantic novels, in which I had encountered various solutions to situations such as Mo's, and I was confident that her predicament was not insurmountable.

"Okay, Mo. Listen now. Here's what we will do."

Mo's due date was fortunately coinciding with our Easter Holidays, and I would arrange to sleep over at her house, as I had on countless school breaks in the past. Once the baby arrived, I would take it, under cover of darkness to the steps of the Carmelite convent, where it would, within hours, be taken in by the Sisters. I had no idea how I would accomplish this, but I believed that I would somehow find a way.

My plan wasn't fool proof, but it was the best I could come up with.

I wasn't unduly alarmed when Mo didn't turn up for school, one Monday early in March, but

when she wasn't there the following day, I called to her house straight after school.

In the high-ceilinged, draughty bedroom Mo appeared diminished, compressed under a pile of bedclothes, her face chalk-white in a tangle of matted black hair, and I was immediately apprehensive.

"Are you sick, Mo?" I enquired, as she began to cry.

"Oh Laurie, thank God you're here! The baby… it came early."

"What?" I dropped to my knees by the bed. "What d'you mean?"

"I -the pains started yesterday evening. They got much stronger in the middle of the night, so I sort of knew then. I went out to the red barn, with - blankets and all the- the things, like we planned. But it was dead, Laurie, the baby was born dead." She clutched frantically at me, a terrible wildness in her face.

"Oh my God, Mo."

My ingenious plan, unravelling – everything spiralling out of control, six weeks too early. I crouched there, shocked and scared, as she continued:

"I wrapped it in an old blanket, to bury, like, but the pain - I just couldn't do it. I thought I might die as well, Laurie."

"Mo, listen - we really need to tell someone now."

Her hand shot out suddenly, seizing my wrist.

"No, we can't tell! He'll kill me. There're can't be a baby, Laurie, don't you understand?"

"What are you talking about? Who'll kill you?"

"He'll go mad! If they find the baby, they'll send me away. Laurie, oh please Laurie, will you do the burying?"

The ensuing silence, broken only by a faint soughing of wind in the ancient beech beyond the thin glass, was, for a few seconds, almost peaceful.

I realized I had no choice - the time had come to honour my part of the agreement - and a dead baby couldn't be left in the hands of the nuns.

It was a quarter past four – I had almost two hours of daylight left in which to execute my task.

"They've all gone to the mart," whispered Mo, "Except Ger. Be careful."

I took Mo's old army jacket from the back of the door, pulled it on over my school jumper, and silently left the house. I crossed the yard, through the disused haggard and down the overgrown path towards the red barn.

This dim and cavernous building was a repository for out-dated and broken farm machinery, rusting tools, barrels, stakes, bales of wire, assorted agricultural paraphernalia, all covered in choking layers of dust and cobwebs. Many games had we played here – ghosts of the children we no longer were flitted from dark corner to creaking rafter, and so I searched for, and found Mo's poor little bundle, wedged behind the turnip-mangle, exactly as she had described. It felt very cold and slightly heavier than I had expected. Emptying my mind of all rational thought, I placed it carefully into a fertilizer bag.

Among the scattered tools was a rusted spade with a short handle, which I hefted on my shoulder, as, laden and perspiring, I threaded across the paddock towards the wood.

Had I encountered someone, I would have been incapable of any kind of coherent speech, but I did not allow myself to think beyond the next step, and the one after that. Upon reaching the edge of the wood, I took the familiar path to the old lime kiln, where once, in our long-ago childhood, Mo and I had had a secret den. It felt like a good place, a safe place. I began to dig. Bending, lifting, bending, lifting, deeper, deeper, deeper. Sweat running into tears running into snot running into blood, as I bit down hard on my lower lip. Keep going keep going keep going.

Then I was walking home through the almost-dark, my schoolbag a crippling burden on my aching back.

"In the name of God?" cried my mother, "Look at the state of you!"

I said that we had been helping Martin clear out a shed, adding that I thought I might be coming down with the flu.

The next morning I awoke with a raging fever, and was out of school for the remainder of the week.

It was Sunday afternoon, when I eventually got to visit Mo.

At first I thought she was asleep. Untouched on her bedside locker, a mug of scummy tea stood next to a curled slice of toast, roughly smeared with purple jam.

The air in the room had a pungent odour, sickly sweet, yet sharp.

"Mo? Mo, I was in bed with flu. But it's done now, Mo, it's all sorted. Are you feeling better?"

Although it was abundantly clear to me that she wasn't.

Hunkering down, I took her, chill, clammy hand in mine. She acknowledged me only with the slightest of nods.

I had never seen anyone look so ill. Glassy beads of sweat glistened on her waxy forehead, her sunken eyes were ringed with a brownish tinge. My heart hammering, I eased back the bed cover. The large bath towel, in which Mo had swaddled her lower body, was saturated in dark red blood. For a few dizzying seconds I stood suspended in indecision, summoning the last of my courage, then I turned and ran downstairs.

Through the open kitchen door, I saw Martin standing over the blackened cooker, throwing something limp and bloody into a pan of sputtering oil.

"Martin?"

He started, frowned, regarded me sharply,

"Laurie!"

"I think Mo needs a doctor, Martin."

"A doctor?"

"She's very sick. She …"

"There's nothing wrong with Mo, that won't right itself after a few days."

Frantically, I shook my head.

"But, Martin…"

"Mo is a strong girl, don't you know that? She'll be grand in a day or two. Now, go home Laurie. Go on."

He turned abruptly away, savagely prodding at the greasy pan. The significance of this curt dismissal alarmed me further - never before had I been ordered out of Mo's house. The words *they know and they know that I know* tumbled about, helplessly, in my head.

From elsewhere in the house I heard the rumble of male voices, raised as if in minor disagreement, as I headed for the door.

At the gate I paused, threw a last desperate glance back at the house. As I did so, a figure moved with furtive haste away from the landing window, out of my line of vision, but not before I saw his face. It was Mo's uncle, Arthur.

The knowledge that hit me then was only partially formed – an impression of something that, in my innocence, I was unable to fully comprehend. Understanding would come in time, and far too late.

The following day, a special whole-school assembly was called for mid-day: a ripple of rumour ran through the senior girls, as the school Chaplin, Father Cosgrave, joined Sister Josephine on the podium. Through a haze of exhaustion, I managed to process the words, third year pupil, tragedy, and sudden fatal brain haemorrhage, before I pitched forward into a rising tide of blackness.

III

Mo had never said whether the baby was a boy or a girl, but somehow, I have always thought of it as a boy. Secretly I named him 'Francis' – after the gentle saint. And it's a name that can be male, or female, just in case.

For nineteen years, the long shadow cast by Flanagan's wood has poured its darkness over my life. The advantage of shadows, is that you can hide in them.

Now, they are felling the wood.

Slawa Rusin - Patrick Cosmos

Day 1

My name is Patrick Cosmos and I'm a stranger here. I come from a planet that is much smaller than Earth. It's a travelling planet, meaning it doesn't have a fixed orbit and it can go pretty much anywhere it likes.

I have been sent here on a project that we are currently working on. It is to see how other planets are doing in terms of overpopulation, and we've been told that Earth isn't doing so good.

Every Friday I will have to report to our Headquarters, which we call 'Base' over there. I can contact them through any phone box in the country.

I can speak every single language on this planet. I can even communicate with animals, but Base told me not to talk to them in public. Apparently humans don't understand them.

The only problem is, I look different. I am seven feet tall and my entire body is covered in fur. I also don't have any ears or a nose and I have enormous lips that look like a squashed tire.

Base told me I could always explain that I suffer from a very severe case of hirsutism - a condition which causes abnormal hair growth. Instead, we invented a pill that can make me look like a human. The pill transforms me into a young college student - Katy. I have to remember to take them every morning and make sure no one finds out what I really look like.

It's summer, so I don't have to study. I just need to find a job.

The hardest thing so far was getting used the smell. I'm going to be honest - humans stink. They stink of cheese and some sweet smell I can't even describe. What surprises me even more is that they are obviously unaware of their unbearable smell.

What I also dislike like are pregnant women. They take up too much space and they must think that they are better than non pregnant people. Base told me that they are the main contributors to the overpopulation issue.

I'm renting a room in a house that I share with a couple from Poland. Marek and Ania Pimpek are their names. Ania works as a waitress and Marek works in a mental hospital. He finishes at seven and comes home twenty minutes later looking sad and disappointed. Ania just looks sweaty.

Day 3

Today I had an interview at a local supermarket. Manager Julie told me that they are looking for a checkout operator. I didn't know what that meant so I asked her to explain. She looked a bit confused.

'Well, Katy,' she finally spoke after a moment of awkward silence. 'You will be sitting on a till and the customers will come to you with their shopping and you will scan their items.'

She then started sliding invisible items on the table. That sounded fantastic! I really do hope they hire me.

Day 5

Happy days! I got the job. I could barely sleep last night I was so excited. I even love my new uniform that is the same colour as the dark burgundy carpet downstairs.

My shift starts at ten. I got dressed and went downstairs to have my breakfast.

Ania was sitting on the sofa in her dressing gown and she was watching the TV. Next to her was a plastic bag with sun flower seeds. She put one in her mouth and cracked it open with her teeth. She then looked at me wearing my work uniform and a sinister smile appeared on her face.

'Hey, Marek!' she shouted. 'Check her out! Her IQ dropped as soon she put that uniform on.'

She then roared with laughter. A piece of sunflower seed must have stuck to the back of her throat and she started to choke. She leaned forward and with her head between her knees she started coughing. I watched as the long strings of saliva escaped her mouth and landed on the burgundy carpet.

'It's your first day today, Katy?' Marek got out of the kitchen. 'Do you need a lift?'

'Thank you, but I fancy a walk.'

It was an introduction day. We were all sitting in the same room where I had my interview. There were about ten new starters.

At the head of the table sat the queen of checkouts, supervisor Kath. She looked very serious. She had blond, spiky hair and she was telling us about the importance of excellent customer service.

'I'm gonna be honest with you guys,' she leaned back in her chair, looked out of the window and pulled her pants up. 'There are a lot of bastards down there on the shop floor. But you need to rise above it and always be polite and offer help with packing.'

On our lunch break Steve, who worked at the bakery, was showing us photos of his new sofa on his phone.

'Four year interest free credit,' he said.

I realized I left my phone at home. Supervisor Debbie was sitting next to me and she was eating her yoghurt. She peeled off the lid and started licking it. For some reason I got distracted by that tongue.

'Are you not eating anything, Katy?' she said to me.

'I'm not that hungry.'

I couldn't sleep that night. I could hear some voices coming from the attic, right above my head.

'Did you see the new guy?'

They weren't humans.

'Yes, I have,' I heard another voice. 'He is not one of them. He is covered in fur, like us and he doesn't stink of ricotta.

'Rats,' I thought to myself and finally went to sleep.

Day 6

This morning Marek came to my bedroom to check the boiler. I told him that they may have rats in the house.

'Rats?' he came out of the closet where the boiler was and sat on the chair next to my desk. 'Maybe there were birds?'

'I am sure there were rats.'

Ania was downstairs in the kitchen making as much noise as possible. She stomped heavily and kept slamming the doors. Marek had just been to the toilet.

'What is that smell?' she said walking up the stars.

I looked at Marek. He sighed heavily.

'I don't buy rat traps anymore,' he said.

'No, you don't!' Ania shouted from the landing. 'Now you just don't bother closing the door to the toilet and you let the smell kill them all of!'

I looked at him again. He had his eyes closed and he put his head down.

'Ania's friend, Magda, is going to be staying with us for a while,' he said. 'She and her husband are getting a divorce. Ania wants to help her.'

I got worried. There were only two bedrooms in this house. Where would I sleep?

'She will sleep downstairs,' he said and then got up and left the room.

Day 8

Today I was working on till number five. I counted two male customers who had their fly undone, which I noticed straight away because their genitals, although hidden underneath their clothing, were at the same level as my head.

'My baby is eighteen months,' said one woman in her early thirties.

'Aren't you concerned with the planet running out of resources?' I scanned a reduced pack of half opened grapes. 'Or that didn't even cross your mind when you decided to have that child eighteen months ago?'

She looked shocked and didn't say anything. Later I found that she complained to the supervisor.

On my lunch break I decided to phone Base.

'Hi Patrick, how are you doing?'

I was so happy to hear his voice again.

'When I ask pregnant women why are they pregnant they don't seem to like it very much. One of them complained to the supervisor.'

'No, Patrick. You can't be that direct,' Base sounded disappointed. 'You need to be more discreet.'

Today I didn't have to walk back home. Marek offered to pick me up after work.

'I picked Magda up from the airport this morning. We will need to help her find a job. She doesn't speak any English.'

For a while we drove in silence.

'Oh, Katy,' he sounded like he was in pain. 'This country is for someone like you. You are honest and a good person and you suck at lying. In Poland, you need to be street smart, you need to know, how to play the game. Do you know what I mean?'

No.

'In Poland you have to fight. For everything. Here, people are kind and honest and they will respect you.'

When we arrived home Magda and Ania were sitting at the table. Magda is fat and short and she looks bored.

I am not that good at small talk so after introducing myself I went upstairs to my room. I closed the door behind me but decided to listen to their conversation.

'I haven't had sex in three months,' I heard Magda's voice.

Oh yes, sex. Apparently it's the reason why this planet is in so much trouble. Base tried talking to me about it but it sounded so disgusting that I asked him to stop.

Day 10

Magda is still looking for work. She sleeps underneath the stairs on a single mattress and she spends her days chatting to lonely, Polish men online.

I haven't made any new friends yet. I have also started to talk to different people online. Mainly men. They all want to know what I look like. I am not naive. I know that they want to see young and beautiful Katy not hairy Patrick. When they say that they want to see me naked I look for photos of random women and send them those instead. They email me back saying how beautiful I am and that they would love to meet me in person. I don't have my own email address so I'm using Marek's or Ania's. They can read all my messages and also see the naked photos I've been sending.

For the past couple of days I have been talking to James. He is in his late thirties and lives in London. He told me he got married last year and that things aren't going so well with his wife. He asked for my photo.

'I need to see another photo, Katy,' he typed. 'You look absolutely stunning. I need to believe this is you.'

I sent him more photos.

Day 11

Today at work I kept daydreaming about James. Once he got a bit excited and told me that he wanted to lick me all over. That wouldn't be good for his health. He would end up with a giant fur ball in his stomach. I didn't tell Base about him.

'This chicken stinks,' said an older lady and started uploading her shopping on my till.

When I got home I found Ania and Marek in the kitchen. Marek was leaning against the counter in his usual submissive pose - head down and eyes closed. Ania was standing next to him in her dressing gown and flip flops and was holding a big kitchen knife. It was then that I noticed how hideous her feet were. Each toe was pointing in different directions.

'When are you going to do something about it?' she turned around and started chopping onions.

'I don't know, Ania,' Marek whispered. 'I really don't know.'

'You are getting fatter. We will need to get you a longer dressing gown belt.'

I went upstairs to my room. There was a message from James.

'Meet me tomorrow. I'll take you to the cinema.'

Day 12

I woke up early today. I am going on a date with James. It's official and I'm going to meet him in person.

He still believes that I'm an attractive college student not a freaky looking monkey from out of space. And I intend to keep it that way.

Precisely an hour before our date I will take another pill, just to make sure I don't start turning into Patrick. I'll be one of 'them'. I will be a normal person who goes on dates and I will finally fit in. Base doesn't know anything about my insidious plan.

I asked Marek for a lift. I told him I'm meeting some friends and we are going to watch a movie.

He dropped me off outside Asda. I told him I need to get few things. There was a phone box nearby. I wanted to call Base but I felt ashamed.

I got inside and closed the door. I looked down on my arms. Good timing because I noticed that the hair started to grow back. I took the pink pill out of my pocket and swallowed it.

I walked slowly through the car park to the cinema. There he was. He looked nervous and bit older than on that photo he had sent me. He was wearing white t-shirt, black trousers and brown shoes and he looked like he could work as a geography teacher. What a disaster. On the photo he sent me he was wearing a nice suit.

'Hello,' I said as he leaned forward to hug me.

'Hi, Katy.'

I stood on his shoe.

'I stood on your shoe,' I said.

'Don't worry about it.'

He wanted to buy me popcorn but I couldn't eat anything.

We talked briefly about his wife. I found out she was five feet two.

'I like your cowboy boots,' he pointed at my shoes slurping coke.

The movie was awful. I wanted to leave and run, far away from here.

After the movie we were waiting outside for a taxi. We didn't speak much and James just kept staring at me.

'We have rats in our attic,' I finally said.

'Rats?' James smiled.

He then moved really close until his nose was nearly touching mine.

'So, are you going you give me what you had promised?'

'Please stop,' I whispered.

He laughed and stepped back.

'I think I'm gonna go home,' I said.

'Not so fast young lady,' he put his hand on my shoulder. 'You owe me a drink now.'

I panicked. I didn't know what else to do so I ran. I ran as fast as I could through the car park and hid inside the phone box. I picked up the phone and rang Base.

'Base, please forgive me.'

I look down at my hands and notice my hair started to grow back. All that stress must have affected my pills and made them less effective.

'What's the matter, Patrick?' he sounded worried. 'Tell me.'

'I don't want it anymore! I don't want to be normal anymore! I went on a date you see.'

'You did what?'

On no. He is disappointment with me.

'You mean someone actually fancies you?'

Duh! Obviously I went on a date as beautiful Katy not hairy Patrick.

'I met this guy online…'

'Oh, Patrick!' Base sounded really angry now. 'What were you thinking? Did he do something to you?'

'You mean you know James?'

'James? Who the hell is James?'

I am getting taller and now I can barely fit inside this phone box.

'Are you crazy?' said Base. 'You are too naive and sensitive to be meeting strangers online! What were you thinking?'

'Base, I just wanted to be like them!' At that point I was crying so hard that the windows steamed up. I had to open the door to let some fresh air in. 'I wanted to know what it's like to be a normal human being and do normal things you know, like buy a sofa on credit or fart on a crowded bus. I just wanted to fit in.'

'Patrick, we are going to get you. Just stay where you are.'

'Are you mad at me?'

'No, Patrick, I'm not mad,' for a moment he didn't say anything. 'The real reason why we sent you and not somebody else, someone who would have been more suitable for this role, was to help you get out of your comfort zone. I knew this wasn't going to work out, Patrick. It was a mistake. My mistake. Don't worry about it. We are coming to get you.'

I got out and looked around.

'Is that a gorilla?' I hear women's voice.

No. I am not a gorilla. My name is Patrick Cosmos and I don't belong here.

James was still standing outside the cinema smoking a cigarette. He looked angry. Then taxi came and he got in. I wiped the tears and waited for Base to come and pick me up.

Sue Whytock - Lord of the Dance

The sun is weakly warm and there are daffodils. The church is packed. People are standing outside. So many adults in black. It must mean my Dad is famous. We walk past them all to our places at the front, like some obscene red-carpet parade. Some reach out to touch me and they are crying, so I have to smile.

Now he will become even more famous. Soon he will become a saint.

Dad was a 'rising star' according to Shirley Williams. His campaign manager was someone called George Galloway.

This is a memorial, it even sounds sad; it sounds mournful and mysterious, like other Catholic words I know: apostolic, liturgy, tabernacle. There is no body, no burial. Just lots of words and his favourite hymn… *dance then, wherever you may be...*

It is at St Teresa's in Colchester, my primary school and our church… *they buried my body and they thought I'd gone, but I am the dance and the dance goes on.*

Ruth Sidlaw, from class 6 examines me from where she sits with the choir. Her face is big and square-jawed; her carrot hair hangs in two long, tight, thick plaits. I scowl at her and look down. She doesn't look away. She will ask me at school and at Brownies, wherever and whenever she gets the chance, if I have stopped crying yet. She means it kindly, but she has no idea how much I dread her questions.

After the service, back at the house, I deliver tea, coffee and, sometimes, whisky to the men in black. I smile at them all and try not to mind them all examining me too.

My Dad was on his way to Scotland. Every month or so, on a Friday morning, he drove to Dundee, his home town, to campaign for his safe Labour seat. He would return on a Sunday evening, often with chips. If we were already in bed, Dad would get us down. They were tightly wrapped parcels in layers of newspaper, when you opened them and spread the paper out it would be flecked with salt and running with vinegar, which collected in the creases in little wells. I would savour every illicit post- bedtime one of them.

The car he was killed in was a brand new, blue Morris Marina which was unusual as our cars were normally always red. The registration was 'SNO', it snowed a lot that winter. I told my class 5 teacher, Mrs. Kennedy about the numberplate. 'How appropriate', she said. I have a photo of me and dad leaning against it outside Aunty Nancy's in the Christmas holidays. He's laughing at me because I'm in a strop. It's probably the last photo.

This is what I think I remember, but memories are sometimes so fleeting I can only just grasp them.

Friday, February 24th. We wave him off in the morning and we go to Nan and Grandads' for supper as usual that evening.

That night, I wake up in my parents' bed.

I don't remember getting there.

Mum and Nan open the door a tiny bit and I see grey light. They are shadows. What's my nan doing here? 'Go back to sleep', Mum says. I must be asleep already. Dreaming.

I wake up again. I know it's early because when I look at their mustard-coloured curtains the big white flowers look like faces in the gloom, appearing and disappearing between the folds in the fabric. If I get in with them and the curtains still look like faces and not flowers, they always tell me it is too early and to go back to sleep.

I can hear a low hum downstairs. It sounds like people talking on the radio and then there are long silences. Maybe it's time to get up; but we don't normally have Brian Redhead and Libby Purves at the weekend. We don't usually have the radio at weekends at all. I lie still and listen. A low mumble again and a louder shout, or a cry; I sit up and call out. No one comes. I get up and go downstairs. I open the living room door and the light is on, it's bright enough to make me squeeze my eyes shut for a moment. My Mum is there with my Nan and Grandad and my brothers. My chest gallops and I can hear rushing and crashing in my ears. Their faces look scary and twisted, like the faces in the curtains. Mum whispers I have to brave and then she tells me, using the same word they used for Uncle Jim. And I'm falling.

A little over a year before, we were told Uncle Jim had been killed. They didn't say he had died. He was killed in a car. I saw my Dad weep and I had never seen a man cry; it made me feel like I was falling.

I remember sliding open the door of the old G-plan sideboard in the kitchen to retrieve more cups and mugs for all the visitors. I remember the 70s pattern on the mugs – repeated in a ring around the middle – a speckled glaze on each one in blue, grey, ochre or green. I don't know how these people knew what had happened. I don't know who called them.

Some other memories are more solid, like a series of tableaux: lying silently on my parent's bed with my brother, Michael. Standing outside the closed door of my brother Stephen's room, listening to my own breathing and heartbeat, but not going in. I was the youngest and I didn't have the words. None of us did.

Some memories are like short bits of film: flinching from the priest, who speaks to me in my parents' bedroom. I don't like this Priest, Father Con. I like Father Michael, although he sometimes comes to talk politics with my dad on a Thursday night when Top of the Pops is on and we have to go upstairs and watch it on a tiny, snowy, black and white portable. That's the only bad thing about him. He is on retreat though, so it is Father Con. I want to wriggle away from him, but I stand still and I try to smile because that is what I sense I am supposed to do. He tells me my father was the best of men. I know that. He doesn't. He tells me that is why he has been taken. He tells me I must be good. I must be brave. I must look after my mother. I wait for him to finish speaking; I look at the big holes on the skin of his nose and the waxy hairs in his ears. Incense and cigarettes.

Ruby and Keith, close friends of my parents, come. Keith is speaking and then he is sobbing. Ruby puts her arm around me and moves me away. I am not supposed to see these things. She talks brightly to me. I am learning that people do not want to see us cry; they want us to be brave.

In the early morning, the awful sound of my Mum. The sound scares me. It seems to tear itself from her and fight to force her mouth open and be heard. She is sleeping in the small spare room on a narrow single bed. I can't climb in with her. Every morning, for a short while at least, I hear those sounds. I go rushing in. And she says she is okay.

I think it was Monday, two days afterwards, when I went back to school. Maybe it was later; but it was definitely within the week. Ruth Sidlaw, in class 6, asked if I was alright. I saw Mick Terry doing some idiotic mime of crashing a car, but he didn't come near me. Everyone else acted the same as always, so I tried to act the same as always too. Nobody mentioned it. None of my friends. None of the teachers. I imagine they had been told not to. Perhaps it was better like that. Everything had changed entirely, but not at school.

Over the next few days and weeks there are streams of visitors to our house; adults and, often, their children. I know some of the children, but others I have never met and I have to be good and brave. I have to entertain them while the adults whisper downstairs. One girl I have never met, plays with my stuff in my room. I am chattering away but she isn't talking.

I remember hating her and wanting her to go.

My Grandad comes upstairs and gives us both a Cadbury's Cream Egg.

It is decided I should not go to the funeral. It will be too traumatic for me, but not for my brothers. I can go to the memorial service instead. The funeral is in Dundee and my mother says now that if she had been able to think straight or resist she would have had my dad's body brought back here. But she doesn't. He is buried in a cemetery on the Old Craigie Road, same place as Uncle Jim, and later my dad's own parents and countless others from our large, extended family. He has a headstone, hard, unyielding which we visit whenever we go to Dundee. It's like he doesn't belong to us.

I begin to secretly think that he might not be dead.

I'll never know if not seeing his body, or not seeing the coffin made a difference to me. Because I have a recurring dream that dad wasn't killed. What happens is this: I come across him in America, where we lived for a while, or in Scotland, somewhere else living a different life. And he always has a new wife and more children. Those dreams are brutal; they swim with sadness and pulse with rejection and betrayal.

Mum gets a job and a new car. She has to leave before I go to school, so I sort myself out. I have a key that is kept in the tumble dryer in the garage. I am a latch-key kid. I feel ashamed every day that I let myself in. I look around frantically to see if any neighbours are watching. Sometimes my brothers, who go to secondary school, get back before me. 'Why didn't you use the key?' they say, if I ring on the bell. Sometimes when I leave the house in the morning, I stand at the open front door and shout 'Bye!' back into the empty hallway and house before I set off.

At the end of the day, I always wait for Mum at the window. I used to wait at the same window for my dad, but I was always excited. I was never worried that he wasn't coming back.

I hear her telling Nan that she doesn't know how she gets to and from work in the car. She says she is on auto-pilot. I think I know what that means and it worries me more. She stops driving the car and takes the bus. This means that she leaves even earlier and gets back even later, but I am relieved. She sells the car and never drives again.

In time, I will also be embarrassed that we don't have a car.

The days turn a bit warmer. I keep seeing my Dad. I see his car but I can't quite see the number plate. I glimpse him, along Straight Road, on my way to and from school. I wonder if the police will come again and say there has been a mistake.

After school, I open his wardrobe and bury my face in his brown corduroy jacket and breathe. Wrigley's Spearmint Gum and cigarettes.I put my feet in his shoes.

The pale Hush-Puppy boots he mostly wore are missing.

Sometimes my legs feel so heavy on the way back from school that when I get in, I go to my bedroom and kneel on the yellow carpet with my face on my thighs and stay like that, in the afternoon sun, for ages. This strange heaviness goes on for weeks, I think. I don't mention it to anyone, though. At some point it stops. At some point things begin to get sharper again.

I develop a fear of meeting new people. The world is divided into people who know and people who don't. The people who know don't mention it, but the people who don't sometimes ask awkward questions.

I start to lie.

These are some of the lies: I have a pet puppy at home, which I keep in my room.

My mum doesn't go to work.

My real name is Susannah, not Susan.

My middle name isn't Carmel, it's the much more familiar Clare.

That type of thing; random lies. I'm not sure why.

The big lie is that sometimes I pretend to new people that I still have a dad. He's not around much. He works away a lot.

My mum carries on working full-time and one winter, a few years after dad's death, she gets the flu. She is really ill: staying at home – shivering in bed – unable to do anything – ill. She is never off work, just as we are never off school. I must be 12 or 13 and I take on the role of nurse.

I take the role very seriously.

I go to her in the middle of the night to check on her. I wake her up to get her out of bed, standing and shaking, while I plump her pillows and smooth her sweaty sheets. I force honey and lemon drinks on her at all times of the day and night. I stand over her while she drinks them.

She cannot bear even the smell of honey now.

She is off work for a whole week and, to my shame, I enjoy the luxury of her being there, albeit in this state, when I leave for school in the morning and when I get home.

Everyone has something to say to me about him. At secondary school my new headteacher has seen my name and calls me in to his office. We called him Big Jones (like Big Brother). He had campaigned with my dad. My English teacher brings in an election pamphlet from years back with us all bunched up on the settee, looking smart. The five of us. Another teacher canvassed for him. A friend's father was a colleague at the university; came to the memorial. When I am 18, I get a holiday job at Christmas time in the sorting office of the GPO. It's brilliant. Back from our first terms at university, loads of my friends and my boyfriend land this job too. The postmen, the permanent employees, are raucous and sing along to Christmas songs on the radio. We get paid each day and go straight to the Hole in the Wall pub when our shift finishes.

The local Tory MP visits the sorting office for a regional newspaper story. He speaks to some of us students. He comes to shake my hand, alcohol sour on his breath and his papery skin, sallow and wrinkled. He asks what I am studying. 'Ah English Literature. Have you read the novels of Benjamin Disraeli?' He asks my name. I give him both first name and surname, my face burning, and I think I see him shaken for a moment.

An opportunity presents itself, but neither of us takes it. And he moves on.

People of an age, locally, notice the surname throughout my life and they ask and then they tell their story. I have to share him. Even in death. Especially in death.

His death continues to shape my life. A life of fearing and anticipating loss; the terror of losing the other parent and then the fear of losing anyone. I now have children of my own and I obsess about them losing one of us. I am alert to danger. Risk averse.

Childhood is another country. That's what they say. But I often think of that exhausted little girl, curled up in prayer pose, breathing in the scent of her knees and half-dozing in the fragile, early spring sunshine.

Tabitha Bast - The Girl Will Fix It

Sometimes, a thing would be broken. A light fitting or a shower or a curtain. And it soon started that Uncle Paul would say "The girl will fix it," and the girl was me.

In the first place it was because Uncle Paul was busy or not bothered enough. He'd have his feet up behind the reception desk and be just rooting to get back to his magazine. But soon I got better at fixing things than anyone else and I took a real pride in it.

Mostly it was men travelling alone who stopped at our motel - truckers and salesmen and the like so I wouldn't go to their rooms alone. Instead I was sent along with John or Joe who'd make small talk. John and Joe had lived with us for as long as I can remember. They were both old and it was hard exactly to say what use they now were, except that they played cards and drank with Uncle Paul in the evenings and knew the best route to anywhere to guide the guests. When I was little I thought they were brothers, but now that I'm a woman who lives in the City and knows all about the world, I think they weren't brothers but something more, and our home was a place they could be themselves without getting nuisance for it.

There was a real art to the small talk, and John or Joe would stand in the doorway asking just the right questions to figure out a bit of a story without being rude. Both of them made it look natural, and they each had their own ways about it. They were both wiry men with grey hair and from behind you maybe couldn't tell the difference if you hadn't known them all your life. The rooms were all more or less the same, and the doorways were all more or less the same. It was just the people inside them who made them new.

John or Joe would lean against the identical doorway and nod and hmmm and John would say, "Oh, is that so?" and Joe would say, "Really now?" and ask whether the highway was busy or had it been an easy ride and had they much further to go?

More often than not the guest or guests would want to say a lot regardless of whether they actually had a good tale. John or Joe would always listen with polite attention, no matter what. John said that those stories made up for the lack of tips in the jar when our customers left.

The times you were least likely to get a story was when the guests were a couple, a man and a woman who just wanted their thing fixed and me out of there. In fact, often they didn't bother telling us anything was broken until the morning when they were leaving and the man would mention it only when he was paying, as if the room didn't matter so much and there was much more pressing business at hand.

If there wasn't a good enough story from a guest it was my Uncle Paul who made the best ones up. He didn't much talk to the guests but to us he loved to tell tales. Sometimes they were so funny and ridiculous that it hurt, and sometimes they were a bit dirty and I didn't quite get them. And sometimes they were just lonely ones that made you want to cry. When he told the sad tales he'd even get himself worked up like he was mixing the stories up with real life in his head.

My story is that one day a lady came all on her own, a rare kind of guest for our motel. She was tall and blonde and what Uncle Paul called "worldly" and to me she looked beautiful and exciting even if she wasn't wearing high heels. Her suitcase was enormous and I was a little starstruck. On reception Joe had to do all the chatting and give the instructions because I was just staring at her.

She was given room 22 which was one of the quieter ones like she asked, but it was only a matter of minutes before she rang through to reception to say her TV wasn't working. I was embarrassed because I wanted everything nice for her, but also pleased because maybe I'd get to see her clothes laid out. Joe sent me along on my own because I didn't need to be kept safe from a man. Again, I was both embarrassed I'd have to do the talking and pleased it would just be me.

"Oh," she said when I came in, "it's a girl!" As if this would be news to us both. "Well, aren't you clever?"

This was before I'd even looked at the TV so it didn't feel a real compliment.

In the absence of another it was up to me to ask some questions and I started with the one about was it far to go now.

"Not so far, no. I do sure feel all dusty from driving for so long today. I wouldn't usually come so far out but I'm on quite an adventure."

I couldn't believe she just paused for so long that I had to ask directly. A trick John had taught me was just taking a bit of what people say then saying it back so nothing could be seen as rude and out of line so I said back "An adventure?"

"I'm going to meet my mother for the first time," she said. "I was adopted as a baby and I've finally tracked her down. I only really know her name and her address so far but I have a photo from when she was young. I expect she's changed a lot now, though. It's a strange feeling, that I'll see her tomorrow, for the first time. Well, not the first time but you know what I mean."

Well, that did seem like a big adventure but frightening as well as exciting. My heart pounded really hard, and it wasn't from the lovely clothes she was laying out on the bed, but because I'd never known my mother either. It had never occurred to me that I could.

The TV; it turned out; was broke for good and even I couldn't fix it. I didn't get upset, though. I just moved the lady into room 18 which was also quiet but the best of all the rooms for the view. You could see the distant town and no matter what time of night someone there always had their lights on which was comforting. But more than the town were the mountains behind it which always had snow on their peaks, even in the hottest summer, like some things were there and forever and unchanging. The lady was perfectly nice about changing rooms, even though she had to put all her clothes back into her case again. I offered to help, but she laughed at me and called me a "total delight."

I couldn't stop thinking about her journey and her unknown mother who could look like and be like anything, and what that moment would be when they first saw each other. And I told my Uncle Paul about it all because I always told him everything.

He was very quiet and lit a cigarette although he was trying to stop smoking. He also poured himself a drink a little early and he took a deep breath. Uncle Paul was a believer in a deep breath, and not rushing in to answer anything that required a little thought.

"Well, my darling," he said. "Sometimes you need to fix a thing that's broken in a room, even if you have to drive into town to get whatever tools you need to repair it because you know - or you think - it can be fixed and so it should. And sometimes, like with this lady, it's best for everyone just to move her to another room and leave the broken thing. Your Ma was a broken thing that couldn't be fixed - not by me and not even by you. But once you came to live with me it turned out you fixed me, even though I didn't know I had a hole in me. But I did have a hole and it was that I was hungry to love someone, to love them fiercely and more than even myself. And when you came to me instead of her, I tried sometimes to mend her too, but every time I tried I ended up myself a bit more broken.

It's up to you if and when you find your Ma, it is up to you. And if you find yourself broken from it, I'll fix you up again as often as you need it. After all, I think a girl like you who can grow as good as you have in a motel with three old men for company can do just about anything."

I went to him and hugged him hard and made his face all wet with my own tears that were both sadness and happiness that he loved me so much. And then I tried to steal a sip of his whisky, which even then I was partial to, but he laughed and slapped me away and I wasn't allowed.

The lady left in the morning and she was full of praise for me that she twittered at John on reception who didn't once say he wasn't my grandad like she presumed. Instead he nodded along as if he was so proud to hear it, even though I hadn't fixed the TV. He loaded her big suitcase into the boot of her car for her and she waved at us as she drove off with the window open as if we were all great friends.

"Now that's a lady who talks a lot when she's nervous," John noted, and I agreed wholeheartedly.

I wasn't one who talked a lot when I'm nervous and I came to decide that I wasn't much like that lady after all. I never needed a big suitcase for a journey, I always had just a small bag of essentials.

I also decided I didn't need to meet my Ma, though if she came to meet me herself I wouldn't say no. I was growing up good enough in a motel with three old men. Sometimes you don't need the small talk of oh where did you come from when you have a lot to say about where you are and where you want to go instead.

I grew up so good that I won a scholarship for college despite nobody in town ever doing something like that, and I had to go away to the city where I still live today. The city was full of women like the one who had stayed. Women with a lot of clothes who were looking for something they felt was missing. I lived in a dorm and often helped the janitor with the trickier jobs about the place, something the other students marveled at and mocked. Usually we fixed it, but when we couldn't we shrugged and left it and I didn't mind a bit. Sometimes in an evening we played cards together, though he always beat me.

John died of prostate cancer in my final year and it's only Joe and Uncle Paul left home at the motel, keeping each other company and grabbing bites of stories from the passing guests. I call every week and visit when I can, and I sleep in room 18 when I do. I've always said room 18 is the best room, even if only for the view.

Terence Lehane - The Turnstile

Rosemarie Laborde, weighed down with a large handbag and a carrier bag full of toys, rolled a pushchair up to the entrance to the Olympiades Metro station in the 13th arrondissement of Paris. She put down her bags, took Thomas, her three year old son, out of the pushchair, folded it up, put it under her arm, picked up her bags, took Thomas by the one free hand she still somehow managed to have, and headed towards the escalator.

Just then a woman's voice came from behind. "*I think you've lost something*". When Rosemarie swung around she saw a young woman in a red coat hunkered down talking to Thomas. In her hand was a navy blue woollen mitten Thomas must have dropped when getting out of the pushchair. "*You have to be very careful with these*" she said "*They're so very easy to lose*". Thomas took the mitten. The woman smiled at him and passed her hand through his hair.

She then stood up and Rosemarie thanked her. "*He's always losing his mittens*" she laughed nervously. The woman smiled, a strange sad smile thought Rosemarie, as if she were about to burst into tears. She then abruptly turned away and got on the escalator. Rosemarie and Thomas followed and stood some steps above the woman as the escalator rumbled downwards.

The high-speed driver-less line 14 of the Paris metro is twice as deep underground as the normal metro lines. Why? Rosemarie had no idea but it just was and three long escalators were needed to ferry passengers down into the bowels of the earth. She had read there were 4 million passengers every day, 48 every second, the magazine said, most of them commuting to work and school between 7 and 9 just as she was. 4 million anonymous faces.

She marvelled at how fleeting those faces and encounters were. Every time she took the metro, she would observe them closely, hooking on to those who fascinated her most and fantasising about where they were going, their jobs, families, boyfriends, girlfriends, husbands, wives…

And then the doors would open and they would be gone! The end of these transient, silent relationships left her with a wrenching feeling. She knew she would never see them ever again.

Rosemarie looked down the escalator at the woman in the red coat. Why was she so sad? She seemed to be looking for something. What was it? Where was it? Rosemarie imagined herself being so bold as to go down and ask her "*What's wrong? You can tell me. I'm a good listener*". But of course she didn't dare. She knew the woman would soon disappear, just like all the others, never to be seen again.

Just then, the woman turned around and looked up towards Rosemarie and Thomas. She caught Rosemarie's eye and stared at her as if she were trying to read her mind. Rosemarie felt uncomfortable and embarrassed but couldn't break away from her gaze. This perfect stranger seemed to want to tell her something, unburden herself of some great secret. What could it be?

The woman got off the escalator, moved to the side and stood still, waiting. Rosemarie's heartbeat speeded up. Was she waiting for her? She was sure the woman would try to talk to her. Rosemarie was so taken with this idea she didn't notice the end of the escalator coming up. Thomas stumbled off but she held him up by the arm. Rosemarie quickened her step, looking straight ahead to avoid any contact with the red-coated woman. She and Thomas got on the second escalator. Thomas was giggling at his near fall and despite everything Rosemarie smiled.

Three and a half years old and just look at him with his tiny duffle coat, scarf and mittens. Rosemarie made sure he was always well wrapped up and protected from the cold. You never know what bugs were going round and at that age children were so fragile.

Today was his first day at school. Rosemarie would drop him off then go on to work. She shuddered at the thought. She feared he would be swallowed up by that huge machine that is the French National Education System. Even if it was only playschool, he was such a delicate and vulnerable little thing. What if he's bullied by the bigger boys? How would he cope? She wondered were all mothers like her. Unable to let their children run free across this minefield of a society, danger lurking at every turn. In her heart of hearts she wanted to keep him safe at home, sheltered from the craziness of this world, but of course she knew this could not be.

So she would diligently bring him to school, knowing the separation would be more painful for her than for him. She knew she would have an awful day, worrying about him, wondering if everything was all right and checking her phone for any emergency texts from the school. Ah… that damned maternal instinct! Did men have a paternal instinct? Did such a thing even exist? If it did, it didn't amount to much.

As the end of the second escalator approached Rosemarie grabbed Thomas's hand to get him off safely this time. After a relatively soft landing they struggled over to the third and final escalator, the one that ended just before the turnstiles.

As she settled in for this final ride Rosemarie's mind turned back to the red-coated woman. She was probably a few steps above them looking down. Rosemarie was certain she had stopped deliberately after the first escalator to get behind them and follow them. Rosemarie felt the urge to look back. She fought against it but knew the woman was there. She could feel her gaze. And that made Rosemarie self-conscious. She looked at her bags, clothes, brushed her coat down, pushed her hair back, tightened Thomas's scarf and nervously waited for the escalator to land.

The turnstiles came into view. This and the sound of the trains arriving at the platform 10 metres beyond the turnstiles combined to awaken the beast in a large number of commuters. Like parched buffalo stampeding to a water-hole, they started to hurry down the stairs passing out those who stood still. Rosemarie had to squeeze in to the side as the herd moved quickly past her, growling and snorting. They were visibly put out as they passed her by, resenting her getting in their way, slowing them down on this, their, escalator at 8 in the morning. They were going to work, she was probably some stay-at-home mum taking her kid to the park. They clearly had priority. So they bumped into her and jostled Thomas without so much as an "excuse me" or "sorry".

As they landed for the third and final time Rosemarie stopped to gather up her things. Streams of commuters passed her by on both sides fanning out as they rushed to find the turnstile with the shortest queue. The 12 turnstiles clicked madly as the crowds streamed through. For the commuters the turnstiles were like Rosemarie - an obstacle they had to overcome as quickly as possible. So they had their passes out in advance, arms outstretched aiming at the scan point. As soon as it beeped the turnstile was released and the two small doors behind the turnstile opened. They moved through the turnstile then through the two doors which shut immediately behind them, only to open nanoseconds later with the next metro pass card beep. The doors opened and closed incessantly like a flock of albatross flapping their wings in a desperate and futile attempt to get airborne. The least delay at a turnstile– an old lady rifling through her bag looking for her ticket - and the queue would scatter over to the other faster moving ones.

With Thomas in tow, Rosemarie was clearly one of the slow cases and the other commuters fled at the sight of her bags, pushchair and child. Thomas was small enough to pass under the turnstile and Rosemarie had him do this and wait in front of the two doors while she got out her pass. She flashed it and the turnstile clicked as it was released. Rosemarie struggled through then turned back to haul her bags and the pushchair over the turnstile. She didn't see that Thomas had moved forward through the open doors. As soon as he got to the other side the two doors shut leaving Rosemarie stuck in the narrow space between the turnstile and the doors and Thomas inside the Metro station.

Rosemarie flashed her pass again but it wouldn't work a second time at such a short interval. She turned to her right to try and get some help but the commuters ignored her in their rush to work and her pleas of "*Ah excuse me…*" fell on deaf ears in the midst of the furiously clicking turnstiles, trains, escalators and rushing crowds. Rosemarie then turned to her left and froze. The woman in the red coat was standing in the turnstile beside her. Rosemarie was desperate now, apprehension slowly taking hold but she said nothing. The woman said nothing either. She just looked at Rosemarie, then down at Thomas, then walked through the open doors of her turnstile and stepped quickly over to the platform.

Rosemarie shouted out to Thomas "*Thomas, don't you move. You wait for me okay?*" Thomas nodded. Rosemarie then turned back again. Surely somebody would help her? Were there any metro staff around? She could see none and her pleas of "*Please, help me…*" still went ignored. She turned back to check on Thomas and came face to face with the woman in the red coat who had come back and was now standing beside Thomas on the other side of the turnstile doors. The woman bent down and picked up Thomas' fallen mitten yet again. This time though, she put the mitten into her own pocket. She then picked up Thomas, hugged him, kissed him and squeezed him tight. A tear rolled down her cheek. Rosemarie's heart pounded as apprehension gave way to panic. She knew exactly what the woman was thinking. She finally found her voice and begged her not to do it. "*No, no, no, don't take my Thomas, he's mine, he's mine, he's mine… don't take him, don't!*". Her pleas were drowned out by the noise of screeching brakes as another train pulled up to the platform.

The woman, her lips trembling, said nothing. Thomas started to cry. The woman turned and ran over to the waiting train with Thomas in her arms. Rosemarie's turnstile doors were finally released by a metro worker.

The train's high-pitched door-closing warning whistle sounded. Rosemarie rushed forward. Just as the train doors started to close her feet got caught in the pushchair, she fell over, knocked her head on a huge stone pillar and everything went blank.

***

Rosemarie lay unconscious with a large white bandage around her head, in a bed with white sheets and white pillows, in a hospital room with white walls and white windows, watched over by a doctor in a white coat. Then a man in jeans and a black leather jacket knocked on the door, entered, nodded in the direction of the doctor and sat down in a chair on the other side of the bed.

Rosemarie's eyes slowly opened.

"*Hello Rosemarie. How are you feeling?*". The doctor said. Rosemarie winced with the pain and raised her hand to her head.

"*Yes, that was quite a knock you got there. Do you remember me Rosemarie? I'm doctor Manier.*" Rosemarie sat up suddenly and cried out "*Thomas! Thomas! Where's Thomas? I want to see Thomas*". Doctor Manier took her hand and turned towards the man on the other side of the bed.

"*This gentleman is detective Dubray, a police officer. Why don't you tell us exactly what happened Rosemarie. Right from the start.*"

Rosemarie turned to detective Dubray "*Are you going to find Thomas for me?*" Detective Dubray's eyes darted over to Doctor Manier who turned back to Rosemarie.

"*Just tell us what happened*".

Rosemarie told her story, ending her account in tears. Where was Thomas? Where was he she cried to Doctor Manier. Doctor Manier squeezed Rosemarie's hand.

"*Rosemarie… you can't keep doing this. We were making progress Rosemarie, real progress. You'd been released from the hospital, allowed to go home. Everything was going just fine.*"

Rosemarie's eyes welled up again. "*But where's Thomas, Doctor, where is he?*"

Doctor Manier swallowed hard. "*Rosemarie, you know Thomas is gone. You lost him two years ago, in the metro. A woman grabbed him from you, ran onto a train and was never seen again. The police investigated, did everything they could…*"

Rosemarie pulled her hand away.

"*No, no! That woman in the red coat, she took him, she took Thomas!*"

Detective Dubray put his hand down into a plastic bag and pulled out a red coat for Rosemarie to see.

"*Is this the coat you're talking about Madame Laborde?*" He threw it onto the bed.

"*Yes! That's it. Did you catch her?*".

"*This is your coat Madame Laborde. This is the coat you were wearing this morning*". Rosemarie shook her head.

"*You didn't have Thomas or any other child with you Madame Laborde. The video surveillance cameras show you were alone. You went to the metro station looking for an opportunity and you found it. A poor woman stuck in the turnstile separated from her child, just like you said except it wasn't you in the turnstile Madame Laborde. You were the woman in the red coat. You grabbed the boy and ran towards the train. That's when you tripped up and knocked your head on the pillar. Luckily the boy, Etienne, wasn't hurt.*"

Rosemarie listened in silence. Doctor Manier turned back to Rosemarie.

"*You have to come to terms with your loss Rosemarie or spend the rest of your life in this hospital. If you don't you will always be a danger to yourself and to others and we won't be able to let you go home. You don't want that do you?*" Rosemarie shook her head.

"*If you stay in denial we can't do anything for you. You have to understand Rosemarie. You have to realise what you did this morning and how serious it is. Well? do you?*" After a long silence, Rosemarie nodded slowly.

"*Good. That means we can continue your treatment. Will you help us make you better Rosemarie?*" Rosemarie nodded again.

Doctor Manier stood up.

"*Very good*". He glanced at his watch. "*First you'll need some time to get over that knock on the head. The nurse will be around shortly with your medication and I'll pencil you in for a session next Monday. Does that sound okay to you?*" Rosemarie nodded again.

"*Any questions?*". Rosemarie shook her head.

"*Fine*".

Detective Dubray picked up the red coat to put it back into the bag. As he did, a navy blue woollen mitten fell from one of the pockets. Rosemarie picked it up, looked at it and smiled. She handed it over to Doctor Manier.

"*Please Doctor, can you give this back to Thomas. He's always losing his mittens*".

Toby Privett - The Great Lockdown Novel

I leap out of bed. Today is the day I will begin my *Great Lockdown Novel.* The flat is cold, so I detour via the thermostat and hunt for yesterday's woolly socks. I upturn the laundry basket, check under the sofa and behind the fridge. Then find them where I left them, on my feet. I make coffee, sit down in front of the computer and check my emails. Someone has sent me a re-purposed, war-time propaganda picture: a strapping man in an armchair, surrounded by smiling offspring.

'What did you in the Great Pandemic, Daddy?'

'I wrote a masterpiece, kids.'

Boosted by this positive affirmation, I delete yesterday's efforts and wipe away everything I've written in the last few lockdown weeks. On a blank page, I type the title of my new masterpiece-in-progress, FORGETTING TO SWITCH OFF THE CAPS LOCK, and begin:

Once upon a time there was a man who got dumped by the woman he expected to spend the rest of his life with.

Her again. Why the hell am I writing about *her* again.

My stomach tightens, but that might be hunger. I go to the kitchen, pluck the least rotten banana off the bunch and return to the screen. As I chew, I wait for the pain to ease, but it doesn't. It's time to move on, but I have no idea where to start.

Twenty year ago, my first guide through the swampy waters of creative writing talked about writing down the bones. Natalie Goldberg's instruction, in times of barricade, was to pick up a pen and write the first thing that came into your head. Then the next, and the next, again and again. Keep that hand moving, and don't stop till the boiled egg timer has lapped itself at least three times. Stop for no man, no woman, nor doorbell, until that crisp sheet of white paper is full of words. Then flip it over like a pancake and keep it on a high heat until the other side is crispy brown. Prise the pages out of the spiral bound notebook, peel the scraps out from under the metal rings, and deposit the daily doings on top of yesterday's excretions. Then file it all away in a colour-coded ring binder:

red for summer, black for winter and green for the breakup that I don't want to write about.

I fire up the egg-timer app on my phone, then stare at the computer screen until my eyes wander off and around the room. I spot a black smudge on the yellow paintwork. It's just below the entry phone that my daughter picks up and answers, whether its ringing or not. I didn't notice the smudge yesterday when the words (about her) were tumbling out.

I go to the kitchen and run a washcloth under the tap, squeeze out the drips, then wring it tight with both hands. Up close, the smudge is deeper and darker than I first thought. This job needs chemicals. She would have the perfect products filed in the cupboard under the sink, but all I have is a bottle of chip shop vinegar.

I wrap a cloth around the top, and shake. Out, out, damn smudge, and with each rub the black turns to grey turns to a pale shade of mud. I roll up my sleeves and scrub till the muscles on my arm bulge up like the lady on the cover of the baking soda box. The smudge is gone, and the egg-timer is ready for its first flip.

But there is a foul smell in the air. I crack open the window and return to my chair. There is a dust ball in the corner, just behind the door. Dust is on my mind now. I could write a treatise on it, but I'm not sure I know what a *treatise* is. I get up again and cross the room in three shuffling steps. I bend down and run my fingers through the dust pile until it binds together like pink sugar spinning around the insides of a candy floss machine. I make a fist around the clump. Walk to the bin. Dispose.

Left to my own devices, I am not the slob she said I was.

It's time to flip the timer again. I count bird shits on the window till the upstairs neighbour comes to a running halt outside. He puts his hands on his waist, red gloves on a yellow jacket, and bobs his head a couple of times, exhaling his post-orgasmic exercise grunts. He's smiling and looking straight at me, but he thinks he's looking at himself.

The windows are coated with privacy film, and I spend my lockdown days spying on the outside world like a celebrity driving through town in a stretch limo or a middle-aged man daydreaming about being a writer.

I hear the communal door bang shut, then count the footsteps on the stairs. Two, maybe three, at a time. Then the flip and flop of the floorboards above my head. He is probably in the shower now, but the flats in this young building are well-insulated and I don't have to listen to him - unlike the old house with its creaking stairs, vintage plumbing and her shouts from the guest room:

'Don't turn the fucking shower on at two in the morning!'

The bottom bowl of the virtual egg timer is almost full, and I have a new idea. I am going to take up running and write about my adventures along the country lanes: passing cars that spit their mud at me, sweat that beads down my neck and lungs that tell me to stop smoking.

I go to the athletic store and ask the guy behind the counter for the best pair of shoes for the job. He comes back a few minutes later with a bright orange cardboard box. I lace up the new shoes and walk around the shop while he watches the creases and bends of my feet. He sends me outside and tells me to run up and down the pavement. Perfect, he says, and rings me up at the till.

Back at home, I put on the new running shoes. They fit even better now, with my feet up on the coffee table. I sit back in the chair and flip the egg timer for one more round. Knockout or submission. My new life as a long-distance runner is stretching out in front of me. Marathon running and novel writing worked so well for Murakami that he wrote a book about it.

Running worked for her too. She used to take our baby girl to the Monday morning *Mum's on the Run* club, racing the red pram around the park perimeter like a supermarket shopper stocking up on pre-pandemic toilet paper, flattening out the natal stretchmarks, coming home with a smiling, sweaty face.

Not me, though. I'm out of breath already. But it's not time to stop. Keep spouting drivel till the end of the line, then cast off onto the next like I'm knitting a woolly scarf to keep my neck warm on those cold morning runs, or a spare pair of socks. Knitting would be a fine hobby to while away the winter nights. I go online to watch a video tutorial and learn about the needles and wool and patterns I will need to source. I remember that her aunt owns a knitting shop in Nottingham, but a family and friends discount is probably out of the question.

The egg-timer beeps to say I'm done, but this yolk is still raw, and the white is pale and snotty.

I suspect that I am suffering from writer's block, so I ask the internet what to do about it.

The gospel according to Wikipedia suggests that a writing project, too explosively large, can cause the cerebral cortex to swell up like a blocked artery and squeeze the flow of ideas into a drip, drip, drip. I step outside to do a little rain dance, but someone walks past as I'm waving my arms in the air, so I pretend I'm checking the gutter for leaks, before hurrying back inside to look for more advice.

I stumble upon Dr Upper's published investigations into the self-treatment of writer's block. The peer review notes that the writing style is flawless, and the manuscript should be published without any further edits. Inspired, I send a copy to the printer, forgetting to open the feeder flap. I un-scroll the blank page onto the kitchen counter, smear it with lemon juice and look closely for a hidden message. But the paper is as blank and soggy as my idea bank.

Edmund Bergler psycho-analysed impotent writers and reckoned that bottle feeding as a baby was to blame. I draft an email to my mother about breastfeeding - an inspired piece of writing that I know she will compliment me on, as mothers usually do - but it does not have the narrative strength for the opening page of a *Great Lockdown Novel.*

I decide to go on a writer's retreat and relocate to the windowless bathroom. With the door shut, there is just enough room to wedge myself on the floor between the shower stall and the toilet bowl, both of which could do with a clean. After a few minutes with my knees wrapped around my ears, I get up to stretch my legs and walk around in tight circles. With each revolution, I come face to face with my chin in the mirror. If I bend at the knees, my face comes into focus.

There used to be four scars on my forehead, but in the dull light I can only see three. The deepest gash, just above my right eyebrow is now as thin as a razor slice. I remember my mother mopping me up with kitchen towels; nurses serving bowls of jelly in the children's ward; the Humpty Dumpty bandage wrapped tightly around my head and the plastic pot, labelled 'stitches', that I filed away in my memory box. One day, my little girl will bump her head and be hurried to the hospital. I wonder if it will happen on my time or her mother's.

The phone that I hadn't plan to take into the bathroom rings. It's a video call from my daughter.

'Move the camera back a little, I want to see your face,' I look for my nose in hers, but her nostrils are flared open and laughing.

'Silly, Daddy! What are you doing in the loo? Are you doing a poo?'

I see her mother in the background, folding laundry.

'Show me your room,' I say, and she carries me up the stairs. I recognise the green leaf prints on her bedroom curtains, and the cartoon character duvet cover on the bunk bed that I put up on a rainy Sunday afternoon last year. She strums a ukulele at me for a few minutes.

Her mother's voice: 'Bedtime!'

'Daddy, why can't you read me a story tonight?'

'You'll be here with me next week,' I say.

'Daddy, why did you leave me?'

'I didn't, my love.'

'But, Daddy, you said you were going to buy me ice cream. But you never came back!'

'I didn't want to go.' I want to hug her right now, and wipe the tears from her eyes, and mine.

'But I don't have a daddy to read me a story tonight.'

The phone beeps. Call disconnected.

I sit down on the toilet seat, paper on my lap, pen in my hand.

Your mother held a gun to my head: 'Have a second child with me. Or leave!'

It's not the opening page of a *Great Lockdown Novel*, but it is the story that I need to write.

Tricia Green - Disco

The disco drew Geraldine like a magnet. She knew that city girls wouldn't think it had much in the way of bright lights, but they were the brightest Killay Cross had ever seen. The old people said all the teenagers would come to rack and ruin …a glamorous state Geraldine often tried to envisage.

The disco was strictly forbidden to Geraldine, although she watched longingly each week as Bridgie and Mona set off on their bicycles. They were old enough to go their own way, Gran said, as all the young ones did these days. But Geraldine, poor motherless child, was still her responsibility, and Mary, Joseph and all the saints would vouch for the fact that she never shirked her duty. Duties, such as Geraldine, had to know their place.

***

"Come and choose your dress from the catalogue, Geraldine."

This was a formality gone through every six months or so. She chose a dress, Gran then vetoed her choice in favour of something she considered suitable for a thirteen year old.

Geraldine looked wistfully at the young fashion pages – she could really do with a bomber jacket and a pair of pedal pushers. She stared at the page long and lovingly.

"Will you see the cut of that!" said Gran. "Think of anyone respectable dressing their youngsters that way – like something out of an American film."

Geraldine did think of it, as Gran filled in the form for a demure long-sleeved dress she could almost have worn in her own young days.

She prayed to St Anthony, the patron saint of lost causes, but without much hope. Most causes she had previously troubled the good saint with had remained lost.

But, for once, St Anthony was on her side. She got off the school bus one night to find Gran in a rare taking.

"What your Auntie Madge wants another baby for, at her time of life, I can't imagine," she said crossly. "But as there's only me, it's me must go, I suppose. Mona and Bridgie will have to look after you – mind you do as they say."

Mona and Bridgie said a great deal for the first couple of hours, then drifted into a wholesome neglect. Praying to St Anthony the while, although she was sure he would never countenance such deceit, Geraldine managed to tear up the slip ordering the demure girlish dress, and replace it with an order for the bomber jacket and pedal pushers. If Gran came back before they arrived, she would think they had been sent by accident, as other things had in the past, and alter the order again. Geraldine would at least be able to try them on and see herself for a few minutes in some real cool gear, instead of Gran's choices or her school uniform. She ran to the post box, before she could become convicted of sin and change her mind.

Gran was some time with Auntie Madge, so long that Geraldine began to actually miss her. She had friends to tea several nights running, buying fresh cream cakes from Maceys, but the novelty soon wore off, she didn't like to see them with their muddy feet up on the chairs, being rude about Gran's old-fashioned furniture. She kept the place tidy as best she could – Mona and Bridgie soon stopped bothering with it.

Then the parcel came. It lay neglected on the hall table. Geraldine jumped with nervous guilt when she saw it.

"Can I open this, Mona? It's some clothes for me."

With trembling hands, Geraldine carried the parcel up to her bedroom. She turned the plaster Blessed Virgin to face the wall, then, with a quick prayer, turned her back again. It was probably a worse sin to want the Blessed Virgin to look away than to deceive one's grandmother. She scrambled rapidly into the clothes, trying not to crease them, and rushed to the mirror. She saw, apart from the timid face and the childish dark fringe, a proper, streetwise teenager. It seemed a shame to enjoy the sight nowhere else but here. Maybe… she flung downstairs and burst in on the girls. Mona raised surprised eyebrows.

"Mona, Bridgie, are you going to the disco tonight?"

"I'm going with me fella."

"In his car? Are you giving Mona a lift?"

"Oh, Geraldine, grow up!"

Geraldine failed to see why only two people needed four seats. It seemed plain greedy.

"Oh, I'll take you on the back of my bike. You'd better cover that lot up, though. Waterproof trousers for you, my girl, by the look of those puddles,"

"Oh, Mona!"

"I'm not taking you if you twist your face up, or if you hang around me all evening. You can fend for yourself once you're there, girl."

***

Geraldine felt a bit sick by the time they got there, either from the bumpy road or from nerves. She ripped off the waterproofs around the corner of the building and bundled them viciously into Mona's bike bag. It was impossible to do her hair in this wild wind, but at least the outfit could be seen in its full glory. She blinked as she went from the cold into the dark and heat. Mona left her almost at once and went to join a little knot of girls her own age, who were clustered around a table in a corner. Bridgie and her man were snogging with abandon over the other side of the room. She hardly seemed like the home Bridgie any more, but someone who belonged to this wild glamorous world.

A strobe light illuminated Geraldine and she stood frozen, like a hypnotised rabbit. Blessing of blessings, kind Clare O'Sullivan from her French set, face a-glitter with make-up, swam out of the miasma to greet her.

"Geraldine! I never knew you came here!"

"Oh, well, you know…" Geraldine affected what she hoped was the world-weary pose of one whose social calendar could seldom allow trips to such minor venues.

"Come and have a Coke."

It was difficult to concentrate with the music turned up so high. Clare and her friends communicated in a sort of high-pitched shriek.

"There's a live musician – really fancies himself – you'll never guess who it is," Clare hooted into Geraldine's ear. "Hughie Murphy!"

"Hughie Murphy from Bog Lane!" Geraldine was hit by a burst of helpless laughter. Bubbles of Coke rushed the wrong way and she ended up sneezing.

"The thing is, we all pretend to fancy him … and he believes us. You watch when he comes on."

After an hour or so of breathless dancing, the elderly D.J. bawled out "Now the time all you girls have been waiting for – it's Hughie Murphy!"

Hughie Murphy was a normally rather nondescript postman. Tonight, though, he wore tight silver trousers and a scarlet shirt open almost to the waist, displaying a hairy chest and a glinting gold medallion. If Geraldine hadn't been primed sufficiently beforehand, she would have thought he looked quite impressive. But you never got to heaven by enjoying the sight of men gyrating their hips around. Pretending to enjoy it was quite another thing. Clare and her friend were red in the face, wiping tears of imaginary emotion from their eyes. Geraldine did a poor imitation of the same. She felt too shy to go into quite the transports the other girls were faking all around her. Hughie glanced at her once and caught her eye. He had very warm, twinkling brown eyes – strange she had never noticed before.

"Well, thank the sweet Lord that's over." Clare flung back her long hair which she had thrown all over her face during her keening. "What's the colour of your money, Gerry? Can you stand a round of Tizers?"

As Geraldine staggered out to the toilets, the coolness hit her like a blow to the face. Almost drunk with the contrast, she reeled along, holding to the wall. It was way past her usual bedtime.

In the spotty mirror in the graffitied toilet she saw only a plain and normal looking Geraldine, hair untidy, face as red as the rising sun. She did what she could to tidy herself, fastidiously picking bits off her new outfit. The cloakroom was rustling with courting couples – so this was a den of iniquity, like Gran said. Maybe she should keep her eyes shut as she hurried past.

"Haven't seen you here before, little girl." The voice was deep and husky. She turned round to see Hughie Murphy, even more embarrassingly good-looking close to. He was walking a little unsteadily and breathing out alcoholic fumes.

"It's my first time here," her voice came out in a thin childish squeak.

"Not your last, I hope, love." He slid an arm across her shoulders and her already choky voice vanished altogether. "I hope they let you come out a lot more."

He led her to one of the alcoves between the coat racks. People's

Wellington boots and overclothes were lying about the floor, kicked into a hopeless muddle. Geraldine had no idea why she went with him, she was as drunk with the strangeness of this world as if her Coke had contained gin. As he tilted her chin up and kissed her she complied blindly. So this was the French kissing the girls talked about. Quite easy really, once you picked up the way of it… How many Hail Marys would compensate for it? She'd never dare mention it in Confession. Hughie was snuggling against her and stroking her back. She got very little affection at home. There'd hardly ever been anybody around with either the time or the tendency to take her on their lap and make much of her. Maybe Hughie really loved her – perhaps at first glance his eyes met hers and he knew she was the only girl for him. Would it be forward to stroke his hair a little, where it curled so thickly around his neck? She reached her hand tentatively forward and the next thing she knew, Hughie was being jerked backwards, away from her, and flung back into the opposite row of hooks.

Geraldine screamed, an accomplishment she hadn't realised she had, and leapt up onto the boot-racks behind her. Hughie was lying on the ground being pummelled by Bridgie's fellow. He wasn't much of a pummeller himself, he just lay there and took it.

"Come here, you." Hughie had rushed for the toilet – he seemed to be crying. Surely men didn't cry? "I never thought Bridgie had a little tart for a sister."

Geraldine found tears trickling slowly down her face. Why did the greatest evening of her life have to turn out so terrible? Bridgie ran forward from somewhere and put her arm around her, for what must have been the first time ever.

"That dirty Hughie– she's only little – just because he can't get a girl old enough to know better. Didn't you know, Gerry? Didn't Gran teach you it's wrong to do those things?"

Geraldine nodded and wiped her eyes frantically, on the back of her hand, rather than the sleeve of her new outfit.

"We can't tell Gran. It'd kill her."

"Let him show his face here again, and I'll kill him."

"Get in the car, lovey."

A ride in the car was a rare treat, but Geraldine had somehow gone beyond treats today. It would help to know whether she was in disgrace or not. They drove home silently.

"Go up to bed now," she was told as soon as they got in. Immediately, as if she was carrying out a holy rite, Geraldine folded the disco clothes ready to be sent back. Tears waited behind her eyelids ready to fall. She knelt upright for extra long on the hard cold tiles as she said her prayers, as a penance.

However, when she got to bed it was laughter, not tears, which sprang to the surface. As she closed her eyes bright lights, crashing music, and the feel of Hughie Murphy's arms and lips accompanied her into her dreams.

Troy Ollis - Masterpiece

My hands drip a crimson stain upon the floor; my heart sinks a mile further. I take a step back and survey the damage. It is beyond repair. A cloth cleans the error from my fingers and the colour mixes with several previously wiped away. This is not my doing; I see no part of my humanity in this deed. I tear the painting from its easel and hide it among the blank canvases. I refuse to witness such mediocrity. I am haunted by a brush and some smears dashed across a page. Or perhaps it is not the tools that whisper wounds, but the subject of their efforts. It seems an impossible task; to immortalise innocence within an image. It is pain, drawing her memory to the forefront of a fractured psyche. I have looked at those tangles of thorns and found only the tearing of flesh, a showering of violence. I am entombed in red. My eyes seek rest, yet my body aches for a little more of that liquid comfort. I decide one must lead to the other and drain the last of the Rosé. My head, now filled with the corpses of bad ideas, has reached the brink and it is time to drain them into dreams. My eyes, once electric, now stained and inflamed, close and I drop away.

An SUV, its skin a lethal vantablack, flashes a toothy grill in my direction. The car accelerates, gaining a metre with every blink. There is a woman beside me; her dress has a brilliance that would envy a canary. She acknowledges my situation and says,

"What are you reading?"

"The Raven," I respond.

"Oh," She frowns, "The one from The Simpsons?"

"Yes," I nod, "though it was a famous poem first."

She shakes her head and dissipates; I call after her as the SUV bears down. Glancing back as it takes off into the sky, the back tire grazes the top of my head.

I am tugged away from these visions and find myself still in the studio. A drummer plays a solo on my brain. My body reacts to a night spent on a cold couch. I grasp for my jacket. Monogramed with my grandfather's initials, M.M., it held no sentiment. The coffee-stained tan of the jacket served to reflect what I had known of his life; a bitter man who detested the ambiguity of art. How ironic that I would be bestowed his name, as well as his jacket. Having conquered the cold, I stand and inspect the room. Several items have been ripped away from the furthest wall. An easel lies on its side. A mirror, once hung by a familiar face, is shattered. But it is the wall itself that stands out against the mess. The usual plain white interrupted by a single painted image at its centre.

A silhouetted figure atop a bike, the head points forward, the body sits hunched. One hand rests on the handlebars; the other grips the second bicycle the shadow pushes alongside. It's frame smaller, its seat empty.

It's a masterpiece. My hand betrayed me while I slumbered and delivered a sketch of magnificent simplicity. I fall forward onto my knees. No tear breaks free, yet I lower my head until it touches the ground. Forcing my gaze upwards, I am overcome with the urge to see the portrait no more. If like the sun, it burns to look upon, I will raise the moon. I cross the room and snatch a brush, its bristles tacked with paint. I dip it into mother-of-pearl and touch it to the wall. I attempt to streak my hand across the painting, but cannot. No one else must see my chef-d'oeuvre, yet I find myself unmoving. I am caught between the desire for destruction and the clemency of confrontation. I decide, if my hand will not make a move against it, I must hide the painting in plain sight. Surround its splendor with those of equal and better value. I find whiskey stashed away in a cupboard and I get to work.

I drink, and I paint.

For two and a half years.

***

My strokes caress her, leaving a stripe of pastel blue. The finishing touch to Masterpiece One Zero One. It sits among the other hundred paintings created by an appendage which never took absence of its duty. To leave these works abandoned was to fear of no return. It has been a time scarcely remembered since I began this toil; working to outweigh the pain of original sin. I have at long last completed my work. Though I still fear the object of my efforts has been in vain, for that portrait still stands stark. The others come close to this piece first splashed upon these walls, but refuse to surpass its allure. Yet, perhaps it is only I who cannot see past its hidden depths. Having poured out myself, drawing from the little that remains in me. Distance is a luxury not awarded to a creator. Could this be how God feels? He produces a race of murderers and thieves, yet gives them a chance at forgiveness. It seems even the Almighty cannot detach Himself from His mistakes. If my mind refuses to be impartial, I must seek one who is. An outsider who can scan the images of this room and have no thought of their intentions. If my masterpiece stands no better than any other in their view, I have succeeded in my deception. It will fade and become nothing in my memory. I will have brought the night and it will cover all from being seen. I move to the door and stumble out into the bright street. I feel myself splattered with achromatic drops; watering my arid skin. Yet when I cast down my eyes, I find floorboards of a suspicious familiarity. Returning my gaze upwards, I discover the door to the street still before me; cobwebs unbroken. My body is dry as before and my colourful friends frown down at me from the walls. They whisper, and they speak truth. I must remain close to this sanctuary. For we do not know what misfortunes may befall us while distant and unable to make swift return. These feet have not breached the threshold since my last rations run. Even then I had felt the insurmountable anxiety rise within and had begged a friendly acquaintance to gather many months of reserves. I handed them my list and several rectangles adorned with famous faces, before retreating. I admit, I felt a sense of great comfort when that door no longer demanded to be unlatched. When the continuous check-ups ceased and the salt-and-pepper spiders spun their homes. Undisturbed at last, I found the opportunity to work without interruption. This coincided with the awakening of the emerald and ruby Dragon; masterpiece twenty-two.

I have worked without disruption since.

My eyes wander over the walls, reflecting on the creation of each delicate design. While some are bottomless pools and others are but shallow mirrors, all are meaningful. Each a represention of memory; events long dismissed. I smile, and drink deep as I celebrate the success of my isolation. Yet, Chronos raises his heads and there comes the sharp sound of knocking. At first my eyes dart from over the room, attempting to pinpoint the origin. A reverberation of fear echoed throughout my frame as I concluded the unbidden din oozed from the famed portrait. I have never given much thought to the idea of madness, yet it is true my only friends had once been liquid. I press my nose against the wall, I can almost smell the two-year old paint. The knocking comes once more, and puzzled, I realise it originates behind me. I turn. Opposite to my position is the studio door, that seconds ago I had resolved never to disturb. I am awash with relief, however it is short-lived. There was now a presence at my door; one who expected to gain access to my sanctuary. My relief turned to agony and I decide to wait out the disturbance. The noise not only continued, but seemed to increase rapidly. It seems a distinct probability I am mad, and yet my desire for knowledge begins to overcome my fear of discovery. My friends are furious. I sense the jealous gaze of each representation as I inch towards the door. I am mocked and chided as my fingers wrap themselves around the handle. I stand petrified for a moment, before flinging the door open into the daylight. The silk strands float through the air.

My friends murmer.

My heartbeat wails.

A long charcoal coat wraps his frame. An equally burnt hat clings to his head, partially hiding what is a combed head of inky hair. He appears as in monochrome; a true old-fashioned gentleman. He stands silently in my doorway. I do not know him yet he stares at me with expectant stygian-blue eyes. He does not wait for my voice to return from its haven. He places a single step over the threshold and enters my gallery. His intrusion awakens the ruby and emerald Dragon. Its terrible teeth glisten as its roar reverberates and a jet of golden fire scorches the air. The other paintings follow the Dragon's cue and come screaming to life. As the dragon thunders, a plume of smoke billows from a chimney, boats chuff through a body of water, a lonely pencil scribbles across a barren page, the dancers dance, the fisherman fish.

The pedals of the bike do not budge.

Masterpiece One continues in its stillness as the others stir furiously. The man shows no indication of witnessing the commotion around him. He continues to study me with those impossible eyes. He opens his mouth and the commotion stops dead, awaiting his words. He stands as a general, commanding an army. I am in awe; I have no such power over them.

"I am a collector," he says, "and your biggest fan."

His voice catches me by surprise. It is as if the words had not been uttered, they had simply appeared inside of me. His eyes scan the walls, drinking in the majesty, but they linger too long a time upon the damned spot. My heart lowers to the depths of my being. Those shining eyes flicker away and my heart becomes raised once more.

I inquire with nervous whisper, "What do you see?"

He replies, his words slow and measured, "What you have created, with those two hands before you, are a marvel to be sure. So much beauty fills my vision; I am overwhelmed into lack of speech."

He falls silent, but continues to regard each painting. I can see that what this man has uttered is not true. He dances with the fire of many words. Some of which would be in languages that were long forgotten or had never existed. My own voice is lost in the vortex of language that surrounds me. My tongue remains chained to my palate. If I were to regain speech I am terrified that it will be nothing but an outpour of the babble that strains my cranium; a linguistical waterfall. It is a small mercy that the man attends to me not, instead having begun to survey my memories. I feel brief empathy for the spiders who have had their homes torn apart, but soon pull myself from the open doorway. I watch the charcoal-clothed stranger as he examines the walls, surely analysing my regrets. I have no doubt he is aware that I am not present at his side and I gingerly approach. He does not turn to acknowledge my advance, but I know that if I were to reach out and rouse him, it would assuredly burn me.

The man, having deducted my position, speaks, "Perhaps it is lent a quality due to the freshness of paint, but this magnificent piece is alive with intention."

I glance past his striking stature and look upon the painting he has selected. Still glistening with fresh paint, Masterpiece One-Zero-One glares down at us.

It depicts a man on the edge of a cliff. The world around him stands bright with colour, yet his eyes are cast down; drawn into the shadowy abyss before him. The chasm is filled with a dark smoke that billows and beckons.

Swiftly, without warning or hesitation, the stranger stretches out a hand and presses a finger firmly against the wall. It sinks deeply into the moist paint and the smoke begins to swirl violently, seemingly to boil. In that moment I am convinced that he has come not to relieve me, but to destroy my creations. A fury builds and I am close to reaching forward and wrenching the abysmal digit from my wall. I summon the resolve to raise my hand against him but am unnerved to witness his finger pulling away from the moist colours, completely unsoiled. Yet his print resided distinct, sunk deeper than the paint layered on the concrete. I glance into that smoky void and I find it still, the hypnotising swirls have ceased. A realisation dawns; this painting will never move again. The remaining One-Hundred sense the death among them and their faint whisper builds steadily into a crescendo, until my senses are overwhelmed by the deafening scream. The burnt hat turns in my direction as my knees hug the floor. There is agony within my ears and my palms slam against them by instinct.

"Come."

The single word sliced clearly through the uproar, forced through my protected ears and appeared inside once again. I raise my numbed appendage and grasp his outstretched hand. To my disbelief, I discover it to be cool. He lifts me to my feet and leads me on to Masterpiece One-Hundred.

It depicts a gilded ring clenched tight between the jaws of a blacksmith's tongs. It is in the process of being melted down, the aurum dripping into a bullet shaped mould.

I have no notion of how my visitor has ascertained the order in which I have marked the surrounding walls, but in the midst of the evenings events it seemed a minor query. I am unsurprised when, wordlessly, the monochrome man reaches forth his hand and lays it once more upon my art. The dry paint liquifies and eagerly absorbs the print, before solidifying to its original state. The dripping of the molten ochre slowly resolves its motion and I am overwhelmed with the panicked cries of my creations. I am held aloft and we continue on this journey, approaching Masterpiece Ninety-Nine together. It is merely seconds until the next print is absorbed and another voice dissipates. We roam my gallery laying paintings to rest; the fish cease their wriggle, the dancers freeze in their painted poses, the ruby and emerald dragon's fire is finally extinguished. The blender within my bowl quickens with each slaughter that brings us closer to the inevitable unveiling. I feel as though my countenance has aged considerably since the visitor violated my solitude.

It is mere moments until I stand, once more, before my original masterpiece; laid bare.

He peers at me, and confesses, "The moment I passed your threshold I was mesmerised by this piece. You spoke to me as I glanced upon you; you screamed of fault and agony, and so I suppressed my interest. It is only now, that we have banished your folly, that I lay myself before you and request, friend, to pour upon me the weight you have supported these long years. Come and share with me the magnificence of your masterpiece."

He takes hold of my hand, and I can feel every crack and wrinkle of his skin upon my own. My body tenses, and pleads,

'You are not ready,. You are but filth, and dirt, and shit'

Yet we are linked. He leads me into myself; and I relive it. I speak it to him, but I relive it for me. I tell of the day I lost her, of the competitive race I'd instigated, the volume of her joyous laugh as our pedals spun. He learns of the torturous road where she lost her soul, about the grill splattered with the precious remnants of her young mind. My voice is but a shriek of anguish, but it makes no difference to him; he hears me clear. He hears until my voice ceases, until I can extract the memories of her mangled frame no longer. At the moment of my vocal collapse, he reaches forward and completes his purpose. The print sinks into the paint. The previously immovable pedals of the painted bike begin to spin, gaining speed with every rotation. Hypnotised, I am compelled to approach the wall. Stretching out my arms to their fullest extent, I lay myself bare against it. My own trembling is soon overcome by a growing vibration deep within the wall. The floor begins to buckle beneath my bare feet and I fail to flinch as a shower of ceiling begins to fall around me. The painting palpitates against my chest. As it reaches a rhythmic climax, the wall explodes inwards and I am thrown forcefully across my studio. My landing is softened by my couch, turned makeshift bed these past years. I feel no pain, despite the concrete that has accompanied my journey and now lay heavily upon my breast. I attempt to breathe and lack the lung capacity to draw it. Too weak to move I struggle to locate the stranger with my eyes, fearful of his fate. I am unsurprised to land upon him, unharmed and perfectly groomed amidst the rubble. He smiles kindly, and in gentle finality stretches out his beckoning palm. He acknowledges that I am prepared and proceeds to fade, becoming increasingly transparent until he has departed. With a clear view, I now stare out into the visible courtyard and watch the bulldozer rumble past.

My chest is relieved of all my burden, and we are reunited.

Tunde Oyebode - Explosions

Lyndsay works at TMLC. It's the most efficient, lucrative and highest-grossing company—operating in many countries. She's the supervising manager on the 60th floor of its UK branch in London. There are 73 floors in this branch and the boss' office is at the peak of the triangular glass building—almost invisible in the sky.

She came in later than usual at 9:32 am. Work starts at 9:30 am. It was Monday and everyone sat at his or her desks, chatting rather than working.

As she walked out of the lift into the work floor the employees ceased their chatting and faced their computers. Straining her bloodshot eyes, she focussed on her desk and sluggishly made her way to it through the expansive aisle that split the row of desks. She greeted each employee with a thin smile. 'Hiya Greg, how was the weekend? Ah Suzie, did you see last night's show? Mark, Mark, Mark, I see you are at it again, crisps in the morning. Careful Susan, you're gonna spill your coffee.'

When she settled at her desk, she buzzed for Jim. He didn't reply so she looked up at where he would've been sitting to find that he wasn't there. Wondering where Jim was, as he's never late, she asked Alana Kipling if she'd seen Jim that morning. Alana, along with other employees who she'd also asked hadn't seen him.

Not a minute after resettling to begin her day, she received a call from the boss on the 73rd floor. She suspected it was something serious, maybe a promotion or more appropriate to the day, a telling-off as she'd been two minutes late and was missing an employee.

It was regarding Jim. He wouldn't be arriving at work because, tragically, he'd been explosive. The boss instructed her that Jim Crawford will be replaced after lunch. Lyndsay heard the boss but stared past his baldhead, through the large panorama window that encompassed the oversized office. All she could see was blue. There were no structures anywhere as tall as TMLC's triangular building. There was no one sat any higher than the bald man before her. He gazed at her from his black leather chair behind the mahogany desk. 'Lyndsay do you hear me?' he said. 'Mr Crawford would be replaced after lunch.' She replied and got the lift back to the 60th floor.

Lyndsay relayed this information to the staff. Many expressed their sympathy for his family and displeasure in the lack of Jim's presence in the office (as he'd been an absolute light), but also expressed jealousy wishing they didn't have to endure a day at TMLC anymore.

'I would like to explode too… maybe with a gun to my temple,' Mark said.

'No, that's messy. A pill is better,' Greg said.

'A pill takes time. Jump in front of a train. That should do it,' Suzie said.

'I would prefer jumping from the top floor of a building,' Susan said. 'At least you feel like you are flying for a minute—you feel free.'

'Enough.' Lyndsay arrested the conversation. 'Return to your desks,' she said.

At lunch, Lyndsay sat alone on a bench opposite TMLC. She retrieved her lunch box from her TMLC tote bag and chewed lazily on a BLT sandwich as she watched the crowd that formed outside the triangular glass building. They protested. Banners high in the air, condemning TMLC. It didn't take long for officials wielding electric batons to appear. Zapping each demonstrator.

When she was done she crossed the littered street: banners, glass, shoes, clothes, everything, everywhere. She showed her badge to the officials and was let through the barricade. Suddenly, the officials guarding the barricade were knocked off their feet. In the chaos, Lyndsay found herself on the ground.

Struggling back to her feet she was approached and pinned down by a man with deranged eyes. 'We must take them down!' he shouted, breathing heavily. He looked at her neck badge hanging on her neck, 'You work here? Why do you work here?' he demanded, gripping Lyndsay by the collar. He glanced to his left then his right and then looked at Lyndsay.

'I can see it in your eyes. The frustration. The exhaustion. You're tired aren't you?' His words were accompanied by sprinkles of spit.

Lyndsay screamed. 'Get off me! Get off me!' But he was resilient, steadfast in his mission.

'Join us. We must fight them! I can see it in your eyes. You're frustrated,' he said, staring at her with ferocious wide eyes.

His weight on her was eased. He tried to break free, but the official who'd come to help her was too strong for him. The official zapped him with his baton and then he fell.

After lunch, the replacement, promoted from the 59th Floor, arrived on the 60th floor. It was Lyndsay's job to get him settled. Her hand trembled from the earlier event as she shook his hand. 'Alex, Alex Higgins,' he said.

'Lyndsay—' she took a deep breath, then let it out— 'this is your desk: table 32 row D. It used to be Jim Crawford's, but he's exploded now. Mine's down there.' She pointed to the solitary desk at the end of the room. 'If you need my help don't shout my name; call me using your telephone and I'll attend to you when I can. You are to arrive no later than 9.30 am. If not you will be fired. And leave work no earlier than six pm. If you wish to stay longer, you can, but no one stays longer. Everyone leaves at six.

If you ever feel like exploding, alert me instantly by pushing on that red button on your desk. It will be disruptive, and inconsiderate of you to explode during working hours. It's inefficient.'

At exactly six, Lyndsay left work. So did everyone else on the work floor and every floor of the building. This affected the duration of her journey back home as it had always done, and after several minutes of navigating through the crowd of people that were in a hurry to get home, she finally made it out of the building only to meet another crowd flocking to the underground station.

The streets were spotless. No sign of the chaos during lunch could be seen—it was like it hadn't happened. Pondering if she'd imagined the deranged man, she joined the crowd to the underground station.

Walking at a snail's pace, squeezed amongst people, she reached the station where the crowd was worse. At least when she was outside she had the benefit of fresh air, but in the underground, it was stifling. Even though it was winter the heat generated by everybody made it unbearable, forcing her to take most of her layers off; her pashmina scarf, her wool trench coat and her navy cashmere sweater.

After, she was left with a white shirt tucked into a wool-blend pair of trousers and black stilettos. Her comfort was only momentary as in no time sweat patches were visible in her underarms. She hated that.

On the platform, futilely trying to conceal her sweat patches as they'd grown beyond concealment, Lyndsay waited for the train.

Everyone waited quietly until a disturbance began. Lyndsay recognised the culprit to be Mark Corfield from work. He kicked the bench next to him, swung his arms around, kicked his briefcase and smashed his laptop; he was in an explosive rage. People encircled him and stared like he was performing a street show.

Officials came running and tried to control him. They zapped him with their electric batons, but that only enraged him further. As the train pulled up to the platform Mark Corfield broke from the officials, pushed through the crowd and jumped onto the train tracks. He was crushed. The clean up didn't take long and within ten minutes the train was ready to depart.

Lyndsay along with the many others on the platform squeezed into the carriages and a team of white-gloved officials pushed at the occupants so that the doors could close behind them.

On the train, Lyndsay sustained sexual harassments in the form of groping. Lyndsay said nothing. It was a regular thing on her daily travel. At her stop, she got out and headed up the escalator to street level.

Amongst the many advertisements that filled the station, she discovered one indicating a change to the transport system. There would soon be women-only carriages on trains. This made her smile—a genuine smile. The smile lasted only a short while as she saddened discovering the service had extra charges—but at least the service would exist.

At home, her husband—a large, dark and round-faced man—sat on the sofa in the living room in his bathrobe and watched TV.

At the corner of the small living room, which colourfully stood out from the white walls and furniture, the baby played. Her husband had put the baby there to play with his toys. He didn't want his TV viewing interrupted. Holograms of unicorns, winged horses and birds floated and danced around in circles above the baby's cot. Lyndsay watched as the creatures appeared and disappeared in an endless loop and cycles—her eyes followed each movement. Then she turned to her husband.

'Has he eaten?' she asked her husband. He shook his head and waved his hand with his eyes fixed on the TV.

She changed into house clothes and sat the baby on the high chair in the living room. Her husband now watched the news, which headlined the usual; rise in population and explosions increasing at an alarming rate. It was also announced that Absolute Pharmaceuticals, a TMLC affiliate had developed a drug under the financial backing of TMLC, which calms explosive people and prevents them from having 'malfunctions'. 'A new era where people are happy, calm and efficient at all times has come upon us. This drug takes away all negative feelings and leaves positive ones behind,' the presenter said. The presenter interviewed a man dressed in a white coat and skullcap. 'We've heard it has some adverse effects,' the presenter said.

The baby fiddled with the strap and cried as Lyndsay tried to fasten him in while watching the TV. She turned and faced him, strapped him and pulled on it to make sure that it was secure.

'Guess what I found out today on my way back from work?' she said to her husband. He didn't respond. His eyes were fixed on the TV. 'Guess what babe?' she repeated, shaking him to get his attention.

He was shocked by this and accidentally knocked an empty hexagonal glass and a little yellow cylindrical bottle that sat on the armrest. The glass fell on the grey linoleum floor and remained solitary, but the yellow bottle rattled as it rolled underneath the TV stand.

'What did you say?' he asked.

'I said guess what I found out today.' she said.

'I don't know, what?' he said.

'There are going to be women-only carriages on trains,' she said.

Her husband nodded. His head was half-turned away from the TV—his eyes were fixed on it.

'What do you think of that babe?' she asked.

'Ah… well I'm happy if you're happy,' he said and then turned his head to the TV. Lyndsay stared at the yellow bottle underneath the TV stand, and then she turned to her husband.

They discussed dinner and after Lyndsay got up to prepare it. She preferred to cook the old fashioned way—like her grandparents had taught her, with real ingredients; spices, herbs and whatnot. This took several minutes longer than readymade, molecularly augmented meals, which could be cooked in a minute in a microwave.

It was therapeutic for her, it tasted better and she was convinced that the explosions were heightened by the molecular augmentation of the readymade meals. So she started cooking and in an hour food was ready and everyone ate to satisfaction.

Soon after she bathed the baby, prepared him for bed and put him to sleep. After, she washed the dishes, with her husband sat on the sofa, not having moved since she first arrived home.

When she was done with the dishes she went to the bedroom and shopped on her portable computer. She projected the clothes with it. They hovered in the air. She stood right in the images and faced the mirror to see how it looked on her. She skipped to the next clothing item after each, until she was done with shopping and bought the items she wanted.

A drone delivered them within an hour. She tried them on again and then sent back the items she didn't want.

With shopping done she lay in bed and waited for sleep to take her to the next morning. It didn't come quickly, and when it did she was awoken instantly by the cries of the baby. She looked at the clock. It was one am. She got up from the bed and went to the living room. Her husband was still watching TV, sprawled on the sofa. She went to the baby's room, rocked him for 20 minutes until he fell asleep and then returned to bed.

Her husband walked into the bedroom. He was done watching TV. He took off his bathrobe and lay beside her. Then he kissed her forehead and gently moved his palm along her smooth thigh. Lyndsay didn't react. She was still and silent. She wasn't quite in the mood. The events of the day tumbled around in her mind.

It was the first time someone she knew personally had been explosive. Yielding to her husband's advances, she lay in bed as he had his way. And as she lay there motionless, without making a single sound, she thought of the explosions and of the people she knew. She thought of the deranged man. His face fresh in her mind, staring down at her as her husband did. She thought of his words; 'join us. I can see it in your eyes. You are frustrated.' She lay there silently with the thoughts tumbling in her mind as her husband finished up. He fell asleep not long after.

She tried to sleep again. It failed her. It had failed her more often now—three to five times a week. So she went to the living room to get a cigarette from her bag, and then she heard the cries of the baby.

She went to the child. And cuddled him to sleep, but again he woke just as she lay in bed. This continued all night. In the morning she was exhausted.

The replacement had settled in at work. The rest of the staff treated him no differently from Jim Crawford—it was like he'd never died. Sometimes they mistook him for Jim, which Lyndsay corrected. It seemed like everything was fine, but suddenly a cracking noise resonated on the work floor.

Zack Kipling was punching his monitor. He ripped it from the table and smashed it against the floor. He ripped the telephone from the table and smashed it too. He jumped on his table, kicked everything; the picture of his daughter, the pieces of paper, the penholder, everything. He swung his arms aimlessly, warding off invisible bees.

Electric baton-wielding officials came. They poked and poked, trying to control him. This enraged him further. Zack evaded them and ran through the row of desks into the window. It didn't break. It cracked. Everyone watched. He ran headfirst into the window again. It cracked a little more, slowly splitting into spidery sections. They poked and poked him, trying to control his rage. He broke free. And again he ran into the glass pane, headfirst. It broke and Zack fell 60 floors to his death.

The clean up was quick—the blood pool, the glass bits, everything. The window was fixed quickly too. Work continued as normal as if nothing happened.

The boss called Lyndsay to his office and informed her that Zack Kipling would be replaced with someone from the 59th floor after lunch.

At the closing time, everyone flooded out in masses. In the large lift, which could take up to 50 people at a time, Lyndsay overheard some of the employees discussing the event of the day.

'That was a new one,' the man in a blue suit said.

'I haven't seen anyone explode that violently,' the woman in the black suit said.

'Looks like it is getting worse,' the blonde man in the black suit said.

The explosions weighed on Lyndsay's mind. She wanted her employees to be happy. She didn't want to be frustrated.

She entered the crowd of people outside and walked at a snail's pace to the underground station.

At the station slowly making her way towards the platform in the crowd, she watched the holograms of displays and adverts that illuminated the station's blank monolithic walls. A man in a neat black suit walked to a triangular glass building.

On his way there his appearance slowly worsened; rumpled suit, bloodshot eyes and overgrown beard. He remained this way as he walked to the triangular building until a man in a white coat and skullcap with a neat pointy beard gave him a yellow bottle. Instantly his appearance improved and the hologram changed to an office where he sat smiling and typing away.

After the advert, an image popped up and a large caption floated in front of the wall: WOMEN-ONLY CARRIAGES. Then smaller letters began to appear below as if typed in real-time; DUE TOO… When the letters stopped a red line formed across ~~WOMEN-ONLY CARRIAGES~~.

It started with Lyndsay punching the man in front of her. Then the crowd cycled around her, giving her space and watched as she kicked her briefcase, then she swung her arms aimlessly as if fighting a mob. After which electric baton-wielding officials came and tried to contain her.

Warwick Sprawson - Sunshade

1997
Tokyo, Japan

Japan streamed past the train window. Rice fields filled the valleys, punctuated by cedarwood houses with graphite grey roofs. Bamboo groves and vine thickets sprawled lushly from uncultivated rises. It was my first time outside of Australia. I was tired from the flight. My eyes were dry and felt deeply recessed into my head.

'Look at that!' said my father loudly. He pointed to an advertising banner hanging from the carriage roof like bunting. 'Calpis. Looks like some kind of drink. Sounds like "cow piss!"' He laughed heartily, head bowed, shoulders shaking.

There is little as embarrassing for a 13-year-old boy than their 43-year-old father, and my father was more embarrassing than most. He was pale and overweight, with receding wavy black hair and gold-framed glasses as unfashionable as his sense of humour. He always spoke loudly, as declaiming to an audience, and I shrank in my seat as the eyes of silent Japanese commuters flicked over us.

'And look at him!' My father nodded to a man slouched in his seat wearing neon green sneakers, oversized army pants, a loose black T-shirt and a pair of bulbous headphones. 'A fan! He knew I was coming.'

On the man's T-shirt was a naked lady with butter-yellow hair wearing a tiara and a headdress of lush indigo feathers. This was the album cover to *Sunshade* by the band Golden Picnic. Twenty years ago, as a young session musician living in the UK, my father had played the flute on one of their tracks, 'Highwayman', a top 10 hit. It was an anecdote he endlessly wheeled out – including to my friends – despite few people ever having heard of the song, album or band.

Big in Japan, apparently.

I resumed looking out the window. As the train approached Tokyo the rice fields were replaced by drab brown apartments, concrete overpasses, ugly powerlines, forlorn little parks and roads busy with boxy cars. An old lady swept a footpath with a bamboo broom.

Japan was not my idea. This was the first significant time Dad and I had spent together since my parents separated. It was his clumsy attempt at… what? Bonding? Bribery? Forgiveness?

The next day my father and I went to Shinjuku Station. I found the ticket office, bought the tickets and located the right platform for Tokorozawa. It was quite satisfying: Dad was totally reliant on me – he couldn't speak a word of Japanese. I'd been learning the language for two years, and while I wasn't that great at speaking, I could read hiragana, katakana and 150 kanji characters. Mrs Takahashi said I had a 'good head for forms'.

Arriving in Tokorozawa we walked the scrappy backstreets east of the station, entering an industrial area. It was a day of drizzly low cloud, but still warm enough for a T-shirt. Thick black cables hung between power poles, sectioning off the grey sky. There were no footpaths, so we walked on the narrow roads, stepping aside for pint-sized delivery trucks. Through the open roller doors of small factories I glimpsed machinery, barrels, pallets, polystyrene boxes, forklifts being driven by men in pastel blue boilersuits.

The Mitutoyo factory was a two storey sheer-faced building with a stained concrete forecourt and a planter box of sickly shrubs. We removed our shoes at the sliding door and put on the slippers provided.

Inside was a showroom. Bright lights shone on cabinets of flutes gleaming like jewellery on soft beds of blue velvet.

A whip thin man in a navy blue suit bowed from behind the counter. Probably in his early 20s, he wore a blue tie patterned with white flowers. His ears jutted out either side of his head like mug handles. I recited the sentence I had practiced, *Sumimasen, chichi wa furūto o kaitaidesu.* Excuse me, my father would like to buy a flute.

Fortunately the man, Mr Nagamoto, spoke perfect English. He maintained a slight smile as Dad droned on about f-stops, lip plates, *Sunshade* and his new role in the Melbourne Symphony Orchestra.

I left them to it and paced around the showroom. There were hundreds of flutes, mostly silver, but also gold and platinum. Behind the cabinets were posters of men and women holding Mitutoyo flutes. Presumably famous flutists, they held their flutes awkwardly, as if holding delicate scientific equipment.

'Toby!' Dad bellowed across the room. 'He says we can go in and see where they make the flutes.'

Mr Nagamoto opened a door at the back of the showroom and we changed into different, more sturdy slippers. Passing through a blue curtain we entered the factory, a large room with two lines of benches in the centre, and lathes, presses, drills and other equipment around the sides. About 20 men and women in grey smocks sat at the tables soldering, filing and polishing tubes and keys. The room smelt of machine oil and hot metal.

A woman in a jaunty red headscarf put a flute to her lips and played a few notes, made an adjustment to a key, and played a few more. Beside her an older man with a weathered face riffled up and down scales, eyes closed.

'Every flute has around 100 different components, said Mr Nagamoto, 'each one handmade. They have to fit together perfectly. That's why every person here, from the cleaners to the machinists, plays the flute. To make a flute, you have to know the flute.' He paused for a moment and then said modestly, 'I myself play a little bit of flute.'

When we returned to the showroom Mr Nagamoto unlocked a cabinet and took out a gleaming golden flute, holding towards my father with two hands, as if presenting a ceremonial sword. 'Try this. Twenty-four carat gold tubing, embouchure, rings, ribs and posts. Maximum quality.'

My father took the flute. He held down all the keys and blew air silently through the instrument three times. He paused, tongue flicking in and out like a reptile, then closed his eyes and played. It was an extended version of his 'Highwayman' solo, starting with percussive bursts of air before breaking into a jerky canter of sound, fusillades of notes, from the breathy depth of the lowest register rising lightning fast to an urgent shriek, his fingers fluttering on the keys, the tension in the tune building, before – where the guitars and the drums would normally kick in – the melody changed to slower arcs of sound punctuated by dramatic scattershots of notes, an 18th century sea shanty dipped in a vat of 70s LSD.

A head appeared at the door to the factory, then another and another. Until nearly the whole factory was gathered in the showroom listening to my father play.

2007

Osaka, Japan

Dad entered my apartment confidently, rolling his suitcase past the kitchen nook in the entrance hall, past the tiny plastic bathroom pod with its shower and toilet, through to the modest main room with its coffee table, TV and couch. 'This isn't so bad,' he said, glancing around at the blue carpet, textured vinyl wallpaper and the stamp-sized balcony. He flung open the double doors in the main room and moved forward as if entering a doorway, receiving a face full of coat hangers.

I laughed. 'That's the wardrobe!'

He slowly closed the wardrobe doors, puzzled. 'So where's the bedroom?'

'There is no bedroom,' I said with perverse pride. 'At night I fold up the coffee table and put it in the wardrobe and take the futon out. I sleep on the floor. You can have the couch.'

It was a 29 minute train trip to Osaka Station. I hadn't seen Dad for over a year, he looked smart in his new tuxedo. He'd lost weight – and his remaining hair – and his new tortoiseshell-framed glasses made him look younger. His Mitutoyo flute, in its sleek black leather case, was on his lap.

Outside the train window the pachinko parlours, convenience stores, shopping malls, vending machines, baseball fields and river valleys were familiar to me. I had been teaching English in Higashiosaka, a suburb of Osaka, for nearly nine months.

Initially teaching had been terrifying. But I soon realised teaching is a kind of performance – you learn your lines, open the door and get on stage in the role of Teacher. There was nothing to be scared of. And besides, Japanese students were uniformly polite and kind.

From the station Dad and I walked to the Osaka Symphony Hall, a huge white tiled structure that – like many civic buildings in Japan – was more utilitarian than elegant. We padded the soft blue carpets, upstairs, along long corridors, past closed doors, to the performers' entrance. I gave Dad a hug and pretended to dust dandruff from his shoulders.

After killing time drinking champagne in the bar area, I settled into a plush seat in the auditorium. Japanese classical music goers seemed more diverse than those in Australia. In addition to the usual oldies in their pearls and knits, there were plenty of people my age and lots of families with young children.

From behind the red curtain the orchestra tuned up. The morose call of the oboe was answered by the lead violin and then the woodwind and brass. The oboe again, and the warm swell of the string section tuning, the sound layering into a warm haze. Tuning was always my favourite part of a concert. Much to my father's disappointment, classical music – and 70s big hair schmalz like Golden Picnic – had never been my thing. Give me pop any day.

The Melbourne Symphony Orchestra were on a seven day tour of Japan, playing Tokyo, Osaka and Nagoya. Tonight they were playing Beethoven's Symphony Number 3, conducted by Tadaaki Otaka.

In the fourth movement Dad had a solo. The Mitutoyo flashed under the lights, as Dad, head nodding, lips pursed, produced a pure sound, weaving and soaring, bolstered by the strings' semiquaver passages, before a final rapid patter of flute and the whole orchestra reigniting, swelling the sound in to a golden howl.

At the end of the concert the orchestra received a standing ovation.

Otaka pointed out Dad with his baton, and my father took a bow.

2018
Melbourne, Australia

Melbourne's Royal Melbourne Hospital was built in the 1940s and then expanded, haphazardly, ever since. In a dreamlike haze I walked the endless corridors, the worn blue linoleum floodlit by fluorescent light. I had only arrived back from Melbourne the day before, a 16 hour flight from Sapporo, where I now lived.

When I finally found Ward 7 West all the nurses were busy. After waiting at the counter for a few minutes I saw room 12 across the corridor. A shared room, the bed near the door was occupied by a man in his 40s with broad shoulders, a jowly face and a blubbery neck like a seal. 'You must be the son,' he said cheerfully in an English accent. He pulled closed his green hospital gown and nodded to the curtain next to him, 'He's in there.'

I pushed through the curtain and found Dad sitting up in bed looking out the window to Royal Parade. I was shocked. He'd shrunk in the 18 months since I'd seen him. His body was thin, almost gaunt, but his face was somehow fuller, his skin pouchy under the eyes. There was a tube in his arm and a mask over his face, the faint hiss of oxygen. He looked mild and defenceless without his glasses.

'I wish you hadn't come,' he said in a drug thickened voice.

'Good to see you too.' I put the chocolates on the bedside cabinet and kissed him on his bald head. Sitting on the edge of the bed, I took his hand. 'I wanted to come. I had to come.' We both looked out the window at a passing tram. 'Why didn't you tell me sooner?'

'I didn't know for sure. Tests and more tests. Scans, blood tests, biopsies, you name it. And you've got your career over there. But they're sure now.'

'But the lungs! You never smoked.'

'I smoked!' Came the cheery voice of Dad's roommate from beyond the curtain. 'Can't say it helped me much.'

My father pulled down his mask. 'Put a sock in it, Peter!' he yelled. 'This is private!' He coughed thickly into his hand. Once he had caught his breath, he gestured me to him and spoke quietly. 'It was just the lungs to start with, but now it's everywhere, in my spine, my kidneys, everywhere.'

'But they're treating it aren't they? Chemo.' I touched the mask at his chest. 'Shouldn't you put this back on?'

'No, they stopped treatment.' He tried a smile. 'I was wearing out their machines.' Seeing the look on my face he patted my hand. 'I *am* happy to see you.'

'Has Mum come?'

He paused for a moment before answering, 'No.'

Dad struggled to sit up, and I stood to help him. 'Open the bottom drawer. Take out the case.'

I opened the drawer and took out the battered black Mitutoyo flute case.

My father held out his hand. He placed the case on his lap and stroked the scarred leather with his fingertips. 'This flute needs a home.'

'A home?'

'A new owner, someone to play it. Not just anyone, the right person.'

'Dad, we can talk about this later. Can you please put the mask back on?'

His voice remained level. 'There is no later. I've tried to find someone, went through the orchestra, through the schools, all my contacts. Sure, a lot of people will take it, but in their voices I can hear they're already counting the money they'll make when they sell it. No, it has to be someone real, someone talented, a person who will love it.'

'Ok, ok. You should lie back down.'

'No!' He struggled to sit up further. 'This is important! This one thing.' He thrust the case at me. 'Take it. Promise me you'll find someone, the right person.'

'Ok! Now put your mask back on. Lie down.'

'Promise me.'

I promised, and from the other side of the curtain I heard Tony say with rich satisfaction, 'Good lad.'

2019
Nara, Japan

Walking north from Nara Station I enter parkland where tame shika deer roam. It's early April and the cherry blossoms, *sakura*, are in full bloom. I'm not someone who gets emotional about flowers, but I feel the weight of tears as I walk beneath the avenues of grey barked trees, the blossoms floating overhead in an ethereal pink haze, too delicate for this world, an impression confirmed by the petals drifting down, one by one, to lay gently upon the damp gravel path.

Nara Centennial Hall is to the east of the park, just off Sanjo-Doi, a dark tiled building with a rounded profile like a sleek 80s boombox.

Through the glass doors is a soaring atrium with a glass roof. After showing my ticket I climb some granite stairs to the auditorium.

About six months ago I had sent the Mitutoyo flute back to

Tokorozawa for a service. I was surprised to receive an email from Mr Nagamoto, who – 22 years after our visit – still worked in the showroom. He asked after my father, who he remembered playing 'Highwayman'. After learning Dad had passed away, he offered any assistance Mitutoyo could provide. He wrote 'your father played the flute with a hot, hot heart'.

Behind the purple curtain the school orchestra is tuning up. The oboe plays a long wavering A, and is answered by a swell of strings. After a moment or two the woodwinds join in, and then, hovering sublime above them all, the beautiful pull of the flute.

Available worldwide from Amazon

Michael Terence Publishing

www.mtp.agency

www.facebook.com/mtp.agency

@mtp_agency

Printed in Great Britain
by Amazon

66997686R00210